"YOU TOLD ME TO INVESTIGATE YOU. DID YOU THINK I WOULDN'T TAKE YOU UP ON THE INVITATION?"

"Breaking into my house is a pretty broad interpretation of what I said. I was hoping for something more direct. More hands-on," Jack said.

"It was a pretty hands-on kind of search," she purred softly, her gaze mocking him, not giving an inch. "Most revealing."

Despite the lingering anger, a bolt of pure, sweet excitement shot through him. Damn! He couldn't remember when he'd last had this much fun with a woman, and they hadn't even taken off any clothes yet.

Yet . . .

"Then I gotta tell you, Diana—I can't wait to see how you'll interpret *this.*"

Before she could respond, Jack pressed her fully against the wall, his hands on either side of her head, and kissed her like he'd never get another chance in this lifetime. . . .

MICHELE ALBERT

GETTING HER MAN

AVON BOOKS

An Imprint of HarperCollinsPublishers

This is a work of fiction. Names, characters, places, and incidents are products of the author's imagination or are used fictitiously and are not to be construed as real. Any resemblance to actual events, locales, organizations, or persons, living or dead, is entirely coincidental.

AVON BOOKS
An Imprint of HarperCollinsPublishers
10 East 53rd Street
New York, New York 10022-5299

First Avon Books paperback printing: October 2002

Avon Trademark Reg. U.S. Pat. Off. and in Other Countries, Marca Registrada, Hecho en U.S.A.
HarperCollins® is a registered trademark of HarperCollins Publishers Inc.

Printed in the U.S.A.

10 9 8 7 6 5 4 3 2 1

PROLOGUE

...

Mandeville, on the north side of Lake Pontchartrain, was an upscale community where the crime rate was low, houses and yards were large and pretentious, and people had a lot of free cash to spend on pricey trinkets.

Exactly the kind of pricey trinkets he wanted, in particular.

The one thing he'd learned early on was that if he wore a repairman or delivery uniform, he became invisible. People let him poke around outside their homes with few questions, and inside as well, depending on how forceful and professional he sounded. And people responded to questions from "official" companies on the phone with far more trust than they should.

It made his job so much easier, sad to say—and the more affluent the community, the more complacent. Unlike the rougher parts of New Orleans, where people routinely trusted nobody else and installed door and window grills, and owned mean dogs, those who lived in these picture-perfect suburbs relied on the security of alarm systems that too often didn't work as well as they thought. Amazingly, some still didn't take any precautions beyond locking their doors and windows.

Tonight's house would make his task unbelievably simple.

No dogs, an out-dated silent alarm system rigged for interior protection only—and yet all inside blissfully asleep, safe and snug in their beds, visions of rising stock markets and juicy returns dancing in their heads.

He targeted the back entrance because the artistically landscaped bushes and vines mostly concealed the door, and because it had a basic lock which took him only seconds to open.

Jimmying the deadbolt took a bit more time, and he closed his eyes as he gently rocked the pick, listening intently, alert to the slightest change. Picking locks was more a science than a craft, with its own laws of physics, and when he felt the familiar give, he carefully opened the door and stepped inside the dark, quiet house.

If not deactivated, the alarm would alert the security company sixty seconds after his entry, and then they'd call the owners. Unless something went terribly wrong, he'd have what he'd come for and would be out the door before that call. All the same, he remained on the alert for any movement or noises. Since he wasn't armed, the last thing he wanted to encounter was an irate homeowner with a shotgun. Or the police.

He moved quickly forward, virtually invisible in the black coveralls he wore over his street clothes, each step silent. He knew exactly where he had to go—he'd been here a week ago to "repair" the air conditioner that, in the wee hours of the morning, he'd disabled by disconnecting the outside fuses. He'd bluffed away until the harried housekeeper had let him in to check the entire house. Once he found what he was looking for, he left, made a brief show of tinkering around outside, and then "repaired" the big central air unit simply by plugging the fuses back into their sockets.

The living room he stood in was huge, and ruthlessly decorated to proclaim how much money the king of this castle—a trial lawyer working in New Orleans and an acquaintance of anybody who was anybody—made each year.

Within several seconds, he'd opened the flimsy lock on the curio cabinet. What he'd come for rested on the middle shelf, artfully arranged on the glass—and next to a silver frame holding a photograph of a smiling couple.

The man's arrogant expression, and the woman's timid eyes and smile, briefly caught his attention, leaving him with a prickling of guilt.

No time for that. He scooped up the necklace into the palm of his black-gloved hand, then carefully wrapped it in cotton, and slid it into his pocket.

He shut the cabinet door, but not before he'd left his "calling card" behind, and then slipped out as quietly as he'd come, and disappeared into the darkness of night.

ONE

...

SIX MONTHS LATER . . .

At the familiar clomp of thick-soled boots, Diana Belmaine glanced up from her desk to see her part-time secretary walk into her office. Luna was twenty-two and pretty, with pale skin and a penchant for dark nail polishes, bloodred lipstick, black hair dye, and black lace. Not surprisingly, she moonlighted as a vampire guide for night tours of New Orleans.

In a disapproving voice, Luna said, "You didn't tell me you had an appointment today."

Diana removed her reading glasses, then sat back, arching a brow. "Because I don't."

"Well, there's this old guy by my desk who says he's here to talk to you."

"Does the old guy have a name?"

"Mr. Jones." Smiling didn't mesh with Luna's image, but humor lit her dark eyes all the same. "I'm thinking probably a close cousin of Mr. Doe and Mr. Smith."

Real clients—those wealthy enough to require her services—weren't keen on announcing to the world

they needed a private investigator. They almost
never came to her; she went to them. Most of her
business deals transpired over café au lait and
beignets at the Café du Monde, at somebody else's
office, on the phone, or in dark bars.

Diana sighed and pushed to her feet, reluctant to
waste time when she had a report to prepare on her
recovery of a stolen Picasso. The insurance company
who'd hired her probably wouldn't be surprised to
learn that the painting's owner—a cheery, white-
haired oil company exec going through financial dif-
ficulties following his third divorce—had arranged
the theft so he could collect on the insurance settle-
ment.

A trick as old as dirt, and people never, ever
learned.

She followed Luna to the small waiting area of her
three-room office suite, which was decorated in ba-
ronial tones of burgundy, navy, and tan, and located
on the second floor of an old St. Phillip Street building, not far from the market. The lazy *whir-whir-whir*
of the ceiling fan blended with the street noise filter-
ing through the filmy chiffon curtains: chattering
tourists swarming through the French Quarter,
beeping horns, and the plodding clop of hooves as a
mule-drawn carriage rumbled past.

An elegant, silver-haired man stood by the window. He wore a conservative dark suit and carried a
large leather briefcase—a lawyer to somebody with
lots of money?

Thank God she'd worn a dress. Its lime green silk
played up her blond hair and lightly tanned skin,
and while the sheath's slim lines skimmed her

curves a bit more than she'd prefer for meeting a potential client, it was still tasteful and businesslike.

"Hello." She walked forward, spine straight,
shoulders squared. The man turned, and she noted a
white rose adorning his lapel. "I'm Diana Belmaine."

"Edward Jones." The man shook her hand in a
firm, brief grip. "You're the private investigator who
specializes in stolen antiquities, I presume."

"Yes, and I also specialize in art, jewelry, heirlooms, and antiques. I handle fraud cases, too,
though not as much as when I worked with
Sotheby's." She paused. "Have you lost something,
Mr. Jones?"

"I'm afraid so."

Diana took in his diamond tie tack, the expensive
suit, and smiled. "And you'd like me to find it."

"Oh, yes."

Her smile blossomed into a full grin. "Lovely.
Let's talk, shall we? This way, please. Hold all my
calls, Luna."

Luna looked amused again, despite her lack of a
smile. "Will do, Boss."

Mr. Jones politely nodded at Luna and followed
Diana into her office. The packed bookshelves and
framed licenses on the wall lent an air of authority to
the room, as did stately chairs in tufted oxblood
leather and the massive oak desk from a cotton ex-
change office that had gone out of business long ago.
The overall impression was one of power. Masculine
power specifically, which helped overcome the annoying handicap of looking more like a Grace Kelly
society girl than a private eye.

"Have a seat." She closed the door. "Would you like coffee or something else to drink?"

"I'm fine, thank you."

Curiosity piqued, Diana sat, pushed aside the clutter on her desk, and asked, "What can I do for you, Mr. Jones?"

As an answer, he hauled his briefcase onto his lap. After dialing in the combination and snapping open the fasteners, he withdrew an accordion file and dropped it on her desk with a weighty *thump*. He didn't push it toward her, and she didn't touch it.

"This file contains all the information you should require to investigate my client's recent loss."

"You're a little ahead of the game here. How about you tell me your client's name, first."

"Steven Carmichael." When her brows shot up, the lawyer smiled thinly. "You are familiar with my client?"

"Of course. Anybody in the antiquities business knows his name. And it so happens Mr. Carmichael approached me a month ago about taking on a case after the police investigation stalled. Something about missing crates of Mayan artifacts, destined for his new gallery." Diana tipped her head to one side. "But he hired another investigator."

That rejection still stung, especially since she suspected that the wealthy and powerful Carmichael had passed her over because he came from a generation that didn't believe a woman could handle a "tough" job. It wouldn't be the first time sexism had cost her a case.

"Ah, yes . . . I am aware of that situation."

"Did Mr. Carmichael ever recover his missing antiquities?"

"Not yet."

She managed not to smile. "That's too bad."

The lawyer fixed her with a hard, assessing gaze. "A most unfortunate affair, I agree, but not the one I'm here about. Mr. Carmichael has an urgent matter he needs addressed at once, and it's of a more personal nature."

"I don't do people," Diana said, repressing a sigh. "If what Mr. Carmichael has lost is a girlfriend or mistress, I can't help."

"Actually, what Mr. Carmichael has lost is something more along the lines of a family heirloom. An ancient one, which I believe puts the matter in your area of expertise, Ms. Belmaine."

"It would help if you'd tell me exactly what it is."

"Nothing elaborate, but it has a great deal of sentimental value to my client. It's a small alabaster box containing a lock of hair and a two-inch-high statuette made of solid gold. It's Egyptian. Eighteenth Dynasty, in particular."

"From a tomb?"

"Yes." Jones cleared his throat. "The Pharaoh Tutankhamen's. And the alabaster box is inscribed with the name of Queen Nefertiti." Jones folded his hands on top of his briefcase. "My client believes the lock of hair is hers, so he is very anxious to get it back."

No kidding.

Nefertiti, the most fabled of Egyptian queens— the mere mention of her name brought to mind images of her timeless beauty and grace, the mystery of her ultimate fate.

At a niggling sense of unease, she asked, "May I ask how Mr. Carmichael came into possession of such an item?"

"Legitimately."

"Completely legitimately, or sort of legitimately?"

The antique mantel clock on her desk delicately ticked away the seconds.

"Ms. Belmaine, a great number of the antiquities in museums and private collections were acquired by less than ethical means. Today they call it looting; back in the old days they called it collecting. It's the way of the world. And my client possesses the required provenance papers and terms of sale."

Official paperwork did make Carmichael's purchase lawful and justified efforts to retrieve it. It was also true that many antiquities, even some on display in world-famous museums, had been plundered— by adventuring British lords, short French emperors, professional looters following family tradition, modern-day organized crime, or even academics who should've known better but couldn't resist temptation.

Of course, the box and its contents could be clever forgeries. But taking on this case would be a change of pace from the half-assed insurance frauds and mundane thefts she'd investigated lately. Life had been awfully tame for the last couple years, and she could use a real challenge. Something, *anything*, to give her wits a decent workout.

"So when did Mr. Carmichael discover the box was missing?"

"Three days ago." Knowing he'd hooked her, Jones's mouth tipped in a small, satisfied smile. "It was stolen from his gallery, the Jade Jaguar, over on Julia Street. You'll find all the details in this file, including the names of anyone with access to the building and a guest list for the gallery's opening night gala, a week ago."

"Parties are always a prime opportunity for thieves—and the timing fits," Diana murmured. "But I didn't know Mr. Carmichael collected ancient Egyptian pieces. I thought his interests were strictly pre-Columbian."

"It's his main interest, yes, but first and foremost he's a collector of rare and beautiful art."

Diana weighed the lawyer's polite, if carefully bland, expression. "You've already hired an investigator to recover the Mayan shipment. Why not have him look into this latest theft, as well? Why did you come to me?"

"My client feels that your expertise is better suited for this situation. He wants this investigation to be discreet and delicate. I'm sure you're aware of the recent trend toward repatriating antiquities to their country of origin. An artifact such as this could explode into an international incident."

Diana raised a brow. "Did Mr. Carmichael report the theft to the police?"

"No."

"Why not?"

Jones made an impatient sound. "Oh, come now. Surely you can understand why my client is reluctant to involve law enforcement authorities of any sort. He doesn't want to risk losing the artifact or the considerable amount of money he paid for it."

Not to mention the possibility of having his moral

character publicly called into question—which certainly explained the man's desire for a "discreet" and "delicate" investigation.

"There is one other thing." Jones reached into his briefcase and removed a plastic Ziploc bag. It held a playing card—the jack of spades. "This was left in place of the artifact, obviously by the thief. My client was careful not to touch it, in case there are prints."

There wouldn't be any, though she'd check to be sure. This case had all the earmarks of a professional and well-planned job.

"May I?" she asked. The lawyer handed over the bag, and she studied the card. It was the thief's signature; an introduction as personal as a handshake, and as unique as a fingerprint. A zing of excitement shot through her.

"A thief with style." She smiled. "My favorite flavor of deviant."

"Forgive me for failing to share your enthusiasm, Ms. Belmaine." Jones removed another file from his briefcase, then clicked it shut. "I've taken the liberty of drawing up a contract for your fees and services. I'll leave both the contract and evidence files for your perusal. You have the night to think it over, and I'll return to your office by eight o'clock tomorrow morning to finalize matters. If that's convenient for you."

Diana peeled back the top of the folder and glimpsed the fee in question. She hoped her eyes hadn't visibly bugged out of her head. "It's convenient."

"Of course you understand that everything we've spoken about is to remain in absolute confidence."

When she nodded, Jones stood, smoothing his suit coat. "Very good. It's been a pleasure talking with you."

Diana stood as well. "One last question, please. Does your client have any potential suspects in mind?"

The man's expression remained neutral, and after a moment he said, "I'm sorry, but no."

"All right." She smiled politely. "Thank you. I'll see you tomorrow, then."

After the lawyer left the office, she looked down at the bulging folder on her desk and frowned. The purpose behind this monster file was clearly to prevent her from asking a lot of inconvenient questions.

The reason could be as simple as Steven Carmichael's reluctance to reveal he owned plundered property that could stir up an international hornet's nest. Then again, maybe he had something more to hide.

She had no reason to trust the man or any of the information in the file, and his lawyer hadn't been telling the truth when he said there were no suspects—his hesitation, the way he'd schooled his expression, said he was hiding or lying about something.

Nothing new in that. The first thing any private investigator learned was that people lied to you. All the time. The boy next door, little old ladies, cops, priests, beggars and rich men, winos and pillars of the community . . . everybody lied.

TWO

...

An hour after officially accepting the Carmichael case, Diana pulled her vintage sky-blue Mustang convertible to the curb outside Tulane University's Anthropology Building, just off Audubon Street. She surveyed the beige stucco two-story building, with its gray-painted trim and plaster embellishment. A number of its tall, narrow windows were open, and the place looked a little shabby, with patches of discoloration here and there.

Diana cut the engine, anticipation coursing through her like a current of energy. After being up most of the night reading through the file and doing preliminary research, she was running on pure caffeine and adrenaline, and welcomed the familiar rush. It had been such a long time since she'd gone on a hunt like this, a hunt that wasn't predictable, safe, or easy.

Before getting out of the car, she glanced at Luna's dog-eared copy of *People* magazine on the seat beside her. It was the annual most eligible bachelors issue, and right there on page 44 was Dr. Jack Austin, professor of archaeology at Tulane, renowned Mayan expert, Discovery Channel regular, and all-around boy wonder. He'd discovered the lost Mayan city of Tikukul when he was only twenty-seven, and it had been his bread and butter for the following ten years—the past five of which had been heavily funded by grants from Steven Carmichael's Ancient Americas Preservation Society.

Judging by his picture, Austin had a rough, unaffected appeal that would attract women but not make men feel uncomfortable: a man's man sort of guy. He wore canvas shorts and a sweat-dampened ribbed tank, and lay sprawled on a slab of vine-encrusted rock, muscular arms and legs spread-eagled, as if he were some sort of human sacrifice.

A strangely erotic photo, in the way the camera's focus drew the eye to certain erogenous zones. Rather like banging a dinner bell: *Come and get it!*

She folded the magazine and stuffed it into her purse, got out of her car, and headed for the building. She'd scheduled a meeting with Carmichael later in the afternoon, but until then she'd work her way alphabetically through the guest list for the Jade Jaguar's opening night bash—a list that had included a most impressive number of wealthy political and society types, artists, and rival gallery owners.

So far she'd learned that the Allens were out of town and the Archers weren't morning people. Now it was Austin's turn, although considering his dependence on Carmichael for funding his excavations, he didn't rate high on her roster of potential suspects.

In a pumpkin orange linen suit and dark brown heels, wearing wide-rimmed oval sunglasses and a Hermès scarf tied in a bow around her long, straight ponytail—Jackie O would've approved—Diana walked with purposeful strides to the departmental office.

Today was not about being surreptitious; today was about making a vivid impression on one of America's most eligible bachelors and giving herself the upper hand by catching the man off guard.

When it came to getting straight answers, this strategy worked a good 90 percent of the time.

The departmental secretary, an older, no-nonsense type in pants and blouse, plainly served as the first line of defense between eligible bachelorettes and the good professor, and her demeanor plunged from friendly to chilly when Diana asked to see Austin.

"I'm sorry, ma'am," she intoned. "Dr. Austin doesn't hold regular office hours, but if you leave your name and telephone number with me, he'll get back to you."

Right. Diana hauled out her investigator's license from her purse. Occasionally, the thing came in handy. "This is official business. I'm here on behalf of Dr. Austin's benefactor, Mr. Steven Carmichael."

Ooh, successful shot. The woman's mouth thinned. "I'm not allowed to give out his office number to nonstudents, but he's teaching his Intro to Archaeology class right now in room 150. You can wait outside and catch him there after class."

While she had no intention of lurking outside any classroom, Diana smiled her thanks and walked away, paying no mind to the secretary's hostile stare.

Rattling cages for a living usually meant annoying people.

Five minutes later, Diana found the room, eased the door open, slipped inside, and leaned against the wall at the back of the room.

Professor Austin stood by the chalkboard at the front of the classroom, facing away from her. He wore a white, short-sleeved shirt tucked into khaki cargo pants, and lectured as he drew a diagram with quick, aggressive strokes of chalk.

". . . which is the theory behind *terminus ante* and *post quem* dating. Let's say you're excavating a refuse pit and want to know how to date it."

Caught up in his subject, he didn't notice the buzz of whispers or the absolute silence that followed.

"The oldest artifact found *in situ* will be—"

Austin suddenly broke off, his body tensing as if he'd sensed a predator at his back, and turned.

Across the room, their eyes met—and Diana's first thought, with surprise and irritation, was that the TV and magazine photos didn't do Austin justice. No camera could ever fully capture this man's energy or magnetism.

The direct intensity of his dark gaze commanded attention first, then she noticed how long days under a tropical sun had added coppery highlights to his dark brown hair. And how his tanned skin and lean strength made even conservative clothing look sexy. If L. L. Bean ever recruited Jack Austin as a spokesperson, their stock in button-down shirts would skyrocket.

With twenty-five pairs of speculative gazes on her—two-thirds of them female—Diana watched

Austin, curious to see how he'd respond to her presence.

After slowly surveying her from head to toe, Austin arched one eyebrow, turned back to the chalkboard, and continued to lecture and sketch diagrams as if a strange woman in orange hadn't just invaded his classroom.

"The earliest, or oldest, artifact found *in situ* is often referred to as the *terminus ante quem*, and the latest, or newest, artifact as the *terminus post quem*. Everything in the pit will be dated after the earliest artifact, but before the latest."

Austin faced his class again, resting a shoulder against the chalkboard. "Some of you look confused, so let me put it this way. In my refuse pit I find dozens of record albums. The earliest, in the bottom sediment layer, is Elvis Presley's *Heartbreak Hotel*, first cut. The album in the topmost layer is a first edition of the Beatles's *Abbey Road*. I know *Heartbreak Hotel* came out in 1956, and *Abbey Road* in 1969. With nothing in the pit earlier than 1956 or later than 1969, the artifacts I find as I excavate the layers between will fall within these two dates. This means the people who tossed their trash in my pit did so during the golden age of rock and roll. Is that any clearer?"

Nodding heads, a few laughs, and a murmur of assent followed. For the remaining fifteen minutes of the class, Diana relaxed and enjoyed watching Austin in action. He had a laid-back teaching style, a deep, slightly raspy voice with a hint of a Boston accent, and no difficulty whatsoever in keeping his students' attention on him rather than on her—

despite the fact he was talking about dating ancient garbage.

This was charisma: when you didn't care if that man thought garbage was exciting; you just wanted to watch him move, hear him talk.

And she bet he'd turn that charisma up to sizzling hot or down to icy cold as the situation demanded. Probably she'd get something closer to icy cold; she often had that effect on men once they realized all the little lady wanted from them was answers to questions.

"That's it for today." Austin parked his butt on the table in front of the room and folded his arms over his chest. "Project reports are due next Wednesday. If you need to talk with me before then, see me after class."

Oh, great. An open invitation to get mobbed—and keep her at a distance until, gee whiz, he just had to move along.

Undaunted, Diana pushed away from the wall and made her way toward the front of the room, paying no mind to the curious stares. Austin, nodding as a young woman spoke earnestly to him, watched Diana's approach with all the warmth of a big bayou gator.

"I'll be in my office at three," he said to the petite student. "You can come by then."

The woman nodded and reluctantly moved away, the expression on her pretty face branding Diana an interloper.

Coming to a stop directly in front of Austin, Diana flashed her most polite smile. "I'm looking for Dr. Jack Austin."

"That'd be me," he said evenly, the look in his eyes telling her he wasn't fooled by her claim not to know him. "What can I do for you?"

"Diana Belmaine. Private investigator." Again, she displayed her license. His gaze flicked briefly to it without any obvious emotion, then returned to her face as she added, "I'd like to talk with you. Alone, please."

He shrugged. "Fine."

No surprise at finding a PI in his classroom? How interesting. She'd read up on Austin, and from all accounts he was something of a hothead. Two summers past, he'd gotten into a gunfight with would-be looters and ended up in a Guatemalan jail for a couple of weeks—and that hadn't been the first time he'd used a gun, or his fists, to protect his excavations.

"Come with me to my office," Austin ordered as he pushed away from the table. He gathered together a few books and papers and walked off without waiting to see if she followed.

Huh . . . maybe he was a little annoyed, after all.

Diana lengthened her strides to match his, which wasn't easy in three-inch slingback heels and a tight skirt.

"Are we in a hurry?" she asked, as they approached the department office.

"No," he said, but didn't slow down.

The secretary watched their approach. "I have a few messages for you, Dr. Austin." The woman's gaze shifted to Diana as she handed over the yellow slips. "I see the lady found you."

Austin folded the messages without reading them

and slipped them in his pocket. "It's okay, Carol." To Diana, he said, "This way."

He led her up a flight of stairs—he took them two at a time, to her annoyance, although she didn't mind the view from behind—and down a long hall. As they passed offices with open doors, Diana glimpsed people craning their necks to watch. Voices abruptly halted in midconversation.

Well, orange *was* an eye-catching color . . . and she supposed it didn't help that her heels sounded sharp and aggressive on the linoleum tile floor.

Finally, Austin motioned her into a small office and shut the door behind him. The room looked comfortably messy and smelled like old books—a great number of which sat on shelves, on the floor, and on Austin's desk. The desk also held a computer, a phone that looked older than most of his students, and a coffee cup with dried residue at the bottom.

Two cheap stackable chairs were angled in front of Austin's old Steelcase desk, and she dropped her purse onto one as he sat. Instead of sitting, Diana examined book titles and admired a series of framed pencil drawings of Mesoamerican hieroglyphs. The drawings were amazingly detailed, but she couldn't make sense of all the stylized curves and curlicues.

Behind her, Austin shifted in his chair, and the atmosphere in the small room all but hummed with his impatience.

After several seconds, Austin said dryly, "You did need to talk with me, right?"

"Yes, I do." Confident she'd regained the upper hand, Diana turned. "Lovely drawings."

"Mayan hieroglyphs. It's a pictorial form of language." He sat back to watch her—or, more accurately, to better check out her breasts and legs. "Have a seat."

Diana smiled, despite her annoyance at his blunt appraisal of her body. She rested a hand on the back of a chair, but remained standing to keep him looking up at her for a moment longer. "I know what glyphs are. I majored in archaeology in college, but it turned out I didn't have the patience for the work. Plus I'm not big on bugs and dirt."

"So you became a private investigator?"

"I'm good at piecing things together, and I specialize in art fraud and stolen antiquities—so I put what I'd learned to good use after all."

The muscles around his mouth and nose tightened, ever so slightly.

"So why do you want to see me?"

"I'm here on behalf of an acquaintance of yours." Diana made a show of sitting down, smoothing her short skirt and crossing her legs. "Steven Carmichael."

Austin leaned back, his chair springs creaking loudly. "What happened? Did Steve lose another couple crates of pots?"

"Something like that."

He rubbed his thumb along his bottom lip, plainly skeptical. "So you're really a PI? This isn't just a way of getting in my office so you can slip me your telephone number?"

Wow; nothing small about this man's ego. She fixed him with a cool look. "In your dreams, Dr. Austin."

Smiling slowly, he looked down, his gaze lingering on her mouth, then lower. "I'm already there."

His frank, wholly male aggression surprised her, then immediately roused her suspicions. On a sudden hunch, she deliberately recrossed her legs. He didn't look down to watch, much less leer.

Well, well. Not exactly Mr. Consistent. Austin was overplaying his interest in her, probably as a distraction—which intrigued her almost as much as that fleeting look of wariness on his face moments ago. She'd go along with him—for now. "You're trying to flirt with me."

He made a face of mock concentration and pointed a finger at her. "Good observation skills. I bet you're one crack private investigator."

Oh, boy. Smart-ass alert.

Not rising to the bait this time, Diana pulled a notepad and pen from her purse, catching sight of the *People* magazine as she did so. On an impulse, she took it out, folded it to the page with Austin doing his pagan sex god impersonation, then tossed it on his desk. He looked down, face impassive, then pushed it aside, out of his direct line of vision.

Almost as if it embarrassed him.

"I'm sure there are a lot of women across the country who'd love to worship you up close and personal, Dr. Austin, but I'm not one of them."

Austin laid a hand over his chest, drawing her attention to his long fingers, dusted with dark hairs.

Powerful hands, more a workman's than a scholar's, and yet somehow still elegant.

"I'm crushed," he said.

Diana clicked her pen with force. "No, you're not. Now, let's get back to business. These artifacts are over three thousand years old, worth a heck of lot of money, and my client wants them back."

He raised a brow in apparent amusement. "It might help if you told me what you're looking for."

In spite of her sudden, irrational urge to lunge across the desk and shake him, Diana maintained her poise. "A small alabaster box with a gold statuette inside. It's Egyptian. Eighteenth Dynasty. Were you aware my client had these objects in his private collection?"

Austin leaned even farther back, resting an ankle across his knee, lacing his hands behind his head—which did wonders for showing off his chest. Oh, yes; the man obviously knew a distraction technique or two himself.

"Steve collects lots of things, including financially challenged archaeologists, but mostly he collects pre-Columbian art," Austin said in that low, raspy voice that seemed to rub against her skin, as soothing-rough as a cat's tongue.

Diana shook off the sensation. "Did you know he owned Egyptian artifacts? Yes or no, please."

Something very like anger flashed across Austin's face. "Yes, although not what you've described. I've seen a few scarab amulets and rings. And I remember him mentioning pottery and a late Roman funerary portrait. That's it."

Nodding, she jotted down his answer, then looked up. "He funds your excavations at Tikukul, doesn't he?"

"His foundation does, in part. I'm high-profile, and the society likes high-profile. Good PR and all that."

Diana detected a coolness in Austin's voice, as if maybe he didn't think too much of his benefactor. "And you also know about the shipment my client recently lost to thieves."

"Who doesn't? I read the newspapers, and I talk regularly with Steve."

He jiggled his foot, drawing her attention to his hiking boots. Well-worn and expensive; boots for someone who did a lot of walking and climbing.

"And just so we're clear on this, Ms. Belmaine, I'm paid to find artifacts, not steal them."

Alert to the tension rising in the room, Diana said evenly, "I never said you stole anything."

"No, but you're considering it." Austin smiled again, but it didn't quite mesh with his intent, watchful expression.

"Nothing personal, Dr. Austin. In my line of work, everybody's guilty until proven innocent."

"Bet that makes you a fun girl to talk with at parties," he said dryly, then shifted in his chair, lowering his foot to the floor with a loud *thump*. "So about this box and statuette, I assume they belonged to someone famous."

"I'm not at liberty to discuss specific details, but yes, they have a definite historical significance."

"I don't have to be an Egyptologist to make a few

guesses here. Are you talking about the last pharaohs of the Eighteenth Dynasty? Tut and company?"

"Let's say that's true." She kept her expression noncommittal. "Who among Mr. Carmichael's circle of acquaintances would be interested in acquiring funerary artifacts from this period?"

Austin laughed, a chest-deep, genuine laugh that made it almost impossible not to want to laugh along with him.

"Come on, you're looking at a select group of wealthy people who obsessively collect old things, and the older and rarer the better. You're gonna need to come up with better questions, Ms. Belmaine."

Tamping back a fresh spurt of annoyance, Diana smiled. Despite his arrogance and attempts to goad her into losing her cool, she couldn't quite resist the pull of his attraction—and it wasn't just his good ol' boy sex appeal, either. Behind the smiles and studied indifference, he was hiding something. She could all but smell the lies he'd wrapped around himself.

"Oh, I don't know. I'm learning quite a lot so far. More than you realize."

At that, Austin sat forward, elbows on the cluttered desk, his face suddenly serious. "Okay. This has been fun, but I have another class to teach soon. How about you tell me why you're really here."

Pushy, pushy. Diana tipped her head and asked, "What time did you arrive at the Jade Jaguar for the opening party?"

"I got there at eight, and left at about ten-thirty."

"At any time did you go upstairs to the offices or storage room?"

"I drank a lot of Steve's free wine, and had to use the upstairs john a couple times when the downstairs one was busy. Other than that, all the action was in the gallery. I didn't want to miss Steve's big night." Again, a hint of irony colored his tone. "Why are you asking?"

"Because the theft likely occurred the night of the gallery's opening. I'm talking with all the guests, starting with the 'A' names and working my way on down."

"Lucky me, that my name starts with an 'A.'"

Diana raised a brow at his sarcasm, then turned her attention to jotting down his answers.

"How good are you?"

Caught off guard by the question, Diana glanced up. "Excuse me?"

"How good are you?" His focus on her had suddenly intensified—almost uncomfortably so. "As an investigator, that is."

Her face warmed at the suggestive tone of his voice—and she didn't like how easily he flustered her. "I always get my man, Dr. Austin."

Most of the time, anyway.

"That's not exactly an answer."

Diana didn't break eye contact. "I just wrapped up an insurance fraud case, and last month I recovered a quarter million in gold bullion looted from a shipwreck off the coast of Florida."

"A quarter mil." Austin's expression had turned speculative, assessing—as if he'd finally decided to take her seriously. "How'd you do it?"

"It takes hard work and determination, though sometimes I don't have to work as hard as you might think. The thieves tried to sell the gold on eBay."

"You're serious?" he asked, incredulous.

"Nobody ever said crooks are smart," she said lightly. "Most of them are pretty dumb."

His focus on her sharpened, and then he smiled. "But you like it better when they're smart."

She shrugged. "It's more of a challenge that way."

"You like the hunt."

"No, Dr. Austin." Holding his gaze, she leaned slightly toward him, and smiled back. "I *love* the hunt."

A charged tension filled the room, and as the silence between them lengthened, she sensed she'd just hit pay dirt. He knew more about what happened at the gallery that night than he was telling; she just didn't know exactly how much yet.

"Are we done?" Austin asked evenly.

"For now. Thank you for taking the time to answer my questions." Diana stood and pulled a business card from her purse. "If you hear anything that might help, please give me a call."

Austin took the card, but didn't look at it. "Will do."

Diana hitched her purse over her shoulder and donned the sunglasses for a touch more attitude. She didn't move away from the desk. "I think you're lying to me, Dr. Austin."

As his smile widened, her temper snapped. She *hated* it when people—especially men people—thought they could toy with her just because she was female and blond.

Walking with a deliberate, languid slowness around his desk, she leaned down, close enough to smell the scent of his soap and shampoo; close enough to see the fine lines around his eyes, the mingled brown-and-copper shades of his hair, the reddish beard stubble . . . and to feel the tension vibrating off him.

A tension thick with as much sexual awareness as anger.

"I'll be watching you," she whispered in his ear, her lips nearly brushing his warm skin. She moistened her lips with her tongue, and he tensed. "And if you did help yourself to a couple extra party favors from my client's gallery, I'll take you down, no matter how much it'll break my poor little heart to see your very fine ass in jail."

In such an intimate proximity, she could feel every touch of his breath. Finally, she stepped away. Though she yearned to knock that damn grin off his face, she coolly blew him a kiss, then strolled out the door and shut it firmly behind her.

THREE

...

Smile fading, Jack stared at the closed door and pulled in a long, deep breath. The sweet, musky scent of her perfume lingered heavily in the air, filling his senses and stirring something inside him that was better left unstirred, dammit. The receding click of her high heels still echoed outside in the hall, and nearly matched the crazy beating of his heart—which wasn't just because of alarm.

Jesus. Letting out his breath, he rubbed at his brows. The day had started out bad and now, thanks to this feral female who'd crashed his classroom and the refuge of his office, it had gotten a whole lot worse.

But his initial alarm began to fade, edged out by a sense of admiration—and a hot bloom of lust. He'd always liked women with a bit of a bite to them; too bad this particular woman could also deep-six his career and his reputation—his *life*—if he wasn't careful. For damn sure, he hadn't seen the last of this hot blonde with the cool blue eyes that saw too much.

She'd caught him by surprise, that was all. While she had a few suspicions and a lot of brass, she had no evidence. Yet, in under fifteen minutes, she'd made him. How had he tipped her off? Had she seen or sensed something, or was it just that he hadn't been able to resist playing with her a little?

Later. He'd worry about this later when he had more time to think.

Frowning, he looked down, and that stupid magazine Diana Belmaine had dropped on his desk caught his attention.

I'm sure there are a lot of women across the country who'd love to worship you up close and personal, Dr. Austin.

Judging from the disconcertingly large amount of mail he'd received over the past few years, most of those "women" averaged about fourteen years of age, and sent letters usually starting with: *Dear Dr. Jack . . . you are SO hot! I saw you on TV . . .*

Off to the side of his desk were more of those letters; they'd piled up all summer while he'd been sweating out the jungle heat at Tikukul. He'd take them home tonight and write back, since not answering wasn't an option. While it embarrassed him to have a starring role in the fantasies of fourteen-year-old girls, he couldn't be such a bastard as to stomp all over their dreams.

A knock sounded on his closed door. Shaking free of his morose thoughts, Jack looked up, and called, "It's open."

The door swung inward, and one of his students poked her head inside, smiling shyly—and reminding him it wasn't only the fragile psyches of fourteen-year-olds he had to be careful with.

"Melissa. Come in." He smiled, trying his best to look fatherly yet distant. As she made to shut the door, he added, "Please leave it open."

Because he had to be careful of his own ass, too. Despite the pretty PI's skepticism, women had offered him their phone numbers—and made a few eye-popping propositions—in the privacy of his office.

"Oh. Okay. Sorry." The young woman sat down, dropping her backpack to the floor, and looked at him expectantly, notebook and pen in hand.

"What's up?"

"I'm doing my project report on underwater archaeology, but I'm not sure what articles to start with? I was kind of hoping you could help me with that?"

Jack reined in his impatience. He rattled off a few names and titles as Melissa wrote furiously, then added mildly, "All these articles are in the library. Try the subject index. If you have any trouble, just go find the reference librarian."

She beamed at him, as if he'd said something startling and profound. "Thank you, Professor Austin. This has been a really big help."

He rubbed at his cheek, hiding a smile. "No problem."

Two more female students followed Melissa, each with equally transparent motives, and after the last one left, Jack shut the door. He was gathering his books and a slide carousel for his next class—a grad

seminar on Mayan hieroglyphics—when a knock
sounded again.

"Yeah?"

The door opened to admit not another student,
but a tall woman with graying dark hair, wearing
sensible pants and an equally sensible blouse—Judith Mayer, the department chair. Never a good
sign.

"Hey, Judith, I'm on my way to class. Can it
wait?"

She shut the door firmly behind her.

Jack grimaced. "Guess not."

"Why was that woman in the orange suit here to
see you? Carol told me she's a private investigator."

"Yup."

Judith gave a heavy sigh. "What did you do this
time, Jack?"

He tried not to scowl. "She's talking to people
who were at Steve Carmichael's opening party at the
Jade Jaguar. I was one of the guests. That's it."

"So we won't get any embarrassing calls from re-
porters?" She narrowed her eyes. "Or the police?"

"Look, I settled the problem in Guatemala over
two *years* ago. It's time to let it go, Judith."

Fat chance of that; she'd never let him forget he
was the only professor during all her years at Tulane
who'd ever been arrested and jailed.

Her attitude pretty much summed up the department's love/hate relationship with him. They loved
the attention he brought since it translated into
funding for other faculty projects, but hated the oc-
casional controversy. He never apologized for his

temper, his opinions, or his tendency to get in the way of trouble or a camera, and while he could've taken a position at any university, he'd wanted to come to New Orleans. It wasn't like any other city in the country, and he fit right in with all the other beggars and thieves, liars and charlatans.

"I can't help always jumping to conclusions where you're concerned." Judith's mouth, outlined in a sensible neutral lipstick, curved in a thin smile. "You're an asset to our department, and your work is top-notch, of course. But I'm not quite convinced that even the time you spent in jail taught you a single thing about being responsible."

Academic envy was at the root of much of her dislike of him, and he tried keeping that in mind at times like this. "Trust me, it taught me plenty. Now, excuse me, but I gotta go impart knowledge and inspire minds."

"One of these days, Austin," Judith said coolly as he brushed past her, "you're going to dig yourself a hole so deep you won't be able to get out."

Just outside the door, Jack turned. He gave her an exaggerated wink, knowing it would annoy her. "Hey—even us brainy guys need to have a little fun."

The Jade Jaguar was the newest of many antique shops and galleries in the Warehouse District, an area reclaimed in recent years from neglect and ruin. The abandoned buildings along Magazine Street had been converted into luxury condos, pricey shops, and galleries. Travel guides called it the

"SoHo of the South," and Diana couldn't visit the district without remembering New York—sometimes a blessing, sometimes not.

She found a parking spot close to Julia Street and pulled in. She was early, which gave her a few minutes to think about Jack Austin. A short while ago, she'd been certain the man had lied to her, certain he knew something about the alabaster box and gold statuette, but now doubts began seeping in.

He'd been awfully cocky, but maybe that was his natural personality. It didn't make sense that a respected, tenured professor would be supplementing his salary with a little black market dealing in ancient artifacts.

Yet she couldn't dismiss the possibility. The mess she'd left behind in New York had come about because she'd refused to believe the obvious when she should have, and by the time she'd faced the truth, it had been too late.

She wouldn't make that same mistake with Austin. Yes, he was good-looking and yes, he appeared to have everything a man could want—but that didn't automatically earn him good guy status.

Diana swung out of the Mustang and locked the door, acknowledging another thought: She couldn't dismiss Carmichael as a suspect either.

Tangling with the rich and powerful was like walking a minefield—too often things blew up in your face—and she wanted the thief to be a gallery employee. The chances of that remained high. Past experience had taught her that if the owner of the "stolen" item wasn't trying to pull something funny, then an employee had seized a moment of opportunity to make a fast buck.

But before interviewing Carmichael's employees, she had to talk to the head honcho himself and quiz him about that stolen shipment of Mayan artifacts. She didn't believe in coincidence; that he'd been the victim of two robberies in such a short time period suggested more than a simple theft of opportunity.

Diana walked quickly past the boutiques, antique shops, and galleries lining Julia Street, anxious to get out of the heat and sticky humidity. She couldn't miss the gallery's sign—a snarling jaguar painted jade green—mounted on the weathered pinkish brick of a square, squat warehouse.

Walking inside revealed an airy, modern gallery. Diana stood in the cool entryway, letting her eyes adjust to the muted lighting.

A young black man wearing a security uniform and a sidearm—a new addition to the security, that gun—greeted her when she walked forward. "Hello, ma'am. Is there anything I can help you with?"

"I'm Diana Belmaine. Mr. Carmichael is expecting me."

"I'll have someone call up to the office and let him know you're here."

While she waited for an employee to escort her to his office, Diana strolled into the gallery. The brick interior walls were painted red, and plants dominated the decor: tall palm trees and large-leafed, potted plants sitting on the floor, as well as hanging from the walls. Display cases held most of the artifacts, although a few had been mounted on the walls, and the larger items—stone steles, architectural friezes, vases, and sculptures—were arranged in freestanding displays. Simple benches lined the walls, and water trickled peacefully from a small, central fountain. The carpeting was a broad-leaf pattern, in shades of dark red, green, brown, and gold.

Junglelike, except for that savage red splash of the walls.

A Mayan jade funerary mask, in a display case in front of the center fountain, caught her attention, and she walked over to admire it. Spectacular, beautifully preserved, and worth a freaking fortune— a museum could build an entire collection around such a piece.

"Lovely, isn't it?"

Recognizing the voice—and its slight Texas twang—Diana turned to the man behind her, a smile disguising her surprise that he'd come himself.

Gray-haired, gray-eyed, wearing jeans and a short-sleeved chambray shirt filled out by broad shoulders, Steven Carmichael looked younger than his sixty-four years, thanks to the best personal trainer, clothes, and haircuts money could buy. Most women would find him handsome and compelling; he exuded the power of a man used to getting his way.

"Absolutely beautiful," Diana said.

"It's part of my personal collection and not for sale. I have it out here because I can't bear to lock it away. It was created for kings and gods, and something this magnificent is meant to be seen."

Not sure what to say, she held out her hand. "Mr. Carmichael, I'm Diana Belmaine."

"I remember you from our last talk, Ms. Belmaine." He shook her hand firmly. "My apologies for being unable to meet with you sooner, but I've had a hectic schedule this week."

"No apology necessary." She turned toward the jade mask. "Late Preclassic period, and in excellent condition. Where'd you buy it?"

"A private auction." He didn't elaborate, and motioned behind him. "Would you like a quick tour of the gallery before we talk?"

"Yes, thank you," Diana said. "The place is gorgeous."

"Most of the credit goes to my manager, Audrey Spencer." Carmichael smiled, which made him look even younger, somehow softer. He really was quite an attractive man. "I'll introduce you to her in a moment. This way."

The tour didn't take long. As she knew from the building plans in the file, the gallery had been designed as one open room, with a central suspended spiral staircase of distressed iron that led to the storage room and offices located on the partial second floor. There were public rest rooms on the main floor, as well as a small gift shop that sold quality souvenirs, calendars, books, and framed and unframed prints. The gift shop had a cash register, but all sales for pricier items were conducted one-on-one in an upstairs office, the ultimate in customer service.

A desk with a computer and phone sat to one side

of the main room, and behind it stood a petite, red-haired woman wearing an off-white linen dress. She smiled at their approach.

"This is Audrey, my right arm and my lifeline. Audrey, this is Diana Belmaine. She's investigating the theft from my office. She'll talk to you after she meets with me."

Diana shook hands with the woman, quickly sizing her up: young, attractive, and single. Plenty of potential motivation right here. Audrey might be decent, honest, and hardworking, but she could also be sleeping with the boss. There were reasons why men like Carmichael hired perky young assistants.

Still, the intelligence in the woman's hazel eyes hinted she knew exactly what Diana was thinking, and her smile chilled a fraction. "I'll be happy to give Ms. Belmaine my full cooperation, Steven."

"I know you will. Ms. Belmaine, this way, please."

Carmichael, unlike Jack Austin, acted like a perfect gentleman. He politely led the way up the stairs, making small talk. While Diana responded, she noted the second floor took up roughly half the space of the first, supported from below by columns covered in leafy vines. She could see almost the entire gallery from the balcony. All the office doors faced the brass-and-Plexiglas balcony—no place to lurk unnoticed—and were equipped with number pad security access.

Carmichael opened the center door and motioned her inside. A massive aquarium took up almost half a wall, its bluish glow filling the room until Carmichael snapped on the lights. It was a spacious office, the walls painted soft white and decorated with Victorian-era prints of ruined cities in jungles, as well as more very nice artifacts, including an Aztec portrait head and an intact Preclassic Mayan vase.

The carpeting was an off-white Berber flecked with brighter colors, and the furnishings Danish modern in honey tones. The L-shaped desk held a computer, fax, printer, and a lot of scattered files and paper. A matching armoire stood to the left of the desk, and two office chairs, upholstered in red leather, were placed in front. A large red leather couch tucked against the far corner, with a coffee table stacked with books and magazines, finished off the room.

The back wall had a line of small windows, all of wire security glass. Not the easiest place to pull a heist, but she never underestimated human ingenuity.

"Have a seat, please." Carmichael pulled out one of the red chairs for her, and she sat, thanking him.

He moved to the other side of the desk and eased down into his chair. "I imagine you have questions."

Diana nodded. "I read the report in the file. From what I understand, the armoire contains a safe, your personal files, cigar box collection, and a few other smaller pieces from your collection."

"That's correct."

The phone rang. He ignored it, and after three rings, somebody answered. Probably Audrey, his gal Friday.

She removed her pen and notebook from her purse. "The box was in the armoire, correct?"

"Yes."

"The file was missing a few important papers. Like proof of insurance."

"That's because I didn't insure this particular item. I'm sure you can understand why," he added. "Considering the potential for controversy, I gambled on absolute secrecy keeping the artifact safe—and I lost."

Well. So much for an insurance fraud motive.

"The report also didn't mention how or where you stored the artifact."

Carmichael smiled, amusement sparkling in his eyes. "I kept it in one of the cigar boxes."

Diana arched a brow. "You kept something worth a small fortune in a cigar box?"

"Not just any cigar box, but one I had specially designed for it. A number of my smaller and more valuable pieces are concealed in the faux cigar boxes to deter thieves. I reasoned that if anybody did manage to rob me, they'd take the safe and leave the boxes, which aren't worth much." His gaze hardened, and for the first time, Diana glimpsed the depth of his anger. "Again, I was wrong."

"May I see the armoire?"

"Certainly."

Carmichael got up, unlocked the doors, and swung them open. She noted no scratches or splinters on the door; a lock this basic would be easy to pick without a need for force. The lowest shelf held a small safe that was bolted to the wood, giving an illusion of security, but in reality a thief only had to saw through the wood and walk off with it. A clever decoy—except it hadn't worked.

The shelf above the safe had been converted to a file rack, and the remaining three shelves were stacked with cigar boxes, some old, some new—a large number of them Cuban, and Cohibas in particular.

She didn't consider it her place to point out the ticklish legal aspects of buying or bringing Cuban cigars into the US. So her client wasn't lily-white; who was? The odds of working for a saintly client were on par with being swept off her feet by a hero on a white horse.

Carmichael motioned at the boxes. "These in front actually contain cigars. I know which ones are just cigar boxes, and which ones are fake and hold coins, jewels, and my other small treasures."

"Why don't you keep them in a safety-deposit box? It's what most people would do."

"I know, but I've always preferred to have my collections close at hand. That way I can show the pieces whenever I want. And besides, I can't bear to lock any of them away."

It was the second time he'd said as much, and he must've seen the skepticism on her face because he smiled.

"I'm a collector and a connoisseur, Ms. Belmaine. I believe objects of beauty, these pieces rich in our past and heritage, are meant to be seen by all, not buried in bank vaults, a rich man's mansion, or in some crate in a museum basement. Call me eccentric, but I believe that since I am privileged enough to have the means to own them, the very least I can do is share them."

Carmichael's benevolent god tone was starting to

irritate her. "Except you weren't planning on sharing the Nefertiti box with John Q. Public, were you?"

"No. Very few people know I own this little memento. Please understand that I don't approve of the fact it was stolen in the first place, but it's passed through many owners over the years. It's mine now. And I will get it back."

He sat down, and Diana joined him. She'd seen what she'd needed in the armoire.

"I can tell you don't approve," he said after a moment.

"My personal feelings aren't important. You hired me to recover stolen property legally belonging to you, and that's what I'll do."

He steepled his fingers, studying her over them, the animated gleam in his eyes at odds with his crisp, authoritative bearing. "Think about it: to have in your possession a family memento of an ancient pharaoh who died when he was little more than a boy, a lock of hair that might have belonged to history's most beautiful queen . . . how could I resist?"

"You don't owe me an explanation, Mr. Carmichael."

Scholars the world over would give almost anything to have a piece of hair that could make clear the mysterious lineages and tangled successions of Egypt's most controversial dynasty. But Carmichael was paying her to find a thief—paying her *very* well—and it'd be smart to focus on that, rather than judging his actions.

Smoothly changing direction, Diana spent the next half hour questioning him, mostly about small details. She'd just asked about the lost Mayan shipment when Carmichael announced he had another meeting. He handed her off to Audrey, asking her to show Diana the rest of the offices and storage rooms.

Diana took Carmichael's brush-off in stride, and, notebook in hand, carefully examined the gallery, questioning the security guard and Audrey as needed. Audrey smiled that same cool smile, but she responded with efficient professionalism. If she was boffing her boss, it wasn't because she was too dim to know better.

After another hour of poking about and taking notes, Diana asked Audrey to show her the upstairs area. The storage room, on the far left, smelled like raw plywood and sawdust and, as expected, contained shelves and lots of boxes. Next she checked over the employee lounge, including the bathrooms, and found everything neat and tidy. While Carmichael's office connected to the lounge, that door had a private security code known only to him and Audrey. The last office, on the right, belonged to Audrey.

"I share the office with our accountant, who works Wednesdays and Fridays," she explained, punching in the security code and opening the door.

Although smaller than Carmichael's office, it had been decorated in the same pale colors and minimalist modern furnishings—two desks, a row of filing cabinets along the right wall, art prints lining the others, and more plants. The same small windows, same security glass. Audrey's desk, which looked neater than her boss's, also faced two red leather chairs.

An unsecured door in the far wall caught Diana's

attention—she didn't remember seeing it on the building plan. "Does that lead to Mr. Carmichael's office?"

Audrey nodded. "Usually we keep it closed, but when Steven and I are working on joint projects it's easier to come and go without the hassle of dealing with the security locks. And without customers seeing us."

"So you and the accountant have access to Mr. Carmichael's office?"

Again, Audrey nodded. "But I rarely go in there when he's not at his desk. The same goes for Martin, the accountant."

"How about the housekeeping staff? The security guards?"

"Of course they'd have access to all the rooms. The housekeeping staff clean during regular hours, and someone is almost always up here. The guards patrol after hours, and their duties include checking the offices." Audrey walked to her desk. "Please have a seat, Ms. Belmaine."

"Thanks." Diana sat, and flipped to a new page in her notebook. "Let's talk about the night of the opening party. Who organized it?"

"That would be me. I'm in charge of most everything at the gallery, from ordering souvenirs to picking out carpet to feeding Steven's fish when he's out of town."

Diana smiled. "No wonder he can't function without you."

Audrey smiled back, a shade more friendly this time.

"What was security like the night of the party?"

"Lax, as you can imagine, although people had to produce an invitation to enter. We had over a hundred guests coming and going between 7 P.M. and midnight, as well as the caterers and waitstaff. We had a guard on duty at the front door and on the balcony. All the offices were locked except for the staff lounge, because we needed to keep the upstairs bathrooms open."

"Makes sense." It also meshed with what Austin had told her earlier. "So you know for certain that nobody entered Mr. Carmichael's office, or your own?"

Audrey said, "Yes," even as a blush slowly colored her fair, freckled skin.

Diana let several seconds pass. "You're sure? When I interview the other guests, no one will remember seeing anybody enter either office?"

"You're interviewing our guests? All of them?"

"I'm an investigator, Ms. Spencer. It's what I do."

Audrey looked down, sighed, then met Diana's gaze again. "All right. I went up to my office. Steven doesn't know, and he'll be angry if he finds out."

Diana couldn't give the assurance of silence that Audrey wanted, so she asked, "Why were you up in the office during the party?"

"You have to understand I've been working my ass off for months on this gallery, getting it ready for the opening. Most days I got in here at six in the morning and didn't leave until ten at night, and that includes weekends."

Diana nodded, encouraging her to continue, and closely watching her. Right now, she read only embarrassment mixed with a little defensiveness.

"So finally the gallery is open, the party is a *huge* success, and all that time and effort I put into things has paid off." Audrey shrugged. "I was finally going to kick back and have a good time, you know?"

Again, Diana nodded; a woman-to-woman-I-understand kind of nod.

"I overdid things with the wine, and this guy was at the party . . . a guy I've been in lust with for *months*." Audrey's face grew even pinker. "Blame it on liquid courage, but I kind of propositioned him. He must've hit the wine pretty hard, too, because he said yes."

"Why is it strange he said yes? You're an attractive woman."

Audrey looked a little uncomfortable. "He's never paid much attention to me before. Not in that way."

"So you and this guy went up to your office for a little privacy."

"Yes, except that . . . well, Steven has a couch in his office." Audrey fiddled with a paper clip, bending it out of shape. "A big couch."

"Ah," Diana said, and managed to hold back her smile.

"Steven would kill me if he knew. Well, not *literally* kill me, but he'd be pretty angry."

"Why? Jealous?"

Audrey blinked. "He'd be angry because I acted unprofessionally. Steven and I don't have a sexual relationship. He might try for that if I gave him the chance, because I know he's not exactly faithful to his wife, but I don't sleep with married men."

The woman's expression was steady, open. Honest. If she didn't sleep with married men, she probably didn't steal, either.

"Who was the man you brought upstairs?"

"I'd rather not say."

"Ms. Spencer, people saw you go upstairs." Diana leaned forward, and said gently, "All I have to do is start asking questions, and eventually I'll find out. It'd save us both a lot of time if you just tell me now."

Shoulders slumping, Audrey looked down. "His name is Jack Austin."

A jolt of surprise hit first, quickly followed by anger, and then a tiny twinge of disappointment. After a moment, she said calmly, "Jack Austin . . . he's that archaeologist from Tulane, right?"

Audrey nodded, a tiny smile curving her mouth; satisfied and smug.

Keeping her temper in check, Diana pasted on a sly smile and played the "sympathetic girlfriend" angle. "Lucky you. I've seen pictures of him. He's really good-looking."

Audrey brightened and leaned forward as well, all hush-hush and conspiratorial. "Oh, God, yes. Every time he calls, every time I see him, I get this little zap, you know? I've been in lust with him ever since Steven first introduced us—"

"Which was when?"

"A few weeks before Jack went to Guatemala for the summer. And this may sound dumb, but he's not just another pretty face. He's smart and funny, and so interesting to talk to. Get a few beers in that man, and the stories he can tell . . . I can't believe I made a pass at him. And I still can't believe he said yes!"

"Oh, I believe it," Diana said evenly.

So the studly Dr. Austin *had* lied to her—and helped himself to a lot more than the upstairs john and Audrey's obvious charms.

Closing her notebook with deliberate slowness, she sat back again. "Ms. Spencer, do you know why I'm here?"

Audrey's smile faded. "One of Steven's Egyptian pieces is missing."

"You don't know exactly what it is?"

The woman shook her head. "Unless it's in the gallery, it's his business, not mine. And I would *never* steal anything from Steven."

"Please understand, these are questions I have to ask," Diana said automatically. "How about Dr. Austin? Would he do it?"

Audrey stared at her. "You're kidding, right? Jack's not that kind of guy, and he and Steven are really tight. Steven treats him almost like a son. Jack wouldn't do anything like that, not even as a joke."

Now this was an interesting bit of news. Judging from Austin's earlier attitude about Carmichael, she didn't expect a father-son type of relationship.

"Besides," Audrey said with a sigh, "we weren't even in the office for ten minutes when Jack's pager went off and he had to leave the party. Something about an emergency with a grad student in the lab."

"When was this?"

"I don't know . . . I wasn't paying close attention. It was after ten, though."

Which meshed with Austin's story. At least he

hadn't lied about everything. Bully for him.

"And the two of you were together the entire time you were in the office?"

Audrey frowned. "He didn't steal anything."

"Please answer the question, Ms. Spencer."

"I went to the bathroom to freshen up." Audrey's demeanor had chilled again. "We didn't do *the deed*, but I had to fix my makeup and hair before we went back downstairs. I let him make his call from Steven's office. I was in the bathroom for no more than a minute or so, Ms. Belmaine. That's it. I can't believe you'd even consider that Jack could do something like that, or be so stupid."

"I'm only doing my job. It's nothing personal."

The reminder seemed to calm Audrey, and she reluctantly nodded. "Sorry. I just know none of Steven's friends or acquaintances would steal from him. It must have been somebody on the catering or cleaning crew. You're talking with them, too, right?"

"Yes." Diana returned the notebook and pen to her purse, then stood. "That's about all I need to know for now, thanks. If I have other questions, is it okay for me to drop by to see you, or call?"

"Sure. Steven said I was to do everything I can to help." Audrey came to her feet as well. She hesitated, then asked, "Do you have to tell him I was in his office with Jack? I wouldn't have done it, except I wasn't thinking clearly. I just . . . the gallery is my dream job. I don't want to risk losing it over one dumb impulse."

The woman appeared genuinely worried, and Diana's anger toward Jack mounted. "If nothing comes of this, then I won't feel obligated to say anything."

Audrey looked relieved. "Thanks, I appreciate that."

Diana followed Audrey back down the staircase. Now that it was early afternoon, business had picked up. A dozen or so people had come into the gallery, including a middle-aged couple intently examining a case of pottery. Audrey went to them, relieving the gift shop clerk. Diana headed for the doorway—and stopped short when she saw Steve Carmichael off to the side, deep in conversation with a man she recognized all too well.

Jack Austin.

Realizing they hadn't yet noticed her, she stopped and watched them together. Smiles, low laughter . . . they seemed chummy enough. And why not? Without Carmichael, Austin wouldn't have the funds for excavating each season. Austin's high profile probably came in handy when Carmichael solicited donations for his nonprofit society. And maybe Carmichael liked Austin as a friend; just because Diana didn't like the guy didn't mean others couldn't.

"Steven," Audrey called from behind Diana. "This nice couple would like to talk to you about the Calakmul vase?"

Both Carmichael and Austin glanced up, catching sight of Diana at the same time. Carmichael smiled. Austin did not.

"All done, Ms. Belmaine?" Carmichael asked as he walked toward her.

"For today, yes."

"Good." He touched her on the shoulder, smiled once again, then made his way to Audrey and the older couple.

After sharing a long and not entirely friendly look with Austin, Diana turned her attention to Carmichael, observing his enthusiasm as he spoke with his potential customers. The man owned an oil drilling and shipping business, a farm, a foundation, and a number of other ventures, but it was plain the gallery was his pride and joy. He didn't need to be here, hobnobbing with his customers, but he loved it.

Turning back to Austin, she caught a fleeting look on his face—so brief, she couldn't really pin it down. But it had tasted . . . tense, nothing like the easy camaraderie she'd glimpsed moments before.

She moved toward Austin, who stood by the glass case displaying the funerary mask, and let anger roll over her. It didn't matter that Audrey propositioned him first, or even that nothing had actually happened between them. This wasn't about Audrey, who was an adult and welcome to screw up her own life. This was about Austin using a woman for his dirty work—and that cut way, way too close to a personal pain she wanted badly to forget.

Diana faced Austin, and, for an instant, something hot and alive and aware flared between them.

"Nice mask, huh?" she said, her tone silky and cool.

"I've seen it before." Austin barely glanced down before adding dryly, "You sure do get around."

"Oh, you'll find I'm very thorough." Diana moved closer into his space, and as his brows shot up in surprise, she placed the narrow heel of her shoe on the top of his boot and pressed down—hard.

Austin's eyes opened wide, startled and pained. "What the—"

"That's for using Audrey Spencer, you son of a bitch." She stepped back, and gave him a cold smile as she walked toward the door. "You're not getting away with it, Austin. I promise you that."

FOUR

...

Diana walked into her office shortly after two-thirty, her arms weighed down with shopping bags, and Luna looked up from her computer. "Uh-oh. Somebody's having a bad day."

After pushing the door shut with her heel, Diana blew a loose strand of hair out of her eyes. "Why do you say that?"

"You've been doing a little retail therapy. Whenever you're grumpy, you go shopping."

She dropped her bags across several waiting room chairs. "Actually I'm way beyond grumpy. I let a suspect rattle me today. I stomped on his foot and basically told him his ass was history."

"Whoops," Luna drawled, her eyes bright with interest. "Guess you tipped him off he's a suspect, huh?"

"Oh, yeah." Diana sighed, more than a little irritated with herself for letting personal history color her reaction to the work. She hadn't made such a stupid, gauche mistake since she'd been a rookie.

"Forget the case. Let's talk important stuff. What'd you buy?" Luna sat straight, eager for the show.

Diana laughed. "Maybe you should ask what I *didn't* buy. I swear I hit every boutique within a five-block radius. The first store I went to had a pair of Anne Klein shoes screaming my name, so I put them out of their misery. And look at this skirt . . . is this a perfect eggplant purple or what?"

"Yup." Luna nodded. "Short, too. I approve."

"Then I went a little nuts at Mimi's. They just got in new suits, so I bought two. And another skirt." Diana pulled her spoils out of the bag, and Luna leaned across her desk.

"Raspberry pink, lemon yellow . . . damn, Boss, we gotta do something about your fruits-and-vegetables approach to fashion."

"Hey, I don't give you grief about what you wear. I *like* bright colors." Diana turned back to rummaging through her bags, tissue paper rustling. "Then I hit Pied Nu and bought more shoes, two scarves, and a new purse. After that, I decided I'd better get back here before I had no money to pay your salary for the week."

"Gee, thanks."

Diana grinned and pulled a pair of shoes out of their box. "Ostrich leather, and hand-dyed. What do you think?"

Luna hesitated. "They're orange."

"Well, yeah. I bought them to go with the suit I'm wearing. It's an almost perfect match."

"We could set you in the middle of a highway

during construction season. Like one of those little cone things."

Diana snorted and returned the shoes to their box. "Lucky you're a whiz with my accounting software and an art major; otherwise, I might find you annoying."

Luna, of course, didn't smile, but still managed to look amused. A neat trick, that.

"Time to get back to business, I guess," Diana said. "Any messages?"

"Nope. It's been quiet."

"Good." Diana gathered her bags again. "I need to make a few calls and do some more research. Give a yell if you need me for anything."

Diana retreated to her office and partially shut the door. After settling in at her desk she dragged the Carmichael file toward her and pulled out her list of numbers to call, including the gallery's cleaning service and the company that had catered the opening night party.

"Honey," said the woman who owned the catering company, "we were hustling our butts off that night. I had my people busy every second from setup to breakdown. I was downstairs the entire time—you can ask the manager, Audrey, or the security guards—and I never saw any of my people leave. We're professionals, and I check my references very carefully."

Diana took the names of the six waitstaff. She'd follow up, even if it didn't look promising, and even if she was fairly certain Austin was her thief.

The upstairs security guard verified the caterer's

claim that the waiters had stayed in the gallery. He assured Diana he would've questioned a nonguest going upstairs, and he also remembered seeing Audrey go into her office with Austin.

The housekeeping staff consisted of three women, all of whom had been with the company for more than five years, and with no complaints in their personnel files. Just three middle-aged women working hard to make ends meet. She left her number with the cleaning service's receptionist and asked that the women call her anyway. Just to cover all her bases, she decided to run more thorough background checks on Steven Carmichael, Audrey Spencer, and Jack Austin.

Diana's gaze fell on the evidence bag with the jack of spades.

Okay. The fact that "jack" equaled "Jack" was *way* beyond obvious, although it seemed unlikely her Boy Wonder would be dumb enough to tip his hand like this. Unless he wanted Carmichael to know it was him, but that didn't make much sense, considering Carmichael was his golden goose. And what were the chances of Carmichael or his dapper legal eagle missing the similarity, as well?

Granted, it might not occur to them unless they were suspicious of Austin in the first place, but Jones's evasiveness, when she'd first asked if Carmichael had any suspects in mind, still bothered her. A lot.

If they *did* know the thief's identity, then why all this pretense? Why not just take matters into their own hands?

She sighed and rubbed away the ache of frustration in her brows.

Really, any number of "facts" in this file could be fake or doctored, and with no crime reported to the police—and the crime scene now hopelessly compromised and pretty much useless—she had to assume there was little to no evidence. Or any proof, beyond Carmichael's word, that the card had been left behind by the thief. It could easily have been planted, although with no insurance fraud motive, the reasoning for that eluded her.

Still, for now she'd progress on the assumption the card was legitimate and had been left as some sort of message for Carmichael. Keeping in mind the possibility Austin was *not* her thief, she'd look at the card from other directions, too.

But first things first: background checks and after that, see if she could find out anything more about her mysterious little alabaster box.

Diana quickly pulled together more details on her client. She'd already known that Carmichael was a Texas oil baron who'd married into an old and powerful Louisiana family, and who'd made a name for himself in art circles by owning one of the largest pre-Columbian collections in the world. She'd also known that eight years ago he'd founded the Ancient Americas Preservation Society, which provided funding for archaeological expeditions like Jack Austin's, and also lobbied for legislation on the preservation of native historical culture.

What she hadn't known was that Carmichael remained active in the political lobbying, or exactly how much money he had. Heck, if she had a personal net worth of 250 million, she could afford ancient Egyptian trinkets, too.

She opened the file and removed a number of glossy color photos, shot from multiple angles, of the stolen box and its contents. After slipping on her reading glasses, she carefully examined each photo again.

The box was roughly three inches by three inches, with a separate curved lid, and carved of the finest alabaster. It was incised with typical Egyptian motifs—stylized papyrus and cornflowers, lily petals, mandrakes, and checker patterns, all painted in black and red. The lid and two sides of the box were also incised with the cartouche of Queen Nefertiti.

Interior photos showed the gold statuette nestled beside a coiled lock of dark, braided hair.

The tiny pharaoh, only two inches high, squatted on a square base, his expression serene. He wore the rounded *khepresh* crown, with its familiar snake ornament, a pleated kilt, and a necklace made of blue beads, and held the crook and flail in his right hand. A photo of the back showed a hook at the neck, so it could be worn from a chain, although no chain had been found. The figurine was amazingly detailed, right down to the crown's pattern, pleats in the kilt, and nails on his fingers and toes. The last photo showed a close-up of the square base, clearly stamped with the cartouche of Amenhotep IV— Akhenaton himself.

Compared to the dainty box and gold king, the lock of hair didn't seem like much. Diana noted it had a reddish tone, and was intermingled with paler fibers she guessed had once been a linen wrapping. Humble as it appeared, this bit of hair was easily the most valuable object in that box—if uncontaminated, its mitochondrial DNA could prove or disprove a relationship to Tutankhamen himself.

If it wasn't a fraud.

She stood and walked to her bookshelves, packed with books spanning prehistoric to modern art, pop culture collectibles, furniture and architectural guides, as well as trade journals and magazines, assorted tax books, fat law tomes, and well-thumbed business, government, and people directories.

After pulling a number of Egyptian art history books, she returned to her desk and flipped through them until she found what she was looking for—a section detailing the contents of Tutankhamen's tomb.

"Aha," she murmured, finding a picture of a statuette almost identical to Carmichael's. "I knew I'd seen something like this before."

The caption read "the squatting king," and identified it as Amenhotep III, Akhenaton's father and, presumably, Tutankhamen's grandfather. More importantly, this figurine had been found in a miniature gilded sarcophagus inscribed with the name of Amenhotep's queen, Tiye, along with a lock of auburn hair assumed to be hers.

The similarity didn't prove authenticity, but stylistically the two figurines were almost indistinguishable. Only lab tests could verify if it wasn't a modern forgery, but from what she could tell, her missing box looked genuine.

And if so, what an incredible piece of history

Steven Carmichael had been keeping in a cigar box in his office.

Diana pulled more books, and was halfway through an article when Luna poked her spiky-haired head through the door.

"Need anything? I've got a quiz in my four o'clock class, so I gotta run."

"Okay. I'll see you tomorrow." Diana looked up from her book, and as she did so, the jack of spades caught her attention again. A sudden thought struck her, and she called after Luna, "Hey, wait . . . I do have a quick question. Do you know anything about card symbolism? Or know anybody who does?"

Luna clomped back into the office, backpack slung over her shoulder. "I know a little tarot, a little cartomancy. Why?"

Diana held up the bag. "A thief allegedly left this behind. I'm just wondering if the jack of spades means something."

"It depends on who you talk to, but usually the jack of spades symbolizes a dark-haired, youthful male with good intentions."

Again, Jack Austin—dark-haired *and* most definitely male—popped to mind, but she pushed the thought away. And it was ridiculous to think a thief, young or not, meant well by stealing anything.

"Doesn't sound too likely to me."

Luna shrugged. "In general, spades mean you're experiencing conflict, or have a need for change. These cards have a sort of negative energy, but they're warning you to move on, to give up bad habits, or let go of a destructive or unhealthy pattern in your life. Too much spade energy means you're in major denial and not making the changes you need to."

"Ah." Diana frowned uncomfortably, recalling why she'd stomped on Jack Austin's foot earlier. "Don't want to have too much spade energy."

"I have a friend named Iris who does card readings in Jackson Square during the afternoons. She's good. Why don't you go see her? Tell her Luna sent you."

Diana considered card readers harmless frauds, but if the jack of spades had a meaning beyond the obvious, it couldn't hurt to ask a few questions.

"I'll do that, thanks. Good luck on your quiz."

After Luna left, Diana continued to stare at the card. Jacks were also known as knaves . . . maybe her thief simply meant it as a joke, calling himself a knave in the pejorative sense of being a villain, or a scoundrel.

Possible, yes, but she didn't like it—too impersonal.

Which brought to mind another possibility. Diana picked up her phone and dialed. "Hi, Audrey. This is Diana Belmaine. I need to speak with Mr. Carmichael if he's there . . . it's important." She waited again until Carmichael came on the line. "I'm sorry to bother you, but I have a quick question I need to ask."

"Shoot," Carmichael said, his tone pleasant.

"I'm working an angle on that card the thief left, and I'm wondering if you've ever had your fortune read by cards?"

"Never. I don't hold by such things." After a brief silence, he added, "My wife is into New Age junk, though. Psychics and auras and all that."

Ah, yes, the wife.

In her haste to hunt down Jack Austin, she shouldn't forget that spouses made good suspects—especially when the other spouse routinely cheated on them. Revenge and vindictiveness were perennially popular motives.

"All right. Would your wife be available to speak with me?"

"She's in California, at some meditation retreat spa. I don't have the number handy, but I can have Audrey call you with it."

"That would be great. One last question—do you ever play cards?"

"Not in years. I don't really have a lot of free time for things like that."

"Okay. Thank you."

After hanging up, Diana sighed again, then muttered, "Oh, what the hell."

She donned her sunglasses, slipped the bag with the card into her purse, and set out for Jackson Square in search of a cartomancer named Iris.

The heat of the day had built to simmering and steamy, warmer than usual for early September, and tourists looked as rosy red and boiled as crawfish in a pot. Even after two years, she wasn't used to the tropical heat, although Manhattan in summer hadn't been much fun, either.

Andy Jackson's equestrian statue reared above the crowds in Jackson Square, and behind it the spires of St. Louis Cathedral stretched toward the blue sky. People packed the narrow streets, sidewalks, and benches, and spilled out from the Café du Monde. The square was abuzz with the usual activities of those who made a living hawking their dubious talents to tourists: the mimes, artists, street vendors, fortune-tellers, and musicians.

It didn't take long to find someone who looked as if she'd be pals with a vampiric secretary. Under a wide umbrella sat a wild-haired young woman dressed like a scarlet gypsy. Her top and skirt were embroidered with beads and small, round mirrors, and she sparkled when she moved. Her features hinted at a mix of both black and white, and maybe a little something else more exotic.

"Are you Iris?" Diana asked.

"Yes, I am Iris." She affected a faint accent, a sort of Jamaican thing.

"Luna Benedetto said I should look you up. I'm Diana Belmaine, a private investigator."

The young woman's slanted, greenish gold eyes widened. Diana supposed that attention from any investigator wasn't high on a fortune-teller's wish list.

"Luna's friends are always welcome at Iris's table. Please sit down. How may I help you?"

Diana sat, and leaned forward. "First, you can drop the act. I'm here for information, not to get my fortune read."

Iris seemed to transform before Diana's eyes, from a mysterious practitioner of the dark arts to a college coed earning tuition money in an unorthodox manner.

"Just having a little fun with you." The young woman grinned widely. "I know all about you from Luna. What's up?"

Diana brought out the bag. "I'm working on a burglary case. This was left behind on purpose by the thief. It means something, but I'm not familiar with card symbolism. What can you tell me about the jack of spades?"

"Whoa, that's like really broad."

"Then tell me everything, please," Diana said with an encouraging smile. "And I'll decide later what's important or not."

"Well, it might be just the jack that means something. Jacks represent youth and youthful attitudes."

Which didn't have much bearing on Austin; he was on the high side of his thirties—Carmichael wasn't exactly youthful, either.

"Jacks also relate to issues of movement and change. They're like restless children, needing to be on the move and to explore," Iris explained, her tone utterly serious. "They're learning and growing, but selfish. They're also neutral, indecisive, and playful, but they can be stubborn and tenacious, too, so it's not wise to blow them off."

"Okay." Diana took a deep breath as she assimilated all that. "Luna told me spades have negative energy."

Iris nodded enthusiastically. "So if the spades themselves are important, it could be a warning that things are going to change. Or it's a challenge."

A challenge made sense. This could be something worthwhile. "And what if it's just a jack of spades? What does that mean?"

"It depends." Iris gave an expansive shrug. "There are almost as many schools of card reading as there are cards in a deck."

"I'd appreciate it if you'd give it your best shot, Iris."

"Well, I follow the Continental school of reading. Being in New Orleans, it seemed to make sense to go more French than English."

"So what do the French say about the jack of spades?"

"It's the knave, not the jack, and it means some kind of disgrace that will be unfavorable to the peace of mind or freedom of the Querent . . . the Querent is the person who's asking to have the cards read, so I guess that would be you," Iris explained. "It can also mean serious complications, or if the Querent is a woman, it can also mean betrayal in love."

Diana thought again of the aura-happy Mrs. Carmichael, even as a tingle of alarm spread through her that had little to do with her client's wife.

Ridiculous; card-reading was nothing but parlor tricks—and yet the bit about "disgrace" and "betrayal in love" had hit too close to the bone. That was twice in one day; maybe she hadn't made peace with her past as well as she'd thought.

"There's something else." Iris scooted closer, and lowered her voice. "If the Querent is asking about a thief, which you are, I'd need all four knaves in the cards I'd use for my reading. Then I could tell you about the thief. Are you sure there were no other cards left except the knave?"

"As far as I know." She made a mental note to find out if a card had been left when the crates of Mayan artifacts had mysteriously vanished.

"This is kind of complicated. You want to take notes?"

"Good idea." Diana dug out her trusty notebook and pen. "Okay. Go for it."

"It's like this: The four knaves, combined with other cards during the reading, will give me information. For instance, if I turn up the ace of spades, the thief is ass deep in danger, maybe even dead. If I turn up the king and eight of spades, then your thief is already in jail. The ace of clubs, king of clubs, and queen of hearts suggest the thief wants to make restitution. A bunch of diamonds means the thief has been arrested, but over something that doesn't have anything to do with you. You following me?"

Diana nodded as she scribbled. "Sort of."

Iris plucked at her lip. "The English cartomancy is different."

"Oh, great." Diana looked up. "In what way?"

"The old English school, which goes back to the fifteenth century, says the knave of spades is a lawyer. Someone to be shunned."

"Lawyers had a bad rep even back then, huh?" Diana smiled—and Edward Jones flashed to mind again, with his pleasant, genteel features, dark suit, and white rose boutonniere. As she'd signed the contract, Jones had mentioned he'd known Steven Carmichael for some thirty years—and that he'd been the one to handle the sale of the Tut artifact.

Focusing on Austin merely because he really, *really* pushed her buttons wasn't smart. She couldn't afford sloppy thinking.

"Did I help?" Iris asked, looking a little anxious.

"You've given me plenty to think about," Diana said absently. Then, smiling, she slipped the young woman two twenties, and added, "Thanks."

* * *

Diana maneuvered her shopping bags through the door of her French Quarter condo, and sighed with relief as its air-conditioned coolness caressed her body. She'd fallen in love with the place's high ceilings, tall windows, wooden floors, and beautiful vintage moldings—and the fact it was big enough to hold all the furniture, antiques, trinkets, and a few of the more esoteric objets d'art she'd collected over the years.

After kicking off her heels, she walked through the living room, her footsteps echoing on the floor, then past the kitchen and dining room to her bedroom. She tossed the bags on the ivory matelassé bedspread, peeled off her clothes, dropped them on the old Persian rug she'd found for next to nothing in Malta, and headed straight to the shower.

As the cool water beat down, soothing her flushed skin, she mulled over everything that had happened that day.

The overwhelming lack of untainted evidence nagged at the back of her mind—and it didn't improve her mood at all that her background checks had failed to turn up anything useful.

Carmichael was a very powerful man, much more ruthless than his benevolent demeanor suggested—and by extension, lawyer Edward Jones wasn't likely to be the Southern gentleman he'd appeared. Tomorrow she'd do some checking into Carmichael's wife.

Audrey Spencer hadn't so much as a parking ticket to her name, and Austin's history revealed what she'd already known: He was a highly intelligent man with a quick temper that occasionally landed him in trouble. He was also so dedicated to his work that it appeared to be his life, which accounted for a string of short-term love affairs, and no ex-wives or children.

Not the usual profile of a cat burglar with expensive tastes.

Still, her instincts were rarely wrong, and since her instincts said Austin was her man, she'd run with it until she either took him down, or evidence convinced her of his innocence.

Which meant she still had work to do—like check out where Austin lived and the kind of car he owned. She'd looked up his university salary, and while not shoddy, it wasn't that much, either. An address on the far fringes of the Garden District didn't necessarily mean he lived in one of the grand old mansions—he might live in a tiny cottage, or rent a flat in a converted old house—but the only way to find out if he was living beyond his means was to go and see for herself.

After stepping out of the shower, she dried off, spritzed on perfume, blow-dried her hair, then drew it back in a ponytail and braided it. She applied mascara and lipstick, then dressed in a pair of heather gray Lycra athletic shorts and a matching tank with a built-in bra. She laced up her running shoes, then grabbed a Saints ball cap and pulled it low over her face, threading her ponytail through the back. A lengthy search finally turned up a pair of wrap-around sports sunglasses. She buckled on a fanny pack, with keys, money, and a camera inside, and a tape player and earphones finished off her outfit.

Fists on her hips, she surveyed the end result in the massive Italian baroque mirror propped against the far wall. Looked like a jogger, would jog like a jogger . . . she'd pass. Even if Austin happened to be outside, he wouldn't recognize her.

Diana left the condo, and walked through the small courtyard and onto the narrow streets of the Quarter. She made her way to Royal, passing antique shops and boutiques, then crossed busy Canal and headed to the stop for the St. Charles streetcar, which was turning the corner as she arrived.

Considering all the beignets she'd eaten—and the double helping of chocolate gâteau after the foot-stomping incident—she should've jogged for real, but the idea of running anywhere held zero appeal.

She paid her fare and joined the tourists and homebound nine-to-fivers jostling for seats, then the old streetcar clanged its bell and shimmied and rattled its way down St. Charles. The swaying motion lulled her, and through half-lowered lids she watched the passing landmarks: Lee Circle, the elegant Pontchartrain and Columns Hotels, Jerusalem Temple, the Academy of the Sacred Heart, and Loyola University. Finally, the car lurched past the pale limestone façade of the Romanesque Gibson Hall, Tulane's signature building.

Lost in her thoughts, Diana missed her stop and ended up getting off the streetcar across from Audubon Park. Grumbling, she jogged back along St. Charles to Calhoun. She ran several more blocks and turned at Prytania, keeping an eye on the street numbers of the graceful old houses, with their carefully tended lawns behind wrought-iron fences.

She slowed as she approached her target, then stopped, pretending to take a rest, stretching a little to make it look good—though the panting part was real enough.

So this was it: a single shotgun cottage, three-quarters of the way through a repainting job from yellow to white, with a mowed and orderly yard. No garage, but she spotted a white-and-gold motorcycle parked to the side of the cottage. The Honda sport touring bike, built for two, looked well maintained, if not quite new. A number of cars and trucks were parked along the curb, none directly in front of Austin's cottage, but that didn't mean he didn't own one of them. Something else to check on.

If Austin was wheeling-and-dealing in black market antiquities, he wasn't spending ill-gotten gains on his house or his transportation. Then again, he was a smart guy. He'd probably know better than that.

She pushed the STOP button on the tape player, cutting off Madonna in midwarble. Unzipping her fanny pack, she pulled out her camera and focused on the house.

One of the advantages of being even remotely near the Garden District was that few people would blink an eye at a woman photographing private residences.

Diana snapped a third picture just as she became aware of an unfamiliar sound coming up fast behind her. A loud clacking, growing louder. She turned in time to see an in-line skater round the street corner, clearing a row of hedges, and shoot past her.

The skater wore a billowing short-sleeved white shirt, unbuttoned to reveal a ribbed tank top, although he'd traded the khaki cargo pants for tan shorts. He also had on a backpack and what looked like a brown Australian drover's hat, pulled low in a rakish angle. Before she could react, he slowed and glanced over his shoulder.

Oh, damn.

After completing a leisurely turn, Austin glided back toward her, wheels *clackety-clack*ing on the sidewalk. Dark aviator-style sunglasses concealed his eyes, but he was smiling a shit-eating grin that put her on the defensive before he even scraped to a halt in front of her. Way too close in front of her.

Instinctively, she backed up—right into a street lamppost.

"Hey, Ms. Belmaine . . . what a surprise finding you here. In front of my house. Taking pictures."

"Dr. Austin." She forced coolness into her tone, trying to figure a way out of this and having no luck. "Just getting home from work?"

He was breathing hard; perspiration gleamed on his face, on the line of his collarbone—and every time his breath molded damp knit to his chest muscles it reminded her that her job would be a hell of a lot easier if he looked more like an ugly thug and less like a pagan sex god.

"You know, some people might call this stalking."

True enough. Sloppily tailing a subject could result in a harassment complaint, although she usually didn't blurt out her suspicions, much less get caught by her suspects. And there *was* the annoying fact that she had no evidence against him.

He knew it, too. That kiss-my-ass smile said as much.

"Some might call it doing my job." She met his gaze squarely—or as squarely as either of them could while wearing dark sunglasses. "How'd you recognize me so quickly?"

"I didn't." He rocked from side to side on his skates, then startled her by leaning close and inhaling deeply. "I smelled you. Nice perfume . . . musky, and sweet. Very distinctive. I got a good whiff of it this morning."

"Back off," she ordered quietly.

Still wearing that cocky half smile, he pulled away, but continued to skate from side to side, with her—standing with her spine pressed against the pole—in the center of his half orbit.

Suddenly, his hand snaked out, grabbing the camera from her hand.

"Hey! Oh, come on . . . don't do that." Her indignation turned to resignation as he pulled the film from the camera and pocketed it, all the while moving in that annoying arcing motion.

"I don't like being spied on, Ms. Belmaine." He handed back the camera, and she didn't need to see his eyes to know they sparked with anger.

"Is that a threat?" She put the camera safely away. "You've got quite the temper, don't you? Barroom brawls, shoot-outs, antagonizing bureaucrats here and abroad. I'm not impressed, Dr. Austin. And I'm not scared."

Before she realized what he intended, he skated toward her, pinning her to the lamppost. Diana froze, very aware of the hard length of him pressed against her; all lean, tensed muscle and damp skin. He smelled male, and hot; she could almost taste the salt of his skin and smell the wind and sun in his hair.

When he pressed his hips and thighs against hers, the motion raw and blatant, her breath caught in her throat.

"It's been a very long day, Ms. Belmaine, and I'm not in a good mood."

His hands settled at her waist. Diana stared up at him, not sure if she should knee him in the balls or scream for help—or see what he intended to do.

Curiosity won out, and she went still, almost anticipating his response . . . but Austin merely plucked her tape from the player.

"What's this?" He glided back a short distance.

Swallowing an odd twinge of disappointment, she retorted, "I'm not recording the conversation. You know, you should see somebody about these paranoid tendencies. They have medication for problems like yours."

"I'm not paranoid." He slid his glasses down the bridge of his nose, fixing her with a piercing—and very angry—stare. "Unless the situation calls for it, and I'd say having a nosy PI taking pictures of my house, stabbing my foot, and accusing me of using women and stealing from my friends is reason enough. You should feel flattered, Ms. Belmaine; I'm taking you very seriously."

Diana moved away from the lamppost. Now was *not* the time to act like a shrinking violet. "How's the foot?"

Something heated and not entirely pleasant flashed across his dark eyes. "Fine."

"So you're not denying you went upstairs with Audrey Spencer to Steven Carmichael's office?"

"I'm saying whatever Audrey and I did together is none of your damn business." He glanced briefly at the tape in his hands, and although his gaze remained hostile, one corner of his mouth hitched up slightly. "*Madonna?*"

"I don't think you're in any position to poke fun at what I listen to," she retorted. What *was* it about this man that roused her anger so easily? His ability to keep her off-balance irritated her—and his crack about Audrey stung more than it should. It wasn't as if she should care if he and Audrey had almost done the horizontal bop.

"I'm just thinking you don't exactly look like the Madonna type."

Diana gave a nongenteel snort. "For the record, I don't want to know what type you think I am."

He studied her from head to toe over his glasses. This morning when he'd checked her out, she'd been amused—in an aggravated sort of way. Now, the unabashed sexual intensity of his look stirred a curling warmth inside her that burned its way up toward her cheeks.

Austin skated close again. He raised a hand—and shocked her into speechless astonishment as he traced the neckline of her top, across the swell of her breasts. The touch of that one finger was like a line of fire along her skin.

"I like this," he said softly.

Recovering—and remembering to breathe again—she slapped his hand away. "Stop that!"

He just grinned. Goaded, she moved to the middle of the sidewalk, forcing him to skate back a little, and demanded, "Why'd you do it?"

When all else failed, go for the jugular.

"Because you look really sexy in that outfit."

She tightened her mouth, gathered her control with a Herculean effort, then said slowly, "Why'd you steal it?"

Austin didn't answer as he slowly circled her, again and again. Diana held her ground, refusing to let him intimidate her.

"Why," he said at length.

"That's what I asked."

"No, *I'm* asking why."

As he continued circling her, she turned to follow, never breaking eye contact, never letting him get behind her back.

"Are you saying I should ask why you *would* steal the box, or why you *did* steal it?"

A subtle difference, but an important one. Judging by that small quirk of his lips, she'd asked the right question.

"You're the hotshot investigator who always gets her man. Here I am. Your man," he said, his voice low and suggestive, his gaze holding hers. On his next circuit around her, he skated so close that his chest lightly brushed her breasts. "So investigate me."

She reacted by instinct, putting her palms on his chest—as much to stop that maddening circling as to hold him at bay. "Touch me like that again, and I'll feed you your dick on a stick."

A young mother with a toddler in a stroller passed them from behind, and the woman stared at Diana, her mouth a circle of shock.

Oh, peachy.

Her hands, still on Austin's warm chest, trembled

as he shook with silent laughter. Incensed, she shoved him away. He didn't so much as stumble.

Diana curled her hands into fists. "Why am I not surprised you can make a simple statement like 'investigate me' sound obscene?"

He laughed out loud this time and tossed her tape toward her. "Lots of practice."

As she fumbled with the tape, trying not to drop it, he sped away, the tight muscles of his thighs and rear moving fluidly, making it look graceful and deceptively effortless.

Diana watched him arc onto the walk that led to his porch steps, where he dumped his hat and backpack, then sat and began unbuckling his skates. They stared at each other for a long moment, and she felt the challenge in his gaze.

With a little finger wave, she spun and jogged back the way she'd come—hoping that if he was watching *her* ass, it didn't jiggle too badly.

Investigate me.

He was playing with her, but he'd also thrown down a gauntlet—one that wasn't sexual at all.

"Why, Dr. Austin," she murmured, "whatever are you up to?"

FIVE

...

Jack leaned his elbows on the step behind him, watching Diana Belmaine's swaying hips as she jogged down the sidewalk. Once she disappeared around the corner, he closed his eyes, flopped back on the porch, and groaned.

Did he have lousy luck or what? A woman finally came along who made his blood zing, and her single objective was to bust him.

Crazy, his wanting her. Crazy, his playing with her like this—because he should be avoiding her, not baiting her. She was a very real threat; her taking pictures of his house proved that, dammit.

Despite the pretty packaging, everything about Diana Belmaine screamed man-eater—in bloodred capital letters—and even if the most primordial part of his brain whispered that one night between the sheets with this woman just might be worth five to ten years in Angola State Prison, he trusted in his survival instincts to prevent him from doing anything too stupid.

For a while, anyway. Jack knew his weaknesses

too well not to pay attention to the warning signs, and she'd been on his mind ever since she'd first sashayed into his classroom that morning.

Her poise and confidence, even that touch of arrogance, fascinated him. She had a cool, patrician beauty a man would notice, and he'd felt the pull of that sharp intelligence in her blue eyes. She also had great legs, and the rest of her looked mighty fine, too. *Especially* in that jogging outfit. It showed off every phenomenal curve, and it had taken all his willpower not to run his hands down her bottom, or along the arch of her back. He hadn't been able to resist touching her that once, although he'd half expected her to slap him.

Christ, he deserved it. Why had she just stood there, wide-eyed, looking like she'd wanted him to do more than touch her?

Wishful thinking. More likely, she'd been too appalled even to move.

Opening his eyes, Jack sat up, uncomfortably hot all of a sudden. He stripped off his shirt, leaving on the tank. Cars puttered past, insects buzzed around him, and humidity sank heavily into his skin. Lost in thought, he stared out at the sidewalk where Diana had stood.

Too bad she'd so quickly placed him in Steve's office with Audrey—that complicated the hell out of things for the next couple weeks. Jack scrubbed a hand over his face and swore quietly. Not one of his finer moments, that little improvisation with Audrey, but he couldn't do anything about it yet. Right now, he had to stay focused on his most immediate problem.

Diana Belmaine appeared as thorough as she'd claimed, but without hard evidence or a motive, she had no case against him—and he intended to keep it that way. If he provided her with the smallest opportunity, she'd make good on her threat to take him down.

Jack looked down at his hands, held loosely between his knees, letting the day's frustration ride over him and feeling damned tired of fighting off the inevitable.

Which was why he'd toyed all afternoon with the idea of turning Steve's pretty PI to his advantage. At least for the next week or two; after that, it wouldn't matter. Despite her cynical attitude, she struck him as honest and fair, especially in how she'd championed Audrey. That, along with her persistence and quick mind, could work to his benefit. If all his careful plans collapsed in ruins around him, Diana might be his best chance of getting out of this with his hide, not to mention his reputation, intact.

Right. There was only one way for this to end, and happily-ever-after wasn't in the script—he couldn't have dug himself a deeper hole even if he'd tried.

Swearing again, he retrieved his skates and backpack, pulled his keys out of his pocket, and let himself into the air-conditioned cottage.

Damned if he wasn't living proof that the road to hell was paved with good intentions.

Jack showered, washing away the day's grime and sweat, then pulled on a pair of shorts. He ambled into the kitchen and nuked the remainder of yesterday's Chinese takeout. After popping the cap off a beer, he stood at the counter and ate moo goo gai pan while sorting through the day's mail, both from home and the office: bills, journals, junk mail, and a letter from his mother, which he read right away. Retirement had enticed his parents to enjoy a second childhood, and her letters always made him smile.

A glance at the clock showed four hours to nightfall, so he might as well put all this edgy energy to good use. He grabbed the stack of "fan mail" and headed to the tiny second bedroom he'd converted to an office—although, at the moment, it looked more like a storage room.

Ever since his last girlfriend had moved out—shouting from the porch, much to the fascination of his neighbors, that she was tired of playing second fiddle to a pile of rocks in a jungle—his housekeeping habits had slipped. Considering he spent his summers cohabitating with bats, snakes, tarantulas, and other creepy crawlies, he couldn't get too excited by a little dust and clutter.

While he waited for his computer to boot up, he searched through the papers, folders, journals, and books on his desk for the telephone book. Opening it, he thumbed to the "P" index. The advertisement was classy and direct, just like her: *Diana Belmaine, Private Investigator. Specializing in Antiquities, Fine Art, Collectibles, Estate Sales. Asset Verification. Insurance Claims. Theft Recovery*.

A prime French Quarter office address meant she made good money. No surprise there. Considering her type of client, he would bet she charged a hefty fee for her services.

He looked up her name in the residence section, but it was unlisted, as he'd expected. It wouldn't take him long to find out where she lived, though.

And when he had her address, then what? Show up at her front door, a bouquet of flowers in hand— she struck him as a tiger lilies and white roses kind of girl—and ask her out for a drink?

Jack grinned. Imagining Diana's response only added to the appeal of the idea.

Maybe he would. Not now, but after he'd squared matters away. What did he have to lose? He tended to scare away the nice, sweet girls. Diana had threatened to feed him his dick, and while a lot of guys would've run for cover after that, Jack considered it an encouraging sign.

Whistling to himself, his daylong funk vanquished, he ripped open the flap of the first envelope. The return address said it came from a Martin Palmer. He didn't get a lot of fan mail from guys, and he began reading with some wariness:

Dear Dr. Austin:

As you know, there is an abundance of evidence suggesting extraterrestrial intervention in the development of the Mesoamerican cultures. I have crucial evidence proving beyond a doubt—

"Aliens," he muttered. "Shit."

Show up a few times on cable TV, and all the goofballs figured you had nothing better to do than listen to their brilliant theories. At least this one knew big words and could spell.

Jack shuffled the letter to the bottom of the pile, then picked up the next envelope, addressed in broad curving handwriting. This one looked more like the usual:

> *Dear Mr. Austin, my name is Jennifer, and I'm thirteen years old. I live in Topeka, Kansas, and me and my friends saw you on the Discovery Channel show. None of us knew digging in the dirt could be so cool. I think you are totally awesome when you put buildings back together and tell stories from the past even if there's nothing left. Someday I want to own a zoo and take care of all the animals going extinct so they won't, but some of the kids at school say it's stupid and won't help. What should I do? I sent you my picture. I hope you like it, even if I smiled too big. Can I have an autographed picture of you? I would love you to write back and tell me where you're digging next and if you'll be on the TV show again soon.*

Jack smiled at her girlishly curly capital letters, the "i's" dotted with little hearts. The small school picture showed a bright-eyed kid with straight black hair and a wide grin. Not at all too big, in his opinion.

While he kept all the letters, he didn't keep the photos or send any of himself—that would be too much—and so he turned over the girl's picture and wrote: *Study hard and stay in school. Best wishes, Jack Austin.*

Maybe it sounded hokey, but he meant it. He then wrote a brief note about his recent season at Tikukul, encouraged her to explore career possibilities from books in the school library—and to hold on to her dreams.

Those dreams might change as she grew older, but he remembered what it felt like to be the kid who never fit in, with interests nobody understood. In sixth grade, crying with anger and humiliation, he'd finally retaliated against his tormenters with his fists. Before sending him to the principal's office, one of the older teachers had told him in a soft voice to hold on to his dreams, no matter how much people made fun of them. She'd said if he believed in himself hard enough, he'd make a difference someday.

He'd never forgotten Mrs. Claire or her words—in many ways, he owed his discovery of Tikukul to her—and always regretted she'd died before he'd found the city's ruins.

As Jack printed the letter, it came to him that Mrs. Claire probably wouldn't approve of how he'd gone about making a difference these past few years.

He glanced up before he could stop himself. "Hey, if you're up there, Mrs. C, it seemed like a good idea at the time."

A touch embarrassed, he pushed aside his broody thoughts and focused on the task at hand.

The thirty or so remaining letters would keep his mind busy for a while. He had one last loose end to tie up tonight, and after that, he'd have more time to figure out how to deal with Diana.

Deal with Diana.

He grinned, liking the way that sounded. It had a certain ring to it.

SIX

...

Diana parked her rental car close to Austin's house. After three days of tailing the man and finding nothing to support her gut instinct about his guilt, it was time to turn up the heat.

She got out of the car and tucked her pink polo shirt, with a *Mid-City Cleaning Service* logo emblazoned in black above the left pocket, into her black chino shorts. Despite the sticky humidity, she wore a white silk tank and blue nylon running shorts underneath—in case she had to ditch the eye-catching hot pink and make a run for it.

The crepe soles of her shoes made no sound as Diana headed up the sidewalk, a canvas tote of cleaning supplies slung over her shoulder.

She'd learned that Jack Austin spent most of his time at work, either in class or in his lab; tended toward the "late-to-bed-early-to-rise" philosophy; and when not working or sleeping, could be found skating in Audubon Park or hanging out at a local campus bar, where a number of his colleagues and grad students often gathered to talk shop.

The acquaintances she'd discreetly questioned had described Austin as forceful and colorful, but after a while, a pattern emerged. Despite his well-known temper, which he unleashed far less than rumor claimed, people liked him. He helped the elderly couple next door with yard work, sometimes baby-sat the dogs belonging to the family across the street, and when he wasn't off prowling jungles, acted as the neighborhood kid-magnet.

Not that a thief couldn't like kids or be nice to old people, but it made him sound like a Boy Scout—and nobody liked busting Boy Scouts.

"Here goes nothing," Diana murmured as she walked up to the house belonging to Austin's elderly neighbors.

Taking a deep breath, she knocked on the door. A few moments later, a smiling, white-haired woman answered the door.

"Hello, can I help you?" The woman's gaze dropped to the logo on Diana's shirt, and a perplexed expression crossed her face. "Oh, dear. I think you have the wrong house. We don't have a cleaning service."

"I'm sorry, ma'am," Diana said, affecting a heavy drawl. "I hate to bother you like this, but I'm . . . this is just so embarrassing!" She put on a hopeful smile, and widened her eyes with sincerity. "I'm supposed to clean for Mr. Austin next door, and I accidentally left his keys back at the office. I was hoping you might have a spare key, ma'am?"

The Evanses most likely did. Somebody had to

keep an eye on the place while Austin was away. If not, she'd have to fall back on Plan B. She hoped not because, frankly, Plan B sucked.

The woman frowned. "Well, yes, I do, but I don't know if I should . . . oh, dear. You might call Jack at work, he—"

"Oh, Gawd, no! Please, ma'am, it's my very first day at this job, and I was so nervous that I forgot all about his key. I can't go back to get it, or call Mr. Austin, without everybody knowing I messed up. I just moved here with my two little girls and I need this job real bad. I can't afford to make any mistakes. *Please*."

The bit about the little girls did the trick, and the woman's worried gaze softened. Success, if not the kind she felt good about—but a job was a job. She'd been hired to recover stolen property, and recover it she would.

"Of course, dear, don't you worry." Smiling, she touched Diana soothingly on the arm. "Please come in while I get the key . . . what did you say your name was?"

"Crystal, ma'am, and thank you *so* much," Diana said, putting a touch of earnest gratefulness in her tone.

"It's quite all right. I'm Mrs. Evans. Jack helps out Mr. Evans and me with yard work, and we return the favor by keeping an eye on his cottage when he's off on his digs. He's such a nice young man."

Mrs. Evans retrieved a key chain from a drawer in a nearby sideboard—a *very* nice Queen Anne reproduction, early 1900s—and smiled again. "I'm glad he's finally admitted he needs help with his housework. You know how men are. Especially unmarried young men."

Diana only nodded in response and followed Mrs. Evans's bright yellow pants and matching shirt over to Austin's cottage.

Although quite aware her actions weren't legal, Diana wasn't obliged to operate under the same constraints of laws and regulations as the police. She just had to avoid getting caught, and if her clandestine searches resulted in closing the case and bagging the bad guys, she considered it ethical enough. The handy thing about turning tables on thieves was that they didn't dare go to the police.

And it wasn't as if she hadn't done far worse.

Shying away from the thought, she gave Mrs. Evans a sunny smile. "It'll take me a while to clean. I'll return the keys when I'm done. You've saved my job, and for the sake of my little girls, bless you."

"Oh, I know how it is, forgetting things like that. My husband is always saying how I'd forget my own head if it weren't bolted on tight."

After Mrs. Evans left, Diana locked the door behind her. If all went as she'd planned, this pleasant, trusting woman would never have cause to feel guilty for her act of kindness.

Sometimes she hated this part of her work. Greed and dishonesty, even when involving white-collar crimes, didn't touch only a few people. Like a stone dropped in a puddle, the rippling effects widened and widened. Thankfully, most people never saw the truly ugly side of it. The dirt pretty much stopped with the police or people like her, leaving the innocents blissfully unaware—and clean.

Shaking free of her thoughts, Diana pulled on a pair of latex gloves, surveyed the living room, then went to work. Quick, efficient, and thorough, she was careful not to obviously disturb anything. The living room didn't take long. Fairly uncluttered and a little dusty, it didn't look as if Austin used it much. His tastes ran toward comfortable, utilitarian furniture that matched the blues and tans of the room. Stacks of journals and books sat beside a recliner situated opposite a small, older model TV and a cabinet holding a new, expensive stereo system. Austin might not watch much TV, but he liked his music. An eclectic range of titles packed the CD shelves, everything from classical music to rap, and a lot of local bands—Cajun, jazz, Zydeco, and blues.

The books were a mix of thrillers and police mysteries, and work-related subjects with dry, scientific titles. No *B&E for Dummies* or *How to Steal: A Beginner's Guide* books anywhere.

An empty beer bottle sat on the coffee table, the local Dixie label. She could imagine Austin sitting in the recliner at the end of the day, feet on the table, the Louisiana Playboys or Dave Koz's saxophone blasting on the stereo, swigging a cold beer as he read over all the juicy details of thermoluminescence dating, amino acid racemization, or paleoclimatology.

The thought made her smile—until a sudden sadness touched her. Austin's conviction and disgrace would leave a gaping hole in his academic community, and she could imagine how he'd feel when someone else took over his ancient city, taking credit for discoveries that should have been his.

What a waste. She'd never understand why people were willing to risk total ruin for money—assuming, of course, that was Austin's motive.

When the living room search turned up nothing, she made her way to the tiny kitchen. Again, a little dusty, but she saw no dirty dishes in the sink or piled in the cupboards, and the trash had been recently emptied. Months worth of junk mail, catalogs, fliers, and personal mail were stacked on the counter in orderly piles. She looked over the addresses, seeing nothing interesting beyond that he had relatives who lived in Key West, and somebody named Patricia had sent him a postcard from Kerry, Ireland.

The only ancient objects she found were a few gourmet sauce bottles and a jar of pickles in the refrigerator. Austin liked Cocoa Krispies, clearly favored quickie microwave meals, and ate out a lot, judging by the pitiful state of his pantry. Still, he owned expensive china—a setting for twelve. He probably entertained now and again. Either that, or one of his ex-lovers had attempted to exert a civilizing influence on the man.

From the kitchen, she walked through the small bathroom—with its quaint old claw foot tub enclosed by an unexpectedly lacy shower curtain—and checked out the next two rooms.

The compact office looked hopeful, as did Austin's bedroom. It took her a while to go through all the stuff he'd crammed into the office. He likely spent most of his time in this comfortably cluttered room, either pounding away on the computer, poring over books and journals, or studying the piles of site maps. Most of the maps were detailed computer printouts, but a few had been hastily sketched on-site by Austin himself, judging by the smudge of dirty fingerprints, water spots, and coffee rings.

Even after ten years, he'd barely uncovered a quarter of his city—but, if she correctly interpreted his scribbles, it appeared he'd found a cache of royal tombs within the last couple of years.

Austin's Macintosh computer wasn't password protected, but her quick check revealed little beyond journal papers in various states of completeness, a simple accounting program that revealed nothing out of the ordinary, archaeology-specific software apps, a couple of computer games, and e-mail. The e-mail program was password protected. She didn't have time to try and crack it, although she doubted he'd be careless enough to leave incriminating evidence on his computer.

It also wasn't likely he'd hide the little Nefertiti box in his own house, but years of experience—and her methodical perfectionism—impelled her to make certain. Just in case.

After her search in the office revealed nothing useful, she headed to his bedroom. Diana hesitated by the bed, feeling uncomfortable.

"Just do it," she muttered, forcing her focus back on the job, on the fat fee she was being paid, and on the fact that cracking this case would go a long way toward rebuilding her reputation after she'd nearly destroyed it with her weakness and self-blindness.

A sweet-talking man never brought anything but trouble to a girl: something she needed to remember as she stood by Jack Austin's king-size bed with its crimson duvet.

She could imagine him lying there. Did he wear anything to bed? Her imagination envisioned him sprawled in the sheets, bare and relaxed. He'd probably exude all that sizzling charisma even while sleeping . . . he was probably a bed hog, too.

And a playful lover; tickles and laughter along with the intensity and pleasure.

Growing warm despite the air conditioner, Diana put a stop to that line of thinking. She was here to outwit a thief, not to have *Playgirl* fantasies in a strange man's bedroom.

Turning, she surveyed the chest of drawers and dresser, both in a clean-lined, modern style. An empty coffee cup sat on the dresser, and more books and journals were lying about, along with a couple dissertations and a stack of comic books. She raised a brow, and thumbed through the comics.

Maybe after plowing through hundreds of pages of a thesis titled *The Ceramics of Pre-Classic Tikukul: Burials, Caches, and Residential Deposits*, Austin needed to wind down by reading something with lots of pictures. Like the X-Men with the furry blue guy on the cover, or—

"Whoa. Catwoman."

The torpedo-breasted, catsuit-wearing woman on the cover, engaged in kicking some serious bad guy butt, made her smile—as did the thought of Jack reading it, lounging on his big, comfortable bed.

What an amazing, fascinating package of contradictions, her Mayan archaeologist.

Too bad he was also a thief.

Carefully returning the comic book to the stack where she'd found it, Diana looked over the rest of the room. Framed prints of Mesoamerican art and photos of temple pyramids rising above the jungle—probably from his Tikukul—lined the walls, alongside family pictures, both old and new. It looked like Austin was an only son, with four younger sisters. She noticed more photos on the shelf above his dresser, mostly candid shots of him on-site with his team, along with a few photos of an attractive blond woman she assumed was the most recent ex-lover.

Maybe he had a thing for blondes. Lucky her.

Austin's bureau and dresser drawers were surprisingly organized. He was a boxer and white crew sock kind of guy, with a wardrobe primarily in tones of tan, khaki, or brown—great for camouflage in any jungle but the urban one. He owned a few nice suits and little jewelry, and no hint of a feminine presence existed anywhere in the bedroom.

Could it be that one of America's most eligible bachelors was living female free? Even celibate?

Annoyed that her thoughts kept straying to the personal, Diana continued her search.

No sign of any little alabaster boxes or tiny golden kings anywhere. The cottage didn't have a basement or garage, much less any hidden trapdoors under rugs or pictures on the walls concealing secret cubbyholes.

Diana rested her gloved hands on her hips, chewing her lip in concentration—and as the pictures on his bedroom wall caught her attention again, the answer hit her with a jolt.

At work, of course. What better place to squirrel

away an ancient artifact? Perfect, simple—and nearly impossible for her to find a way inside.

Frustration welled within her, but she pushed it back, reminding herself to take one problem at a time.

Diana glanced at her watch. Time to go, in case Austin decided to skate home early.

She retrieved her cleaning bag and let herself out of the cottage, locking it behind her, then returned the keys to Mrs. Evans, thanking her once again in that same thick drawl.

After driving a few blocks, she pulled to the curb under the shade of an old oak and stripped off her disguise as she mulled over her next step. She'd head home to grab a quick bite to eat, check for messages, then return to watch him again tonight.

She'd tail him through the weekend if she had to, but it was getting old. If she turned up nothing by Sunday night, she'd have to attack this from another angle.

Four hours later found Diana, still in her rental car, parked as close as possible to Austin's cottage without him being able to spot her easily, and sweating in the heat as the sky clouded over. Next to lying to nice little old ladies, surveillance was the worst part of the job, boring and tedious. She occupied her time playing "what if" scenarios in her head, but was still stuck on the "why" question he'd thrown at her earlier in the week.

Not much progress on that front, either.

The lack of sleep was beginning to wear on her, and she had other cases she couldn't put off for much longer. More reasons to try a different tactic if he didn't do something interesting soon.

Just as she contemplated what that other tactic might be, she glimpsed movement at Austin's cottage. When he rolled the motorcycle out toward the road, Diana straightened.

It looked like her boy actually intended to go somewhere—high time for a little action.

The motorcycle rumbled past, without Austin even turning his head toward her. She waited a moment, then started her car and followed the red flag of his T-shirt and white flash of his motorcycle.

As Diana followed Austin's taillights down St. Charles, a misty rain began to fall, slowly dampening his shirt. She tailed him across Canal, appreciating how his wet shirt adhered to the strong muscles of his back. Not surprisingly, Austin drove like he owned the streets, giving her reflexes and driving skills a good workout. He headed toward the parking ramp off St. Peter, and she scrambled to find a parking place—always more difficult with a car than a motorcycle.

She lucked out, as a car had just pulled out around the corner from where Austin had parked. He'd already lowered the kickstand as she'd passed him, and from her mirrors she watched him pull off his helmet.

The front of his T-shirt was even wetter than the back, and as he ran his fingers through his dark hair, muscles flexing with each movement, his hard-edged good looks packed a hot, visceral punch.

Oh, great. Her libido was finally showing signs of life again, but now was *not* the time for her body to remind her she hadn't had sex in the two years since Kurt ended up in the slammer for robbing half her clients.

Diana blinked, refocusing, and by the time she parked, Austin had reached the stairs exit. She waited a brief moment before she followed him through the door, tracking his cheery whistling and the leisurely echo of boots on the steps.

With resignation, Diana followed him to Bourbon Street, and reluctantly closed the distance between them before she lost him in the mass of people crowding the street, clutching go-cups as they reeled between smoky bars, noisy music clubs, and cheap strip clubs.

The drizzle had eased into a gentle rain that nobody seemed to mind, Austin included. Diana spared a brief thanks for waterproof mascara and wished she hadn't worn a silk tee—when wet, it wouldn't leave much to the imagination.

Austin's damp T-shirt didn't leave much to the imagination, either, but she didn't mind the view. Or, for that matter, the *entire* view from the rear. After a day like she'd had, sitting for hours in a hot car, searching his house all the while her heart pounded in her throat, jittery with fear of being caught, the least she could do for herself was enjoy—

No, no, no. That tight, very nice behind belonged to a thief, and unless she wanted to end up in another disaster, she'd better not forget it.

Primal urges to the back of the bus, please . . . civilized intelligence to the front.

Maintaining a firm grip on her shoulder bag—and her good sense—Diana elbowed and weaved her way through bodies in various states of inebriation. Ahead, a man outside a strip club called out to Austin: "Beautiful girls inside! Best topless dancing and hottest girls in town! No cover!"

Diana hoped a strip joint wasn't Austin's destination. She'd stick out like a neon arrow in a topless bar, and if by some chance she'd spooked him into meeting with someone tonight, she wanted a look at the person. By now, she recognized most of the local second-story guys and fences on sight.

Which reminded her: How on earth would a college professor, especially one as high profile as Austin, connect with a fence to begin with? Her mind boggled at the implausibility of such a thing.

Although Austin grinned at the caller, he didn't go inside. As she passed the open door of the strip club, the heavy beat of dance music filtered out, along with the stink of cigarette smoke, stale booze, and something more sour and unpleasant.

Austin meandered through the crowds, past bars and clubs and ticky-tacky shops, moving alternately through shadows and the rain-blurry glare of neon lights. He didn't appear to have a destination in mind, or to be in any hurry.

The Old Absinthe House was only a block ahead. Maybe he wanted to listen to wailing blues while sucking down a cold one in the dark, cluttered ambience of a two-hundred-year-old bar.

A small jazz band made up of scruffy locals played on the next street corner, surrounded by people shaking plenty of booty and oblivious to the rain. Austin walked into the heart of the dancers, their gyrating bodies swallowing him, and Diana followed a moment later.

The crowd closed around her. For several frustratingly long seconds, swaying arms, legs, and bodies trapped her, forcing her into a standstill. A man grabbed her by the waist, laughing, and she shoved him back. He laughed at that, too.

Finally, she broke free, and then stopped.

"Damn," she said quietly.

Austin was nowhere in sight.

She hopped up several times to see above the press of bodies, but didn't spot a familiar red T-shirt. She quickly checked out several nearby gift shops, but didn't find him.

No longer concerned with being stealthy, Diana hurried toward the Old Absinthe House, looking all around and hoping for a glimpse of her quarry. When she reached the bar she checked both downstairs and upstairs, but saw no sign of Austin.

He'd vanished, just like that. One minute he'd been in front of her, and the next, poof. Gone.

Not only was the day's search a bust—a big risk for nothing—but her tail was a big, fat flop as well.

Seething with frustration, Diana turned and headed back toward the parking ramp. It took longer, going against the flow of human traffic. Shoulders and elbows jabbed her, people bumped into her and cut in front of her, but she marched forward in a stride too determined to encourage any but the drunkest idiot to shout suggestive remarks at her.

The only option now was to again stake out

Austin's place in the increasingly slim hope that he'd meet with someone she recognized as a bad guy. Or that he'd do something even remotely suspicious.

Diana pushed open the parking ramp door and climbed the steps, fishing the key chain out of her purse. Distracted with her thoughts, she dropped the keys. Turning, she bent to retrieve them—and saw a familiar pair of scuffed hiking boots, strong, tan legs beneath damp khaki shorts, and a red T-shirt clinging to a lean, muscular chest and broad shoulders.

And, finally, she met dark eyes hot with anger—and a spark of something else.

She froze.

"Hey, Diana." Jack Austin stood inches away, a slow, wolfish grin curving his mouth. "Lose something?"

SEVEN

...

Those pretty blue eyes widened in shock, then narrowed in understanding at what he'd done. That look on her face was absolutely worth getting soaked, and almost—*almost*—made up for the fury and disbelief that had shot through him when Ellie Evans had told him how much she approved of him hiring a cleaning service, and he didn't mind that she'd let that nice young lady into his house, did he?

Nice young lady, his ass.

Jack hooked her keys over a finger and held them out, repeating, "You lose something?"

Or someone, sweet thing?

Her expression chilled, and she straightened, folding her arms across her chest in a gesture both defensive and aggressive—and sexy as hell.

Jack dropped his gaze to her breasts, nicely framed and lifted by her arms, and he could see the pattern of her lace bra beneath the wet fabric, as well as a hint of taut nipples.

"You played me."

At her flat statement, he looked up again. "You broke into my house."

Her sudden smile surprised him.

"So what are you going to do about it, Austin? Call the cops?"

Her taunt hit home, but he couldn't hold back an answering smile—as much at the outrageous irony of his situation as her smooth response. "Guess I can't do that, huh?"

A smug expression crossed her face. "Guess not."

Jack let his smile fade, and tightened his mouth. "Don't be too proud of what you do. You live off other people's misfortunes, and you know what that makes you?" He stepped up against her, crowding her soft, warm body against the cold concrete wall. "A parasite."

Her lashes lowered, but only briefly, then she lifted her chin. "But you have to admit I'm much prettier than most parasites."

He continued to stare at her, his anger melting away before the force of that insane, gut-deep lust she always roused. Fast, hot, and, close against her like this, undeniable.

Diana acted calm and cool, but he felt the rise of her breasts against him as she took a quick, shallow breath.

Not as cool and untouched as she'd like him to think.

"I don't know why you're so upset," she all but purred. "You told me to investigate you. Did you think I wouldn't take you up on the invitation?"

"Breaking into my house is a pretty broad interpretation of what I said. I was hoping for something more . . . hands-on."

Emotion flitted across her face, masked too quickly for him to read—but it didn't look anything like fear.

"It was a very hands-on kind of search," she said softly, her gaze mocking him, not giving an inch. "Most revealing."

A bolt of pure, sweet excitement shot through him. Damn; he couldn't remember when he'd last had this much fun with a woman, and they hadn't even taken off any clothes yet.

Yet . . .

"Then I gotta tell you, Diana—I can't wait to see how you'll interpret this."

Jack pressed her fully against the wall, his hands on either side of her head, and kissed her like he'd never get another chance in this lifetime.

She stiffened, but her lips were as warm and soft as he'd imagined. Lips meant for kissing, nibbling, and other things his imagination had no trouble conjuring. She smelled like rain and female, and something else almost sinfully good, and the feel of her damp body against his made him want to grind his hips against hers.

If she'd kissed him back, softened even a fraction, he would have. After a moment, when she didn't, he pulled back. The look on her face was as unreadable as ever, but he knew for sure it wasn't fear. She kept her hands rigidly at her side, and even if she hadn't kissed him, she *had* closed her eyes. He'd watched her lids flutter shut the instant before his lips touched hers.

"You'll steal anything?" Her soft words broke the heavy silence. "Even kisses?"

"I'd like to steal a whole lot more than kisses," he said roughly, and satisfaction settled over him when she went very still. "You feel it too . . . this thing between us. I know you do."

Her eyes went slitty again. "If you think your kiss is enough to befuddle my poor little brain and stop me from going after you, you're wrong."

"Good. I'm counting on you coming after me."

"Don't crowd me." Her tone dripped with disgust, and she made a movement with her hands, as if she wanted to push him away but couldn't bring herself to touch him. "And if you think I'm all excited at feeling every bump on your body, you're wrong about that, too."

"Bump?" Jack arched a brow. "If I were a less secure kind of guy, that might hurt."

He stepped away, though; he wasn't anxious to give her a chance to knee him in the balls.

"Stop it, Austin," she snapped. "If there's something you want from me, then *tell* me."

Jack leaned forward until their noses almost touched. "What I want is to get you up against a wall in a dark alley, in the back of my truck, or in my bed, and do things to you that'll make us both lose our minds."

Her eyes widened, then she blinked once, slowly.

"How's that for honesty and truthfulness? Does it earn me any points?"

She moistened her lips, drawing his attention, and he watched her mouth form the words: "Not in the column you're hoping for."

"Do you always have to get in the last word? Like this is some sort of pissing contest?"

Those full, soft lips thinned. "Give me back Steve Carmichael's Egyptian box, and we'll call it even."

Jack regretfully shook his head. "I admire a single-minded ambition to succeed. Trouble is, I'm pretty driven to succeed, too. I don't suppose you'd consider backing off?"

She merely looked at him as if he were the biggest idiot alive.

"I didn't think so, but I had to ask." He took her hand, pressed her key chain into her palm, then closed her fingers around it. "It's been fun, but I have a lot of work waiting for me at home. Are you going to follow me back? Because if you are, I can go slow again so that you won't lose me."

Her face paled, except for the bright red flush on her cheeks. "Don't underestimate me, Austin. The last man who thought he could use sex to distract me is currently serving a five-year prison term. He was pretty hot in bed, but that didn't stop me from setting him up and letting New York City's Finest take him down."

Jesus, she wasn't lying.

"Then I'll have to be smarter than he was, and hotter in the sack."

With studied casualness, Jack brushed past her and headed up the stairs to his bike, aware of her staring at his back. The memory of her mouth on his, the press of her warm body against him, remained vivid and sharp, and he ached at the absence of something he'd not even known until moments ago.

So much for a restful night's sleep, much less concentrating on finishing that overdue journal article.

He swung his leg over the bike's seat and started it up, feeling the engine's power pulsating between his legs. The engine's rumbling growl echoed through the parking ramp and faded as he pulled on his helmet.

Diana still stood by the door, watching him with all the focused intensity of a jungle cat about to strike. He really liked how she looked in that little bit of top and shorts, but he'd like even better how she'd look wearing nothing at all.

Crazy or not, it would happen. She'd end up in his bed sooner or later. And considering he might not be a free man a couple weeks from now, he'd better see about making it sooner rather than later.

As Jack roared past Diana, he gave her a jaunty salute.

She gave him the finger.

He was still grinning when he parked the bike and walked up the stairs into his quiet, dark, and empty cottage that, if he closed his eyes and imagined hard enough, carried the faintest wisp of her sweet, musky perfume.

EIGHT

...

Wiping the sweat out of her eyes with her arm, Diana took another jab at the punching bag, then spun and kicked it twice, her yell drowning out the lively beat of Capercaillie's *Whinney Hills Jigs*.

Kickboxing was great for abs and muscle tone—and for cutting loose when a way-beyond-PMS bad mood hit.

She'd barely managed a few hours of sleep last night after another uneventful stakeout of Jack Austin's house, and this morning hadn't improved her mood at all. Even a fleeting thought about what had happened with Austin three nights ago spiked her blood pressure into the red zone. He'd made her feel like a fool, and she had only herself to blame. She'd gotten soft and lazy these last two years, and far too complacent.

She attacked the bag with a flurry of punches, taking pleasure in the thud of leather against leather.

Never, in all her years as an investigator, had she been pursued by one of her own suspects. Except for Kurt, but that had been different. He'd studied her for months, learned her weaknesses and habits, and then made his move into her life, her bed, and her heart, and finally into her client files so that he could plan his robberies from a smorgasbord of choices.

It was the move into her heart she'd never forgive.

Three more punches, then she jumped and kicked the bag hard enough to rattle the base.

And now Jack Austin came strutting along, thinking he could play with her head and her libido.

Two more roundhouse kicks, and the jolt of the impact vibrated through her muscles and bones.

He would *not* take her by surprise again.

"Remind me never to do anything to piss you off."

With a yelp, Diana whirled, her heart pounding.

"You," she snarled when she could breathe again. "What the *hell* are you doing here?"

Jack Austin leaned against the doorjamb of her exercise room. In a ray of pure golden morning sunshine, he gleamed like something otherworldly. Then he pushed away from the door and ambled into the room, and the illusion vanished. He wore the ubiquitous boots with crew socks, khaki cargo shorts, white ribbed tank top, and a dark green unbuttoned camp shirt. A fringe of dark chest hair brushed the neckline of his tank, and that familiar, maddening grin split his face.

"Looks like I'm breaking into *your* house."

For a second or two, she could only stare at him, overwhelmed by his sheer audacity. Finally, she managed, "How?"

"Unlike you, I didn't lie to any sweet old ladies. I just picked the lock."

Diana shook her head, then demanded, "And how did you learn to pick locks, Austin?"

"Shouldn't you call me Jack?" He moved closer, but wisely kept the punching bag between them. "After that kiss, and your going through my underwear drawer, I think we've moved beyond the formal stage."

True; but calling him Jack sounded way too intimate. If she continued to think of him as Austin, she still had a chance to keep her wits about her.

A very slim chance, she realized with a small shiver.

"How?" she repeated icily, and gave the bag a vicious jab. Releasing her confusing emotional energy this way was far more dignified than screaming.

"It's amazing what kind of books you can buy on Amazon."

She made a low sound in her throat, and he laughed, moving slowly back, all grace and sinuous strength. She'd often heard the phrase of someone "moving like a cat," but had never, until this moment, understood what it meant. It meant a determined stride that demanded attention and triggered an instinctual wariness; a self-aware arrogance that came from simply being a human male—the most dangerous animal on the planet.

Go on and run, that walk said, *and make it fun for me . . .*

"You want the truth?" he asked.

"That would be a nice change of pace," she said, her tone thick with sarcasm.

Austin lifted his broad shoulders in a lazy shrug.

"I had a very talkative cellmate for a few weeks one summer."

"You learned to pick locks from some thug in a Mexican jail?"

"Guatemalan, technically, and you've been listening to gossip." At her pointed look, he added, "The basics, yes. I had to practice to perfect my technique. Research, research, research—that's what we academic types are good at."

"I'm sure the board of regents at Tulane would love to hear it."

His smile faded a fraction, and those dark eyes hardened. "There's not much I can do that will surprise them, anymore."

"I think stealing priceless Egyptian artifacts will raise a few eyebrows. Even for you."

"We'll just have to keep that a secret, then."

"Not anxious to have your double life exposed by little ol' me, Jack?"

"No, but if there's any other part of me you'd like to expose, feel free to help yourself."

Diana imagined pushing up his tight knit tank, what it would feel like to touch the hard warmth of his belly, to run her fingers over his muscles and crisp chest hair.

Then she let out a yell of pure frustration, and the bag thumped under a perfectly executed side kick— a very poor substitute for grabbing him and having her way with him.

Diana turned and stalked to the other side of the room, as far away from him as she could get. She knew—just *knew*—that he'd bring energy and daring and fun to his lovemaking. He'd like it fast and hot, slow and sweet, playful and uninhibited. No-holds-barred, cut-loose kind of sex, and, God, she really wished she could let herself fall for this man.

It had been so long since she'd let anyone close.

"You kickbox to Irish jigs?" Jack asked, breaking the tension.

She'd forgotten about the music. It had faded before the thudding of her heart and the shivery sensation that had taken hold of her when he'd walked into the room; a hot, jittery sensation made up of excitement and anger—and desire.

"Jigs have a good workout tempo," she said stiffly, not sure if he'd asked simply out of curiosity, or to poke fun at her. After turning down the boom box's volume, she removed her boxing gloves and tape, then grabbed a towel and patted away the perspiration from her face and neck, still scowling at him.

As if it did any good. He didn't even bother hiding the fact he was checking out her boobs and butt. Heated embarrassment washed over her, knowing her sweat-dampened blue Lycra tank suit hid nothing.

Potent sexual awareness shimmered between them, so strong it raised goose bumps along her skin and brought the memory of Friday night's kiss rushing back—that body-whooshing, toe-curling, rock-my-world kind of kiss. It had taken every ounce of her self-control not to kiss him back.

"Did you know I was home, or were you hoping to paw through my underwear drawers in privacy?" she asked, proud of how cool her voice sounded.

"I called your office. Your secretary was very

helpful. She said you were still at home and wouldn't be in until later in the morning."

"And how exactly did you find out where I live? I don't list my home address anywhere."

"I took a tip from the master." A gleam brightened his gaze, and she could've sworn he was trying not to laugh. "I told your secretary I had flowers to deliver, but that I lost the address, it was my first day on the job, and I felt like such a fool, but I had this sick mother I had to support and—"

"You lied to my secretary."

"I'm a quick study."

A reluctant smile tugged at her lips, and Diana quickly ducked her head. The last thing this overgrown delinquent needed was even a wisp of encouragement.

"For the record, I didn't like lying to your neighbor. I'm sorry about that, but not sorry for why I did it." She straightened, uncomfortable with having let him glimpse even that much. In her line of work, it was best never to let anybody see a soft side. "Okay. You're here; you've made your point. Now get out."

"What point is that?"

She closed on him. "That you're not going to make this easy for me. But make no mistake, Jack, I will find out the truth."

"Sweetheart, I'm counting on it."

"Even if it means your arrest?"

"Even then."

Nothing playful gleamed in his eyes; he seemed absolutely serious.

Warily, she moved even closer. "What kind of game are you playing?"

"Wish I knew. The truth is, I'm pretty much making things up as I go along," he said, his tone wry. "The master of improvisation, that's me."

Diana stopped in front of him, inches separating her body from his. She could feel the warmth of his skin and smell his fresh, outdoorsy scent. He *should* smell like smoke and brimstone.

"If I accept this challenge you've thrown out, and excavate your many layers, will I like what I find in the end?"

A corner of his mouth tipped up. "I sure as hell hope so."

Diana considered his comment, her gaze dropping to that faint, self-mocking grin, then lower along the strong, sun-browned neck to the dark chest hair above the tank's neckline, and the well-defined muscles beneath it. She liked a man with a lean, powerful build, the kind that came from regular physical activity rather than hours pumping iron in a gym.

What better way to figure out his angle, than to play along?

She reached out and placed her hand against his chest. He arched a brow, but she could feel the jump of his heart under her palm. She wanted to shake his rock-solid confidence—to make him sweat, make him ache, and make him feel the same itching, yearning need she was feeling at that very moment.

"Then let's get started peeling away your layers," Diana murmured as she gathered a handful of his tank, then pulled him down and kissed him.

After his first jerk of surprise, he wasn't shy about kissing her back. She let herself enjoy him, guilt-free. He tasted even better than he had the other night, since she wasn't so tense or surprised. And could he ever kiss! Not too wet, not too dry. Not too hard, not too soft. Not too much tongue, but not too nice, either.

Jack made a low sound of satisfaction and closed his arms around her, one hand between her shoulders, the other on the small of her back, fingers brushing her bottom.

Her inner alarm sounded weakly, lost in a hot rush of urgency and desire. She had a fleeting thought that she should pull away, that after a workout she wasn't exactly daisy-fresh, but he didn't seem to give a damn—and neither did she.

Moving her hands down his chest and stomach, eyes closed, she pulled the tank free of his waistband, and touched bare skin.

Warm, taut, and vital; simply touching him reduced her to sighing with pleasure.

"You feel great," Jack muttered as if he'd read her mind, then kissed her with a rough urgency that sent everything spiraling out of control.

Vaguely, she knew he'd lowered her to the exercise mat on the floor. Vaguely, she knew it wasn't a smart thing to let him do. She should put a stop to this . . . but not yet.

Eyes still closed, nibbling at Jack's mouth, Diana slid her hands beneath his tank to his back, where the muscles bunched under her palms. He had one forearm on the mat to support himself, his other hand on her side, just below her arms, thumb caressing the side of her breast.

She shifted, peppering his mouth with swift,

hard kisses, wanting him to touch more, and he groaned, the sound rumbling from deep in his chest. Suddenly she became aware of his arousal pressed against her, and how her own hips arched to meet him.

Struggling to regain her self-control, she went still—and at once Jack pulled back.

"Shit," he said after a long moment, his voice low and raspy.

Diana stared up at his face, still only inches away. His eyes were deep and black, filled with a mix of heated need, confusion, and wariness—and for once he didn't have a grin or a smart remark.

Pushing herself up on her elbows, Diana took a deep, steadying breath, hoping he hadn't noticed the rapid rise and fall of her breasts, couldn't hear her hammering heartbeat.

She could almost feel the tension thickening, the silence weighted with reassessment, and the realization that this was no game.

Neither one of them could win without the other losing, and she saw in his eyes the moment he realized it.

Jack settled back and slowly stood. Diana followed, coming to her feet with less grace than usual because her legs had gone all rubbery on her.

"You weren't faking that," Jack said at length, his voice very soft.

Briefly she considered braving it out, going for flippant or icy. Instead, she shook her head. "That was about as real as it gets."

She stood still, waiting, her pride keeping her from asking what she wanted to know.

Again, it seemed as if he could read her mind, and he cursed under his breath, then sighed. "God help me, but I really do like you, Diana."

Excitement and pleasure flared, sharp and sweet and intense.

And stupid! His liking her was *bad*, not good.

Her lips still tingled from his kisses, and she moistened them. "I think you'd better leave." He was almost to the door when she said, "And Jack, don't ever pick my locks again."

He stopped, and glanced over his shoulder at her. "Then the next time you want to come into my house, have the guts to walk up to the front door and knock."

Diana burst through her office suite door and charged past Luna, who sat at her desk flipping through a *People* magazine, a Tootsie Pop in her mouth. "I have to make a private phone call. Please don't disturb me until I open my door."

"Okay. I have a message for—"

"I'll take it later!"

"Whoa. Good morning to you, too," she heard Luna mutter.

Diana slammed her office door shut, sat at her desk, and pulled her phone toward her. Oh, God, she was in trouble. Seriously bad trouble, and she needed help: the kind of help only lifelong friends could give.

Cassie and Fiona would help her sort out this muddle.

She punched in Cassie's number, biting on her

lower lip, trying not to think about Jack biting that same spot only a short while ago.

When that failed, Diana closed her eyes, forcing herself not to dwell on how good it had felt. She'd only get all panicky again if she did.

The phone on the other end rang with a deep, long trill.

"C'mon, Cassie, pick up," Diana whispered.

She'd met her two best friends during her freshman year at Ohio State, and they'd stayed close over the years, sharing triumphs and tears, shopping trips and vacations, being there for each other through marriages and divorces, births and even the deaths of loved ones. Fiona and Cassie would understand. Oh, they'd yell at her, but after the scolding stopped, they'd help, even if that meant just listening to her rant and rave.

The phone range for the eighth time. Where the hell was Cassie? It was only ten o'clock in Wyoming; she should—

"Hell Creek Fossil Company. This is Cassie Ashton."

At the brisk, unconsciously sultry voice, an image of Cassie flashed to mind: long, curling dark hair surrounding a hopelessly cute face, her broad smile, and wide hazel green eyes that brimmed with all the force of her blunt, earthy personality.

"Cassie, it's Diana, and I'm in such a mess!"

"Hey, it's okay. What's wrong? Is Fiona on the line?"

"Not yet. Can you hang on while I ring her shop? It's nine in L.A. She should just be opening up."

"You bet."

Diana put Cassie on hold and dialed Fiona, who answered after four rings, sounding slightly breathless: "Hello, Kennedy Antiquarian Books."

"Fi, it's Diana. Help!"

"Oh, God." The cultured voice still carried a strong lilt even after almost fifteen years in the US, and if ever a woman personified Irish, it was Fiona, with her dark red hair and fair, freckled skin. "I haven't had my first cup of coffee yet. Is this a five-cup alarm?"

"I think so." Diana relaxed back in her chair, relieved and happy despite her panic. She pushed the conference call button. "Cassie, you still there?"

"Yup. Fiona on?"

"I'm here, Cassie. How's it going?"

"The fossil business is booming, God bless Steven Spielberg and *Jurassic Park,* but it's a slow day in the shop. Good thing you called now. What's all this about a mess?"

"I think I'm having a Kurt Bentley rerun."

"Oh, shit," Cassie said in a tone of disgust. "Diana, you dope."

"This calls for something stronger than cream in my coffee." Fiona sighed heavily. "I'm putting you on the portable so I can find a chair and my whiskey."

"What happened?" Cassie demanded, while Fiona made a lot of noise over the line, the scrape of a chair on the floor, then a liquid, pouring sound.

If she closed her eyes, Diana could almost smell the dusty old-book scent of Fiona's dim rabbit warren of a bookstore, and the pungent, bitter aroma of her favorite espresso.

She took a deep breath. "It's a case I'm working on—or bungling, is more like it. I lost my temper, and told the guy outright he was a suspect. I can't seem to tail him without getting caught, I can't find any evidence against him even though I know he's a thief . . . He's brilliant, he's gorgeous, and he kissed me Friday night. And I kissed him back just now. A lot."

"Why the hell did you do that?" Cassie sounded more bemused than shocked.

Diana sighed. "Because I thought I could make a point about not playing around with me."

"Which didn't work," Cassie said dryly.

"Not the way I intended it to, no."

"And why else did you kiss him? Come on, love. 'Fess up."

Something about the tone of Fiona's voice made Diana shift uneasily in her chair. "I admit I wanted to kiss him. I mean, *any* woman above the age of puberty would be attracted to the guy."

"And this does raise a few problems, I agree." Good old Fiona, ever calm and diplomatic.

Unlike Cassie. "I don't believe this. Why are you always attracted to such jerks?"

"I'm attracted to forceful men." Diana couldn't help sounding slightly defensive. "It's not my fault that most forceful men also happen to be jerks."

"So you think this guy is pulling another Kurt on you?" Fiona asked.

"Well, not exactly." Diana vented her nervous energy by tidying the piles of papers and folders on her desk. In the center was the Ziploc bag with the card inside, and she began fiddling with the zipper, moving it back and forth, back and forth.

"He's not really denying anything," Diana said. "Or pretending to be something he's not. This guy isn't even hiding the fact he wants to get me in bed, and he doesn't seem to think that my investigating him rules out the possibility of . . . well, whatever."

"But he's a bad guy." Cassie plunged right to the heart of things.

"He's a bad guy," Diana admitted, squeezing her eyes shut. She could still vividly recall that serious, intent look on Jack's face as he'd pulled away from her. "Or at least he wants me to think he is."

Neither of her friends responded for so long that Diana said, "Um, hello? Are you still there?"

"Yes," Fiona murmured. "How peculiar."

"That about sums it up," Diana agreed.

"I don't get it," Cassie said. "He's either a baddie or not, right?"

"Oh, I'm sure he's my thief. What bothers me is *why* he did it. I have this odd hunch that he has some sort of good intentions in what he did."

There. She'd put into words the indistinct feeling that had troubled her all along.

"You mean like Robin Hood? Stealing from the rich and giving to the poor?"

When put that way, it didn't sound very plausible. "Something like that."

"You made excuses for Kurt, too," Fiona said quietly. "I'm sorry, Diana, but I have to wonder if that's not what you're doing all over again."

"It just doesn't seem the same," Diana insisted. "I know I shouldn't feel this way. You're right; I'm being a dope, but he . . . intrigues me. He *wants* me to investigate him. Why would he want that, unless he thinks I can find something that will help him?"

"He's using you," Cassie said, her tone sharp. "Kick his ass into next week, Diana. I mean it. Lose the loser."

Exactly the advice she'd give Cassie and Fiona if their situations were reversed. "Maybe you're right, but—"

"Oh, shit," Cassie said abruptly. "Dinosaur Hunter Incorporated just pulled up in front of my shop, in full bad-ass mode. I wonder what long list of ethics I've breached this time."

Taken aback by the shift of the conversation, Diana asked, "Who are you talking about? Is it that paleontologist you keep locking horns with?"

"Right. And he doesn't look happy." Cassie laughed, and it wasn't pretty. Over the line came the sound of a door crashing open, and a male voice yelling Cassie's name in a distinctly unfriendly tone. "Uh-oh. I gotta go. I'll call you back later. You take care of yourself first, Diana, and give 'em all hell."

"You always say that," Diana said, smiling.

"And I always mean it," Cassie retorted cheerfully. "Toodle-oo, girls! We have *got* to get together again soon."

The line clicked.

"Well," Fiona said after a moment. "That was abrupt."

"You know Cassie."

"Yes, and don't take her advice. I adore her, but the woman's a chaos magnet. Take my advice instead—stay far away from this man. Better yet, find yourself a nice, normal job before you get hurt again. Please don't take any more risks."

Diana frowned. "There was a time you wouldn't have said that."

After a short silence, Fiona laughed softly. "I learned my lessons the hard way. Not that it matters; you always do what you want, anyway. We all know that."

Fiona was right; she'd already known what she had to do before she'd called her friends. She'd simply needed to hear their voices, to talk it out with someone who'd sympathize, no matter what.

"I don't think I want to stay away from him," Diana admitted.

"Oh, I figured that from the start." Fiona's voice held a note of resigned humor. "But I agree with Cass about one thing—take care of yourself, first and foremost. Be careful. We worry about you. And remember, if you need to get away for a while, you're always welcome here."

A small lump rose in her throat, and Diana blinked away a sudden stinging in her eyes. "I know, Fi. Thanks. Love you guys bunches."

Fiona chuckled. "Ditto. Call again soon. Keep us posted."

"Will do."

After hanging up, Diana sat back. She felt much calmer now; her palms weren't all sweaty, and that awful fluttery sensation in her stomach had faded, edged out by growing curiosity.

Was Cassie onto something? That Jack Austin was acting as some sort of misguided Robin Hood?

The recovery of Steven Carmichael's Nefertiti box suddenly seemed a lot less interesting than figuring out what Jack Austin was up to.

Still deep in thought, Diana stood and went to open her door. "I'm done with my call, Luna. Sorry for snapping at you. This case . . . it's turning out to be more complicated than I anticipated."

Luna nodded. "It's okay. You looked a little hot when you came in, so I figured something was up. And by the way, that's a great dress, in a nonfruit sort of way."

"Thanks. I think." Diana glanced down at her leopard-print knit tank dress. She'd worn it because of the hideous heat; there wasn't much to the dress, and it also matched her hissy mood. "You said I had a message? And did any more calls come through while I was on the phone?"

"Just the one message. Some guy named Jack."

Diana froze as a sweet, betraying heat rolled over her. Luna appeared not to notice.

"He wouldn't leave a last name, and didn't really leave a message, either." Luna shifted the Tootsie Pop to the other side of her mouth. "He said you'd know who he was, said he was sorry and wasn't, and that you'd know what he meant. Well, what he actually said was that you'd decipher it."

"Okay."

Luna looked curious. "That's kinda weird, Boss."

"Yeah, well, weirdness is my stock-in-trade. Thanks." Diana went back into her office, shutting the door quietly behind her.

So Jack had called, with a "sorry, but not sorry" message. She stared down at the folders and papers on her desk, smiling. She'd said almost the exact same thing to him—although she'd meant lying to his neighbor, not nearly kissing him out of his clothing.

Her restless gaze settled on the jack of spades, and her smile slowly faded as understanding dawned.

Of course it would be spades. Decipher, indeed.

"Cute, Jack. Very cute." Exasperated, she shot to her feet and grabbed her purse. "God, I really hate games."

NINE

...

Later that afternoon, Diana ran Jack down at the Columns, the old hotel's stately, slightly musty lounge. He sat at the bar, drinking beer with four young men—most likely his grad students, as they had that slightly scruffy, hungry look about them.

She walked past the tables lining the patio and through the darker interior nooks and crannies, and insinuated herself into the group as if she'd been invited.

"Hi, boys." She smiled sweetly, and the grad students stared like they'd never seen breasts or legs before. To their credit, they tried not to be obvious about it, but had a little trouble keeping their focus on her face. "I need to talk to Professor Austin. Alone."

The students exchanged startled glances before turning to Jack for guidance, and he nodded. "Go find a table, and I'll join you when I'm done here."

They went off, beers in hand, still looking a little confused, and Diana sat on the recently vacated barstool next to Jack, smoothing the leopard knit over her thighs.

His gaze tracked her hands and settled on her breasts, although he didn't look particularly happy to see her. Even these parts of her. "If it isn't Sheena, Queen of the Jungle."

"You're quite the charmer. I bet all the girls just beat a path to your door, especially with you being such a famous eligible bachelor and all."

Why the *hell* had she said that?

Diana tucked a wisp of stray hair behind her ears, trying to quell the flush warming her body and seeping upward to her cheeks—and hoping it was dark enough that Jack wouldn't notice. But it was hard to act cool with a guy who'd had his hands all over her that morning.

"Fishing?" A corner of his mouth tipped up in a half smile. "Sorry to disappoint you, but the only girl anywhere near my door lately has been you."

She didn't like the little tickle of relief his words brought, and she was in no mood to spar with him, either. She removed the card and placed it, in its bag, beside his beer.

He didn't move; didn't so much as twitch a muscle. Finally, he looked at her. "What's that?"

"It's a jack of spades."

"I can see that. So?"

"It was left in place of my client's recently liberated Egyptian goodies. My first thought was that jack equals Jack—meaning you—but I couldn't see you being that stupid. Guess I was wrong. How disappointing."

He took a swig of beer. "If you have a point, I'd appreciate your getting to it sometime soon. It's been a long day, and I'm kinda beat."

"Are you in a hurry to get rid of me, Jack?"

Amusement gleamed in his dark eyes—along with a controlled, yet frank sexual interest. "I'd say that depends on why you're here. If it's to continue what we started this morning, you can stay and we'll lay bets on how quickly I can get you out of this very sexy dress." His gaze dropped to the hemline, which was hiked high along her thighs, his look as hot and tangible as a touch. "If not, you can leave me in peace with my beer and my hard-on."

Diana couldn't help looking at his groin, any more than she could ignore that inner curl of desire. The palms of her hands tingled with the remembered feel of his skin, and she closed them. He sat too close, his warmth and nearness raising goose bumps along her arms, and he smelled delectable.

"Didn't your mother ever tell you it's not nice to talk about your penis in public? Why men are so crude, I'll never know."

"I may be crude, but I'm honest about it. More honest than you," he said, and took a swallow of beer.

Looking away from the strong lines of his throat, she tamped back her irritation at the sting of his words—and with an effort, resisted the urge to kiss him and taste the malty richness of beer on his lips.

"Before your very obvious attempt to misdirect me, I was talking about this jack of spades, and about to say that cards are kind of like hieroglyphics."

That got his attention; unease briefly flashed in his eyes before the familiar amusement returned. "That's a stretch."

"The queen of hearts has an iconic meaning, 'jokers wild' is another word for unpredictability, and the ace of spades symbolizes aggression and power. Granted, I'm not a wonder boy like you, but I don't think it's such a stretch to say card symbolism and hieroglyphics are roughly similar in concept. I even talked to a fortune-teller in Jackson Square about cartomancy, which was interesting, but that was just making it more complicated than it really was. Don't you hate it when that happens?"

Jack looked across the bar, as if the shapes and labels of the booze bottles held a sudden fascination.

"A 'spade' is another name for a shovel, and you're a digger, aren't you, *Jack*?" She leaned toward him, close enough to feel the soft cotton of his shirt rub against her bare arm, and lowered her voice. "You're using the card as a personal hieroglyph. Clever, clever boy. Too bad Carmichael hasn't figured it out.

"Or maybe he has, but he doesn't want to believe that the man he's been funding for five years, the man he treats like a son, is stealing from him."

A muscle in his jaw hardened. "Hell of an imagination you've got there."

"But I'm right."

"And there's nothing wrong with your ego, either."

"It's a little something we have in common, Jack."

He abruptly swiveled on the barstool to face her. "Can I buy you a drink?"

Diana stared at him for several seconds, then sighed. "That little tussle on my floor this morning probably left you with a few misconceptions, so I think it's time to chat about the game rules here." Again, she leaned closer and spoke each word slowly and carefully: "I'm the good guy. You're the bad guy. I hunt you down. You run and hide—you really shouldn't offer to buy me drinks."

"Is that a no?"

His persistence and that too-bland expression made her smile, even as some uneasy part of her wondered who was the cat here—and who was the mouse. "Oh, what the hell . . . it's hot, and I'd love a Louisiana lemonade, thanks."

"A Bloody Mary seems more your type."

"Very funny."

Austin grinned, and ordered her a drink. After it arrived, he swiveled again to face her. "Do the bad guys always run away?"

She shrugged, playing with the straw. Her favorite drink back home had been a Captain Morgan's spiced rum and Diet Coke, but since she'd migrated south of the Mason-Dixie line, she'd developed a fondness for the tart, sunny vodka and lemonade. The tropical heat of New Orleans likely had something to do with that.

"Sometimes they yell at me, or threaten me. Every now and then, things degenerate to pushing and shoving. I deal with white-collar bad guys, so things stay civilized for the most part."

"There wasn't anything civilized about that kiss you gave me this morning. Were you trying to scare me off?" He took another long swig of his beer.

She watched the smooth, gliding muscles of his neck as he swallowed. He had a great, guy kind of neck.

The icy glass in her hand suddenly felt good. It would feel even better pressed against her cheeks. She took a quick gulp. "Not exactly."

"You want to tell me why, exactly, you kissed me?"

Fat chance of that. "No."

He grinned again, raising the dark bottle to his mouth. "You've got the hots for me, sweet thing. Just admit it."

"Don't call me sweet thing, and I'm not admitting anything. *Your* ego certainly doesn't need any more stroking." The second the words were out of her mouth, she realized how he'd interpret them, and held up her hand. "Don't say it. Don't even think it."

"Too late. I've already got the visual, right here." As Jack tapped the side of his head, Diana noticed he'd buttoned his dark green shirt since she'd last seen him, and she couldn't decide if that was a blessing or a pity.

Looking away, she rested both elbows on the bar, chin in her hands, and took a long sip of her drink through the straw. "I've been thinking."

"Uh-oh. Isn't that dangerous for you blondes?"

She didn't even bother with a glare or a frown. "You've been excavating at Tikukul for the past ten years, right?"

"Give or take a few months, yeah."

"And you've been on-site for each season?" When he nodded, she added, "Then people down there must know you pretty well, maybe even treat you like one of the family."

"You could say that."

"Especially since you probably employ the locals on the site and give back a little to the community and all that?"

A small frown appeared between his brows. "Yes."

"So explain to me how you ended up in jail for over two weeks, and why somebody from the US Consulate's Office didn't hustle their butt down there to get you, an American citizen and rather well known university professor, out of the local pokey within a day or two."

An emotion darkened his face; one that read a lot like anger. Jack picked at the label on his bottle, then finished off the beer. He signaled for another, still avoiding her gaze. "That's a question I asked myself. Turned out, I didn't much like the answer."

Diana blew out a breath in frustration. "Why don't you ever give me a straight answer?"

"Because I'm having fun." Jack swung around to face her fully, one elbow resting on the bar.

"You're stringing me along as a delaying tactic, Jack."

"That too," he admitted, and laughed.

Jack *was* enjoying himself—and that facet of his personality fascinated her as much as anything else about this maddening man.

"So why the delay? What are you waiting for? Or are you planning to make a run for it soon?"

He shrugged. "You can keep asking questions, Diana, but I'm not answering them."

"Maybe you should," she said quietly.

For a long moment, Jack said nothing, then he

leaned close enough that their noses almost touched. "When you start asking the right questions, then I will. I really do like you, despite my better judgment, and I'll also admit I want nothing more than to get you in my bed. But I don't trust you enough to believe you'll put my interests before your own, especially after that admission about sending your ex-lover to prison. I'm just looking out for my own ass."

"Fair enough. I don't trust you, either." That fluttery sensation returned to her stomach—and it wasn't because she'd knocked back a drink before dinner. The nearness of his mouth, and her imagination kicking into overdrive, was intoxicating enough. "Though I think you're a pretty likable guy, too . . . for a thief and a liar and a manipulator."

And sexy, a great kisser, fascinating, and smart . . . definitely smart. Jack was working an angle, and as much as she wanted to crack his secrets wide open, she enjoyed matching wits with him.

"You're a damn good flirt, Diana," he murmured, so quietly that if she hadn't been so close, she'd never have heard him. "But your pickup lines need a little work."

"I'm not trying to find a date." It suddenly struck her that if she leaned over even a tiny bit more, he'd have to kiss her. "I'm trying to catch a thief."

"And when you catch him, what are you going to do with him?"

As his expression turned serious, the fun suddenly fizzled out of their conversation. Diana didn't have to respond; they both knew the answer.

Jack pulled back and took another swig of beer,

eyeing her for a long, uncomfortable moment. Then he stood, dug into the pocket of his shorts, and slapped a twenty-dollar bill on the bar.

She let out a breath she hadn't even realized she'd been holding.

"Stay or go, or have another drink, it doesn't matter to me. I've kept my grad students waiting long enough. If you want to continue our conversation, come knock on my door later tonight."

As if she trusted herself to go anywhere within a mile of Jack Austin's bed, with its crimson coverlet, when he was within pouncing distance.

Diana watched him walk away with his beer and sit at the table with his students. She finished off her drink as their discussion quickly turned serious, with much hand gesturing and bodies leaning intently forward. Within minutes, Jack had a pen in his hand to sketch out something on a small notebook he'd pulled from his shirt pocket.

A suspicion began forming: one she didn't like, but made too much sense for her to dismiss. Finally, she collected her purse and stepped down off the stool. She walked out without looking at Jack again—although she could feel his gaze on her.

With the windows rolled down, Diana sat in her car on the Canal ferry, tapping her fingers on the steering wheel as she stared out at the brown, sluggish waters of the Mississippi. A huge freighter barreled past, diesel engines rumbling, the bow plowing a high furrow around it. Dusk had settled over the city, but she was too preoccupied to appreciate the sparkling beauty of the view.

A cop buddy lived in Algiers Point, and he might help her find information on the theft of Steve Carmichael's Mayan artifacts. Calls to her informants had so far turned up nothing useful, and she needed details—among them if any playing cards were left behind—and she doubted Carmichael's other PI would appreciate her horning in on his investigation.

She also had a feeling Carmichael wouldn't like her poking around a case he wasn't paying her to investigate.

After the ferry docked, she drove toward Pelican. She couldn't remember the exact address, but knew to look for the double shotgun that, like Austin's place, was in the middle of a repainting project. Since she didn't have Bobby's new phone number with her, she'd have to take the chance he'd be home. It was well after six so he should be off work, although city detectives didn't always keep regulars hours.

She found the house and saw his red Bronco parked outside by the curb, in front of a mud-spattered black pickup. She parked behind the truck, then walked to the house, where voices and strains of lively Zydeco music filtered through the screen door. Halfway up the porch steps, remembering it wasn't wise to sneak up on a cop, she called out, "Hello? Anybody home?"

A beer in his hand, Bobby ambled out onto the porch. He'd recently cut his blond hair, and it looked like he'd just come home from work—he still wore tan pants, a white short-sleeved shirt, red suspenders, and a crawfish-print tie.

She'd never met another cop who dressed like

Bobby Halloran—which she considered a good thing.

"Where y'at, darlin'," he drawled, laying it on thick in his best good ol' Alabama boy guise. His gaze flicked past her to the Mustang, and he whistled. "Looking good."

"Hey, Bobby," she said with a grin. "What's looking good? Me, or my car?"

"Pretty women are a dime a dozen, but it's not every day I see a Mustang looking that fine."

"No wonder you can't keep a girlfriend." She let out an exaggerated sigh, then flicked the garish tie. "And I hope you didn't go to court dressed like that today. You'll give cops a bad name."

"Too late. This is New Orleans; we already have a bad name." Bobby flashed her the wide, engaging smile that had fooled many a gullible bad guy. His eyes, pale blue like those of an Alaskan husky, brimmed with good humor, despite the weary lines on his face. "Today wasn't a court day. It was a sit on my ass and make phone calls and write reports day." He took in her curve-hugging sheath. "Nice dress you're almost wearing. Hot date?"

"No. I've been working." Diana poked him with her elbow. "And I've exceeded my suggestive comment threshold for the day, so no hooker jokes. And don't even think about flirting."

She might as well have told him to stop breathing. Bobby Halloran had emerged from the womb with a wink and a grin.

"Bad day, huh?" he asked.

Diana sighed. "You have no idea."

"Probably do, but we won't argue that."

Before she could ask him what was wrong, a woman inside the house asked a question in a cheerful tone, a deep, male voice responded, and a child laughed.

"You've got company?"

"Some friends who've come over to help me work on the place. I provide the beer and food, and we work until there's nothing left to eat or drink." Noticing her pointed look at his bottle, he added, "I just got home. You want something to drink?"

"I can't stay and work." She gave an apologetic shrug and smiled. "Sorry."

"Come on in and have a beer anyway."

He looked so tired, and since she'd dropped in without calling first, the least she could do was share a sociable beer before pumping him for information.

"How's the remodeling going?" she asked once inside the old house he'd inherited from his great-uncle, a thirty-year veteran of the NOPD. The place smelled like paint and freshly cut wood, mixed in with a whiff of grilled hamburgers.

"I'm still living in Uncle Walt's side of the place. I've got this side pretty much torn up."

The left side was gutted, period. "Looks as if you're making progress," she said encouragingly.

He grunted. "Like glaciers move."

"Second thoughts about leaving your apartment?"

He shrugged, looking faintly uncomfortable. "It's not so bad, it's just what the hell am I going to do with all this space? It's a family kind of house, and I'm not exactly a family kind of guy."

Prone to picking the wrong kind of women, was

more like it. Given his mood and the fact they weren't alone, she made a mental note to drag him out to a bar or a car show soon and cheer him up.

As she followed Bobby around a corner, Diana spotted three people sitting on the bare plywood floor: a woman with long auburn hair, a toddler pushing around a Tonka dump truck, and a dark-haired, powerfully built man in jeans, a white T-shirt, and well-worn work boots. A construction worker, and just off work, judging by the line around his hair that had been flattened by a hard hat.

The man looked up, and Diana nearly swallowed her tongue. Not just any construction worker; a Chippendale version of one—she'd never seen a man so absolutely drop-dead gorgeous.

"Hey, *chère*," the man said in greeting, his deep voice colored with a Cajun accent. He didn't appear to notice her near gawking.

The woman looked up then, as did the little boy. The wedding rings registered almost the same moment that Diana noticed the kid was a spitting image of his old man, God help all little three-year-old girls the world over.

She smiled and walked forward. "Hello. I'm Diana."

The woman stood and brushed sawdust off the back of her shorts. She was tall, with a strong, athletic build. She smiled back and said, "I'm Dulcie Langlois. This is my husband, Julien, and our little boy, Sammy."

So *this* was Dulcie.

Diana glanced at Bobby, but he had his head in a rattling old refrigerator, banging around bottles and avoiding eye contact. She'd heard a lot about this woman from Bobby—namely that she'd shattered his heart. It appeared he'd gotten over it, but she'd always had a feeling he hadn't told her the whole story.

"Nice to meet you." Diana resisted the urge to stare at Dulcie Langlois—or at the Cajun hunk still hunkered down behind her.

How on earth did the woman deal with it? Diana didn't consider herself overly vain, but she wouldn't like being married to a man who looked more gorgeous than she did. And the worst of it was that he probably woke up looking that good, too.

"Hi," said the kid on the floor. "I got a dump truck."

"I see that." Diana looked away from Dulcie and smiled at the boy. She didn't know what else to say. Kids made her a little nervous, and the younger they were, the more unsure she felt around them.

"It dumps," the kid added, and demonstrated by depositing wood bits, sawdust, and a McDonald's Happy Meal bag on the floor.

"How about that." Diana hoped she sounded suitably impressed, and glanced at Dulcie, who watched her son with a soft, indulgent expression.

Langlois smoothed back his son's dark hair, the gesture tender. Then he looked up at Diana, gaze skimming her dress, and grinned. "You don' look like you're here to paint none, *chère*."

The amusement in his smile sharply reminded Diana of another man. While Jack Austin might not be as model perfect in his looks, she bet he could hold his own against Julien Langlois in a roomful of women.

"I'm here to talk business with Bobby. I'm a private investigator."

Bobby returned with a Dixie, and Diana took it as Langlois came to his feet with a grace Diana wouldn't have expected of a man of his size. He was taller than Bobby, and more muscled—although Bobby Halloran was no slouch in the looks department.

"A PI? Oh, Bobby." Dulcie sounded both amused and exasperated, and when she glanced at Diana, her expression was a little less friendly. "You're not into something that'll get you in trouble again, are you?"

"No," Bobby retorted. "Diana's a friend. I help her out now and then, that's all. Mind your own business, Dulcie."

The irritation in his voice almost made Diana smile, although she understood the sentiment behind Dulcie Langlois's question. Bobby engaged in a little creative law enforcement from time to time, which didn't always go over well with his superiors. Art theft being international in nature, she'd worked with a lot of cops over the years—big-city cops, small-town cops, Feds, Interpol, and Scotland Yard—and she considered Bobby Halloran not only one of the most dedicated cops she'd ever met, but one of the best.

Besides, she sympathized with his trouble handling the team-player concept. Her inability to play well with others had been the main reason she'd left law enforcement after a year. Too bad she only thought of him as a friend—Bobby, in all his golden gorgeousness, would be a lot healthier for her than Jack Austin.

Bobby nudged her with his elbow, his expression still faintly annoyed. "How about we go sit out on the porch."

"Sounds fine. This shouldn't take long." Diana smiled again at Dulcie and Julien. "Nice to finally meet you two."

"Halloran's been tellin' tales." Julien Langlois's grin widened, and suddenly he didn't look half so intimidating—unlike Jack Austin, who alarmed the hell out of her the instant he cracked a grin.

Langlois slipped a hand casually into the back pocket of his wife's shorts, and she leaned back against his body with a comfort that came of long habit and complete trust. The little boy squatted between his father's legs, making truck noises as he reloaded the back of his toy.

Diana couldn't help feeling a brief twinge of exclusion.

Shaking off the sensation, she walked outside with Bobby. Once she was out of hearing range, she leaned toward him, and said, "Jeez, how do you stand looking at them? They're such a picture-perfect little family, I almost want to hurl."

Bobby grunted. "You get used to it."

He eased down onto the porch swing and Diana sat beside him, facing the slowly darkening sky and a homey scene of quirky old houses and flower gardens. The chains of the swing creaked as they gently swung back and forth.

"So what do you want from me?"

The abruptness of his question stung. Even if she'd come for information, the way he'd put it made her sound so grasping—especially since she was still smarting over Jack calling her a parasite. While she had no illusions about the nature of her work, it had hurt, all the same.

"Nice to see you, too, Bobby."

"Darlin', it's not me you're here to see, as you always seem immune to my spectacular good looks and Southern charm."

She smiled. "It's just that all that charm and good looks are attached to a cop. No offense. I still think you're a pretty decent guy."

"Thanks. You're a pretty nice girl, too, for a sleazy private eye."

Ouch . . . why was everybody picking on her job lately? Eyeing him, she said, "Taking a wild guess here, but work's not going so well?"

He looked away, balancing the beer bottle on his knee. "There are days I wonder if what I do out there does any damn good, and why I'm busting my ass if it doesn't. Other than that, life's grand. And you? Bagging all the bad guys?"

At his blatant evasion, she let out a long sigh. "Okay. Since you don't want to spill your guts about what's bugging you, and now that we have all the polite chitchat aside, I do need your help."

That got a grin out of him, and he seemed to relax. Of course, sitting on a porch swing with a cold beer went a long way toward soothing away the day's cares. "All right then. Let's get down to business."

"Do you know anything about several crates of

Mayan antiquities that were stolen from a ship a few months ago?"

"Steven Carmichael's boxes of pots? Yeah, but it's out of my district."

She nodded, aware of that. He'd recently transferred to the First District, keeping busy working a steady caseload of violent crimes. "Carmichael just hired me to investigate another theft, one that he hasn't reported to the police because it's . . . delicate."

Interest sharpened Bobby's pale eyes. "Delicate as in illegal?"

Diana gave him a reproachful look. "You know me better than that. If I thought anything about the case was illegal, I'd have turned it down. I'll admit there's a sticky area that concerns him, but he legally owns the artifacts that were stolen." She sounded convincing, even to her own ears. "I need to know some specifics about the investigation on the ship case, and since it's ongoing, it'll be easier if I can get what I need through inside sources."

"Meaning me."

"Yeah, meaning you." Diana took a deep breath, and smelled the thick, sweet scent of honeysuckle close by. "Besides, Carmichael hired another investigator to hunt down the missing crates, and I don't want to step on any toes . . . or let my client know what I'm doing."

Bobby laughed softly. "I do like your style."

Coming from a ruthless, relentless cop, that didn't strike her as a compliment, exactly. "Can you help me with this?"

"Sure. I can ask around, see what's up."

"And can you ask if there were any playing cards

left behind on the ship, where the crates had been stored?"

Bobby eyed her curiously. "Cards?"

"I have a hunch the two thefts are related." She sighed again. "You know that old poem, about coming to the fork of a path in the woods?"

He nodded.

"Well, that's where I'm at in this investigation. It's starting to feel deep to me, and whether or not the cops found any cards on that ship will determine which path I'll take."

And just how much shit would hit the fan.

"I'll get on the phone tomorrow, call in some favors from a few buddies over in the district."

"You've got all my numbers, right?"

He nodded. "Cell phone, home phone, office phone, and pager, I got 'em all. Are you looking for a smuggling ring?"

"For the artifacts in the crates, yes. For the other thing, I'm not so sure."

Bobby rubbed his thumb over a blond brow. "If you're talking smuggling antiquities by ship, you should talk with Customs and the Coast Guard. That's their territory."

"It's too early for the Feds, but the Coast Guard can tell me who owned the ship, right? I bet it was one of Carmichael's, but I want to check for sure. You wouldn't happen to know anybody in the Coast Guard who might be inclined to clear that up for me?"

"It so happens that I do."

"Female?" When he grinned, she added, "Not another one of your damsels in distress, I hope."

"Not this one. She's straight as an arrow."

She thought she detected a note of frustration, but she'd always found Bobby difficult to read. "And off-limits, then, seeing as how you're a little bent?"

He stared at her for a long moment. "I don't have any former lovers doing time in a state penitentiary."

Friends always knew exactly how to make a maximum impact.

"I guess I deserved that," she said stiffly.

"Uh-huh. Guess the pot can't call the kettle black," Bobby agreed mildly. Then he gave her an exaggerated puppy-dog look, with a coaxing grin. "C'mon now, no sulking."

"I'm *not* sulking!" She tried holding back an answering smile—and failed. "Damn that Southern charm. It gets me every time."

He laughed at that. "Okay, seriously. I promise I'll start calling around first thing tomorrow morning, and get back to you as soon as I can."

"Thanks, Bobby. I appreciate it."

"You owe me one."

"How about a shopping trip to the men's department at Dillard's or Lord & Taylor, with my fashion expertise for free? If I see another tie like that, I may not survive the shock."

Wholly unperturbed, he said, "Nope. I have my own style, and I'm sticking to it."

"Okay, how about a six-pack and a day's worth of house painting?"

"Deal. So are you going to tell me why you still look worried?"

Diana shifted, avoiding his direct gaze. "It's my

suspect, I guess. There's something going on with him."

And me, she almost added, but thought better of it. She wasn't entirely certain how he'd react, as a cop or as a friend, but either one could be a problem if he took it upon himself to interfere.

Bobby frowned. "How about some parameters here, darlin'? A good something? Bad something?"

"I'm not sure." She rubbed her forehead, which ached with tension. "But he doesn't taste . . . dark. Bad. Evil. Whatever."

"Interesting choice of words." Bobby fixed her with a sharply speculative look.

Diana glanced away again. "All I know is that I'm positive he's my guy, but it still feels and tastes all wrong. Something doesn't fit, and I'm going crazy trying to figure out what."

"You got a gun, right?"

Startled by his unexpected question, it took her a moment to answer. "Yes, of course. And I target practice once a month. I'm very good at it."

He grinned, which annoyed her all over again. She checked her watch, then stood. "You know, I *hate* it when you cops get all macho and superior like this."

"Just making sure you can protect yourself if you get in a tight spot."

"I'm a big girl. I can take care of myself." She handed him her half-finished beer. "I have to go if I want to catch the next ferry. Thanks for the beer— and for the help, Bobby."

"Anytime, darlin'."

She frowned, and lightly touched his cheek. "And take it easy, okay? You look like you could use a little downtime."

He caught her hand in his, and kissed her knuckles as if he were some old-time, smoothie Hollywood star. Diana rolled her eyes, but smiled.

As she turned and walked down the steps toward her car, he called, "Diana!"

She glanced back, stopping abruptly when she saw his grim expression.

"You watch that pretty ass of yours, darlin'."

"And here I thought you'd be watching it for me," she said lightly, despite her discomfort—and alarm.

"I mean it. Smuggling is serious shit. There's big money in it, and very bad people involved."

"I know." She gave him a grateful smile. "And I will be careful. I promise."

TEN

...

On Wednesday, Diana finally tracked down Carmichael's wife, Rhonda, but all she learned from that brief, strained conversation was that the Carmichaels didn't like each other, and the missus considered her husband's priceless collections a waste of money.

After that, she forced herself to take a break from the Tut case. She needed to catch up on her backlog of insurance work, as well as several minor cases for lawyers—the usual verifications of authenticity and value, with some theft and fraud investigation thrown in to keep things interesting. Working on other projects would give her mind a chance to rest, and maybe when she came back to the case she could approach it from a fresher angle.

Shortly before noon, while taking notes on an insurance case involving the verification of $200,000 worth of eighteenth-century French antiques, Luna buzzed her on the phone intercom.

"Hey, Boss, there's a cop out here to see you."

Diana's knee-jerk reaction was defensive, as she

and the local police merely tolerated each other. Then she remembered Bobby, and jabbed the intercom button. "I'll be right out."

When Diana opened her door and walked into the waiting area, she found Bobby sprawled in a chair and Luna holding out her arms toward him, wrists and hands pressed together in an old-fashioned gesture of supplication, just like a cover illustration on some Victorian penny dreadful.

"Luna, what are you doing?"

"I want him to arrest me." Luna batted her dark, mascara-thick lashes. "I *need* him to arrest me."

"Ah." Diana folded her arms over her chest, and shared an amused glance with Bobby. "You're wasting your time. He only dates damsels in distress."

"I'm distressed," Luna insisted, not lowering her arms. "Seriously distressed. You should see what she pays me. And I have no coffee and no chocolate in my apartment."

Bobby, grinning by now, looked quirkily handsome in gray pants, a dark purple shirt, and a pale yellow tie. "Luna, how old are you?"

"Twenty-two."

"It breaks my heart to have to say this, but I don't associate with women under thirty." He pushed himself to his feet, and Luna tipped her head back to watch, her mouth slightly open. "I'll tell you this, though, you'd have me on my knees if you were ten years older."

"But I have an old soul," Luna said mournfully, her eyes sparkling with flirtatious humor. She slowly lowered her arms and heaved a dramatic sigh. "Oh, all right. Leave me depressed *and* distressed. See if I care."

Diana, still smiling, motioned with her head toward her office door. "Bobby, come on inside. Luna, please hold any calls."

"Sure thing, Boss. And I'll scare away any stray people who might wander in, too."

She probably would, without having to say a word. Diana took in her secretary's stark makeup, spiky black hair, bloodred T-shirt, short black stretchy skirt, fishnet stockings, and black boots. Next to Luna's Goth darkness, she felt practically invisible in her flax linen pants and peach silk tank.

"Just don't bite any clients," Diana said, and firmly closed her door.

Bobby chuckled as he dropped into the chair across from her desk. "She's something else. Where'd you find her, Vamp-Mart?"

"Through an ad, and you of all people should know better than to judge by appearances alone." Diana sat down. "Luna's incredibly organized, actually understands accounting, and majors in art history. I adore her, even if her fashion sense makes me want to weep." She crossed her legs and leaned forward. "So what's with the personal visit? I expected a call."

"A slow day, and I wanted to check out your digs. You've never invited me over, you know."

He looked around, nodding with approval, and Diana noticed how his shoulders took up most of the wing chair's broad back.

"Nice. Maybe I should quit police work and take

up private investigating. Looks like you make a hell of a lot more money than I do."

"Only because I specialize." She leaned back, picked up a pen, and absently tapped it against her thigh. "Do you have news for me?"

"Yeah. You wouldn't have any Coke around here?"

Although near bursting with curiosity, Diana reached into the small, dorm-size fridge behind her, stocked with soft drinks, iced tea, lemonade, and bottled water, and handed him a Coke.

"So what did you find out?"

As Bobby popped open the can, his expression turned serious. "You were right about the card. The detective I talked to near busted a gut when I asked. It's a detail they've deliberately kept from the media, and he wasn't too happy that I wouldn't tell him about your case. Or your name."

Diana leaned forward again, excitement prickling along her skin. "God, I love it when I'm right."

"It gets better." Bobby took several deep swallows. "Besides the ship theft, there've been four residential burglaries of Mayan artifacts in Louisiana over the last eighteen months, and a jack of spades was left behind each time. Word on the streets is that somebody's passing around big bucks, looking for stolen Mayan pieces."

"There's always interest in that, Bobby. A lot of the galleries I worked with in New York had stopped dealing in pre-Columbian stock because most of it was looted or stolen. There's big money in it."

"I know the black market antiquities trade brings

in millions every year, right up there with drug smuggling and gunrunning. But what I'm hearing in the rumors is that somebody isn't looking to buy, they're looking to get something back, no questions asked." Bobby set the soda can down on her desk, his expression intent. "You want to tell me what this is about?"

Diana simply hadn't expected something of such magnitude, and a cold fear settled over her . . . along with a bitter, ashy disappointment. She'd so wanted to believe Jack was a Robin Hood. One of the good guys.

The chances of that still being true didn't look so good right now.

"When was the most recent burglary?" she asked at length.

Although plainly irritated at her evasion, he answered, "Last Tuesday, from a condo over in the Warehouse District. Some funerary jewelry and a jade headpiece belonging to some banker guy who's still yelling up a storm because the stupid, bumbling cops haven't recovered it."

Last Tuesday was when she'd first met Jack. "Bobby, where did this banker buy his pieces?"

A slow smile spread across his face. "You're gonna love the answer to that question."

"The Jade Jaguar?"

"You got it."

"Oh, shit." Diana let out her breath in a long sigh. "And the others?"

"Steven Carmichael's lawyer handled one sale before the Jade Jaguar opened, one was bought through a private auction, and the last came from a gallery in Baton Rouge." He paused. "I'm gonna ask again: What's this about?"

"I'm not entirely sure." Diana frowned, tapping her pen against her desk.

"Want to take a shot at explaining it?"

"No, not yet." She ignored his annoyed expression. "Were all the thefts funerary artifacts?"

"Why should I answer? I'm being cooperative, and you're holding back."

"Just answer this question, please. Then I'll answer."

Bobby pulled a folded piece of paper from his pocket, set it on her desk, then settled back, resting his ankle over his knee. "This lists jewelry, some pots, a couple little statues, stuff like that. I'll get you a more comprehensive report in a couple days. You think it's tomb looting? And does it tie into that other theft you're working on?"

Diana rubbed the pen against her lip, thinking. "Sounds like tomb looting to me. As for the other theft, it's Egyptian, not Mayan."

"So much for a pattern."

"There's still the jack of spades," she reminded him quietly, "and that ties them all together."

"Your thief's been a busy guy."

"That he has." Diana tossed the pen aside. "It's smuggling, all right, and I bet if I dig deep enough, I can tie all the stolen jewelry, pottery, and statuettes to Steven Carmichael."

Or his lawyer. She couldn't rule out Edward Jones's involvement yet.

Bobby's brows shot upward. "Are you telling me one of the richest and most powerful men in Louisiana is a cat burglar? Stealing back bits and pieces he's already sold to people? I know this is Louisiana, where we like our rice dirty and our politics dirtier, but I can't see this, Diana. Not at all."

"Carmichael didn't pull any of these jobs. That much I know for certain."

"But you know who did."

Diana sighed. "Indeed, I do."

"Then you need to tell me." His eyes had gone cold and unyielding, friendship taking a backseat to his oath to uphold the law.

"I can't do that, Bobby."

"Why?" he demanded.

"Because," she snapped back, "until I understand his motive, I cannot, in good conscience, tell you anything."

Bobby swore under his breath. She didn't like holding out on him, but she held Jack's reputation, maybe even his life, in her hands, and she couldn't, wouldn't, endanger him.

"Are you in any physical danger from this man?"

"No," Diana answered without hesitation.

"Will any other individuals be placed in physical danger?"

She hesitated, not because she doubted Jack, but because she didn't know what he was involved in, or the extent of it. "Not from my suspect, no."

"If you become aware of the possibility of bodily harm or further loss of property, you will alert me."

It wasn't a request. Diana gave a short nod. "Yes."

He scowled, looking as grumpy and tired as he had the other day, then suddenly grinned. "Dealing with you, darlin', is never dull."

Diana didn't trust that assessing gleam in his eye. "Don't bother tailing me, Bobby. I'll know if you are."

Unperturbed by the warning, he asked, "Do you need help?"

"For now I have everything under control."

More or less. But the kind of control she was in danger of losing wasn't the kind she'd willingly admit to Bobby, even though she knew he'd understand. He was just too good a cop to trust.

Bobby stood. "Thanks for the Coke. I gotta get back to work, even if there's not much to do. I guess it's been too hot for any killing, maiming, or raising cain."

"You almost sound sorry." Diana stood as well, relieved that the tension between them had eased. She walked with him to the door.

"Not really. I needed a chance to catch up on my paperwork."

Outside in the waiting area, Luna perched on her desk, with what was obviously a flower delivery.

Luna held the paper-wrapped bundle toward Diana. "For you . . . and this time I didn't tell anybody where you lived, I swear it."

Diana wished the girl hadn't brought up the subject: she could all but feel Bobby's radar humming.

"Who are they from?" he asked, his expression deceptively mild.

"I don't know, and it's none of your business any-

way." Diana made a shooing motion at him. "Don't
you have to go protect and serve or something?"

"I am protecting and serving. Now open up. I
want to see."

Great. If she refused, she'd only hike his suspicions up into the danger zone—and Bobby could be
a tenacious son of a bitch. But she didn't want to
give away Jack, either.

If Jack had sent her flowers. That was a big assumption on her part, and the delivery could simply
be a mistake, too.

"Did you recognize the delivery guy?"

Luna gave her a strange look. "It was a delivery
gal, and no, I didn't recognize her. Why would I?"

"Never mind." Diana mentally bit the bullet, and
ripped open the pretty pink floral paper to reveal a
crystal vase bursting with dozens of brilliant orange
tiger lilies—and a single white rose.

After several seconds of silence, Luna whistled.
"Whoa. You must've done something pretty good to
deserve that."

Hoping no one noticed her unsteady hands, Diana took the small envelope and quickly opened it:
*To Sheena: I couldn't find any leopard lilies, so I impro-
vised. Come knock on my door.*

Thank God he hadn't signed it. Following on that
rush of relief came a warm tickle of delight.

Come knock on my door? Of all the outrageous, arrogant—

"Who's Sheena?"

Bobby's question, directly in her ear, made her
jump. Flashing him a look of irritation—she had to

get a grip; she never would've let Bobby that close if she'd been thinking rather than mooning—Diana stepped away from him as Luna pouted, and said, "Sheena? Does that mean they're not yours? We can't keep them?"

For a moment, Diana considered taking the easy way out. But something—purely female satisfaction or pride—kept her from denying Jack's flowers were meant for her.

"What's with this 'we' thing? Of course they're mine. No doubt about that."

"Excellent! Because they are *gorgeous*." Luna leaned forward, sniffing exuberantly. "You don't see tiger lilies much, and I like that they're different. A girl can get so tired of plain old roses."

Diana touched the single white rose with the tip of her finger.

"I wonder if it's a message," Luna said. "You know, flower language."

Diana turned to her, avoiding Bobby's observant gaze. "You read flowers as well as cards?"

"Yup. Practitioner of the arcane arts and all that." Luna leaned back on her desk, her fingers gripping the edge, the short nails painted black. "A white rose usually symbolizes innocence and purity, but since I don't see how that applies to you, maybe your secret admirer is saying he feels worthy of you. Or he could mean secrecy and silence. That's the other thing a white rose symbolizes."

"Or maybe he just got a good deal on a leftover rose." Bobby grinned.

Diana fixed them both with a quelling glare.

Secrecy and silence . . .

Unexpected and eerie in its truth, and a tiny shiver rippled over her. "So what do tiger lilies mean?"

"Pretty much what you'd expect from a tiger," Luna answered. "Pride."

Hmmm. Modesty wasn't exactly one of her defining traits. "Well, they're lovely, whatever they may mean, and will look even lovelier sitting on my desk." Diana finally met Bobby's eyes over the splash of deep orange. "I thought you were going to work."

He slid his hands in his pockets and rocked back on his heels. "I thought you had everything under control."

She heard the suspicion, but smiled anyway. "I do. Thank you."

"And if you get into trouble, who you gonna call?"

"You. Super Cop." Diana laughed. "Now go away so I can 'oooh' and 'aaah' in private. It's been ages since anybody's sent me flowers."

Flowers that truly *meant* something personal, rather than offered out of a sense of obligation or habit.

Bobby sauntered out the door, and when it closed behind him, Luna pushed away from the desk.

"Where do you meet guys like that?" she asked, slightly petulant.

Diana stroked a long, curving lily petal. "Not in cemeteries after dark, that's for sure."

Luna snorted. "I meet nice guys at work. Like Mike."

Tall, thin, white-blond Mike with his black Van Dyke beard. Diana had seen him several times when he came by to pick up Luna, and he appeared pleasant enough, if slightly vague.

"Are you working a tour tonight?" Diana took her flowers into her office and set the vase on the middle of her desk.

Perfect, and a nice touch of whimsy and color to the otherwise severe room.

"Yup. A whole bunch of Japanese tourists from the Sheraton," Luna answered from the other room. "Some of these tourists really get into the whole ghost and vampire scene. I love it when that happens."

"Just be careful, and remember you're a pretend vampire. Those cemeteries are dangerous. I worry about you out there, even when you're with a large group of people."

"Yes, *Mother*." Diana easily imagined Luna rolling those big dark eyes, embarrassed by even this small display of emotion.

Tough; she'd grown fond of the kid, and needed to voice her worries from time to time.

"Hey. Is there something weird going on with you?"

Burying her nose in the sweet scent of the rose, Diana smiled at Luna's question. "Nothing you need to worry about."

"Diana."

Surprised—because Luna almost always called her "Boss"—she looked up to see her secretary standing by the doorjamb, a look of concern on the face that, under the dramatic makeup, was so very, very young.

"Is everything okay? I'm seriously asking here."

"It will be." She hoped so, anyway. "I have a few more phone calls to make, and then how about you and me walk over to the Court of Two Sisters for lunch? My treat."

"Hell yes, if it's your treat. Can I have dessert, too?" Luna brightened, all concerns apparently forgotten. "Because I wasn't joking when I said I didn't have any chocolate at my apartment."

With a three-hour break between his grad seminar and Aztec-Mayan Lit class, Jack grabbed the opportunity to get the hell out of the office and work off the tensions crowding in on him.

And he knew just where he wanted to go.

He headed first to the campus gym at Reily Center, where he changed into a pair of black Lycra bike shorts and a loose-fitting gray tank, and buckled on his skates. He stashed his boots in his backpack, along with his keys and wallet, pulled on his Australian Akubra hat, its brown felt stained by years of sweat and wear, then slipped on sunglasses.

After leaving the gym, he skated fast and hard across campus, crossed St. Charles, and headed into Audubon Park. He cruised along the park's paved boulevards, packed with joggers and skaters, bikes, trikes, and strollers, families with kids out for a day at the park, and tourists wandering around. Adjusting his stride to a more leisurely pace, he skated toward the zoo.

The ticket sellers at the gate knew him on sight. They always offered to waive the entry fee, and he always refused. After entering the zoo, Jack sat down on a bench amid a swarm of excited kids on a field trip, all in their school uniforms, and changed back into his boots.

Slinging the backpack over his shoulder again, he headed for his favorite thinking spot: the Jaguar Jungle, an acre and a half of jungle and Mayan ruins right in the heart of New Orleans.

Once he passed through the imposing Jaguar Gate into the darker, quieter interior of the jungle habitat, the temperature cooled as the dense, broad leaves of caryota palms blocked out much of the sunlight. A sense of the sinister, of the mysterious, advanced with the encroaching shadows.

Through a heavy mist, Jack followed a winding path over a quiet stream and past crumbling Mayan "ruins" entwined with vines, cannas, orchids, bromeliads, and other delicate flowers. Over the distant sounds of youthful laughter came the chatter of spider monkeys and the piercing cries of exotic birds. He took a deep breath, his senses filling with the moist, dense scents of earth and jungle.

Too clean, too manufactured, but it still smelled like the one place on earth where he could always go and just be . . . himself.

Most people wouldn't consider a dark, mist-shrouded corner of a jungle an ideal thinking spot, but it isolated him from all the white noise and petty annoyances. Here, where zoo visitors and children rarely ventured, he could relax and let his thoughts wander. He could sit by himself and sift through the detritus of daily living until he zeroed in on what was important. Or troubling him.

Pushing back his hat, Jack perched on a smooth rock surrounded by curling ferns, and leaned back

against the slender trunk of a caryota. He had Diana
on his mind—and a few other equally sticky issues.

Not only did he like her a lot, he couldn't stop
thinking about her. If it weren't so pathetic, it might
be worth a laugh—that he was falling hard for a
woman who was so damn right for him in so many
ways, and at the same time, his worst nightmare.

The attraction wasn't one-sided, but he wasn't
naive enough to think that would make a difference.
Regardless of how strong her personal attraction to
him might be, her professional ethics were stronger
and she'd turn him in if he gave him the opportunity.

He *was* a thief. A damn good one, too, and he enjoyed the planning and outwitting, the rush of
adrenaline at each risk, small or large, and the incredible irony of it all. He'd found that heady rush
addictive—and it had been his undoing. He hadn't
stopped when he should have, and now he'd pretty
much backed himself into a corner.

God, he wanted to come clean. The rush had lost
its spark, and the triumph of tricking the tricksters
didn't mean so much anymore. The constant tension and need to watch his back wearied him, and if
that wasn't enough, his need to get closer to Diana—
physically, emotionally, any way he could—dogged
him.

He wanted a chance with her, a *real* chance, but
the only way to do that meant revealing evidence
that would prove his own guilt. Even then, the evidence he had was weak—he wouldn't have hatched
this half-cocked scheme otherwise—and no matter
what direction he came at it, he couldn't see a way
out of his catch-22.

Except for Diana—a double-edged sword if ever there was one.

Jack couldn't tell her just to trust him, and she had no reason to believe his motives were altruistic. In her work, she probably heard excuses all the time.

The only thing he could do was try and point her toward the truth without implicating himself—and hope she wouldn't hate his guts in the end.

And she was close. Frustratingly close. If only she would ask the *right* questions—

A sudden, icy sensation of being watched prickled over him, and Jack twisted around.

Diana Belmaine stood barely two feet away from him—he'd never even heard her approach—her eyes wide with surprise.

Jack stared back, not moving. She was wearing a little pinkish top neatly tucked into tan pants and held a small purse, looking beautiful and sophisticated— and so damn clean.

"What are you doing here?" he asked finally.

"I wanted to talk to you, and stopped by your office—I even braved the dragon lady in the main office—but you weren't around. I lucked out and ran into one of your grad students who remembered me from the other day at the bar. He wouldn't let me into your lab, even though I said pretty please. You warned them about me, didn't you?"

A nervous ramble if he'd ever heard one. Alone with him in a jungle, she wasn't nearly as sure of herself, and he smiled inwardly. "I might've done something like that."

"He told me you'd gone to the zoo."

"How did you get him to tell you that? Threaten him?"

"Not very much." A puzzled expression crossed her face. "And at first I didn't believe him. Why are you at a zoo?"

"Why else? To get in touch with my inner animal."

She flashed him an I'm-not-that-stupid look, but like hell was he going to explain. She'd probably think he was crazy. Or more crazy than she already considered him.

"The zoo's a pretty big place. How'd you know where to find me?"

"Really, Jack, give me more credit than that. Where else would I find a Mayan archaeologist than at a Mayan habitat?"

"Now that you found me, what are you going to do with me?"

Anger flared in her eyes, quickly replaced by exasperation. "I recently came across new information, and we need to talk about it."

He looked away as his tension gathered, pushing relentlessly to the forefront. Another interrogation, another go-round with Diana, wanting her so bad, with unease riding close to the need, anticipation spicing his danger, his gut knotting.

"I came here for a little peace and quiet," he said at length, his voice low. "I don't suppose you'd grant me a stay of execution and take a walk with me."

Diana frowned, looking both curious and impatient. She was easier to read now than when they'd met a week ago. Either he already knew her too well, or she wasn't bothering to hide her emotions.

Finally, she let out a long sigh. "I suppose we could walk for a while. It's not like I don't expect you to evade every question I ask, anyway."

Jack pushed up from his thinking rock, pulled his hat down, and set out toward the center of the jungle, Diana at his side.

The walk seemed to take longer than usual, and he couldn't shake the strangeness of how her presence made him both tense and content, and just how good it felt not to be alone on a walk he'd taken a hundred times before. He liked having her at his side like this.

He didn't have a desire to talk, and Diana, perhaps sensing his darker mood, asked no questions and made no comments. But he was still aware of her, of her warm body, her musky-sweet perfume, the pull of his need to move closer and brush against her. Finally, he led her to the Jaguar Plaza at the heart of the "jungle," and stopped to watch the two big cats pace with restless grace, growling, clearly agitated.

He could sympathize; he wanted to growl, too.

Several more seconds passed before Diana broke the charged silence. "I also wanted to thank you for the flowers. They're lovely, and I have them on my desk, though I think I'll take them home with me tonight."

"You're welcome," he said quietly, staring at the male jaguar, who seemed to stare right back at him from eerie, golden eyes. "I'm glad you liked them."

Suddenly the male flattened his ears and screamed, and Jack froze at the raw, bone-chilling sound. Beside him, Diana jerked back with a loud gasp. He moved protectively in front of her, his hand touching her shoulder, ready to push her away from danger.

And almost immediately he felt like an idiot. The jaguar wasn't a threat—and even if he had been, there wasn't much Jack could've done about it; he'd just acted on pure instinct. Still, Diana didn't try to shake off his hand, and even moved nearer, her soft, fine hair brushing his face.

"Please tell me he doesn't think I look like a big, juicy peach."

Exactly.

In answer, Jack moved his thumb in a slow, soothing gesture along the curve of her shoulder. Her peachy pink top felt silky, and her bare skin above it warm and soft.

"I didn't mean to jump like that, but he's so *close*, and I swear he's watching my every move." She darted a glance at Jack, finally easing away a little. "I know I'm safe, but . . . it startled me. Sorry."

"Nothing to be sorry about."

Jack dropped his hand to his side as nearby spider monkeys, anxious over the big cat's agitation, erupted in a frenzy of chatter and rustling leaves and snapping twigs.

"Every time I hear the scream of a jaguar, I freeze up. Just the sound of it shreds the air like it's muscle and bone." The big male paced back and forth, powerful muscles moving beneath its dappled fur, and Jack couldn't look away from those hypnotic, unblinking eyes. "Deep inside us there's something so ancient that we remember what it was like to be hunted, a part of us that knows all the technology in the world doesn't mean a damn thing. We're back hundreds of thousands of years in some dark cave, with nothing but a sharp rock and our wits."

Diana stared at him with a wary, mystified expression—as if she were seeing him for the first time.

"You just made my hair stand on end," she whispered.

"That means you've got good instincts. But you already know that. And so do I." He held her gaze for a moment longer with a wry smile, before looking away. "The word jaguar means 'a beast that kills with one leap,' and they were holy to the Mayans. Jaguars symbolized the night sun of the underworld, and acted as intermediaries between the living and the dead. The Mayans also believed humans and animals shared coessences, and jaguars were the protectors and companions of kings and warriors. Seeing them up close like this, it's easy to understand why."

Diana moved toward him again, and the scent of her perfume shot straight through him to that same ancient, instinctive part of his brain.

"I'm a dedicated city girl, and I'll never give up hot showers and coffeemakers and phones . . . but I've always wondered what it would be like, living in a jungle like you do, week after week."

"Noisy." Jack smiled and motioned at the trees above them. "Sometimes the howler monkeys sound like a bunch of frat boys throwing a kegger up in the canopy. But there's no howler cops to call, and the best you can do is pull your pillow over your head. And when the bats come swooping in, thousands of them at a time . . . man, think Hitchcock and *The Birds*. It's creepy as hell, hearing the flurry of thousands of wings slicing through the air."

She shivered. "I'm not real big on bats. Or bugs."

"Then you wouldn't like the jungle. Lots of bugs. Big ones."

Her lip curled back. "Ick."

Jack shrugged. "You get used to it, and for me, being in a place untouched by technology, living in the same world the Mayans did, walking the same trails and drinking from the same rivers—it's like time doesn't exist anymore. There's no longer this huge, black void between me and the guy who ruled that city over a thousand years ago, or the people who went to its markets, worshiped its gods, raised families, worked, and died there."

"Do they . . . come alive for you?"

When he saw the intensity in her eyes that told him she truly wanted to understand, his heart seemed to skip a beat.

"Sometimes, yeah." Closing his eyes, Jack tipped his head back and took a long, cleansing breath, letting himself remember, tasting the feelings, the tug of nostalgia. "Sometimes at night, the air around me suddenly seems . . . old. And I swear I can feel them around me, as if I could look outside, and Tikukul wouldn't be empty and in ruins. But it's only my imagination. Just me wishing I could sit down by a temple and debate with Jaguar Claw the Great, talk shop with a priest, or with some old woman who sold fish in the market."

Suddenly feeling awkward, Jack opened his eyes and focused on a beetle creeping along a palm leaf. "Maybe it sounds stupid, but that's what drives me—it sure as hell isn't the money or the glamour. All I ever wanted was the chance to make these people live and breathe again. In a way, I'm all they have. Like the old jaguar god, I'm the intermediary between the living and the dead. Their protector."

Maybe he sounded like some half-baked dreamer, but he couldn't explain it any better. She would either understand, or she wouldn't.

Yet he waited, oddly tense, for her response.

"I don't think it's stupid at all, Jack. You sound like a man with a great passion for his work."

Passion.

A word people mocked these days. It wasn't "cool" to feel passion about anything. Even sex had become commercial, a commodity rather than an experience two people shared, heart and body and soul.

He sensed Diana would understand "passion" in all its many guises; maybe even how passion could drive a man to do something he shouldn't.

"Most people never get a chance to see or experience half the things I do," he said, his enthusiasm gathering steam. He turned and caught the sharp interest on her face, obvious even in the murky light. "Do you know what it's like, to clear away the debris of a tomb and look into the face of a man who died over a thousand years ago? To know you've rediscovered a king that history has forgotten?"

She shook her head; a small, brief movement, and slowly, Jack's muscles began to relax. "It's a hell of a feeling. I can make a dead man speak again . . . if even only through his bones and pieces of broken pottery. God, Diana, there's nothing like it. *Nothing*."

As he heard the forcefulness in his words, the awkwardness came sweeping back.

He'd gotten way, way too personal, so he flashed a grin, falling back on the tried and true—and the safe. "Except maybe sex. Sex is pretty damn good, too."

He expected that to break the intimacy of the moment; expected her to roll her eyes or coolly arch a brow. What he didn't expect was the sudden shock and confusion on her face.

"Oh my God, Jack. What have you done?"

At her hushed question, he froze. Then he looked away, as a bitter, inner voice answered: *What I had to do.*

All the heat of passion faded away in the face of cold reality. He stared hard at the pacing jaguar, angry with himself for letting her see this part of him, for giving too much away. She'd only use it against him, although he couldn't hold it against her. She was what she was; in the same way that cat slinking through the ferns could only be what it was.

"You make it sound like you almost give a damn, Diana." The words were out before he even realized he'd spoken aloud.

"I do give a damn." Her hand lightly touched his cheek, but her long, slender fingers were strong and forced his chin around so that he faced her.

Her eyes mirrored his own frustration, his own sense of loss, and suddenly he couldn't think of a single word to say.

"I shouldn't care, but I do, and I have this awful,

sinking feeling . . . what the hell are you trying to do, save the whole world?"

Diana's low voice shook with anger, but another emotion ran deeper than the anger, and he couldn't look away from her gaze, too confounded, too wary . . . too damn hopeful.

Jack had to swallow away the dryness in his throat before answering. "Not the whole world. Just my little part of it."

Her eyes searched his, and she stood close. Too close. He reached out, cupping her chin in his hand, and rubbed his thumb over her bottom lip.

He bent, lowering his head, and he thought she whispered, "Oh, Jack" in a sad-sounding voice. But maybe it was just the rustle of leaves in the breeze. She tensed as his mouth brushed hers, but she didn't try to stop him.

The jaguar screamed again, and the spider monkeys responded with a crescendo of calls. Somewhere close by, children shrieked with laughter, and the harshly discordant sounds shattered the mood.

Diana pulled away, glancing quickly over her shoulder as if expecting the approaching nuns, who were chaperoning the schoolkids, to come over and scold her.

When she looked back at him, something inside his chest squeezed tight, making it hard to take a deep breath. Something that he couldn't deny, even if he wasn't willing to face it head-on.

"No smiles? No smart one-liners?" she murmured, her expression cool, as if what had just happened meant nothing.

But he could feel the faint trembling of her body.

"I'm fresh out of one-liners at the moment." In an effort to get a grip on his pounding heart and uneven breathing, he glanced at his watch—and swore softly when he saw the time. "I need to head back to campus. I have a class at four."

She closed her eyes and made a low sound. "Wait. I came all the way over here to—"

"Grill me, I know. Come to my class. After that, I'll let you inside my lab, and you can search it to your little heart's desire."

Her annoyance melted away to suspicious astonishment. "You're serious?"

Jack walked away as the schoolchildren crowded by the jaguars, talking loudly with excitement. "There's nothing in my lab that doesn't already belong there." She still looked doubtful, and he blew out a breath. "Do you want to come back with me or not?"

"You know me well enough by now to know the answer."

Jack almost said, *I'd like to know you a whole lot more*, but he just couldn't put on an act right now. "Are you parked nearby?"

Diana nodded. "Do you want a ride back to the Anthro Building?"

"To the gym. I have to shower and change."

"All right. I've waited this long for answers, I can wait a little longer. And I'm glad you don't go to class dressed like that." She smiled faintly, her gaze skimming his tank, lingering on the tight Lycra of his shorts. "Although I'm sure your female students wouldn't mind it one bit."

His face went warm. "Let's go."

As they left the jungle behind, the palm trees and vines and lush greenery thinned, letting the golden warm rays of sun shine down again. Some of his dark mood lifted, and with Diana beside him, Jack passed the archaeological "dig," where another group of schoolkids were having a high old time looking for fake artifacts, if the din was any sort of measure. One of the park workers caught sight of Jack and waved him over.

"This happens a lot when I come here," Jack said to Diana, with a brief, apologetic glance. "I'll just be a few minutes."

"Hey, kids, do you know who this guy is?" the guide asked, as Jack walked toward him.

A chorus of "no's" and lots of shaking heads and giggles followed, although one young, pretty teacher said, "I do!" and grinned, her cheeks pink.

Damn. He wished he'd worn something other than bike shorts, especially since that near kiss with Diana had left him less than completely decent.

"How many of you kids watch the Discovery Channel?" the guide asked.

Excited murmurs answered him, and grubby hands shot into the air.

"Great! Then maybe you'll remember watching a show with Professor Jack Austin. He's a real-life archaeologist who works at a real lost Mayan city every summer, and I bet Dr. Jack would be happy to show you guys how a real archaeologist digs for artifacts. This man's magic with a shovel."

Jack looked over at Diana, catching her smile, and his tension faded as he surveyed a sea of awed little faces staring up at him. "Be happy to. What school are y'all from?"

Dropping his backpack, he hunkered down in the oversize sandbox with the boys and girls, asking more questions to loosen them up, answering the barrage of questions that soon followed, and demonstrating how archaeologists excavated artifacts— and all the while very aware of Diana behind him, watching.

"Okay. You have to be real careful with your trowel and not poke too hard into the ground," he said, meeting the wide, solemn eyes of a cute little black girl with pigtails. "You know why?"

She shook her head, soaking in his every word.

"Because you don't know if any other artifacts might still be hidden in the dirt, and you could break them. So you scrape away the dirt gently. Pretend your trowel is a feather." He wrapped his big hand around her tiny one, and demonstrated. "Move like your whole body is whispering."

He glanced at Diana. A faint blush colored her cheeks, and the soft look in her eyes made him turn quickly back to the little girl, who was mimicking his scraping motions with painstaking care.

"Good job, sweetheart. Just remember that buried artifacts are very old and sometimes fragile. You know what fragile means, right? Easy to break?" He turned to a blond boy with brown eyes and freckles across his cheeks and nose. "Do you ever eat crackers with your soup, buddy?"

The boy nodded. "Just with chicken noodle soup, not tomato."

Jack managed to maintain his serious expression. "And you crush your crackers, right? Until they're just pieces and cracker dust?"

The boy's eyes brightened. "Yeah. I crush 'em good!"

"That's what would happen if you get too rough with an old and fragile artifact. It'll break apart to pieces and dust. It's pretty hard to glue dust back together. Think about it, guys."

The kids giggled, talking about how they'd glue dust together—the suggestions getting ever more fanciful—and resumed their digging with gusto. The teachers soon joined in, and Jack let himself go with the flow, buoyed along by the energy and enthusiasm of the children.

After a few minutes, he checked his watch again and stood, brushing the sand from his hands and knees. "Time for me to move along. I have a class to teach soon."

"Children, what should you say to Dr. Austin?" the young teacher asked, and the kids answered with a piping chorus of "Thank you, Dr. Austin!"

"You're welcome. Don't dig up *all* the good stuff, okay?"

He joined Diana, and she fell into step beside him. Although that earlier tension between them had eased, he could still feel a low hum just beneath the surface.

"You're really good with kids," she said at length.

Her quiet comment took him by surprise. "I'm a teacher, Diana. I like kids. Little ones as well as the older ones."

"I envy you that. I never know what to say around kids, how to act."

"An only child?" He moved a fraction closer, so that he could smell her perfume. Nothing wrong with looking, smelling, and dreaming, even if he shouldn't touch.

She nodded, not looking at him—which meant he could enjoy the sight of her breasts bouncing as she hurried to match his pace.

"My parents are both professionals, and very image-conscious. When I was little, I always had to dress the right way, our house had to look just right . . . none of my friends ever liked to come over and play."

She frowned, then sent him a slanted, unreadable glance. He looked away from her breasts just in time.

"I don't know why I said that. I adore my parents, faults and all. They love me, the good and the bad, and I didn't mean to sound whiny. Ignore me."

"You're not the kind of person who's easily ignored." Jack slowed his pace, and she flashed him a quick, grateful smile. Maybe it was that smile, or maybe it was being out in the sun again, but his mood lightened even more. "I have four younger sisters, though you probably already know that."

Her expression turned slightly guilty—and he almost laughed.

"When I was a kid we had two dogs, two cats, a herd of gerbils, and a snake named Axel. When you grow up with the noise and the chaos, the bickering, and all the affection underneath it, relating to kids is easy."

"You didn't feed any gerbils to Axel, did you?"

"Axel was a bug-eating snake." He caught her amused look. "Though once I did put a gerbil in Axel's cage, as a kind of experiment to see how the gerbil would respond to adverse stimuli."

"Adverse stimuli? Jeez, Austin, you must've given your parents more than a few gray hairs." She shook her head, then asked, "So what happened?"

"The gerbil wasn't happy, and my sisters nearly lynched me. They might've been younger and smaller, but it was four against one. From an early age, I learned to take girls seriously."

Diana slanted a look up at him. "Not to mention how to charm and sweet-talk them."

"You got it," he admitted. "Though it was more of a survival mechanism than anything else."

"Survival is what it's all about," she agreed, her tone dry. "Stop. This is my car."

Jack stopped. And whistled. "A '67 Mustang convertible, in baby blue. Not exactly a surveillance kind of car. Especially when there's a hot blonde behind the wheel."

She pulled keys out of her purse and opened his door, amusement lighting her eyes. "I left my spy car at home today. Hop in, and try not to get dirt on the seats. I just had them cleaned."

He made a *tsk-tsk* sound, and critically surveyed her pristine pants and icy-pale shirt. "A little dirt never hurt anything. You look like you could use some mussing up, sweet thing."

"Call me that again, and I'll hurt *you*." She slipped on a pair of little black sunglasses, smiling, and when she closed her hand over the stick shift, stroking it, Jack burst into laughter.

"You and I are two of a kind, Diana. We should get together just to save all those nice, innocent people out there a whole world of grief."

Diana's smile widened as she started the car, its engine making a low growling rumble. "Buckle up, Dr. Jack." She put the car in gear. "And you might want to take off that hat."

"Aw, man, you're killing me," he said, but his words were lost in the roar of the engine as she mashed the gas.

ELEVEN

...

Diana slipped toward the back of Jack's Aztec-Mayan Lit class while he went to the front. His hair was still slightly damp, and he looked as casually sexy as ever in his usual urban adventurer uniform: dark green canvas shorts, white tank under a tropical print shirt in tones of green, tan, and black—which he'd buttoned into respectability before walking through the door.

Jack greeted his class and settled right down to business. "Sorry, I know I'm late, so let's get started. Today we're continuing the discussion on the Mayan creation myth from the *Popul Vuh*."

Diana tried to concentrate as he talked about gods whose names she couldn't pronounce, much less spell—of course, he had the advantage of speaking Spanish like a native and was fluent in ancient Nahautal as well.

"In last week's cliffhanger episode, we left the disgraced Lady Blood, impregnated by the very dead and yet amazingly virile Maize God, exiled to the earth's surface . . ."

He never stayed in one spot, and it distracted her, drawing her attention to the curling ends of his hair above the shirt collar, his broad shoulders and chest, the well-defined muscles of his legs . . . and what was he wearing under those shorts? One of the solid color boxers? Or a plaid, paisley, or other guylike print?

"And in today's episode, the beauteous Lady Blood gives birth to the twins Hunahpu and Xbalanque, who'll grow up to be your basic monster-killers and tricksters. But luckily they'll also play a kick-ass game of underworld football . . ."

Why was she thinking about his underwear?

Because she'd plainly left her good sense back at the office. Or maybe back in the jungle, where he'd almost kissed her.

Guiltily, she glanced up at Jack's face, half-afraid he'd take one look at her warm cheeks and read her mind. But, perched on a table, arms folded across his chest, he didn't even look at her as he continued his lecture.

". . . which is why it's important to remember the Mayans considered time cyclical, not linear, as we do. To them, creation wasn't a onetime gig. And this is where things get fun . . ."

As he launched into a complicated explanation on how the Mayans computed dates, Diana looked down again, examining the chipped frosted peach nail polish on one finger.

Forget his boxers; she had other, more pressing things to brood over. He clearly wanted something from her, beyond getting her in the sack. Sexual attraction she could manage, but his other, unknown need for her badly unnerved her.

Not letting herself get emotionally close to Jack would be hard. Maybe even impossible.

Move your whole body like a whisper . . .

Innocent words, spoken to a child—and yet incredibly erotic, drawing a taut, aching thread of desire through *her* body, head to toe.

What that man could do with simple words, and so . . . unexpected.

When the jaguar screamed, and Jack's low, raspy voice had painted such vivid pictures in her mind, she'd actually shivered—and not just from imagining huge claws shredding her flesh. He had allowed her a glimpse of the poet's soul hidden beneath the rough-and-tough machismo and cocky grins.

A part of him, Diana suspected, that he ordinarily kept under lock and key.

Even more sobering had been the fierce dedication and protectiveness toward his work that he'd revealed. His talk of making the dead speak again left her with no doubts at all that he'd never, *ever* risk his work or academic standing by becoming a thief.

Not unless he had a good reason. Not unless what he'd taken had already been stolen, and he was attempting to fix a wrong outside the limits of the law.

Not the whole world . . . just my little part of it.

What else could he possibly have meant?

No wonder he kept dodging her questions; he was treading a very dangerous precipice indeed. The worst of it was she still didn't know *why* . . . and Jack obviously wasn't going to confess. At least not until he had her where he wanted her.

Which meant all she had to work with were the myriad "why's" bouncing around inside her head: why he'd taken up thievery to start with, why he hadn't gone to the police . . . why she wanted so badly to feel his arms around her again, and why in hell she couldn't ever seem to involve herself with ordinary, law-abiding guys.

"You ready to go to the lab, or do you want to sit here all day and stare at the floor?"

Jack's question yanked Diana back to the here and now, and she looked around the empty classroom. Despite her embarrassment at being caught wool-gathering, she smiled and stood. "No way would I miss seeing what you have on the slab in the lab. Let's go."

The Center for Archaeology, which housed his lab space, was part of the Anthro Department, so she didn't have to follow him very far. Which was a good thing, because the silence between them grew heavier and more tense with each passing second.

"This is it." He stopped at a door and leaned down until they were eye to eye. "You don't interrogate my students. And you'll be careful looking around. We do conservation work here, and some of these artifacts are very fragile."

"I know how to handle myself, Jack. I've been working with antiquities for over ten years."

"All right." He opened the door to a small lab crowded with tables, shelves, boxes, and cabinets with roll-out drawers containing everything from pottery to human bones. Diana assumed there was some organizational system in place, but she couldn't figure it out. Two young women worked at a table, assembling pottery shards. A young man sat at a computer running a statistical analysis program. Another student, hunched over a microscope, explained he was examining a small pile of soil for preserved organic remains. They all smiled politely as Jack made the introductions.

"Ms. Belmaine is here to look around, that's all," he told them, and sent another long, unreadable look her way.

It made her feel like an invader, something she wasn't used to experiencing. Private investigators were supposed to be immune to such feelings, but searching Jack's lab might very well end up being one of the most awkward, difficult thing she'd ever done, if not quite up there with luring good old Kurt into the NYPD's net.

Diana took a long, steadying breath and smiled. "Well. I'll get right to work, then."

After a good hour of ignoring the silent curiosity of the students, hearing Jack's minimalist answers to her questions, poking through a dizzying array of pre-Columbian artifacts and human remains, and examining corresponding records, she found nothing that raised a red flag of suspicion.

No surprise; he'd warned her of that. If he had stored any stolen loot in the lab, including the little box with its tiny gold statuette and lock of hair, he'd since moved it all or managed to hide it very well. Which raised a few questions, because hauling around crates of artifacts wouldn't exactly be inconspicuous.

Where had he stashed it all?

"Done?"

At Jack's terse question, Diana turned from the Tikukul site logbook—and caught something deep, dark, and wholly unreadable in his eyes. It made her uncomfortable, as if she'd violated something between them.

She put the logbook aside and returned her notepad to her purse. "For now, yes. Thanks."

With a polite nod to the students, she followed him out into the hall, and after walking a short distance away to frustrate any potential eavesdroppers, she stopped. "Jack—"

He turned, and held up a hand to silence her. "No questions here. It's too public."

Diana tamped back her impatience. "Are you done with work for the day?" When he nodded, she said, "Good. I'll give you a lift home. We'll talk in the car."

"Only if you let me drive."

"For somebody in as much trouble as you are, you sure make a lot of demands."

"I have something you want."

She eyed him shrewdly. "And I have something *you* want—and it's not just a good time in bed. Is it?"

"True." Jack moved closer. "But I'm the one with the most to lose if I don't get what I want."

Some battles were just not worth picking, and Diana sighed. "Fine. You can drive."

When they reached her Mustang, parked with its top down, Jack ran his hand across the shining hood, his expression openly admiring. "This is such a great car. It suits you."

"I'm glad it's not a Barracuda, then." At his surprised look, she laughed and tossed him the keys. "I know old cars. My dad collects them, and his interest rubbed off on me. I have a friend—a cop, by the way—who sometimes goes with me to vintage car shows, and last year I had a case involving a stolen 1932 Dusenberg. It was a gorgeous old car, a true work of art, but I've always had a weakness for Mustangs. They're just so darn cute."

"As I said, the car suits you."

Jack opened the passenger-side door and helped her inside. She appreciated the old-fashioned gesture—and liked the feel of his warm, sure hand resting against her back.

"Speaking of rides, you own something else besides a motorcycle," she said, as he opened the driver's side door and angled down onto the low-slung beige seat beside her.

He grunted, and cranked the ignition. "How the hell do you figure these things out?"

"I usually call my contact at the motor vehicle department and ask her to run a check." Diana buckled her seat belt. "But that night in the parking garage, you told me you wanted to get me into the back of your truck. Ergo, you have a truck of some sort."

"I said that?"

When she nodded, Jack swore softly. After glancing over his shoulder, he put the car in gear and pulled away from the curb. "So I had you trapped against a wall in an empty stairwell, which would've made most women at least a little nervous, and you were taking notes on everything I said."

"It's a job skill."

Somehow she kept her voice cool, even as she remembered both the panic and excitement of being pinned by the damp heat of his body that night.

"Doesn't do much for my male ego." He turned onto the street and into heavier traffic.

"Which I've noticed is pretty healthy, anyway. So what kind of truck do you drive?"

"An old Jeep. How fast can this little beauty go?"

"Fast enough, but you will *not* experiment in the middle of traffic."

Despite peeling rubber out of the zoo parking lot earlier—Jack had the strangest effect on her—Diana wasn't a flashy driver, and, to her relief, he didn't do anything more than wink.

Which made her stomach fluttery. She sighed again, loudly this time. "Jack, we have to talk."

"Hope it's about something good for a change." He glanced at her, his gaze lingering briefly on her breasts.

"Would you stop that? This isn't about sex or lust, this is—"

"The hell it isn't. Diana, you and me . . . it's going to happen. You know it. And you know it's going to be good. Better than good; it's going to be phenomenal."

He drew out each syllable of that word, and Diana briefly squeezed her eyes shut, shifting in her seat with discomfort—though it was definitely the *good* kind of discomfort.

How could it be anything but phenomenal, with Jack Austin in the driver's seat, so to speak? His blunt, straightforward approach to sex and his raw, energetic animal appeal excited her. The feel of his hands on her earlier flashed to mind, along with that kiss in her exercise room, and how it had left her shaken, overwhelmed by the sheer power of her physical need.

She must've been silent too long, because he added quietly, "And I'm not the only one wanting it. You can't deny that."

She glared at him, torn between irritation and that intense, almost painful pull of desire. She wanted him so badly she couldn't believe he even had to ask. "You are such an arrogant son of a bitch."

"Yeah, but I'm a cute son of a bitch." His glanced her way, then back to the road. "Which reminds me. I'm sorry for calling you a parasite the other night."

The apology took her by surprise—and touched her. "It's okay. Private investigators don't usually win popularity contests. Most people regard us as a necessary evil. I'm used to it."

"It doesn't matter. I still shouldn't have said it." He shrugged, a touch defensive. "I was just so pissed off that you'd broken into my house and gone through my mail and my trash and my bedroom . . . how the hell can you do things like that? Just bull-doze through people's private shit?"

"The same way you break into people's houses and *steal* their shit," she shot back.

"People's houses?" He kept his focus on the traffic ahead of them. "Sounds like you're accusing me of stealing more than Steve's Egyptian box."

Reality dampening her softer mood, Diana sent him a dark look. "Eighteen months ago, Baton Rouge.

A year ago, Shreveport. Six months ago, Mandeville. Two months ago, a ship in the New Orleans port. A week ago, a condo off Magazine. Ring any bells, Jack?"

He didn't answer, but the line of his jaw tensed—barely.

As a hollow, sinking feeling settled in her chest, she forced herself to remember the reason this man was sitting in her car to begin with. "A jack of spades was left behind each time. I know it was you, so don't bother denying it. I want to know why. Do you have good reasons? Or did you get involved in something you shouldn't have, and now you can't get out of it? Why the Egyptian box, Jack? What does that have to do with the other Mayan thefts? Or is it something to do with Steve Carmichael? Or his lawyer or wife?"

His shoulder muscles tightened; again, ever so slightly.

Diana zeroed in on it. "Is it Carmichael? He appears to think of you like a son, and he's given you opportunities most archaeologists can only dream about. Why would you steal from him? Do you even like him?" She paused, studying his stony profile. "Am I asking *any* of the right questions?"

Jack braked at a stoplight, unresponsive. Frustrated, Diana glanced away—and suddenly registered that they'd long since passed his street and were heading away from the Garden District.

Alarm tingled through her. "Where are you going?"

"I'm hungry. I figure you're hungry, too, so we're going out for dinner. There's this great rib place up in Mid-City that serves a hot sauce that'll make you sweat. I guarantee."

"Dammit, Jack, I need answers from you! Enough of this; it's not a game."

"You're asking the right questions, and I'll answer one. *One*." He held up his index finger for emphasis. "But not until after dinner. We're going to relax and have a nice time. Got that?"

She stared at him. "Do I at least get to pick which one you answer?"

"Nope."

"I think I feel a scream coming on."

He laughed softly. "Pop a tape in, sweet thing, and let's have some music to cruise by."

Diana gave a snort of exasperation. "This is not a date. You're kidnapping me and taking me against my will to a greasy rib joint."

Ignoring her complaint, Jack glanced down at the car stereo system. "There's already a tape in the player. What is it?"

Before she could stop him, he'd popped it out, and she sighed—again.

"*More* Madonna? I guess your great taste in cars and clothes doesn't extend to music."

He made a move to throw the tape out of the car, and with a shocked gasp, Diana grabbed him, feeling the strength of his muscles as she yanked back on his arm.

"Hey! Don't you *dare*—"

"Just razzing you." He tossed it on her lap. "Pushing buttons."

Despite her best efforts, a high-pitched, mini-shriek eked past her tight lips.

"You need to relax. Really." With one hand still on the wheel, Jack reached out with the other and pulled the peach ribbon off her ponytail.

The wind ripped through her loosened hair. Swearing under her breath, she grabbed at the wildly flying strands, trying to push them out of her eyes as he pitched the bow on her lap beside the tape. The ribbon almost flew out the car, but she snatched it back in time.

"Diana, what's the point in having a convertible if you can't let the wind whip through your hair? Feels great, doesn't it?"

It *did* feel wonderful. His light teasing and infectious good humor kicked something loose inside her, and her laughter bubbled out.

Jack grinned, and a moment later, he began sorting through her tapes. "What's with all the Irish music?"

"You have something against Irish music?"

"It's damn depressing."

"That's not at all true!" God, Fiona would light into him for *that* crack.

"Yes, it is. Or it's political; same difference."

"I think Irish music is beautiful and lyrical, *and* I have a friend who's Dublin-born-and bred, so watch what you say."

"Okay. Then I'll just sing." He winked at her. "Our song."

She stared at him, still feeling light, ridiculously happy. "News flash, Jack. We don't have a song because there's no *us.*"

"The hell we don't," he said, and then sang loudly, "Here's a little ditty—"

"Oh, my God."

"—about Jack and Diana-na-naaaaa—"

"Stop, please!" She laughed, to take away any sting her protest might have. "And a word of advice: Don't give up the day job."

"I can't sing worth shit, I know," he said, plainly not offended. "But you gotta admit it's still *our* song."

She pushed her hair out of her eyes—for what little good it did. "As they say, you are mad, bad, and dangerous to know."

"And you're too serious. Too careful." He wasn't smiling now, and her lighter mood faded. "That bastard you told me about, he walked all over your heart, and now you're afraid to let any man close. Even me."

"*Especially* you. That bastard was a thief." She turned in the seat, looking at him through the blowing strands of her hair. "He used me to get what he wanted, and I let him. So you can see the problem with this you-and-me thing."

He glanced at her, then back to the road. "Yeah. It's crystal clear."

As Diana tried to gauge his mood, he reached over to turn on the radio, and it struck her all over again how strong and elegant his hands looked— and how very much she wanted to feel his fingers touching her bare skin.

She gave a little sigh. "Why is passion never tidy or rational? Life would be so much easier if it were."

"Seems to me, all the things worth having in life

are messy." He flashed a sweetly mischievous grin that made her breath catch. "And hard."

Diana rolled her eyes, praying her outward calm didn't betray her deep, inner thrum of desire. Oh, yes, he knew exactly how to push her buttons. Especially her lusty-hot ones.

Several seconds passed as she listened to the heavily synthesized sounds of some pop diva's dance tune. "All the smiles, the jokes . . . you hide behind them so people won't see what you don't want them to see."

Jack lifted one shoulder in a shrug. "I'd rather laugh than cry. Wouldn't you?"

As he slowed for a stop sign, she looked down at her lap, seeing her hands nervously balled into fists. "In my experience, you can't have one without the other."

The warm touch of his fingers brushed her face. Surprised, Diana looked up again, going still as he stroked the curve of her cheek ever so lightly with his thumb.

"I'm going to try like hell not to hurt you, Diana. If you believe nothing else I tell you tonight, believe that."

Amazingly—and probably unwisely—she did.

"I sense the good in you, Jack, even though I also know you're guilty as hell. All I want is to understand why—" At his pointed look, she stopped, smiling ruefully, and shook her head. "No questions until after dinner. Sorry. I forgot."

Behind them, a motorist laid on the horn. Jack muttered something crude, then put the car in gear.

The rest of the drive passed in an unspoken truce as the radio played catchy pop tunes. Finally, Jack pulled up in front of a dive—it really could only be classified as a dive—and switched off the engine.

Diana surveyed the old, peeling paint, crushed-shell parking lot gone to seed, and the neon beer sign in the window flashing D-I-E, instead of D-I-X-I-E.

"You've actually eaten here?" she asked doubtfully.

"And lived to tell about it. I know it doesn't look too good from the outside, but inside is a different matter. The food is excellent. Dinner's on me, so order whatever you want."

Until she walked through the door, Diana had fervently hoped there was a basic salad on the menu. But once inside, the potent and spicy scent of barbecue sauce made her mouth water and her stomach rumble.

Only a few tables remained open; the rest were filled with families and blue-collar workers. The small place had the feel of a neighborhood diner that the locals wanted to keep as their own little secret.

The jeans-clad hostess, a teenage girl likely related to whoever owned the place, greeted Jack as if he was a regular. She led them to a small table close to the window, sandwiched between a loud group of young construction workers and a couple with two middle-school-aged children.

"There ya go," the girl said, handing over two dog-eared menus as she checked out Diana, her gaze curious. "Liza will be right with you."

After the hostess left, Diana picked up her menu

and eyed Jack over its top. "I guess you come here a lot."

"I'm not much into cooking, so I support local businesses . . . and you better not order just a wimpy salad."

"To hell with that. I'll have ribs and send you the dry cleaning bill."

He laughed, and a moment later their waitress arrived to take their order. Without even looking at the menu, Jack rattled off: "A full order, jerk seasoning, extra spicy. Loaf of bread and salad, Italian dressing on the side, and iced tea. No sugar."

"Same for me." Diana handed her menu to the waitress, who left them with a smile. "Sounds yummy, but if I eat all that you'll have to roll me out the door and to the car."

Jack sipped his glass of water, slouched back in his chair, looking sexy and confident. He slowly unbuttoned the top three buttons of his shirt, smiling a lazy, comfortable smile, and Diana suddenly felt unsure of herself, uneasy with the rapidly increasing intimacy.

This wasn't a *date*. And it wasn't like they were old pals, catching up on lost time. She really didn't know any more about Jack than he knew about her. If she couldn't fall back on work and question him, what on earth would they talk about for the next hour or two?

As if sensing her discomfort, Jack put his water glass down and sat forward. "How long have you lived in New Orleans?"

"About two years. And you?"

"Twelve," he said. "I came here to do my graduate work, and stayed. I was born in Pennsylvania, where my family had one of those small farms that's more of a hobby than anything else. Dad was a dentist, and my mom stayed home with us kids. We moved to Boston when I was eleven, and I went to Boston University as an undergrad."

"I was born in Columbus, and like a good little Buckeye, went to Ohio State. I dropped out my junior year after I realized I didn't really want to do the college scene. I went to live in New York with an aunt whose husband was a bigwig pediatric surgeon. I decided to be a cop, so I joined the academy, graduated, and worked the streets for about a year."

"A cop?" Jack repeated, brows raised. "*You* were a New York City cop?"

"Uh-huh. But I wasn't much of a team player."

"That doesn't surprise me." He scratched his chin, regarding her with curiosity. "So how did you go from an archaeology major to a cop to a PI?"

"It took me a while to figure out what I wanted to be when I grew up." Diana shrugged. "My family is pretty well-off, and my aunt and uncle especially so. They were into the New York art scene, big-time. I went with them once to a gallery opening, where I met a private investigator who worked with Sotheby's. We struck up a conversation, I was fascinated, and when he heard about my background, he told me to give his office a call. So I did, and I worked with him for the next four years, then struck out on my own."

"So that makes you what? Thirty-four? Thirty-five?"

"I'm at the far end of thirty-four, and thank you *so* much for asking. With all those sisters, you should know better than to ask a woman about her age, her weight, or the size of her butt."

"You're not concerned about being thirty-four," he said, his tone comfortable. "Or your looks. In fact, you're one of the most self-confident women I've ever met, and I gotta tell you, it's sexy as hell."

Her mouth went dry, and she took a quick sip from the iced tea the waitress had just brought. "Thank you."

"That and the fact I haven't yet managed to scare you off."

Although he was smiling, it didn't quite touch his eyes—and Diana had a sudden, irrational urge to reach across the table and squeeze his hand in reassurance.

"I don't think your girlfriends leave because you scare them off. You probably overwhelm them, or make them feel invisible. You *do* have a forceful personality—and lucky for you, I like men with forceful personalities."

"You like pushy, arrogant bastards? Damn. I'm in love."

Diana blinked in surprise, then frowned. "You're getting all your 'L' words confused, Jack. You sort of *like* me, but you're not in *love*. That's just *lust*."

"A guy's gotta start somewhere."

She couldn't tell if he was serious or not, and when that so-called self-confidence of hers failed to produce a snappy comeback, Diana took her napkin and busied herself with smoothing it over her lap.

"Okay. Erase that. Back to start. Nothing too personal . . . hey, here comes our food."

Thank God.

The ribs were beyond excellent—if nothing else, Jack Austin could be trusted to nose out a really good restaurant—and throughout dinner, the conversation remained on safe topics like his classes and digs.

"How'd you find Tikukul, anyway?"

"Dumb luck," he admitted. "We had all these cryptic hints in the records, and one camp of academics believed it meant an undiscovered city, the other argued it was an alternative name for a place we'd already found. With all the modern technological advances, it didn't seem likely an entire city had escaped detection."

"But obviously it had."

"Yeah, and here I was, this young gun, so damn full of myself I don't know how anybody put up with me. But I really believed I could find Tikukul, even though most of my colleagues thought I was nuts." He sat back, his face softening, the memories obviously fond ones. "I'd narrowed the search area by using geographical and economical criteria, figuring a city had to be within relatively easy travel distance of the other major sites, and near water. I spent two years tromping through jungles, getting wet, dirty, and bitten by a million bugs, and in the end only found it because my guides got lost."

"So much for being the intrepid adventurer."

Jack spread his hands wide, palms up, before dropping them back on his lap. "Like I said, dumb luck. The city was so overgrown we almost missed it, and Tikukul was smaller than I expected. Some of my colleagues disagree that it's even a city-state. They think it was either a religious center or a rural estate of a powerful ruling family. But it has the layout and buildings of a typical city; it just never got a chance to grow before the Spaniards arrived."

Diana shook her head. "Considering how badly the Spaniards were outnumbered by the local population, you have to wonder why the Mayans and company didn't kick some Conquistador butt."

"One of history's greatest mysteries. Right up there with why Heloise and Abelard named their kid Astrolabe."

His comment startled a laugh out of her, but she didn't let him misdirect her. "Judging from the site maps I've seen, you still have a lot to excavate."

"Hell, yes." Jack picked up his iced tea. "We've been collaborating with a team of Guatemalan archaeologists for the past five years, but the site is pretty remote, and it's slow going."

"Good thing you have plenty of funding from Steve Carmichael."

He stared at her over the glass for a long moment. "I couldn't have done it without him, and that's the God-honest truth."

Diana itched to quiz him further—but a deal was a deal. "It also looks like you've discovered a cache of royal tombs."

Jack nodded, returning his glass to the table. "And it came at a good time, since funding enthusiasm had started to taper off. Royal tombs always attract a lot of attention."

"The night you shot up those looters, were they breaking into the tombs?"

A slow smile curved his mouth. "Diana, Diana."

She sighed. "I can't help it. Asking questions for a PI is like breathing for most people."

"You worked for Sotheby's, right?"

"Time to change the subject . . . and you're *so* subtle about it." Amused, she reached for the bread basket. "Yes, I worked for Sotheby's. And a couple of other auction houses here and abroad."

"You must've traveled a lot."

"I still do, sometimes on short notice, and often enough that I keep my passport with me all the time." Diana tore off a chunk of her miniloaf, which was still warm and chewy, and popped it in her mouth—and almost moaned in ecstasy, it was so good. "I've worked in New York, London, Paris, Rome . . . they're all hot spots for antiquities, and were home for me at various points in my life."

"So why do you do it?"

Diana looked up, licking a spot of spicy sauce from her fingers. The napkin was long since history, and everybody else in the joint was doing it, so when in Rome . . .

"A lot of my reasons were strictly practical. I have an eye for art, good instincts, and a background in law enforcement. You can always make good money when you specialize. Even more so when that specialty brings you into the orbit of extremely wealthy people."

"That's not the real reason, though."

She stopped chewing, intrigued by his observation. "Wanting to make money isn't good enough?"

"For some people. You're not one of them."

He was right—but how had he known? "Why do you say that?"

"You told me that I had a great passion for my work, which I do, and you're the same way. Passion is rarely motivated by money . . . the money's nice, and you like making it, but it's not why you do it."

She sat back. "It's an interesting question. Nobody's ever asked me before."

"I am, and I want an answer."

"You'll get one. Just give me a minute." After considering his question for several seconds, she shrugged. "I like beautiful things, especially beautiful old things. They're a bridge to the past, to those who've gone before us. They weren't mass produced in factories or sweatshops, but were made by true artisans, men and women who took pride in what they created. These objects *are* the craftsmen . . . in them, I see people. If that makes sense."

"You personalize it."

"Yes, I suppose I do. To me, they're not just trinkets worth four, five, or six figures. Each object holds the essence and heart of the man or woman who crafted it, or the person who placed such value in owning it."

Diana looked beyond his shoulder toward the street, absently watching the passing traffic. "My first case involved a Roman mirror stolen from a private collection. I tracked it down within a week. I remember seeing my reflection, and wondering about the woman who'd looked in that polished bronze mirror some two thousand years before I was even born, checking her makeup, her hair, just like me. I wondered what she'd looked like, if she'd had children, a husband who treated her well. If she'd been happy, what kind of life she lived . . . that sort of thing."

Silence fell between them. Faintly embarrassed that she sounded like some romantic sap, Diana focused her attention on her plate.

"And then you just like catching bad guys," Jack said at length.

"I do like being on the side of the angels," she admitted, looking up again. "I sleep easier at night."

"I sleep fine."

Diana smiled. "Probably from the sheer expulsion of all that energy all day long."

"Are you implying I don't have a clear conscience?"

"You're baiting me. That's not polite."

He laughed—she never tired of hearing his laughter—then sipped his iced tea. "Hanging around all those rich people must've been interesting."

"It's a lifestyle. From a distance it seems glamorous and exciting, but in my experience, having a lot of money doesn't exempt a person from being seriously screwed up. When poor people steal, I can make sense of it—some kind of desperation is usually the motivator. Which doesn't make it right, of course, but when rich people steal, it's just greed, and greed is never pretty."

"Were you sorry to leave that part of your life behind?"

She looked at him in exasperation. "It's not fair if you can ask me all these questions, and I can't ask you any."

"I never said you couldn't ask me personal questions. Just not questions that related to work. You're off the case right now."

"You don't know many PIs, do you? We're *never* off the case."

"Were you sorry to leave the jet-set lifestyle of thwarting antiquity thefts?"

"Mine was hardly a jet-set lifestyle," she retorted. "But yes, I was sorry. I liked my job, and I liked being in the heart of the action. The Boyfriend from Hell pretty much wrecked my credibility, since it's hard for my kind of clients to trust a woman who's shown such appallingly bad judgment as sleeping with a professional thief. Anyway, I came down here to reestablish my practice and my reputation. The stakes aren't as high, the money isn't as good, but I'm doing all right. I've branched out to do more insurance work, more antiques and collectibles." She looked down, at her hands knotted tightly together on the table, and slowly loosened her grip. "And I'm getting used to the slower pace of life down here. That was probably the biggest adjustment of all."

The waitress approached their table. "Ready for dessert? We have a pecan pie that I guarantee is the best in all of Louisiana."

Jack glanced at Diana, and she shook her head. "Not for me. I'm stuffed."

"We'll pass," he said. "Thanks."

"Do you want me to wrap up those leftovers for you?" the waitress asked, and when Diana nodded, the woman took away her plate.

"Now what?" Diana asked.

"Home."

"I'm driving. I don't trust you not to take us to Memphis or something." She hesitated. "Thanks for dinner. It was absolutely wonderful. Are you sure you want to pay for my part? I can—"

"I know you can, and I'm sure. How'd the pants come out?"

Diana surveyed her clothes, but didn't see any obvious sauce spots. "Not too bad, all things considered."

The waitress returned with a Styrofoam takeout box and the check, which Jack paid with cash, leaving a more than generous tip. Then he escorted Diana outside.

Night had fallen, but the sky hadn't completely darkened yet. On the horizon she could see fading bands of orange and violet blending into darker purple, then black. A smattering of stars twinkled around a nearly full moon hanging high in the sky.

It hadn't seemed as if they'd been inside for that long. She'd vaguely been aware of diners leaving, new groups arriving and leaving as well, but she'd been so caught up with Jack, she hadn't given the passing time much thought.

Diana unlocked his door before going to hers. She'd put up the Mustang's top, not wanting anybody to swipe his backpack, hat, or skates, and the air inside felt warm and stuffy. She slid into the seat, readjusted it for her shorter legs, buckled her seat belt, rolled down her window, and started the engine as Jack dropped into his seat and buckled up.

She pulled out of the parking lot and headed back toward the Garden District. Traffic was lighter, and she drove at a good clip.

After several minutes she squirmed a little, as the silence and Jack's presence pressed solidly against her. It must've been the darkness, or maybe because she'd put up the top, but the car suddenly seemed much smaller than it had before. She couldn't ignore the warm pull of his body, or how his shoulder nearly brushed hers. He was so close she only had to drop one hand from the steering wheel to touch his thigh, run her hand along it.

Imagining his response, she smiled.

"What? You've got that Cheshire cat thing going on here. Wanna share?"

"Mmm, no. Not really."

He made a low, growling sound. "Good thing you're driving."

Diana glanced at him, speeding up a little to get through a yellow light—and not missing how his foot stomped down on a nonexistent brake. "Why?"

"Because if I was driving, I'd park in a dark corner of a parking lot and find out just how much a guy can get away with in a car this small."

"I knew I'd regret asking." Again, that rush of heat—but in the dark interior, he wouldn't be able to see a blush. "When you're not thinking about sex, which appears to be about 95 percent of the time, what *else* do you think about?"

"Sleeping or eating, I guess. And work."

Diana laughed, but kept her focus on the glowing red taillights in front of her. She had fast reflexes—she'd driven in most of the world's cities infamous for hairy traffic—but Jack distracted her more than she liked. "I think that whole nineties sensitive male thing passed you right by."

"Probably while I was hacking my way through jungles. It's hard to be sensitive when you know that local highway robbers, guerrilla fighters, and drug runners won't hesitate to shoot you on sight."

"Wow. Is it really that dangerous?"

"Real enough that we have armed guards whenever we go long distances. I don't travel rural areas without a gun."

"Nobody can question your dedication," she said dryly, turning onto St. Charles. "Which reminds me. That question—"

"When you pull up to my house."

"You better not be jerking me around, Jack."

"I told you I wanted us to enjoy a night out. I'm just making it last longer."

A little tingle of pleasure shot through her. "Fine. But the minute I pull up to your place, you answer."

"You got it," he said quietly.

The rest of the drive passed in silence, except for the radio playing a boy band singing about love with all the yearning naïveté of kids barely out of high school, who didn't have a clue as to what love really meant.

How confusing, terrifying, inconvenient, exhilarating, and challenging it could be; how much work it took, how devastating it could be, how hopeless and yet ever hopeful.

Well. What a cheery thought.

Diana turned onto Jack's street and made an effort to shake off her moodiness. She rolled to a stop in front of his cottage, then put the car in park. After shutting off the engine, she turned to him.

She couldn't clearly see his face, hidden as it was

in shadows, and now that the time for his answer had arrived, a strange, empty feeling had settled in her stomach. As if she didn't really want to know the truth.

"Well?"

He let out his breath in a short sigh. "One question."

"One," she agreed evenly, waiting, her muscles knotting with tension.

"You asked if I liked Steve Carmichael."

Diana almost groaned. Of all her questions, this would be the most useless, dead-end piece of—

"And the answer is, I hate him," Jack said, his voice low.

Coldness washed over her, raising goose bumps along her arms. Without really thinking about what she was doing, Diana snapped on the dome light.

No smiles, or laughter. No humor gleaming in his eyes, only a dark rage—and something else so fleeting she nearly missed it.

"I hate him like I've never hated anyone in my life."

TWELVE

...

Jack opened the car door and stepped out so he wouldn't say more and put her in a no-win position. At least not more than he already had.

He walked toward his cottage without a backward glance, although he wanted to kiss her good night—and more. That he couldn't be with her made this gnawing hunger even harder to bear. His footsteps pounded on the wooden steps leading up to his porch, but he didn't give a damn that it made him sound pissed off.

He pulled out his keys from his pocket, rammed them in the lock—and felt a touch on his shoulder.

Startled, he turned to see Diana standing behind him. In the moonlight her blond hair looked silvery white, her face pale, her clothing blanched so that she seemed almost statuelike: Diana, goddess of the moon—and of the hunt.

Her parents had named her well.

She held his Akubra in her hand. "You forgot it."

Jack took his hat, careful not to touch her, and laid it on his backpack. "Thanks."

"You're in serious trouble, aren't you?"

He went still at the openly concerned expression on her face, and guilt hammered him. If things didn't work out as he'd planned, he could hurt her, and that was the absolute last thing he wanted.

"It wouldn't be the first time," he said tersely. "But I'm a big boy. I don't need you worrying about me. Good-bye, Diana."

She moved closer to him, into the small space between the open screen door and the front door. The keys, still dangling from the lock, jangled as Jack backed against them.

"You started this, but we'll finish it *together*. And I'll worry about you if I want to," she whispered. "It's not good-bye, just good-night."

Then, standing on tiptoe, fingers brushing his cheek, she pressed a soft kiss on his chin.

His *chin*.

Almost without thinking, he looped an arm around her waist. "A couple inches higher and to the left would be a helluva lot better."

She sighed, and he could feel the tension in her muscles. "Jack—"

Tightening his hold, he drew her closer. At first she resisted, although not very hard, then gave in.

Ah, what the hell.

Jack leaned down—and Diana tipped her head back and closed her eyes. He pressed a soft kiss on her warm mouth, resisting the urge to touch her lips with the tip of his tongue, and waited to see what she'd do.

She kissed him back. Not much more than a nibble at first, and then she opened her mouth in an unmistakable invitation. Jack pulled her against him and kissed her in earnest—insistent, exploring, intent on going as far as she'd let him.

And hoping it was all the way.

But more than sex sparked his need to touch her, to feel her body against his erection. Through the haze of desire and a driving need to be inside her, a sense of contentment, of rightness, took hold of him.

"You feel so good," he murmured against the side of her mouth. "I want to touch every part of you . . . outside you, inside you."

A tremble rippled through her, and her breasts pressed against his chest as she took a long, shaky breath. "I want to touch you, too . . . God, I've never wanted to be with a man as much as I want to be with you."

Then she licked his lip and tugged his tank free. Jack inhaled sharply as she slipped her hands underneath, flattening her palms against his belly. Her lips curved in a small, all-female smile of triumph— a green light if he ever saw one.

Jack kissed her again as he moved one hand lower, cupping her bottom. She leaned into him and ran her hands all the way up his back, her silky-soft shirt brushing against his skin. She made a purr of pleasure, muffled against his mouth as she fiercely kissed him back.

That small sound and the increasingly urgent touch of her hands on his bare skin was all the encouragement he needed.

Jack slid his other hand to the soft underside of her breast, and moved his thumb until it brushed against the taut peak of her nipple. He slanted his mouth against hers in a hungry kiss, catching her soft sigh as he caressed her again, this time more firmly.

She moaned, shifting so that he could cup her breast, not once breaking their kiss. Her erratic breathing matched his, her muscles as taut, her hips moving against him, wordlessly urgent.

Hot, wet, insistent . . . she kissed like his wildest fantasies, and all he could think of, all he wanted, was to ease her past this door, as far into the house as was decent, then get rid of her clothes, open her legs, and push himself into her hot, tight warmth as far and as deep as he could, again and again and again.

Impatient, he pulled at her shirt, freeing it from her pants, and managed to get his hand underneath. She clutched his shoulders, fingers digging into his skin, and shuddered when he slid his fingers beneath her bra and palmed her soft, warm breast.

As he rubbed his thumb over her nipple, she wriggled and sighed. It didn't seem physically possible he could get any harder, but it sure as hell felt like it.

"Diana," he said, roughly, her name coming out like a benediction, a curse. A plea.

Jack took his hand from her bottom, and fumbled behind him with the keys, their tongues still busily engaged in exploring. The lock wouldn't open, and he almost groaned with frustration. He could pick any lock in under three minutes, but couldn't get his own damn door open. Finally, it gave, and he turned the doorknob slowly, partly because they'd both fall otherwise, and partly because he didn't want her noticing yet that he fully intended to steal a piece of heaven tonight if, God willing, she let him.

Jack eased back, taking Diana with him into the darkness of his cottage. She didn't protest, or pull away—she only held on to him more tightly, as if she didn't want to let him go.

Somehow he managed to prop himself against the wall, his hand still on her breast, still kissing her, and kicked the door shut.

Diana had him full against the wall, her hands on his shoulders, fingers digging into his muscles, giving him free access to her breasts. He slipped one hand around to unfasten her bra, but his usually steady fingers failed him again. It took several tries before the hook-and-eye fasteners gave way. A moment later he had both her bra and her shirt off, and she pressed her hips against his, kissing him like she never intended to stop, as he ran his hands across her breasts and teased her nipples with his fingers.

"Off," she whispered, as her shaking hands plucked at his shirt.

Jack eased back just enough to yank off his shirt and pull the tank over his head. Both landed on the floor somewhere in the dark, with her top and bra. Then he took her by the shoulders and shifted until she was back against the wall. Lowering his head, he traced her erect nipple with his tongue, felt her body jerk in response, heard her moan. He closed his eyes as she slid her fingers into his hair, urging him closer, her back arching.

Her heated skin released the musky-sweet scent of her perfume, and it surrounded him. Her whole body moved against his, seeking and straining. With a last kiss against the swell of her breast, he ran his tongue up the middle of her chest, along the column on her neck, along her chin, and took her mouth again in a hard kiss.

The feel of her breasts rubbing his bare chest was almost enough to send him right over the edge. Diana chose that moment to slide her hands down along his belly, and touched him through his shorts.

"I like how you touch me," he murmured, pushing against her deftly stroking hand. "But take it slow."

She unzipped his shorts. "I don't think so."

Jack swallowed, eyes closing as her hand eased beneath the elastic of his boxers. He stopped breathing for a long, delicious moment as her fingers explored him, from tip to shaft, and lower.

A groan slipped out, and he sucked in a long, shaking breath as the tension of release surged over him again.

"Wait. Stop." He lowered his head until his forehead rested against hers, hardly believing he'd just said that. "We better take this into the bedroom."

Her stroking stopped abruptly, and Jack kissed her again, more gently this time but still determined, tasting the inner heat of her mouth. He opened his eyes, and rubbed the tip of her nose with his.

"I want to make love to you so damn bad it's killing me," he said quietly. "But the first time is going to be right, not up against the wall."

In truth, he'd take her any way he could . . . but she needed gentleness, care. For all he knew, he'd be her first after that bastard who'd so badly used her, and if he took time to treat her as she deserved, there'd be time later for raunchy play, too.

He wanted so badly to kiss, touch, and stroke every bare inch of her skin while she lay on the sheets of his bed. He wanted to bring her pleasure with his fingers, his mouth before he even came inside her, and the image of her beneath him hit with such intensity that he had to squeeze his eyes shut and take a quick breath.

"Let's go in the bedroom," Jack said quietly. "I want to be with you tonight, and I'm really hoping you feel the same way."

Her gaze searched his, and he wanted her to see the truth—the desire she'd roused in him, the sharp, deep loneliness he hadn't realized even existed until moments before, and how much he wanted to make love to her.

A small frown drew her brows together before she looked away, and at that small but telling gesture, he realized he'd lost her.

"I can't," she whispered. "Please. I can't. Not this . . . not yet."

He could still feel the trembling of her body, but even this evidence of her inner struggle didn't ease the sharp bite of his disappointment.

It wasn't like he'd expected her to say yes. Every time she looked at him, she probably saw that son of a bitch who'd betrayed her, and even though her rejection left him bitter, angry, and frustrated as hell, he really couldn't blame her.

He'd pushed her right to the limit, and he'd known, all along, where she'd draw the line.

"I'm sorry, Jack. I didn't mean to lead you on, I just—"

"Forget it." He couldn't help the sharp tone of his voice. "You still don't trust me, do you?"

When Diana pushed against him, he released her. She took several steps back, and even in the darkness he could see her wide eyes, feel her turmoil.

She turned away, looking for her clothes, and as she moved through patches of moonlight and streetlight, he glimpsed pale, smooth skin, the rounded fullness of a breast.

Jack zipped his shorts, wishing he could just bang his head back against the wall.

"Kissing and petting are one thing; making love is something entirely else," she said after a moment. "And as much as I want to be with you, there are too many secrets between us for that kind of intimacy. At least for me."

Knowing better than to try and argue, Jack leaned his shoulder against the wall, still uncomfortably aroused. Diana dressed in silence, and he saw how her hands shook as she fumbled with her bra, the sheen of perspiration on her skin when the light caught her just right.

She was fighting it; fighting it hard.

All he had to do was touch her, kiss her again, gently nudge her toward the bedroom—and she'd go. Maybe a part of her wanted him to do that, to take away the responsibility, make the choice for her.

It tempted him; God, he wanted to believe a quick tussle in the sheets would make everything right between them. He'd get what he wanted: a release of the mind-numbing pressure, of the almost blind need to be inside her.

He pushed away from the wall, moving toward her. She went still, watching him—and he could see the rise and fall of her breasts, hear the rapid sound of her breathing.

All he had to do was touch her, slowly move her back.

And she'd hate him in the morning; hate herself even more.

"Do you need any help?" he asked quietly.

Diana let out another soft sigh. "Thanks, but I've got it."

There wasn't much to say after that. Jack waited as she ran her hands through her hair, adjusted her shirt again, and picked up her purse.

"I'll walk you to your car."

"I don't think that's a good idea right now, Jack."

Because he understood her kind of pride, he nodded. He did follow her out to the porch, though, and watched her walk down the steps with her back straight, her shoulders square—never for a minute letting anyone think she might be less than totally in control.

Man, she was something. Even now, rock-hard, disappointment biting keenly, he had to admire her guts and conviction, her style and grace under pressure. Her integrity.

At the bottom of the steps she turned. "I *am* sorry, Jack," she said quietly. "I want . . . I just need you to understand that if I could, I'd stay with you tonight."

Jack only nodded. If he opened his mouth, he'd probably start begging.

Ah, well. At least she wouldn't sleep any better tonight than he would.

He watched until the red glow of her taillights faded into the darkness, then he rubbed tiredly at his eyes, retrieved his backpack, hat, and the keys he'd left outside, and walked back into the cottage.

After dropping everything on the rug, Jack shut and locked the door. Not feeling like turning on any bright lights, he made his way in the dark to the kitchen, grabbed a beer from the fridge, then went back to the living room. He turned on a lamp long enough for him to pick out a Billie Holiday CD, and when he put it on the player, he shut off the lamp again.

As Billie's rich voice, full of pain and unfulfilled yearnings, filled the room, he twisted off the top to his beer, eased off his boots, then dropped into the recliner and closed his eyes, resting the cold bottle on his chest.

He could still taste her, still feel the smoothness of her skin, the swell of her breast beneath his hand, the push of her hips against his. Desire coiled inside him, taut and full and thick, making his pulse pound, and as he took a deep breath, the lingering, provocative scent of her perfume on his skin filled his senses.

The phone rang, breaking the moment. Jack reluctantly opened his eyes, but didn't get up. The answering machine picked up, and then a voice with a slight twang he knew all too well said, "Hey, Jack, it's Steve. Listen, we gotta talk. It's important. You come on by the gallery tomorrow after noon." A pause. "Be there, buddy."

Anger exploded, white-hot and violent, and he forced back the urge to hurl his beer bottle at the phone and listen to the satisfying, brittle shatter of glass.

Losing his temper might ease some of his fury with what Carmichael had done, but wouldn't solve any of his problems.

Especially not his most immediate problem. The only cure for that was a night with Diana in his arms, him moving in her, bodies hot and slick with perspiration, sheets twisted and rumpled, her sighs and moans sounding sweeter to his ears than even Billie's perfect blues . . .

"Shit," he said in disgust, pinching the bridge of his nose.

After a moment, he heaved himself off the chair. The only way to take the edge off this sharp, aching frustration was to do it himself—a lousy substitute for the real thing, but if he didn't do something soon, he'd go fucking crazy.

And now, more than ever, he had to stay sharp.

Diana let herself into her office, keys clinking against each other in the silence, and snapped on the lights. Luna had tidied up before leaving, and the scent of lemon Pledge hung in the air.

When she reached her desk, she sank slowly down onto the chair, surrounded by the smell of leather—and Jack. A hint of his cologne still scented her skin, where his bare chest had touched hers, and it made something low and deep inside her ache, and her breasts feel tender, hypersensitive. She closed her eyes, running the pad of her thumb over her lips, remembering his mouth on hers, and felt them curve as she smiled.

Maybe it hadn't been smart or sensible, but it had been *wonderful*. That faint, electrical tingle still buzzed through her, her legs still wobbled, and her stomach still fluttered with that marvelous, awful sensation that followed a moment of recklessness—and narrowly escaping danger.

That man could kiss like nobody's business, and those beautiful, clever hands of his . . .

She'd almost forgotten every hard lesson she'd learned these past few years. She'd come so close, all for a moment of pleasure that, while it promised to be incredible, would've lasted for twenty or thirty minutes, or maybe half the night—and then what?

The ugly intrusion of reality, that's what.

Had Jack pressed her, whispered just one little "please" in her ear, she'd have melted. He'd known it, too. She'd seen the knowledge in his eyes, in the tension of his muscles. And she'd wanted him to do it. For one brief instant, she'd prayed wildly that he'd force her hand—but he hadn't.

Why? He'd been powerfully aroused and more than ready and willing.

Diana slowly opened her eyes. Minutes passed as she stared out across her office, shadows lying thick in the dim light, lost in thought.

Finally, she slid the phone toward her.

One of these days, she'd have to buy a conference phone for home. At the rate she was going with Jack, she'd be on the three-way with Cassie and Fiona so often, she might as well set up a cot in the corner of her office.

Massaging her brows, Diana wondered what she'd tell them.

That Jack acted on her like a mind-altering drug? He did, in a way, and although the allure wore off quickly and good sense always returned, she was lost while she was in its grasp.

That the sex was beyond fantastic? It would be, but if it were only sex, only the lean strength of his body and rough-edged good looks that attracted her, it wouldn't be a problem. That she enjoyed Jack's company, sense of humor, and seemingly endless supply of energy; that she looked forward to spending time with him, matching wits with him; that she was drawn to his intelligence, and charmed by his blunt honesty and glimpses of a deep, very real honor—*that* spelled trouble.

Or should she try to explain that, somewhere along the line, she'd come to care about him, and her hunt for a thief had turned into something else? Jack needed her help, even more so now that she realized Steven Carmichael was involved.

Carmichael.

Diana had a pretty good idea what was really going on, and it didn't make her happy. It wouldn't be the first time she'd encountered a gallery that looked upright and honest, but was actually an elaborate front, a clearinghouse for smuggled antiquities.

If Carmichael was dealing in illegal sales, and Jack had found out about it, she didn't have any trouble imagining him losing his temper and doing something reckless.

With a sharp inhalation, she sat up straight, suddenly remembering what Jack had said when she'd asked why he'd languished in jail for weeks.

It's a question I asked myself, and didn't much like the answer.

"Oh, boy," she said, her low voice echoing in the empty office. "I don't much like it, either."

Several seconds passed, her mind whirling, stomach tight with tension now. Then, taking a deep breath, she picked up the phone.

First she dialed Fiona at home, but only hooked up with her answering machine. So she tried the bookstore, and got the answering machine there, too.

Wondering where Fi had gone—she'd turned into quite the little homebody since her husband had died—Diana dialed Cassie at home. While Cassie spent long hours scouring mountains, ravines, and deserts for fossils, or working in the family's shop, she was also a single mother with a young son, and the evening hours were always earmarked for family time.

Cassie picked up on the fifth ring. "Hello, it's me."

"Hey, you. It's Diana. I need to talk again. Do you have a few minutes?"

"Sure. Travis just went to take a shower before going to bed. Is Fiona on?"

"No. She's not at home or the store."

"Really? Wow. Do you think she has a *date*? That she's finally getting past her guilt over that selfish jerk she married?"

"It's not nice to speak ill of the dead."

"Tough." She didn't sound at all sorry. "Even after all this time, it still makes me mad . . . no, don't get me started on him, or I'll be frothing at the mouth in no time. So what's up? Still man trouble?"

Not sure where to even start, Diana merely sat like a lump, her words all jammed up.

Several seconds passed before Cassie said, "That's a guilty silence if I ever heard one. I told you to give this Robin Hood of yours the boot."

"Why should I listen to your advice?" Was that her voice? Sounding so . . . peevish? "It's not as if *you* ever have man troubles. Guys follow you around like puppies."

Men seemed irresistibly drawn to Cassie's beguiling mix of cute and sexy. It sometimes annoyed Diana, how the three of them would hit a bar, and before long Cassie would be surrounded by guys while she and Fiona ended up having deep, meaningful discussions over their beers about global warming or Elizabethan politics.

"Not *all* men," Cassie said dryly. "But we're talking about you, not me. Tell me what Robin Hood did this time."

"Maybe you should ask what he didn't do."

"Uh-oh."

"Well, except *that*," Diana said quickly. "Not really. We . . . oh, to hell with it. Let me start from the beginning. We spent most of the afternoon together, and we had a really good talk. Several good talks, come to think of it. He took me out for dinner, and I had a nice time. He's so interesting, and sweet, even if it's in a crude sort of way, and he's—"

"A thief. Let's not forget that pesky little detail."

"I'm not," Diana retorted. "Anyway, after dinner I drove him back to his place and he said a few things about the case that shook me up a little, and I . . . kissed him."

Cassie groaned.

"I know, I know! But Cassie, he's *incredible*. Everything about him fascinates me, and it's more than that he's great looking and sexy and—"

"Did you just kiss?"

"Nothing this man does qualifies as a 'just' anything." Diana closed her eyes again, smiling a little, and leaned back. "He asked me to spend the night."

"Wow. That Robin's a go-getter."

"I'll say."

"Wow," Cassie said again. "He asked you to have sex with him, huh?"

"Well, not in so many words, no."

"So what *exactly* did he say?"

"He said, 'I want to be with you tonight, and I hope you feel the same way.'"

"Hmm . . . sounds like a line to me. How did he say it? Was he serious, and not just putting on an act, trying to get in your pants?"

"He sounded serious, he wasn't smiling. And believe me, he smiles and laughs a lot, so when he doesn't, I pay attention. As for the rest, he's been trying to get me in bed almost from the start. I already told you that."

"So is he a good kisser or what?"

Diana laughed, no longer feeling quite so foolish, so gullible. So alone. Thank God for friends. "Oh, yeah. He should patent whatever it is he does. When I'm with him, it's like I'm the total, exclusive focus of his attention . . . I can't explain it more than that, but it works on me like a charm, every damn time."

"I am *so* jealous. I haven't had a decent kiss in

ages." Cassie sounded wistful. "Did you do anything good and nasty? Did you get to feel him up any?"

Diana grinned. "Yes, and yes."

"I hate you." Cassie sighed. "So spill already. What's the package like? Small, medium, or large? Fast or slow?"

"He's not into hurrying, and he felt just right to me."

"Lucky, lucky you. Didja get naked?"

Diana sputtered, laughing, and Cassie said, "Aw, come on, have a little pity. I spend my days and nights with cold rocks and fossilized monsters. I *need* all the vicarious thrills I can get."

"Bare skin was definitely involved, and that's all the details you get."

"Sounds like a fun time was had by all. So how come you didn't hit the sheets with this guy?"

"Well, gee, let me think," Diana said, her tone sarcastic.

"Hey, you can't use the old 'professional conflict of interest' or 'poor me, Kurt skunked me' excuses. Sounds like you practically got it on, then spooked. Don't tell me it's because you suddenly remembered you're not being paid to screw your suspects."

Diana slumped back in her chair. "I hate it when you ask these questions."

"Yeah, I'm such a bitch. But that's why you keep me around; to keep you honest." Cassie's tone gentled. "What's really going on, Diana?"

"I . . . he gave me a chance to say no. If he'd just pulled me to the bedroom, I'd have gone."

Several seconds passed, and Cassie said, "But he didn't."

"No, and all of a sudden, I'm there, half-naked, seriously hot and bothered, and remembering that this guy hasn't told me the truth at all. Even though I know why he won't, I still can't trust him enough to go that far. I just *can't*."

"Good for you," Cassie murmured. "So he did the decent thing, your Robin."

"Yeah, he did." A little spurt of hope shot through her. "You don't think he's coming on to me this strong just because I keep pushing him away?"

"Could be part of it. Some of us, and we won't name any names here, can't resist a challenge—but his letting you go when he's that close to getting some . . . that's a 'whoa' moment. Guys don't give in like that unless they really want to be with a girl, really care what she thinks. If it was just sex he's after, he'd have hauled you into the bedroom, not caring how you'd feel about it afterward, or he'd have moved on to easier prey by now."

"But what about how he needs my help?"

Cassie made a "hmm" sound. "I don't know. What do *you* think about it?"

This was the easy part, as she'd been giving it a lot of thought lately. "He wants me to find the truth, but he can't give me the details without implicating himself. I don't blame him for that. If it came down to it, and I had to swear an oath of truth in court, I'd have to tell everything I knew."

"No, you wouldn't. Not if you were involved or something, right? Couldn't you plead the Fifth or something?"

"Except we're not involved in that way, and I'm supposed to be a professional investigator." Diana frowned at the phone. "Perjury is a serious offense. I feel very strongly about justice; I wouldn't be in this business if I didn't. And he knows it. In his own way, I think he's trying to protect me if things go wrong."

"Hmmm," Cassie said again. "So what the hell is Robin up to?"

The million-dollar question.

"I think I was brought in on a small piece of a much bigger puzzle. There's so much that doesn't fit otherwise. I can't go into details, but I have a feeling my guy is stealing artifacts that were looted. Why, and what he's doing with them once he has them, I don't know for certain. But I have a few ideas."

Cassie picked up the misgiving in her voice. "So what's the problem? What's *really* got you worried?"

"Somebody powerful, with lots of money, is behind this. Or somebody very, very close to such a person."

"Oh, boy. You do *not* want to go head to head with rich, unscrupulous bastards. You know how it'll turn out."

Diana sighed. "I know."

Though she did her best to right wrongs, the perpetrators often weren't prosecuted. The victims belonged to the top echelon of society, and the average working stiff didn't have much sympathy for the über-rich who spent thousands, even millions, on old knickknacks. They didn't want their hard-earned tax dollar wasted on hunting down thieves who preyed upon the rich and pampered, while drugs were sold in schoolyards, and rapists, killers, and pedophiles roamed the streets of Our Town USA.

And when the *perpetrator* was rich, it made things

that much worse. Yes, rich people did end up serving time now and again, but it was by far the exception rather than the norm.

"The truth has been right there in front of my nose all along," Diana admitted. "But the thought of risking another scandal or lawsuit so soon after that nightmare with Kurt . . . I just didn't want to see what else might be going on. But I can't stand by and do nothing."

"If you go after someone with money and power, you could lose everything," Cassie said quietly. "And this time you might not be left with enough of your reputation to build it up again."

"Believe me, I've thought about that." Diana suppressed a small shudder. "There's something else. What if my feelings for Robin, as you call him, are making me see things that aren't really there? Because I desperately *want* to believe he's one of the good guys?"

She squeezed her eyes shut against a sudden sting of tears. "I don't want to believe he's lying or manipulating me, but I can't act like it's not a possibility, either."

"Robin's using you." Cassie voice hardened. "Not in the same way Bentley did. Nope, this one's using you as his lifeline, and I want you to be real careful that he doesn't drag you down with him when he falls."

"If he falls."

A long silence followed. "Do you really believe this guy is a thief?"

"Yes," Diana answered without hesitation, opening her eyes.

"Then if you help him, and he gets caught, you're an accessory, right?"

"Maybe," Diana said reluctantly. "But like I said, he's been very careful about what he's told me."

"If he really cares for you, he'd tell you the truth. Or he'd stay the hell away from you."

"I'm beginning to realize he did tell me the truth, although in a pretty roundabout way. What he said tonight made everything a lot clearer. He knew *exactly* what he had to say to get me thinking."

Several seconds passed as she and Cassie pondered the implications of that.

"I still don't like it. Not at all, not even if he did the right thing by you tonight, not even if he's trying to protect you."

Diana stared out her door at the empty office. "I trust my instincts," she said at length. "And my feeling is that he won't hurt me. But if I can help in any way to shut down what I'm beginning to suspect is a major smuggling operation, I'll do it. I just can't turn a blind eye."

"Do you like him?"

At Cassie's abrupt question, Diana closed her eyes again, remembering the look on Jack's face when she refused to spend the night with him, and his words to her in the Jaguar Jungle, letting her glimpse the real man few people ever had a chance to see.

And what they'd just done . . . how she'd kissed him, how her senses had opened to him, and she'd lost all awareness of where her body had ended and his began. For those few, fragile seconds, nothing had mattered but the shape and feel of him beneath her fingers and the encircling strength of his arms, the warm taste of his mouth, the sun-and-wind scent of his skin, hearing only her heartbeat, the rapid sound of her breathing.

She hadn't wanted to stop, and when she did, a strange, almost airy feeling had settled over her, as if he'd kept some part of her, leaving an emptiness behind.

That overwhelming sense of loss, brief as it had been, had made her turn tail and run. Distrust existed at the back of her mind, yes, but that hadn't been the main reason she'd panicked. Not if she were honest with herself. She lied to suspects, sometimes even fibbed to clients or others to get the job done, but she never, ever lied to herself.

"I want him so badly it scares me to death," Diana admitted. "I don't like needing anybody that much. It makes me feel helpless, and I *hate* that."

"I'm not talking about sex. I asked if you liked him."

Without hesitation, she answered, "I like him a lot. I think maybe I'm even falling a little bit in love with him."

"Oh, shit."

"That about covers it." Diana heaved a dramatically loud sigh. "The thing is, we have so much in common. It's uncanny, really. He even said as much to me today. That we're two of a kind, and we belong together."

"Look, I'll give Robin the benefit of the doubt, because you really like him, and that's what friends are for. But the second you *even* suspect he's taking you for a ride, you bail. Promise?"

"Promise."

She and Cassie chatted for another fifteen minutes, the conversation moving to good movies they'd seen, Diana's last shopping splurge, the puppy Cassie had bought for Travis because he'd improved his grades, and ended with the usual promises to call or e-mail again soon.

After hanging up, Diana sat forward, elbows on her desk, chin in her hands. Glancing down, she saw a number of phone messages that Luna had left on the blotter. A message from Bobby, one from a fence she'd called, and one from Steve Carmichael. She picked it up, reading the scrawled message: *SC wants to meet tomorrow afternoon on progress. Pls call to set up a time.*

Good. She had a few questions she wanted to ask her "client"—even if she was half-afraid of the answers.

Picking up the phone again, she dialed Bobby's pager. He called back within a couple minutes.

"Hey, Bobby, it's Diana. You rang?"

"Twice. Where the hell have you been?"

"Working, what else? You on your car phone? The signal's not very good."

"Yeah, I'm at the drive-thru at Popeye's, picking up some fried chicken for dinner."

Diana glanced at her watch. "It's a little late for dinner, isn't it?"

"I was on call, and it's been a busy day."

"What did you want to talk to me about?"

"I need to . . . hold on a second."

As he shouted his order at the drive-thru receiver, she mentally cataloged the calories. It wasn't fair that he could eat junk like that and still look so good.

"Okay, I'm back," he said. "I talked to some people about this case of yours, and you and me need to go over a few things. I can stop by your office tomorrow at two. Will you be there?"

"I'll be here." She said good-bye and hung up, mulling over the grim tone of Bobby's voice.

Something was up. The pieces were coming together, and she had a hunch she'd soon be able to see a whole picture. But it didn't do much good to have the whole picture if she couldn't legally do anything with it, and she still hadn't turned up any real evidence. For that, she needed Jack's cooperation.

After her chats with Carmichael and Bobby, she'd have to face Jack again, which would probably be unbearably awkward.

Diana stood, grabbed her purse and keys, shut off the lights, and locked the office door behind her. She checked her watch again as she stepped outside, thinking she could still squeeze in a quick exercise session tonight—she had to work off that dinner, not to mention sexual frustration—and headed for her car, parked several blocks away.

The Quarter was never quiet, and the Café du Monde, which never closed, lured coffee drinkers no matter what the hour. She weaved through thinner crowds of tourists, thankful the heat of the day had eased, and as she neared her car, a tall man in a suit emerged from a black car parked behind her—illegally parked, at that. When he moved into the light of a streetlamp, she recognized him.

"Mr. Jones," Diana said, and Steve Carmichael's lawyer nodded at her in a polite response. "Were you waiting for me?"

"Of course."

"I have a phone, you know."

The lawyer smiled faintly, and in the darkness his face didn't look nearly as mild or unassuming as she remembered. "What I have to say is best delivered face-to-face."

Diana kept a careful distance between them, even if he didn't look or feel dangerous. She had pepper spray, and she moved her purse forward so she could more easily reach it.

"I mean you no harm, Ms. Belmaine."

"When men approach me on dark streets, I don't take chances."

The lawyer smiled. "I suspect you could do far more damage to me than I could ever do to you."

"What do you want, Mr. Jones?"

"Merely to impart a word of advice, nothing more." He moved slowly forward, hands clasped in front of him, his demeanor unthreatening. "You and I, Ms. Belmaine, are professional people. And we're practical, worldly creatures. We have no illusions and see things as they are, not as they should be."

Diana maintained her distance. "And your point?"

His gray, bushy brows drew together in a small frown. "I've known Steven Carmichael for almost thirty years. He's a friend, but first and foremost, I'm his lawyer. I know this man better than you ever will, and he didn't build his fortune, or survive challenges, by being careless. I strongly advise you to recover the Egyptian piece you were hired to find, and nothing more. My client will not press charges against the thief. He merely wants his property back, no questions asked. It's very simple, really—find the thief, and deliver the message. Do you think you can manage this?"

Her muscles tensed as she struggled to contain her anger. "You know what he's doing. How can you stand there and let it happen?"

Jones tilted his head to one side. "My work for my client is well within the boundaries of the law. All the records, all the business deals, all that he owns and sells, is legal and more than adequately documented."

Diana smiled. "That's just semantics, Mr. Jones."

"No, Ms. Belmaine, that's just a fact of life. An imperfect world full of imperfect people, doing what we must." The lawyer smiled back. "Now be a smart girl, and do as you're told."

Diana watched as Jones returned to his car, and after his taillights disappeared around a corner, she opened the Mustang's door and slid inside. Instead of starting the engine, she stared out the window at the spot where Jones had stood.

Now be a smart girl . . .

A fresh burst of anger shot through her, and she slammed her fist down on the dashboard. It didn't help, and she gave her hand a shake as she muttered, "Ow."

Clearheaded again, she mulled over Jones's genteel warning to stop poking around where she wasn't wanted.

Steven Carmichael wanted the Tut artifact returned beyond a simple desire for repossession. Maybe he saw the Nefertiti box as some sort of threat, like blackmail.

Even if he "legally" owned the personal mementos of an ancient pharaoh, the Egyptian government would kick up a fuss to get it back—especially when DNA tests could answer questions scholars had been asking over the seventy-five years since Tutankhamen's tomb had been uncovered. And considering that his foundation aggressively lobbied for the preservation of antiquities, the resulting media scrutiny would be embarrassing, to say the least. It could cost him his credibility, maybe even force his gallery or foundation to close under public pressure.

It might also invite closer scrutiny of certain other activities he wasn't keen to have brought to light.

Except Jack had no interest in blackmail. Granted, she didn't know *what* he wanted from Carmichael or why he'd stolen the things he had, but blackmail didn't feel right.

No; this felt like more of a personal vendetta. A private war.

Edward Jones had lied from the start. That, as well as the subtext of tonight's warning, told her the lawyer knew about Jack. And if he knew, Carmichael had to at least suspect.

Oh, yes. Things would get real interesting real soon.

"Dammit, Jack," she muttered as she started the car. "What kind of mess did I let you drag me into?

THIRTEEN

...

"**I**'m pleased you were able to make it," Steve Carmichael said as he pulled back the red leather chair for Diana. "It was a short notice, I know."

He wore a pale gray suit tailored to accentuate the breadth of his shoulders and his well-maintained body, and she couldn't help hoping she'd look half as fit when she hit her sixties.

Catching the direction of her gaze, Carmichael grinned and made a dismissive motion at his suit. "Board meeting, meeting with a group of investors, and a talk with the mayor. And it's barely after lunch. But I've managed to sneak away from all that boring business to play a little at my gallery."

Diana smiled back, in part because there was nothing fake about his enjoyment. That much about her client was real.

"I work for you, Mr. Carmichael," she said pleasantly as she crossed her legs. Carmichael sat behind his desk—waiting, as usual, until after she'd done so. "Whenever you need to see me, I'm more than happy to oblige."

She wore her new eggplant purple skirt with a short-sleeved, silk charmeuse top in an abstract pattern of vibrant jewel tones, the predominant colors being purple and gold. In a concession to the heat, she wore her hair in a chignon.

The palms of her hands were damp, and her heart pounded, making her light-headed. It wasn't fear, exactly. More like a hyperawareness, along with the effort to act as if nothing was out of the ordinary.

"While I do appreciate the daily phone updates you've provided since I hired you, I think it's a good idea to touch base personally, now and again. Don't you?" At her nod, he added, "Then let's hear it, Ms. Belmaine."

This would be the easy part. She'd spent most of the morning preparing answers, anticipating his responses, and figuring how to work it to her advantage.

"When I'm hired to investigate an alleged theft, the first thing I look for is motive." She settled back, hands clasped loosely in her lap, going for a comfortable, in-control, professional demeanor. "Most criminal activity can be categorized, and even predicted, depending on the situation and facts."

Carmichael raised a brow in interest. "I can't help thinking what a fascinating job you have in comparison to mine, where I spend entire days behind a desk. I envy you that sense of . . . adventure and action."

"The job certainly has its moments." She let him buy into the romantic fallacy, not pointing out all the hours she spent at her own desk, or in dusty libraries and city halls. "I look for the obvious motives, which in this kind of theft is almost exclusively for profit, though occasionally we get a crazy acting on impulse. When the goal is monetary, it typically involves insurance claim fraud, or resale on the black market for big bucks. Since you didn't insure the box and its contents, which I verified with your insurance carrier, that's one motive I can essentially eliminate."

Carmichael smiled, his eyes bright with amusement. "I knew you would investigate me."

"Of course you did." His almost boyish delight didn't surprise her. For powerful men, controlling outcome was nothing more than a game. "There's always the possibility you insured it with another carrier, which you'd conveniently remember or your attorney would rediscover at some point down the road, but I have my reasons for finding that unlikely."

Carmichael sat back, crossing one leg over the other as he folded his arms across the chest. He still looked amused. "So aside from eliminating me as a suspect, what have you come up with?"

The familiar thrill of excitement spread through her. She was back on the hunt.

"Quite a lot, actually. I can rule out a crazy for obvious reasons, but I can't as easily rule out a crime of opportunity. Although few people were aware you owned the Nefertiti box, people *did* know, so it wasn't entirely secret. People talk, let things slip . . . it happens. And the burglary appears to have been committed by someone familiar with you, your habits, and this building." Diana leaned forward.

"The problem is, crimes of opportunity of this nature almost always fall under the 'get rich quick' scheme of things—and that's where I run into trouble."

"I'll be damned. You *are* efficient at this, aren't you?"

The comment stung, but she didn't let it show. "You knew that. You had me thoroughly investigated before you even called me that first time."

"You do have a . . . singular reputation, Ms. Belmaine."

At least he respected her enough not to deny checking her out. Resisting the urge to rub her damp palms along the glossy silk dupioni of her skirt, Diana gave him a slow smile. "I'll take that as a compliment."

"As it was intended to be," Carmichael said, and everything about him—his posture, his tone of voice, his expression—was one of benevolent indulgence. "I admire your tenacity. After that scandal and the loss of your credibility, it would've been much easier to quit than to get back in the saddle."

Anger burned through her at his arrogance, and she couldn't wait to show him up for what he really was.

"Well. Let's get back to business, then." She casually recrossed her legs, watching as Carmichael's gaze flicked downward. "In antiquity thefts, stolen items have a value, even without legitimate provenance papers or terms of sale. An Attic black figure vase is always an Attic black figure vase—it's a type and a style easily identified. Same goes for an Etruscan bronze, an Egyptian Coptic vase, and so on. Your alabaster box is valuable because it's inscribed with Nefertiti's name. The same goes for the statue of Akhenaton. But their value is increased in association with that lock of hair. That's the truly priceless item, and unlike a box or a gold figurine, DNA material can't be forged."

Carmichael smiled, his gaze frankly appreciative. He liked her, Diana could tell, and it left her with a strange mixture of anger and regret.

"In other words," she continued, "if a collector is hot to own a lock of Nefertiti's hair, you can't prove that hair belonged to her without scientific analysis. Expensive, very technical analysis."

"Ah," said Carmichael. "I see where you're going with this."

"Exactly. Few collectors, even those who purchase through unethical channels, are willing pay big money for what can't be authenticated."

He showed no discernible response at the word "unethical," but she hadn't really expected it to be that easy.

"Provenance papers are forged all the time, but even unscrupulous collectors are savvy. They're sometimes fooled by clever forgeries, but the only way a collector can prove that hair came from a member of Tutankhamen's immediate family would be through DNA analysis. You can't do that without getting DNA material from royal mummies, and you can bet the authorities at the Cairo museum wouldn't be cooperative. They'd demand the return of the box and its contents, threaten legal action . . . the media would have a field day with a story like this."

Carmichael's expression was flat, assessing. A

niggling doubt crossed her mind that maybe he *didn't* feel threatened by any revelation that he owned the thing—except that from the very start, she'd been warned by Edward Jones to be discreet because Carmichael wanted to avoid unflattering publicity.

Then again, the reactions of a man who'd been ruthless in business wouldn't be easy to interpret, and she couldn't read anything beyond that he was studying her as closely as she was studying him.

"So you're saying the thief doesn't intend to sell my box."

"That's my take."

"I don't see why someone would go through all that trouble if they didn't intend to sell it."

"It's possible the thief took it merely as a prestige theft, and possession is the end in itself. But I don't see that, either. The thief left behind a calling card for you to find, presumably one you would understand. This theft was directed at you personally."

"Me? Why?"

Carmichael appeared genuinely surprised, which she hadn't expected. She had anticipated that he would get dodgy at this point.

"That's something I'm hoping you can help me understand, Mr. Carmichael. Do you think the theft of the Tutankhamen artifact and the theft of your Mayan shipment are related?"

He gave her a speculative look. "I've not given that much thought."

"Is that a yes, or a no?"

Carmichael's brows drew together, his eyes narrowing. "No."

Obviously, he was more used to giving orders than responding to them.

"There's been a string of thefts over the past eighteen months involving stolen Mayan artifacts, all from private residences. The police have no leads, no suspects. The stolen artifacts haven't turned up anywhere else to date. One of the thefts involved items from a sale handled by your lawyer, Edward Jones."

"Yes, I did know about that. The police questioned Ed and me about it, and we were given the impression it was nothing more than a random robbery. Most likely drug-related."

"Isolated, it doesn't look like much, but when you connect it to the other thefts, a pattern emerges. Except for the Nefertiti box. I admit that puzzles me, unless, as I suspect, it's personal. A little twist of the knife, so to speak."

Carmichael tipped his head to one side. He played the part of the potentate very well—he managed to look perplexed, yet still in control. Very much the man on top of all things.

"To my knowledge, nothing I've sold or auctioned, privately or through the gallery, has been stolen after the sale—except for Jim and Nikki Cluny's funerary pottery."

Funerary pottery—on Bobby's list, it had been described as just pottery. And the most recent theft in New Orleans had been funerary jewelry. A definite pattern.

Time to rattle some cages—but delicately.

"Mr. Carmichael, do you have any idea who might have left the jack of spades for you to find?"

"No, I'm sorry. And I don't see why I would. If, as you say, there have been other similar thefts, why should the card have any more significance to me than any of the other victims?"

"Good question." She even smiled a little, because it *was* a good question. The man was quick-thinking. "It could be because three of the thefts can be directly linked to you. The others involved artifacts which may or may not have been in your possession at one time. Something which will be easy enough to substantiate."

"Are you suggesting somebody is out for revenge? To frame, discredit, or embarrass me?"

Diana leaned forward slightly. "Perhaps. What do you think of that?"

"I think it's very possible. Men like me make a lot of enemies over the years, Ms. Belmaine."

"Any recent ones? Close acquaintances or family? Friends?"

"No."

He answered without hesitation, although he had to know it was Jack. The man was lying—he was just better at it than most people.

How far to push about Jack's involvement? Instinct warned her, loud and clear, not to be too direct yet.

She debated with herself for a moment longer, then smiled. "This has been very helpful, Mr. Carmichael. Before I go, do you have any more questions for me?"

He smiled back. "How close are you to getting my box back?"

"Very close."

"And how close is close?"

So much for stalling. "I have some loose ends to tie up, a couple more leads to check on. Until I verify a few crucial facts, I need to keep my suspicions confidential. In case I'm wrong, we want to avoid annoying lawsuits. I'm sure you understand how that is."

"Of course I understand," he said, the hesitation so brief she might've missed if she hadn't been looking for it. "I know you won't disappoint me in this, Ms. Belmaine. You're a bright young woman."

Diana came to her feet, hearing more than a simple compliment behind his words. Such as yet another subtle warning to behave.

"Thank you for your time and your patience. I'll keep you updated on any new evidence or leads." She headed toward the door, and Carmichael, gentlemanly as ever, hurried to open it before she got there. She stopped short, and snapped her fingers as if she'd just remembered something. "Oh, wait. I do have one more question."

Carmichael waited, his expression politely inquisitive. He smelled wonderful, and even standing still, radiated a sense of power she found faintly disconcerting.

"The investigator you hired to track down the Mayan shipment—I know Danny Palmer," she said. "He's a good PI. He usually handles worker's comp frauds and other injury-related insurance cases, and he doesn't have a lot of experience in antiquities. I guess—" She glanced away, hoping she looked convincingly embarrassed. "It's a matter of professional pride, so I can't help wondering why, knowing my reputation as you did, you just didn't hire me?"

"But I did," Carmichael said lightly as he opened the door.

For a moment, their eyes met, and Diana had no doubt whatsoever that he knew what she was really asking.

Maybe she'd tipped her hand too far.

"I see. Well, then, I'll just have to live with my bruised ego, won't I?"

"Bruised egos happen to the best of us." Carmichael kept his hand at her elbow as he walked her down the stairs. "Huh . . . my next appointment is here already. Early for once, which I'm marking on my calendar, since it's never happened before."

Diana looked down, and faltered—only a little, and she hoped Carmichael hadn't noticed.

Jack stood leaning against the gallery desk, talking with Audrey Spencer. He wore faded jeans, his usual boots and white tank, and a short-sleeved chambray shirt—unbuttoned, of course.

He looked acutely uncomfortable, and Audrey, in a cinnamon-colored sheath dress, appeared pink-cheeked and flustered.

A sudden and sharp jealousy lanced through Diana, and she pretended not to see them—or her client's glance at her.

When they were in the gallery, Carmichael called out, "Jack, buddy—you're early."

Jack glanced over his shoulder, and Diana could've sworn he froze for a second. Then he said something to Audrey, who nodded, and smiled a little.

What had he said, to make her smile like that? Or, for that matter, *blush*?

Jealousy twisted her gut.

"Hey, Steve." Jack walked over to join her and Carmichael in front of the trickling water fountain.

"Ms. Belmaine, have you met Dr. Jack Austin? He's the damn best Mayan archaeologist in North America." Diana didn't miss the change in Carmichael's demeanor; from über-CEO with her to good ol' boy buddy with Jack. "And since my foundation has been supporting his excavations for years, I can say with confidence I'm as proud as hell of this boy's accomplishments."

Diana smiled, and said, "Dr. Austin and I know each other."

As if Carmichael already didn't know that.

Jack smiled politely back, but his expression looked tight, even wooden.

"Really?" Carmichael said, with perhaps a bit too much surprise. "When did you meet?"

"When she asked me if I'd stolen your Egyptian box," Jack said.

"You? Jack, my man, why ever would you do such a thing?"

The sudden silence all but crackled with tension.

"It was routine," Diana said, hastily. "I questioned a number of guests who were at the gallery's opening night party. Dr. Austin was one of them, and while I was at it, I also consulted with him on a few preservation concerns I had on your box."

Carmichael glanced between the two of them, brows faintly elevated. "It's a small world, that's for sure. Jack, I need you to give a presentation next week to the society board members about last season's dig. Would you like to attend, Ms. Belmaine?

I'm sure you'd find it very interesting. Jack is quite the showman, and an exceptional speaker. The stories he can tell . . . sometimes, you could almost swear he's telling the truth."

Diana couldn't bring herself to look at Jack, and with an effort suppressed a sudden, cold niggling of doubt.

Damn Carmichael for being such a low, manipulative bastard.

"I'd love to," she said, with a studied calm. "Thank you."

"Let me walk Ms. Belmaine to the door," Carmichael said to Jack. "Then you and I can go upstairs."

"Sounds good," Jack replied, his tone as neutral as hers.

Diana gave Jack what she hoped passed for a friendly good-bye smile, avoiding meeting his eyes, and headed toward the front door, Carmichael at her side. As she passed the display case with the jade mask, she stopped, turned, and walked back to it.

Pale, shell inlay eyes stared out at her from the stylized face of a man who'd died long, long ago. The mouth was open, as if it wanted to speak.

After a moment, Carmichael came up behind her. "Is there something wrong?"

"No. It's just that I'd really love to know where you found this piece."

Diana looked up, meeting Carmichael's gaze—and saw nothing beyond a polite inquisitiveness.

Oh, he was good. Very, very good.

"Sorry, that's confidential information, but you know how it is." He gave her an exaggerated, conspiratorial wink. "Private source, quite legitimate—and easily verified, if I had anything to prove."

"I'm sure." Despite her pounding heart and damp palms, she smiled back. From the corner of her eye, she could see Jack, watching them both. "Have a good day, Mr. Carmichael; I promise you I'll be in touch soon."

It was the closest to a warning she'd give. Diana stepped out of the cool, dim gallery and into the stifling humidity, bright sun, and traffic congestion of Julia Street.

Facing the snarling jaguar sign, she blew out a long breath, and muttered, "Oh, damn."

Jack watched Carmichael wave to Diana, then walk back toward him, smiling. The cocky bastard was enjoying this—the master of ceremonies, in his element.

Anger hit like a punch to the gut, but Jack wouldn't give Carmichael the satisfaction of letting it show. And he had no intention of letting the man corner him alone anywhere. "I have a faculty meeting in a half hour, so I can't stay. If I'm late, Judith will have my ass. I'm not exactly her pet professor."

"No problem. I just needed to let you know you have to report to my board next week."

"My schedule's tight, it would be better the following—"

"You're flying to London, I know." Carmichael loosened his tie. "I checked with the department secretary, who said you were giving a talk at the Institute of Archaeology there. She also said you'd be back late Thursday, so I'm thinking Friday night at seven will work for you."

"I guess I'll be there, then," Jack said after a moment, his voice cool, deceptively soft. "Since you've already taken care of all the details."

"It's what I do best. Bring along a few nice artifacts to pass around, and I want slides. Get one of your students to whip up some flashy chart graphics and maps, too. Just remember to keep it simple. These people are businessmen, not archaeologists."

"I know the routine, Steve. After five years, I know exactly what you want from me."

"Do you?" Carmichael asked slowly. "There are times I wonder. You're something of a wild card, Jack."

Only a few people were in the gallery. Audrey stood at the desk behind them, close enough to hear what they were saying. The new gift shop clerk, dusting countertops a few feet away, looked a little nervous at having the big boss around. A couple of customers wandered through the displays, talking quietly.

"It's perfectly clear," Jack said, letting Carmichael make of it what he would. "Like crystal."

Carmichael nodded. "You're a fine archaeologist. One of the best. I thought so from the moment we met. You have drive, ambition—and vision. That's a rare quality, and the reason I singled you out, why I've done all that I have for you. I built you, Jack. I'm the one who put you on TV, in the spotlight. I'm the

reason you go back to your beloved Tikukul, year after year."

With an effort, Jack forced back his temper at the
warning couched in the tones of paternal-sounding
pride. "I couldn't have done it without you, Steve.
That's what I always say."

And it was the bitter truth.

"I'm glad we're clear on that." Carmichael
glanced over his shoulder toward the door, and
when he looked back at Jack, he was grinning. "She's
a beautiful woman, isn't she? Your Ms. Belmaine?"

Your Ms. Belmaine . . .

Cold fear hit midchest, then radiated outward,
dark and pervasive, and settled heavily in his gut.

"And she's smart, too."

"Yes, I'm beginning to realize that. Very sharp."
Carmichael's smile faded, then he gave Jack a com-
radely slap on the shoulder. "I'll see you next Friday
night. Don't forget to bring everything. And Jack . . .
I do mean everything."

At the more direct warning, Jack's anger returned, burning away that chill fear. "I'll try not to
forget anything you want."

"I'm sure you won't. Have a good trip to London."

"I tracked down the information on that ship, and—"
Bobby Halloran rested his palms on Diana's desk
and leaned toward her. "Darlin', are you listening?
You seem kinda preoccupied today."

Shaking free of a multitude of uneasy thoughts,
Diana flashed a brief, apologetic smile. "Sorry. A lot
of stuff going on. So who did you talk to?"

"This woman I know in the Coast Guard. She checked the registration on the ship that Steve Carmichael's stolen pots were on. It's a bulk freighter, the *Maria de Santiago*. Carries mostly grain."

"Is it his?"

"In a roundabout way." Bobby sat, and leaned back. "Flies a Peruvian flag, officially belongs to some Greek company, which in turn is run by some guys from Sweden, but when Susan dug a little deeper, she found that the Swedish freight firm belongs to Carmichael. I don't know if it means anything or not. Could be a dummy company. But a lot of small foreign businesses are owned by larger businesses from somewhere else."

"I'm sure it's strictly legitimate," Diana said, recalling her chat with Edward Jones. "Paper trail and all. But it means the captain and crew would be following Carmichael's orders."

"What's going on?"

"I think Steve Carmichael is doing a nice side business in black market antiquities through his gallery. Specifically, pre-Columbian."

Bobby stared at her for a long moment, then scrubbed a hand across his face. "Oh, shit. You sure about that?"

"I don't have any hard evidence, and the evidence I *do* have isn't likely to be cooperative," she answered wryly. "If he talks, he faces burglary charges."

"I'm not following you here."

"I'm just now putting it together, and this is what I think is happening." She gave a small sigh and leaned forward, resting her elbows on her desk. "All those artifacts stolen in the last eighteen months, the ones with the jack of spades, were originally looted, and I bet they can all be tied back to Carmichael if we dig deep enough. My suspect is retrieving stolen property, and I have a hunch he's trying to either return it to the rightful owners or has them stashed for safekeeping."

"Why?" Bobby demanded. "Steven Carmichael has money up the ass, a hell of a lot of clout. And doesn't he run some political group on the preservation of native cultures? Why would he get mixed up in shit like this?"

"I don't think it's just for money, though I'm sure that's a big factor. I have a feeling he believes he's being all noble by putting these artifacts in the hands of people who 'appreciate' them." She made air quotation marks with her fingers. "He's said a couple things to me in the past that make me think he doesn't have much use for universities or museums. A lot of their collections are in storage, so the public—and other 'appreciative' people—never see them."

"What's the connection to that Egyptian theft you're working on?"

"I'll get to that in a minute. Carmichael hired Danny Palmer to track down his stolen shipment. Do you know Danny?" Bobby shook his head. "Well, I do. He works mostly with employee insurance fraud; he has *no* experience in antiquities. Carmichael actually approached me about taking on that case, but didn't hire me. At the time, I thought it was just basic sexism: Blond chick can't handle the tough stuff. But now I'm thinking he did it because he knew I'd have asked questions he wouldn't want to answer."

"Huh," Bobby said. "So he hired you to find this Egyptian thing because he really does want it back, but hiring this other guy was just for show?"

"I think so. Plus, I think he'd begun to suspect who the thief really was, though I'm not sure at what point he figured it out."

"You gonna call the professionals in on this?"

She glared at him. "I *am* the professionals. But no police. They're likely to laugh at me, considering all I have are gut feelings and a suspect who's living a double life. And as you say, Carmichael is rich and powerful. We both know the chances of ever bringing him in are practically zero."

"So why are you telling me all this?"

"Because you and I aren't the type to roll over and play dead when we hit a brick wall."

Bobby laughed, and tugged at the knot of his tie—which had smiley faces on it, some of them sticking out tongues, and which actually matched his pale yellow shirt and navy pants.

"I want to know more about the Egyptian part of this."

Diana sat back, letting out her breath. "Steven Carmichael owns a small alabaster box, about this big." She used her hands to show him the size. "It's inscribed with the name of Queen Nefertiti and contains a solid gold, two-inch-high figurine of the pharaoh Akhenaton. More importantly, the box contains a lock of hair that might be Nefertiti's, which scientists could use to help clear up the parentage of Tutankhamen."

Bobby didn't look impressed. "And we care who his mom and pop were?"

"It's not a matter of life and death, but historically, it's a very big deal. Trust me on this. Besides, the box had to have been stolen from Tut's tomb back in the 1920s, and no matter how you look at it, grave robbing and vandalizing the dead are highly unethical. The Egyptians will want it back."

"Why would anybody steal this thing in the first place?"

"Why then, or why now?"

"Now."

"Because somebody is pissed off at Steven Carmichael."

"This would be your suspect, right?" When Diana nodded, Bobby slowly smiled. "I'd like to meet him. You gotta love a bad guy with a sense of style."

At that moment, shouting erupted outside her office door: Luna, arguing with a man. Diana froze, recognizing the man's voice just as Luna yelled, "Hey, you can't go in there! I said she's with somebody and—"

The door banged open.

Bobby turned, his hand going for his gun. Diana lunged forward and grabbed his arm. "No! It's okay."

Jack Austin stalked into the office, livid with anger. Luna stood behind him, her face a mask of helpless shock, dark eyes wide.

Still holding on to Bobby's arm, Diana shot Jack a warning look, then said to Luna, "It's fine. Just close the door, please."

Wordlessly, Luna did so. Very carefully.

"Darlin', let go of my arm. I won't shoot him. I promise."

Recognizing the understanding in Bobby's eyes—no way could she talk her way out of *this* one—Diana cautiously released him. When he didn't suddenly lunge at Jack, she walked around the desk, putting herself between the two men. Just to be safe.

"Who the hell is he?" Jack demanded.

"A friend of mine. *Detective* Bobby Halloran," she said pointedly.

"A cop, in case you're not clear on that," Bobby added, also coming to his feet. "And you must be the bad guy."

Wariness replaced the anger on Jack's face, and he glanced at Diana before answering. "Depends on how you look at it, I guess."

"I guess," Bobby agreed mildly. He turned to Diana. "You want me to arrest him?"

"For what?" Jack raised a brow, injecting an unhealthy dose of insolence in that one little gesture. "Cussing at a cop?"

"Works for me." There was no humor at all in Bobby's voice or in his eyes. "Once I have you locked up, I'm sure I can find some reason to keep you there."

Oh, boy.

"Everything is okay, Bobby. Really."

"No, it's not. And we need to talk." Jack's gaze swung back to Bobby. "Alone."

Bobby didn't appear particularly intimidated. "That depends on what the lady says. Diana?"

"I'll be all right," she said. "You go on. I'll call you later."

Bobby nodded, making his way slowly toward

the door. "And what we were talking about . . . what do you want me to do?"

"Nothing for now. Just give it some thought. That's what I plan to do, and if I get any brilliant ideas, I'll let you know."

At the door, Bobby turned and stared narrowly at Jack, who still stood by the desk, hands fisted, radiating barely concealed anger.

"Do I know you? You look real familiar."

Diana's tension eased. She even almost smiled. "You ever watch the Discovery Channel?"

"Sometimes," Bobby said, looking thoughtful.

"Dr. Jack Austin." Jack folded his arms across his chest. "I'm a professor at Tulane, and I'm on TV every now and then."

"Jack's a Mayan archaeologist," Diana clarified.

"You're kidding, right? An *archaeologist*?" Then the light went on in Bobby's eyes. "Ahh . . . that does make a few things a lot clearer." He shook his head, grinning broadly. "You call me, Diana. Nice meeting you, Austin. I'm sure it won't be the last time."

Bobby let himself out of the office, and the instant the door closed, Diana rounded on Jack.

"What the *hell* do you think you're doing?"

"That's just what I was going to ask you." In a few strides, he closed on her and took her shoulders in a hard grip. "Why were you at the gallery?"

Along with the anger and frustration on his face, she also saw what looked a lot like fear. "Doing what you want me to do. Finding out the truth about Steve Carmichael. He's running stolen antiquities through the Jade Jaguar, isn't he?"

"Yes." The word was hard, clipped. "But you were supposed to go to the *cops*, not to Carmichael!"

"He's paying me, remember? I can't tell him to get lost when asks me to meet with him and provide a status report—which is what I was doing. And in case you didn't notice, I *did* go to the cops."

He released her shoulders, took a step back, and ran a hand through his hair, obviously still agitated. He blew out a breath, then sat heavily in the chair Bobby had just vacated. After a moment, Diana perched on the edge of her desk beside him, leaning back, palms flat on its surface.

"You know, when I was ten," he said, looking up at her, "my parents took us kids to see the circus."

What the heck did a *circus* have to do with any of this?

"There was a performer who balanced spinning china plates on poles . . . in his hands, on his chin, on his forehead. All these plates, spinning like crazy, and if he made one wrong move, they'd all start wobbling, then come crashing down, shattering into a million pieces." His mouth curved in a half smile, despite the tension shadowing his eyes. "That's what I feel like right now. My plates are wobbling."

Diana sighed. "It doesn't matter what I said to Carmichael. He *knows*, Jack."

"About me, yes, but I didn't want you charging in there and taking him on. And you did, didn't you?"

She didn't bother denying it. He'd see the truth, somehow.

Jack rubbed at his brows as if he'd suddenly developed a whopper of a headache. "Jesus, I knew it. Look, we really do need to talk. I have a few things to take care of first, but I'll pick you up from your place at four. I'll have the motorcycle, so put on something you'll be comfortable wearing for a ride."

Just imagining sharing a ride with Jack, wrapping her arms around him, warmed her with anticipation—and a fluttery desire.

"Does this include dinner?"

"Yeah—and by the way, what size do you wear?"

Startled, she blinked. "A ten. Why?"

"It's a surprise."

At that husky promise in his voice, the tingly, fluttery warmth turned hot and taut, making her breath catch.

"Am I going to like this surprise?"

"I'm counting on it."

Terribly intriguing, this mysterious manner of his. "Okay. I'll be waiting."

He stood and made his way toward her door. She hurried to catch up with him.

"Jack?"

He turned, hand on the knob, and raised a brow.

"Are you okay?"

Tension still marked his face, but he gave her a warm, genuine smile that went a long way toward easing the worst of her fears. "Yeah, I'm okay, wobbly plates and all. See you later."

Jack headed into the waiting area and she followed him to the office suite door. She expected, absurdly, a peck on the cheek or something, but he didn't say a word as he shut the door behind him.

FOURTEEN

...

Silence settled over the office, and all the pent-up apprehension left her in a rush. Suddenly weak-kneed, she settled back against the door, catching Luna's stare.

"Do you know who that was? That guy who just left?" Luna leaned forward, eyes wide with awe. "That was Professor Jack Austin!"

"Yes, I know."

"Ohmigod! He's so *hot!* I took a class on Mayan art last year just so I could stare at him. Half the women on campus have a thing for him. I am so jealous. How do you do it? All these great-looking guys!" Luna flopped back in her chair, shaking her head. "When I grow up, I want to be just like you, Boss."

"No, you don't, unless you really like a lot of stress and surprises in your life." She pushed away from the door, feeling a little less shaky. "I have to go. What time are you leaving for class?"

"In about twenty minutes. But what about Professor Austin? What's—"

"No questions right now, Luna. Just lock up behind you, and make sure the answering machine is working. It's been acting up lately."

Heading back into her office before Luna could protest further, Diana gathered her pile of notes and folders, shoved them in her shoulder briefcase, and locked up her desk and file cabinets. She shut the door behind her.

"I'm off. I'll see you tomorrow."

"Are you hooking up with Professor Austin? For real? God, don't leave me hanging like this. I *have* to know!"

Under the barrage, Diana had to laugh. "It's not a date. It's work."

Luna called out as Diana shut the door, "Whatever you call it, I want to hear *all* the details, and they better be good. Don't disappoint me!"

Diana walked the short distance to her condo, her mood darkening again, and once in the privacy of her own place, she leaned against the wall and stared out at nothing.

Jack had really been angry—and worried. About her? Or that she'd told Carmichael something Jack didn't want her to reveal?

Damn. If she had more time before Jack came to pick her up, she'd put on some soft music, sit in her favorite chair, and piece all these confused thoughts into some sort of whole that made sense.

With any luck, Jack would finally tell her in detail what the heck was going on. She couldn't operate in the dark like this any longer, and she had to decide what to do about Steve Carmichael.

And Jack. The time had come to make a decision about where they were going, as a couple.

Pushing away from the wall, Diana headed to the bathroom and spared a few moments to relax under the pulsing warm water. Afterward, she slipped on a pair of faded jeans, a cotton tank, and a bright madras plaid shirt. She rolled the sleeves up around her elbows and tied the shirttails in a knot around her waist. Riding a motorcycle could be cold even in hot weather, when the wind started slicing through you on the open road.

She also donned thick sport socks and a pair of running shoes, pulled her hair back in a ponytail, and braided it. Then she sat back to wait for Jack, constantly checking the clock while her mind buzzed with questions and concerns.

At five after four, a firm knock sounded on her door. She hurried and opened it. Jack rested his shoulder on the doorjamb, arms folded over his chest. He hadn't changed, although he'd hung a pair of sunglasses from the neckline of his tank.

Again, she felt that absurd wish that he'd lean over and kiss her.

"Ready?" he asked, not making any move to come in, much less kiss her.

"Let me grab my things." She picked up her sunglasses and her purse. "You have a place to store this on the bike?"

He nodded. "I'll pack it away. Give it here."

Diana handed him the purse, then locked the door behind her and followed Jack down to the street, where he'd parked the white-and-gold bike. Jack handed her a spare helmet.

She pulled it on and waited while Jack packed her purse in one of the roomy leather saddlebags.

"Okay," he said, grabbing his own helmet. "You've ridden on bikes before? You know what to expect?"

Diana nodded. "A few times. I like it."

Jack finally smiled. "I figured you would."

He pulled on his helmet, visor still up, then swung his leg over the bike seat and motioned her to join him.

"Put your arms around me," he ordered, and started the engine. The bike roared to life beneath her, the sharp scent of exhaust stinging her nose.

Diana closed her visor, then leaned forward and slid her arms around his waist, taking in the warmth of his body, the lean muscles of his back and belly.

"Ready?" he yelled over the rumbling engine.

She nodded, and he snapped his visor down and took off.

A little thrill shot through her and she tightened her grip around his waist, shamelessly enjoying the feel of him in her arms as he drove through the Quarter at a leisurely pace. He increased speed when they left the congested streets, and kicked it up again on the expressway.

The engine vibrated most pleasantly against her bottom as the wind whipped against her, plastering her clothes to her body. She loved feeling the power of the machine beneath her—and the hard, warm body of the man in her arms.

God, being with Jack . . . no words could describe her feelings just then, except there was no other place in the world she'd rather be than with him.

Too bad he might end up in prison before all this was over.

But she didn't want to think about that, not yet. She hugged him tightly, caressing his chest. He glanced back at her, but she couldn't see his expression through the tinted visor.

Then he took one hand off the handlebar and briefly squeezed hers before gripping the handlebar again.

Such a simple gesture, and it filled her with a bright burst of pleasure, fun, recklessness—and if not for the fact they were going almost seventy, she'd have slid her hands a little lower.

Caught up with enjoying the ride, it took a while before she realized they'd left the city behind and crossed into the next parish—and that her bottom was going a little numb.

Releasing one hand from Jack's waist, Diana glanced at her watch. It was after five; they'd been riding for nearly an hour.

She looked around at the highway unwinding behind them, in front of them, surrounded by the flat expanse of swamp. They were deep into bayou country, heading south toward the Gulf.

A sinking feeling settled in her belly, quickly followed by anger and frustration—and, finally, resignation.

She tapped his shoulder. When Jack glanced back, she jerked her thumb toward the side of the road, telling him to pull over.

With a nod, Jack switched on his turn signal and swung to the shoulder as the cars behind them whizzed past. He stopped, idling the bike, booted feet on the road, and pulled off his helmet.

Diana jammed up her visor. "Where are you taking me?" she demanded, raising her voice as a semi-truck roared past, kicking up swirls of dust that made her cough.

"Someplace safe." He half turned toward her, his profile hard and inflexible. "Just for a few days."

She shook her head. "Jack, you can't do that. You can't take me away like I have no say in my own life!"

"The hell I can't, considering I'm the one who put you in danger."

Diana frowned. "Danger? What are you talking about?"

"Steve Carmichael. You put yourself right in his crosshairs today, and no way am I going to just stand by and let him hurt you."

She went cold. "You can't be serious. He wouldn't harm me; he's not that stupid. Too many people have seen me with him for him to kill me, and—"

"He wouldn't kill you," Jack snapped. "That's not how he operates. But he'd ruin you, Diana, to get back at me. That career that means so much to you? That reputation you're trying to rebuild? It'd be gone, just like that. He's got the money and the connections to bury you so deep you'd never get out."

Stunned, Diana stared at the unyielding set of his jaw, filled with alarm, then with an odd sense of wonder that he cared enough to protect her, even if she didn't need any protecting.

"My career?" she finally asked. "You kidnapped me to keep my career safe?"

He wouldn't meet her eyes. "I know what it means to you, sweetheart, and why you do it. How damn good you are at it. No way is he touching you, and you're not going to make a target of yourself. I can't let you do that."

She should be angry. He had no right to dictate her actions, any more than he had any right to jeopardize her career and reputation to begin with. Yet all she felt was a little tickle of hope.

"Why do you care one way or another?"

His mouth tightened. "Why do you think?"

"I don't know. And even if I did, I'd still need to hear it from you."

For a long moment, he said nothing, then he twisted around to fully face her. "Because I care what happens to you. Because I did something stupid, and now I have to try and do what I can to make everything right again. Because I'm crazy about you."

Seeing his rueful, wary expression, warm tenderness spread through her—and, for the first time, a sense of complete trust.

"That makes two of us," she said, and only then did the tension finally leave his body. "So . . . where are we going?"

"Grand Isle. To the beach." He pulled the helmet back on and faced forward again. "Just you and me for a few days."

And nights . . .

He didn't say it, but the look in his eyes before he turned away told her he'd been thinking about more than protecting her job.

FIFTEEN

...

Nearly three hours after leaving New Orleans, Jack crossed the causeway bridge to the barrier island of Grand Isle, often referred to locally as the Cajun Bahamas. The only year-round residents were commercial fishermen and oil workers, but in the summer, the population swelled by the thousands as vacationers flocked to the beaches and vacation homes. His parents had owned a little beach house there for the past fifteen years—another reason he'd settled in New Orleans.

Out in the Gulf, he could see shrimp boats chugging back at day's end, hopefully loaded down with "pink gold." The water was calm and dotted with pleasure cruisers, small fishing boats, sailboats, and a few big freighters or tankers. He glimpsed the tan sand of the beaches, fronted by a motley assortment of garishly painted summer homes raised on piers, their only protection from the frequent storms and hurricanes.

And this was definitely hurricane season. Hopefully the weather would hold while he was here with Diana.

He was anticipating a good time—providing she was still talking to him after what he'd done.

She hadn't seemed too mad there on the side of the highway, though, and when they'd stopped to eat in Golden Meadow she didn't ditch him. Right now she had her arms wrapped around his waist, her body snug against his, and for the last ten or twelve miles, his fantasies had been going off in all sorts of erotic directions.

If he could've seen any other way out than going high-handed and dragging her down here, he'd have taken it—but if Carmichael got even a whiff of how much he cared for Diana, the man wouldn't hesitate to threaten her. And no matter what might happen to him, he'd get her out of this mess unharmed.

Once he boarded that plane on Monday to Cairo—not London—he'd be in the clear. But since Steve had probably figured out what was up by now, the only way to ensure their safety was to disappear for the rest of the week.

He'd have to tell her about his plans, but first and foremost he owed her answers. The whole truth, from the very beginning, and he could only hope that afterward she wouldn't send him packing.

Or call the local cops.

He slowed, and turned onto a narrow street lined with beach houses. He could already smell the salt air, and behind him Diana twisted around, checking out everything.

As he pulled up beside a bright pink house with turquoise shutters and trim, he was almost sorry the

ride was over. He'd liked having her behind him—
especially when she'd let her fingers roam.

After lowering the kickstand, Jack killed the engine and pulled off his helmet. He turned to see
she'd done the same, pushing strands of loose hair
away from her face.

"We're here," he said, as if it weren't already
obvious.

Diana nodded as she tipped her head to the side,
looking past him with astonishment. Jack couldn't
help smiling. When he'd seen the place for the first
time, he'd stared, too.

Above the turquoise front door, a hand-lettered
sign read: THE LAST FLING-AMIGO. The pink-and-
turquoise color scheme was loud enough, and then
his mother had lined the stone walkway with plastic
pink flamingos—all of them dressed. Some wore
Hawaiian leis, others skirts or hats—and unless he
was mistaken, the baby-sized ball cap over to his left
had belonged to his youngest nephew, Mark.

"Is this yours?" Diana asked, and he didn't miss
the note of caution in her voice.

"It belongs to my parents. It's one of their play-
grounds. I come here when I need to get away from
the city. My sisters and their families visit sometimes, too."

"It's . . . very colorful."

"It's ugly as hell, but it fits right in. Everybody
tries to outdo their neighbors in coming up with the
most obnoxious paint jobs."

Jack swung off the bike, and Diana followed. Her
face was flushed, her eyes bright, and it hit him, low
in the belly, just how beautiful she was—and how

badly he wanted to make love to her, to be with her for far more than a couple of days and nights.

"The flamingos are cute. And some are looking very chic." She grinned, her nose wrinkling. "I like the one in the grass skirt, though the one with the Groucho Marx glasses and mustache is . . . unique."

"My mother has this thing for flamingos. She collects them." Jack grabbed the bags off the bike. "Come on. Let's get the stuff inside, then we'll go take a walk on the beach. There's things we need to talk about."

Diana's smile faded along with the mischievous glint in her eyes as she followed him up the long, creaking steps to the porch. He sorted through his key chain until he found the one he needed, opened the door, and stood aside so she could enter first.

Jack let the screen door bang shut behind him. The place smelled musty and closed-up, the air heavy with heat and humidity. "I'll open the windows and get the air conditioner running."

"I can help," Diana offered, a little too hastily.

That she might be nervous was unexpected, since this wasn't the first time they were alone, and she had to know how the day would end—if he was lucky.

As they opened windows, waiting for the air conditioner to kick in, Jack gave Diana a quick tour. The cabin was similar to his own place in layout: living room first, then the kitchen, followed by a small bedroom, bathroom, and the master bedroom. This last room faced the sea, with a door on the far wall, framed on either side by windows. The door opened onto a small porch, and another long flight of stairs led down to the beach.

While not big, the bedroom looked open and airy. It had a king-size bed with a white wicker headboard and white eyelet coverlet bedspread heaped with flamingo pillows, some bird-shaped. A white wicker chest of drawers, vanity, and high-backed chairs with fat, pink-and-white-striped cushions finished off the room, and a pink rag rug covered the white-painted plank floor.

Framed prints of flamingos dotted the walls, and a brightly colored, oversize sombrero from his parents' most recent trip to Mexico City hung from the vanity mirror, along with an assortment of Mardi Gras beads.

"I thought we'd sleep in here," Jack said, finally breaking the awkward silence.

Not exactly suave or smooth, but he saw no reason to pretend he wanted her to sleep anywhere but with him.

Her color still high, Diana walked to one of the tall windows by the door. The white cotton curtains, with their pink ball fringe, billowed with the breeze.

"It's a sweet little place," she said softly, staring out at the beach. "I bet your mother laughs and smiles a lot, just like you."

He came to stand beside her, fists in his pockets. Close enough to feel the heat of her body, but not to touch, even though he wanted to unbraid her hair, run his fingers through it, and feel its length spread across his bare chest.

Swallowing, he said, "She's always been one to enjoy life to the fullest, so I guess I inherited that from her. My dad's more serious, but lately he's loosened up. Retirement agrees with them."

"Where are they now?"

Cool air blasted his feet, swirling through the small room. Jack reached over her shoulders and slowly closed the window. With his arms still braced on either side of her, the smell of her filled him as he listened to her rapid breathing, felt her tension. After several seconds, he backed away.

"They're in Germany, drinking beer, eating bratwurst, and doing whatever tourists do in Germany."

Diana turned, leaning back, her palms flat against the wall. "I'd love to meet them sometime."

His gaze caught hers, and held it as he considered the deeper meaning of her words.

"I'd like that, too." Feeling strangely awkward, Jack moved back farther and motioned to the bag he'd tossed on the bed. "You can unpack and put your things in the dresser now, or later if you want."

"I still can't believe you bought me clothes." She dropped her head back, a small smile curving her mouth. "You're full of surprises, Jack Austin."

"I thought about picking the lock to your place and grabbing a few things, but this seemed easier—and if I'm going to prison for breaking and entering, it's going to be for stealing something more manly than your panties."

She laughed, as he'd intended, and seemed to relax a little. Jack busied himself by unpacking his clothes and storing them in the dresser, leaving room for her things. He hadn't brought much, just a few shirts, shorts, socks and underwear, and a pair of nice pants and a more dressy shirt. He put his swim-suit in the back of the drawer, keeping it rolled up so she wouldn't see the condom packages. He was al-ready presuming a hell of a lot, and he didn't want to risk offending her by appearing too sure of her.

After a while, Diana joined him. With half an eye, he watched her examine what he'd bought—halter tops, shorts, lacy underwear, a pair of sandals, a flowery sundress that laced down the front, a sexy teddy she wouldn't wear for long, and a leopard-print, one-piece swimming suit with a plunging neckline and a deep-cut back.

"For Sheena," he said. "You like it?"

She held it up, chewing on her bottom lip. "It's beautiful, if very daring."

"Daring looks damn good on you."

Her face softened, her eyes warm, deep, and inviting—and he caught himself leaning toward her. Reluctantly he pulled back, because if he kissed her now, they'd never get out of the bedroom.

"Change into something cooler, and we'll go take that walk. While you're dressing, I'll check the kitchen for food. Mom and Dad usually keep it stocked since my sisters come down here a lot."

Turning on his heel, he walked out of the bed-room, leaving her staring after him with bemuse-ment.

He checked out the cupboards and turned on the fridge. As expected, he found a lot of canned goods, snacks, dry mixes, cases of soda, beer, ready-made margarita mixes, four bottles of wine, and a bottle of champagne.

Perfect.

"Anything to eat?"

At Diana's question, Jack turned—and gave a low whistle of appreciation. She'd put on lipstick and re-braided her hair, and slipped on sandals, the floppy Velcro fastener kind. She'd also changed into denim shorts and a halter top that didn't leave much to his imagination, and his body responded in a heartbeat.

"You look really nice."

"Thank you." She walked closer. "So do we?"

Confused, he asked slowly, "Do we what?"

"Have anything to eat?"

Jack, old boy, get that mind out of the gutter now . . .

"Nothing exciting, but it'll do for now. You hungry?"

"No."

She wasn't visibly smiling, but he could *feel* her smiling. The air in the small kitchen almost seemed alive with the laughter she was keeping inside.

"Okay. I'll go change."

Alone in the bedroom, annoyed with himself, Jack took his time to dress. He had to get his shit to-gether, stop staring at her chest, stop imaging how easy it would be to come up behind her, slip his hands beneath that halter top, and glide them around to cup her bare breasts—

Right; like *that* was going to help. Briefly squeez-ing his eyes shut, he muttered, "Damn."

He'd be lucky to put three words together that made sense. God help him if she asked any ques-tions that would require him to think.

He exchanged his jeans for shorts, and tossed his shirt on the bed, deciding to leave his tank on. After scrounging around in the closet, he pulled on a pair of old flip-flops that belonged to his father. By then most of his blood was back in his brain, where it belonged, and he headed back to the kitchen.

Diana had gone outside to the porch, and she leaned over the railing, her bottom rounding out the seat of her shorts, the blond braid a thick line down the center of her bare back.

Jack took a deep breath, and said, "Let's go."

As he walked down the steps and around the house toward the beach, Diana fell into step beside him. Like the time in the Jaguar Jungle, neither spoke. He supposed she was enjoying the brisk breeze, and the view of the sun as it began to sink into the watery horizon.

The scrubby grass gave way to soft sand. It was nearing the off-season and the crowds were sparser, although couples still strolled along the beach, body surfers rode the waves, and children splashed and laughed close to shore. Sun worshipers lay on blankets and beach chairs, intent on stealing even the fading rays of sunshine, and every now and then the wind brought a hint of coconut oil just beneath the scent of the sea.

Jack headed toward where the surf licked the shoreline. He kicked off his flip-flops, and as his toes sank into the wet sand, warm water sluiced over his bare feet.

"How's the water?" Diana asked.

"Perfect."

She removed her sandals and joined him, the frothy surf whirling around her ankles, the sand coating the tops of her feet. She grinned at him, look-

ing young and girlish and achingly beautiful, and
Jack captured her free hand in his, squeezing her fingers as he smiled back.

Hand in hand, they meandered along the beach,
kicking at the water, stopping now and again to
watch a speeding boat, splashing kids, or to look at
seashells.

Just holding hands filled him with contentment.
He still wanted to get naked with her, but he liked
this a lot, too. He liked how she looked up at him
through her lashes, as if waiting, wondering what he
would do next. He liked how she smiled so freely,
and how she laughed loudly when a more aggressive
wave sprinkled them with spray. He liked her hand
curled warm and tight around his, fitting just right.

And he liked the way other men watched her, and
the dark, primitive satisfaction that came from
knowing she was *his*.

For now, anyway. Jack took a deep breath, hating
to end the peace of the moment, but unwilling to
draw out the inevitable any longer. Time to come
clean.

"I owe you an explanation."

"Mmmm," was all she said, her hand still warm
and soft in his.

Jack squinted out to sea, where the setting sun
sparkled with a dark, golden brightness on the water.
"I met Steve six years ago at a department party. He
was a major donor already then, and he showed a lot
of interest in my work. I was flattered by the attention and, of course, hoped I could translate his interest into funding. I got my wish, and the next year the
foundation gave me a grant to excavate at Tikukul."

He checked for her reaction, but she seemed focused on her toes, on the eddy of water and sand.

Jack looked back out at the line of pale beach stretching before them. "During the first couple years, a few of the nicer pieces of jewelry, pottery, and figurines went missing. I thought we'd maybe made a mistake in labeling or storing them. Out in the field it can get confusing, especially when working under primitive conditions. But when they didn't turn up after we got home, I realized they'd been stolen."

"He set you up from the very beginning." Diana brushed an errant strand of hair away from her mouth. "And used a legal excavation as his own private shopping ground."

"Exactly, and he was careful and organized, positioning his people on my team as laborers." It impressed him how quickly she'd put it together, considering it had taken him years to catch on. "So I didn't see it right off. I figured we'd been hit by looters. It happens: people get greedy, things disappear, and there's not much you can do beyond stepping up security. But nothing I did seemed to work."

Jack stopped, staring blindly out to sea until Diana pressed against him. He blinked, and pushed away the bitter memories.

"I kept losing pieces, a few here, a few there, but never found any trace of the thieves. When we uncovered a group of royal tombs two years ago, I knew I'd have to be even more careful. I expected looters to hit them."

"Carmichael *ordered* the tombs looted?" Diana asked, with disbelief.

Jack shrugged. "I think all he wanted was a few

showy pieces he could sell for big bucks, but somebody went too far. It was about three in the morning
when the alarm went up. I grabbed my rifle and ran.
All the noise was coming from the tombs, and I
swear, it felt like a stone had dropped in my gut. I
started firing, aiming high to scare off the looters.
They started shooting back, so I stopped aiming
high, and things got tense there for a while."

An understatement. Throughout the gun battle—
the longest ten minutes of his life—he'd expected to
die.

"I wounded a couple thieves, but they all escaped
into the jungle. I almost cried when I saw what
they'd done. The first tomb was ruined. They'd
hacked artifacts out of the ground, shoved bones
aside in a heap, broken vases apart to get to the contents . . . we lost everything, the data, the grave
goods. Everything."

"Oh, Jack . . . I don't know what to say."

Her soft voice was soothing, and he took a long,
calming breath. "The next day, while I was trying to
salvage what I could, I was arrested for winging a
few so-called innocent workers. They claimed it was
one of those 'friendly fire' deals, where I mistakenly
shot my own people. They said I had to go see the
authorities, just as a formality. Except I ended up in
jail for two weeks."

"And in the meantime, Carmichael covered his
tracks."

"You got it. All the drawings, photos, and notes
disappeared. There was nothing left to document
what had been in the tomb. My crew reported my
trailer had been ransacked, but they figured the loot-

ers had been looking for something else. Nothing to tie it to Steve ... nothing that would hold up in court."

"Smart," Diana murmured. "If a bit grandiose. So you figured out what was going on while you were in jail?"

Jack nodded. "After a couple days of not being allowed to use the phone or have visitors, I realized someone had bribed the local officials to keep me out of the way, and it didn't take long to figure out who that was. The rest of it came together pretty quickly after that."

They started walking again, clasped hands swinging between them, and she said, "Do you think he believes he's 'rescuing' these artifacts from being stored in a crate in some dark basement for years on end? From the few times I've talked with him, I get the feeling he doesn't have a lot of respect for how museums and universities handle their collections."

"You picked up on that, too?" He glanced down at her with no small amount of admiration, even though he'd known she was shrewd and quick. "That's my guess. Plus, the more money you got, the more you want."

"Isn't that the truth," Diana said with a sigh. "Greed ... I told you it wasn't pretty."

"I remember, but it looks to me like ol' Steve outsmarted himself by hiring you to bring me to heel."

She didn't like that; he could see it in her narrowed eyes and the rigid line of her back. "Are you saying he used me, too?"

"Diana, he knew I was with Audrey, and he knew you'd pry it out of her within days, if not hours.

Then you'd go after me, and he'd have me where he wanted me—in a no-win situation. He'd be generous, offer to drop charges if I behaved. And if I didn't, then he'd get me arrested, haul you into court, let you trot out your evidence, and ruin me. And if you balked, all he had to do was make a little noise about your past mistakes."

"Shit," Diana said in disgust. "I hate it when I get played."

"Believe me, I know *exactly* how you feel."

She leaned against him suddenly, and poked him with her elbow. "But he didn't count on you charming me, did he?"

Jack smiled. "Nope."

Or him falling for her like a load of bricks.

"He probably also didn't count on you figuring out what he was up to in the first place, and even if you had, that you'd do something about it. Or at least not in the way you did," she said.

Jack couldn't tell if she were disappointed in him or not, and he kicked a clump of sand, wondering how he could ever explain. They walked in silence for a while longer before he said, "I was mad as hell, and turning his own game against him seemed like the only solution. I couldn't do anything about the data we'd lost when the tomb was ransacked, but I could get those artifacts back and salvage something . . . *anything*."

Even now, thinking about the wealth of information forever lost to history, just because of one man's greed, brought a lump to his throat.

"I know I can't save the world, Diana. I can't even prove he's been systematically looting Tikukul for years. It's just my word against his, and who will people believe? Maybe I can't prove Steve's a smuggler, but he can't prove I'm a thief, either."

"You stole the box to make him angry. To goad him with the knowledge that he couldn't control you."

Jack saw only understanding in her eyes—and suddenly he felt as if a great weight had been lifted off him. He nodded.

"Steve bragged about the piece, knowing damn well I wouldn't approve. I don't think he could help rubbing my nose in the fact that he was untouchable, and I knew stealing it would get his attention. It didn't matter if he lost a few pots or chunks of jade—he could always get more from good ol' Jack—but the box I took couldn't be replaced, ever. For Christ's sake, he owns an ancient family heirloom that could settle a seventy-five-year-old academic controversy. And he just sits there, all smug and laughing about it."

Again, she squeezed his hand in comfort. "When did he figure out it was you?"

"Probably when I hit the crates. But he still thinks he can control me, that I owe him for all he's done for me. Steve can't grasp the possibility that I'd risk losing everything by challenging him."

Abruptly she stopped, pulling him up short. As he turned, she wrapped her arms around his waist, squeezing him tightly as she rested her head against his chest, and whispered, "I'm so sorry for what he did to you, Jack."

A hard, painful lump rose in his throat. He swallowed it back, then leaned down and kissed the top of her head. Her hair was soft, shampoo-scented, and the tension from his muscles eased as he held her close.

For a long while he just stood there, wrapped in Diana's arms, looking out across the top of her head toward the sea. When he registered how quickly the light was fading, though, and how far they'd walked, he pulled away.

"We'd better head back before it gets dark."

A small frown pulled at her brows. Uneasy at the shift in her mood, he asked quietly, "What's wrong?"

"Nothing's wrong. I'm glad you told me the truth, but I wish you'd trusted me with it earlier."

"Are you mad?"

"A little, but I can't really blame you for being cautious. You have a lot to lose."

"Only if I get caught with that damn box." He started walking back toward the pink cottage, taking her hand in his again. "It's the only thing anybody can prove I've stolen."

"And where is it right now?"

Jack let out his breath slowly. "If you know the answer and I end up getting busted, I don't want you facing accessory charges. And let me repeat that if you piss off Steve enough, he'd wreck any chance of your ever operating as a private investigator in the free world. I guarantee."

She was quiet for a moment. "But you do have it."

"Not here."

"Good, because I really don't want to lose any sleep worrying about what you have stashed in your sock drawer."

Not that he planned on letting her get much sleep

that night. "No contraband in the sock drawer. I swear it."

When they were halfway back to the cottage, Diana said abruptly, "I was wrong about you."

"About what? Being a thief, a liar, and a manipulator?"

He hadn't forgotten her words, and they'd bothered him more than a little.

"Hardly. You're all three, if you want to get picky. But you're not one of the bad guys. I've been so sure of myself, so self-righteous, when all along you're the one who's been trying to do the right thing. I'm just—" Diana broke off with a short, forceful sigh, then added quietly, "I'm sorry for giving you such a hard time."

"I appreciate that, but technically I *am* a thief."

Admitting it out loud at long last didn't make him tense up, as he'd expected. Instead, the ever-mounting strain and pervasive sense of failure that had dogged him for so long eased even more.

"I could be found guilty and convicted, lose my job," he added, because this needed to be said, too. "I'm not going to pretend what I did was right. There's a good chance I won't be able to pull this off, and I recognize the consequences could pretty much rewrite my whole life."

Diana shot him a sharp look. "Yet you did it anyway. Because you were trying to right a wrong."

"For the Tikukul artifacts, yes. The other thing was basic revenge. Nothing noble about that."

"I wouldn't be so sure of that."

The walk back had taken less time because they

hadn't stopped, and Jack spotted familiar pink lights wrapped around the Last Fling-Amigo's back porch railing.

Diana stopped short again, and when he turned to her, she said, "I'm going to have to call Luna tomorrow to tell her I won't be in. I have other clients I'm working for, and if they call, they'll need some sort of answer."

"Don't tell her where you are. Say unexpected business took you out of town. She seems like a nice kid, but she can't lie worth a damn."

"Okay." She started walking again. "But after that incident with you in the office, I don't think she'll believe I'm out of town."

"It doesn't matter, just so she doesn't know where you are."

"And where does your department think *you* are?"

"I've been called home unexpectedly to be with my mother while my father undergoes some tests for a condition that will happily clear up in a few weeks. I asked them to cancel my classes. I'm also expected to be in London until next Thursday, giving a guest lecture."

"Are you really going to London?"

He hesitated, but only briefly. "No, I'm going to Cairo, but nobody else knows that."

"Steve Carmichael seems to think you'll be around all of next week."

"Not exactly. Steve knows I'm going out of town, and knows when I'm supposed to be back."

"If he tries to contact me and can't, and tries calling you and finds you already gone, he's going to put it together."

"That's why you won't tell your secretary where you are. Got it?"

She nodded, not looking entirely happy. "Got it."

Jack stopped. "For the rest of the night, no talking about Steve. Let's relax a little. Deal?"

"Deal." When she approached the porch, Diana smiled. "Pink flamingo lights? This is too much. It's tacky, but in a cute kind of way."

"Mom had her fun here, that's for sure." Jack followed her up the long flight of stairs, his gaze lingering on her swaying hips, the bare skin of her back and legs. He shut the door, and the echo of the lock clicking into place sounded oddly loud in the silence of the room. "You want some wine?"

Diana stood in the middle of the bedroom, as if suddenly not sure where to go, what to do. "Please. I'm a little . . . you know—"

"Nervous."

She sighed. "Yes. Why, I can't say. I know what I want, what I like, and I sure as hell know what to expect, but this just feels . . . different."

"I can sleep in the other room. If that's what you'd prefer."

Diana turned, and he wished he had more light to see her face; that pale pink glow didn't help much. She canted her head to one side, as if seriously considering his offer—an offer he could hardly believe he'd made.

But if she asked, he'd do it. No questions asked.

"I'd like that glass of wine."

Was that a yes or no? "Okay. I'll be right back."

Jack headed to the kitchen, poured two glasses of Merlot, and hurried back to the bedroom, as if half-expecting she'd have vanished in the interim. When he walked into the room, Diana was leaning against the window, looking out at the nearly dark sky. He came up behind her and handed her the glass. She took it with a murmured thank you, and sipped it.

"Am I the only woman you've brought here?"

Jack froze, the wineglass half way to his mouth. Finally, he said, "No. I've had a couple girlfriends I brought to the beach."

She glanced back at him with a small smile. "Don't panic. I'm not jealous, except maybe about Audrey Spencer, and I didn't think you'd been celibate for all these years. But it's good you told me the truth, Jack. I really needed to hear the truth from you tonight."

"Nothing happened between me and Audrey, and I had no intention of having sex with her. I used her to get into Steve's office, yes, and I felt like a bastard about it. When you saw me with her today, I was apologizing. That's all."

"I sort of knew that. I'm glad you made things right with Audrey. She seems like a nice person."

Still not certain of her mood, he took a quick sip of his wine. "I'm clean. From diseases, if that's what you're worried about. I've been careful."

"I wasn't after your medical history, though I appreciate your honesty on that, too. I've been careful myself. These days, nothing is simple." She took another casual sip, still looking out the window, but her hands trembled faintly. "I guess sometimes a girl just wants to hear she's the only one."

Confused as hell, he just grunted and nodded.

"I haven't been with a man since I left New York.

I've had some dates, but I haven't been able to really trust a man again. Not intimately, anyway. Pretty pathetic, huh?"

What she was trying to say finally made sense, and a powerful rush of protectiveness took hold of him, shot through with shame for how he'd treated her at the start of this "game."

Jack put his empty wineglass down. "You *are* the only one for me." He plucked her glass from her hand and put it aside, then reached over her shoulders to pull the curtains closed. "And I'm the only one for you."

The words came out harsher than he intended, perhaps because he didn't want to be reminded of the other men she'd been with—and especially the one she kept comparing him to inside her head, if not out loud.

"For now, anyway." She looked back over her shoulder at him, her face serious, maybe even a little sad.

Suddenly, it mattered a great deal to show her that she meant much more to him than a brief interlude at the beach. Resting his hands on her shoulders, her bare skin soft beneath his palms, Jack turned his face into her hair, smelling flowery shampoo, the lingering tang of salty fresh air—and the sweet, heady scent of a woman's skin.

"Maybe we have something good here. Good enough that I want to see where it'll go. Give me a chance, Diana. That's all I ask."

The alarm clock on the dresser ticked away the seconds, one after the other, before she whispered,

"If you'd tried to charm me, been anything less than honest, I'd have known. And by now I'd be walking out that door."

"I know." Unable to hold back his need a moment longer, hearing the surrender in her answer, Jack lowered his head and kissed her.

It was an awkward angle, with her back to him, and Diana arched to kiss him. Her defensive shell melted away into the wild-edged heat he'd sensed from that very first day, when he saw her at the back of his classroom. Parting her lips with his tongue, he explored the smooth, moist heat of her mouth.

He ran his hands along her sides and over her arms, hungry for the feel of her skin. For a few minutes it was enough, then his fingers brushed the small of her back and against the bottom tie of the halter. With a quick tug he loosened it, then pushed the laces aside.

With a last kiss, he stepped back until he had enough room to slowly slide his hands up her back, pressing down, causing a heat of friction between his skin and hers, and listened to her little sighs of pleasure.

Again, he slid his hands down, with that same slow, massaging pressure, but this time moved his hands around to her belly, and up her front.

Diana sucked in her breath as he lightly skimmed her breasts and taut nipples. The sharp hiss of her response, the soft roundness of her breasts in his hands, and the feel of her back close to his chest, but not quite touching, shot a hot sizzle of need straight through him, head to toe.

"Jack," she whispered.

He didn't know if it was a question or a plea, but he moved his hands up to her neck, pushed aside her heavy braid, and untied the top of her halter. He tossed it aside, then rubbed his hands along her shoulders, kissing the side of her neck, breathing in the scent of her, and watching the high, round breasts and stiff nipples rise with her every breath.

It took an effort, but he didn't touch her breasts or take his tongue to their dark tips. Instead, he slowly unbraided her hair until it lay free, rippled and soft, over her back.

Diana tried to turn to face him, but Jack didn't let her, wanting to draw out the moment as long as possible for her.

He combed his fingers through her hair, and then, because he couldn't resist any longer, cupped her breasts again, taking pleasure in their weight, and how completely they filled his hands.

She leaned back against him, her head on his shoulder, eyes closed while he caressed her. As she made soft sounds of satisfaction, he moved one hand lower and popped the snap on her shorts, and slowly lowered the zipper, spreading it wide with his fingers. He slid his hand along the soft satin of her underwear, and lower, where he could feel her heat and her desire.

Diana moaned, arching her hips against his hand, and he gave her what she wanted. He touched her beneath her panties, and she moved her legs farther apart so he could glide a finger along her sex, tracing the folds, the moist center of her.

She said something, too soft for him to understand, and Jack wrapped his other hand around her chest, rubbing one nipple between his thumb and forefinger as he held her in place. He kissed the sensitive place right below her ear, tongue touching the skin, and eased his finger inside her at the same time he pressed his erection against her bottom.

Diana bucked, and he matched her rhythm, going slow, so slow. A primitive satisfaction took hold of him as she moaned, her breathing sounding erratic, and he could feel how she trembled and strained.

"Come for me," he whispered, then lightly bit her lobe. "That's it, sweetheart, let go. I want to hear you . . . God, you're so beautiful."

He slid a second finger inside her, pushing deeper as he pressed his palm downward. She arched, breath catching, and he could feel her muscles tensing, sense her inner pressure building, and he was so damn hard and hot himself he had to force himself to take it slow.

Suddenly she grabbed his hand, guiding him, pressing harder. He followed her unspoken plea, moving his fingers faster until she jerked back against him with a high gasp, and shuddered before sagging against him.

Sliding his hand upward, he kissed her warm, damp temple, then wrapped his arms around her tightly in a hug.

"Hey," he whispered into her hair. "You okay?"

"Mmmm . . . never been better."

Jack grinned at that low, throaty purr. "We'll see about that."

SIXTEEN

...

Diana closed her eyes, shamelessly enjoying the heavy, swirling sensations of sexual contentment and the comfort of Jack's arms around her, the warmth of his lips against her skin as he kissed her cheek.

A split second later, her eyes flew open in shock as he turned and bent, putting his shoulder under her hips, then stood. She gasped, finding herself slung over his shoulder. Before she could protest, he dumped her on the bed amid the colorful flamingo pillows.

Something squeaked, and she jerked aside, startled. "What the—?"

"One of the stupid birds has a squeaker." Jack loomed above her, wearing a grin—and all his clothes. "I forgot."

She sat up, groping behind her until she found the offensive pillow: a tiny bird-shaped thing with plastic wiggly eyes. Smiling, she gave it a couple good squeezes. "Sound effects?"

He snorted. "Not exactly the mood I'm aiming for."

"I know how to fix that." Diana swept her hair back over her shoulder—and watched his gaze drop to her breasts. She grabbed the waistband of his shorts, and pulled him closer. "Time for Jack to get naked."

In seconds, he'd stripped off his tank, and with a quick yank, she took care of his shorts. God, he was gorgeous. Long-limbed, lean, his muscles well-defined, and dark hair lightly covering his chest before narrowing to a thin line down his belly.

"That didn't take long," she murmured, eyeing him with appreciation.

"That's because Jack's easy."

The breezy comment made her smile, and when he tugged at her shorts, she lifted her hips so that he could easily remove them. Then he joined her on top of the white eyelet spread, and kissed her slowly, tongue probing. With a sigh, she closed her eyes and kissed him back. She wanted to explore every inch of him, to enjoy fully the friction of skin on skin, the sensation of her breasts rubbing against his chest hair, the feel of his muscles moving beneath her hands.

The kiss deepened, growing hotter, more insistent, and Jack abruptly pulled back, his gaze heavy-lidded, his hair mussed from her fingers.

"Better take care of business before I forget," he said, and Diana admired the view as he went to the dresser, then returned with a small package.

"Ah . . . I wondered if you'd remembered necessities while you were off buying me slinky stuff."

He eased down on the bed beside her. "I had ulterior motives in bringing you here."

Diana laughed softly at his admission. "No! I never would've guessed."

Jack gave her that wide, uneven grin that never failed to make her go all warm and weak, then nudged her. "Roll over. After the long ride down here, and after putting up with my high-handedness all day, you deserve a Jack Austin Special."

"Well, that depends on what a 'Jack Austin Special' is," she said suspiciously, resisting his nudges.

"A massage, head to toe. I'm pretty good at it, so you should say yes."

With a small sigh of approval, Diana rolled over. "The magic word. I'd kill for a good massage."

"Lucky for you, that won't be necessary," Jack answered, his tone amused. His fingers lightly brushed her hair aside, and then he knelt over her, legs on either side of her hips.

She tried to peek over her shoulder at what was bound to be an eye-goggling sight—Jack Austin, naked and splendid, straddling her bottom—but he pressed his thumbs between her shoulder blades, holding her down. She sighed again in contentment as he slowly moved his thumbs upward in a circular motion, working the muscles at the base of her neck.

"Mmmm . . . that's nice."

"We're just getting started, sweetheart."

The rumble of his voice made her shiver, and the touch of his hands—rubbing, massaging, kneading her muscles, the heat of friction between her skin and his as he ran his hands up and down her back—

filled her with a slow, spreading warmth of pleasure and satisfaction. And a growing desire.

He continued his massage along her arms and legs, even the arches of her feet, his touch sure and steady, not rushed. Taut awareness tingled whenever his fingers brushed the sides of her breasts, cupped her bottom in his palms, or ran his thumb along the inside of her thighs. She wanted him inside her, but the anticipation was too delicious, so she just made little humming sounds and waited.

"How's that?" he asked softly, bending to kiss the side of her neck, just below her ear, his erection brushing against her bottom.

"I think I'm melting," she mumbled into a pillow. "It's wonderful."

"Melting is good." He squeezed her bottom. "Have I told you how much I like this pretty little ass of yours?"

Diana smiled, although he couldn't see it. "Mmmm, no. Not that I can recall."

"I do." He eased her legs apart, and she let him, her breath catching. "Then again, I like all of you."

He brushed his fingers between her thighs, and she arched to meet the caress, sighing.

"Do you like that?" he asked, his mouth close to her ear, and she shivered again.

Diana swallowed. "Yes."

His finger traced her, rubbing that most sensitive spot, then glided slowly, gently, inside her. Her breath caught in her throat.

"Better?" he whispered.

"Oh, yes . . . only one thing would be better."

"We'll get there. Let's play first. I like to play."

Again, that slow, inner stroking, and Diana squeezed her eyes shut, very aware of his legs on either side of her hips, of the crisp texture of his hair against her smoother skin. "Do you always talk this much when you make love?"

A low laugh. "Until I get to the point where I can't think anymore, yes. Does it bother you?"

"No."

While none of her past lovers had talked much during sex, she found his doing so arousing, even endearing.

Jack continued to coax her, urging her to tell him if it felt right, if she wanted more or less, harder or softer. His questions required her to focus more intently on her body's sensations, how she responded to his every touch, stroke, every pressure—and she liked that it mattered to him, that he listened.

"More," she whispered. "Harder."

She was close . . . so close to the edge, and he urged her legs farther apart, slipping two fingers inside her, the stroke deep and rapid. She arched upward, but he kept his hand on the small of her back. As the pressure quickly built, her breathing high and fast, she grabbed the side of the bed, squeezing harder and harder until the climax rocked through her in a liquid hot rush.

For a moment she lay on her stomach, panting into the pillows, as the cool air raised goose bumps all along her damp skin.

Jack gave her little time to recover. She felt his hands on her hips, raising her to her knees, moving against her, and then the thick, hard pressure of his erection inside her, filling her. She made a soft sound in her throat as her hands fisted, and she dropped her forehead down onto the pillows.

"You okay?" he asked in a low, tight voice.

He thrust into her again, his hands hard on her hips, and she moaned, "Oh, yes."

She could hardly believe how quickly her body responded again, but the crowding pleasure soon edged out any other thoughts. With him behind her and her body angled downward, he could move more deeply inside her, and every slow, steady thrust nudged her closer and closer to another orgasm.

"Faster?" he asked.

"No." She panted, eyes still shut, wholly focused on the taut, sweet tension building within her. "Slow. Just like . . . this . . . please."

Jack gave a short, rough laugh. "You got it, sweetheart. This one's all for you."

He moved one hand from her hip, sliding it upward as he thrust slowly into her. He rolled her nipple between his thumb and forefinger, and desire shot through her with white-hot intensity.

The release came over her gradually; a low, drawing pleasure, then it gathered, and when he filled her again, her muscles went taut. She cried out from the rippling force of her pleasure, and when it had faded, it left her trembling and damp with perspiration.

Only Jack's hands kept her from collapsing facedown again. Slowly she became aware that he'd pulled out of her, of his hand stroking her hair away from her face, and then he eased her onto her back. In the dim light, she could see her breasts heaving, and the glint of perspiration on his skin. He was still erect, breathing hard, and tension radiated off him in waves of heat.

For a moment, the strangely intimate, unguarded expression in his eyes made her uncomfortable. Not quite ready for the heavy stuff, she almost looked away.

But she didn't, and let the deep emotion in his eyes soothe her, hoping he'd find the same peace in her own acceptance.

After a long moment, he whispered, "You liked that?"

"As if you didn't notice. I thought . . . I was going to pass out there for a second." His teeth flashed, and she returned the smile as she opened her arms. "You've been a very good boy. Now it's your turn."

"Damn good thing, too, because I don't think I'm gonna last much longer."

Jack moved between her legs, resting his elbows and forearms on either side of her head, then bent and kissed her. A deep, full, hungry kiss as he entered her again. Once he began moving, he broke the kiss, breathing against her ear, the harshness of it exciting her.

Suddenly, Jack rocked back on his haunches and took her ankles over his shoulders. Diana moaned, closing her eyes as he thrust again, his hips meeting her sensitive flesh. She arched her back, the ache almost painful, one hand grasping the headboard, the other closing over a pillow.

"God," Jack breathed, moving hard into her. "You feel good . . . so damn good."

Then his breath caught, and she felt his orgasm in the sudden, still tension of his muscles, sharp arch of his neck backward, and the jerk of his hips.

After he let out his breath in a long, unsteady sigh, he kissed her ankle, and eased her legs down onto the bed. He followed, propped on his elbows, his body warm and solid over hers.

Her gaze met his again as he cupped her face, his thumb gently stroking her forehead, the gesture unexpectedly tender.

Then Jack kissed her on the nose. "Hey. Thanks."

Diana smiled, warm and relaxed with contentment, her limbs oddly heavy and limp. "No problem . . . very glad to return the favor."

She released the headboard, her hand flopping onto the bedspread, and realized her other hand still held a pillow in a death grip. She held up one of the bird-shaped flamingo pillows, its head angled sharply to one side.

"Oh, no," she said as Jack's laugh rumbled through her body where his chest rested against hers. "I think I killed it."

"No loss." Jack rolled over onto his back, sweeping his hand over the bed and scattering pillows onto the floor with soft little *thumps*. He made a low sound of satisfaction. "Man, that was—"

"Phenomenal. Absolutely phenomenal."

He reached out and scooped her closer with his arm. "I told you so."

"You're such a modest guy," she said dryly, but couldn't hide the laughter in her voice.

"Sweetheart, the first time you strolled into my classroom, throwing off attitude like electricity in a thunderstorm, I knew how it'd be between us—if I could get past that small problem of you wanting to throw my ass in jail."

"I said your *very fine* ass." Smiling, Diana reached around to pat his rear—a firm, possessive, pat. "And it's even finer than I imagined."

Surprise briefly flashed across his face. "You were checking out my . . . assets?"

She rolled her eyes. "Oh, please. Do I have a heartbeat?"

"Damn." He grinned, looking absurdly pleased. "Now I don't feel half so guilty about eyeing yours every time I saw you."

Jack pulled her into a close embrace, her head resting on his chest, his chin on the top of her head, and she was content to lie in his arms like that, as the little bedside flamingo clock ticked away the seconds.

Finally, Jack broke the comfortable silence. "There's something I've been wondering—you figured out I was the thief before you'd even talked to Audrey. How'd you know?"

"You're a lousy liar. Carmichael's got you beat hands down in that area. I can never tell for certain when he's lying, but you have a very expressive face." She drew circles on his chest, liking the feel of his chest hair beneath her cheek, the musky, soothing scent of him. "When I told you the reason for my visit, you reacted defensively. The entire time we talked, I could tell you were hiding something, trying to distract me, and my instincts connected the dots. Later, when Audrey admitted to the tryst in the office, I knew that's how you'd pulled it off."

She tapped her fingertips on his chest, frowning

at a strong, sudden spurt of jealousy. Although he'd sworn nothing had happened—and wouldn't have—it bothered her that he'd kissed Audrey Spencer enough to mess up her hair and makeup.

"Did you enjoy kissing her?" she asked abruptly.

Jack let out his breath. "It wasn't exactly a hardship. I mean, I like her. She's a decent person, and I think she's pretty. But she's not my type."

"Hmmm. What *is* your type?"

He squeezed her, hard. "Tough, mouthy chicks. Like you."

"I'm tough?"

Maybe he meant it as a compliment, but it made her sound . . . hard.

Not so long ago, she'd wanted to be harder—but not anymore, and she hadn't realized she still came across that way to people. Even to Jack, even now.

"I don't want to be like that," she said quietly. "Hard or cold."

"I meant it in a good way, and believe me, sweetheart, you're anything but hard and cold." He tightened his hold on her as she opened her mouth to speak. "Trust me on that."

She searched that expressive face, looking for any wisp of untruth, tempted to ask what exactly he thought of her, but she didn't have the energy to pursue it. Or maybe the guts.

"Okay." She wriggled a bit until he released her. "I need to go clean up."

After she finished in the bathroom—decorated with a flamingo theme and a palm tree print shower curtain—Jack went in. While he ran water in the sink, Diana piled the pillows on one of the chairs, then pulled back the coverlet and slipped beneath the cool pink sheets. He joined her a few minutes later and she snuggled back into his warmth, fitting her bottom against his hips, her back to his chest.

She lay quietly, relishing the feel of him against her, listening to the low, even sound of his breathing. But she wasn't sleepy at all. In fact, she was now wide-awake and wanted to talk again.

"Jack? You awake?"

"Sort of," he mumbled.

"Can I ask you a question?"

His chest rose and fell against her back as he gave a near-silent sigh. "Sure."

"Just how did you steal the box from Steve's office? I'd really like to know."

"Nothing complicated. I programmed my computer to dial my pager at 10:20, and my original plan was to ask Audrey if I could use her office to return the call."

He shifted, fingers brushing her breast as he rested his hand across her belly.

"I'd tell her it was confidential, so she'd leave me alone in the room. Then I'd pick the lock to Steve's office, open the armoire, and grab the goods. I figured it'd take me three or four minutes, total."

"But Audrey got drunk and made a pass at you, and you altered your plans."

"It gave me a believable reason to be in the office if Steve happened to be watching. I held off Audrey for as long as I could, then at ten suggested we go somewhere private. I knew she'd take me to Steve's office, and I'd only have to keep her occupied for a few minutes before my pager went off."

"Slick."

"It was a shitty thing to do," he said, his voice tight, "but I'd just intercepted those crates, and Steve was beginning to put it all together. If he thought I was only trying to score with a drunk, pretty girl, he might not be suspicious enough to follow me and catch me red-handed."

"So after your pager went off, you got rid of Audrey for a minute or so."

"I made sure to mess up her hair so she'd have to fix it before we went back downstairs. It didn't take me long to pick the armoire lock, then I grabbed the box and put it in my pants' pocket. I left Steve my calling card, to make sure he got the point, closed the doors, and shoved my plastic gloves in my other pocket just seconds before Audrey walked in. I thought I'd gotten away with it, until you told me exactly what I'd done. Man, you floored me. I couldn't believe you'd figured it out that fast."

"My past history helped clarify the situation," she said evenly. "What are you going to do with the box? Since you're going to Cairo, I presume you're taking everything back to the museum there?"

"That's the plan."

She pulled back to meet his gaze. "When, exactly, are you leaving?"

He took a moment to answer. "In a few days."

His evasiveness raised her suspicions, and she almost demanded an answer—but she didn't want to spoil the moment. "And you expect the Egyptians to accept it back, no questions asked?"

"I'm not unknown, Diana, and the archaeology community is a small one. It helps that I went to school with a guy who now works in the museum. I trust him to listen to me and help me out. I hand over the box, get on the plane home the next day, and they take care of business, nobody the wiser. It's the only way to do it without causing a lot of trouble. You know that."

"And you feel this is worth risking your career? Possibly wrecking your life?"

"I'm an archaeologist, dammit. The past belongs to all of us, not just one individual, and the dead should be treated with respect and dignity. Ripping off a tomb just so you can have a really cool souvenir is *wrong*, and if I can right that wrong, I'll do it."

Diana couldn't help smiling at his tone, sheepish and angry and defiant. She leaned over and kissed him quickly. As she lay down again, she rolled onto something sharp. Wincing, she groped around in the sheets, and pulled out the slightly flattened condom box.

"Now here's my idea of safe sex." She tossed it to Jack, and he neatly caught it against his chest. "Losing the condoms at the foot of the bed."

"Who says it's the only box?" Jack stuffed it under his pillow, then hitched up onto his elbow, head propped on his hand, looking heavy-eyed and well loved. "Hey, that reminds me of a joke."

Taken by surprise, Diana raised a brow. She'd never had a lover who told jokes after sex. "Joke?"

"Yeah, you know, something that's supposed to make you laugh." With his free hand, he reached out and took a lock of her hair, twirling it around his finger, rubbing his thumb against it. "What's a blonde's idea of safe sex?"

She groaned, pulling the sheet over her chest as she sat up. "I'm not sure I want to know, but . . . okay, what is it?"

"Locking the car door."

"That's really low, Austin." Still, she laughed, then lightly smacked his chest, tossed back her hair, and said, "But I can beat it. What's a man's idea of safe sex?"

Jack shrugged, a smile pushing at the corner of his mouth. "I've no idea. Enlighten me."

She gave a sniff of disdain. "A padded headboard, of course."

He rolled onto his back with a snort of laughter, grabbing her as he did so. Diana landed on top of his hard chest with an *oomph*, grinning like a kid, feeling like a kid again, happy and carefree.

As she looked down into his smiling face, she felt a familiar, half-forgotten longing. God help her, she was hopelessly falling for this man—and he might only have a few days of freedom left to offer her.

More than anything, she wanted this moment to last, wanted to see where it might lead—and the crowning irony was that in order to do so, she had to make sure her thief escaped the long arm of the law.

SEVENTEEN

...

Jack awoke in the darkness with a start, sharply aware of something missing. Rolling over, he saw Diana had gone.

Unease hit with a jolt, and for a second his heart seemed to stop. He squinted at the clock, seeing it was after three in the morning.

Where the hell was she?

Diana wouldn't turn him into the cops, not after everything they'd said and done tonight—but even as he swung out of bed, he couldn't completely squelch a small, niggling doubt.

Jack grabbed his shorts off the floor and slipped them on. He checked the bathroom first, then the rest of the cabin, but didn't find her. A quick glance out front showed the motorcycle still parked where he'd left it.

That left only one place to check. He headed back to the bedroom, opened the door, and walked out onto the porch facing the beach. There, barely visible in the pink glow of the lights, halfway down the stairs and wearing only a shirt, sat Diana.

Relief swept over him, then another wave of guilt. What the hell was wrong with him, that he could doubt her like that?

He shut the door quietly behind him, and made his way down the creaking stairs. She had to have heard him, but she didn't turn. He hesitated, then sat next to her on the step.

"Hey," he said at length. "Trouble sleeping?"

Diana nodded, still not looking up, and a different kind of unease touched him.

"I woke up, then couldn't get back to sleep. I didn't want to disturb you, so I came out here."

The wind stirred, and as the ends of her hair tickled his bare arms, he realized that, for the first time since they'd met, she wore it loose and straight and heavy.

Finally, Diana turned to him. "You look worried. Did you think I'd left?"

"It's three in the morning," he said carefully. "I didn't know where you were."

"Did you think maybe I'd slipped out to call the cops on you?"

What the hell could he say to that?

"The possibility concerned me at first." He paused, struggling to find the right words for her. "I don't believe you'd do anything like that now."

"But the thought crossed your mind."

He let out his breath slowly. "Yeah, for a second or so, it did. I'm sorry."

"Don't be." She added quietly, "Of course I wish you hadn't thought that, but I'm not really surprised you did."

Then Jack noticed she'd been crying. His gut

clenched, and he reached out and traced the drying tracks of her tears. She ducked her head, her hair falling down to hide her face. "It's okay. They're the good kind of tears."

"If you say so," he said warily.

Diana leaned forward, elbows on her knees, resting her chin in her hands. "I'm like a lot of people in thinking I'm right more often than not, that if I run into trouble, I'll keep my cool, fight the good fight. But until you actually find yourself in a crisis, you really don't know how you'll respond.

"Some people would've bounced right back from having the proverbial rug pulled out from under them." She sat so very still, seeming to pull further into herself. "Much to my surprise and everyone else's, I wasn't one of them."

Suddenly understanding where she was going, Jack had to look away. She was a strong woman, but right now she seemed so very fragile, and all he wanted was to take her in his arms—but he knew better than to do so.

"What Kurt did to me . . . it was one of those major turning points in life. There's everything up to that moment, and then everything after, and you can't ever go back to being the same person, even if you try. We were together for almost a year, and the entire time he was helping himself to my client files so that he could plan his thefts."

She took a quick breath. "I loved him, I really did. And I trusted him. We talked about getting married, about having children. He told me—" Her voice broke. "He said he wanted a baby girl first."

Anger shot through him, at how she'd been hurt,

how he couldn't do anything about it—but mixed with the anger was an unexpectedly sharp, biting jealousy.

"I'd never had my trust broken like that. I expected to take it all in stride and get on with life. He was an amoral creep, I was a good person, none of it was my fault, and I wouldn't blame myself."

Jack couldn't keep quiet any longer. "It *wasn't* your fault, Diana."

"I know. I knew it then, too, but the funny thing is, it didn't help. Instead of bouncing, I made myself hard. And rigid. I kept people at a distance, except for a few friends I'd always trusted. I walked away from that part of my life as if it never existed. Big-time denial. Deep down, I understood it was my way of healing, and I'd get past it when I was ready. I just didn't expect it would be like this. With you." She straightened and sighed. "You're the first man I've let myself wholly trust again, Jack. Please, please don't ever let me down."

His chest tightened with guilt—and a piercing, desperate frustration. "That's a lot to ask. I'm not a saint, any more than you are. I can't promise to never disappoint you, but I can sure as hell try to always do right by you."

"I know you'll try. And this is also a roundabout way of telling you that's why I wasn't upset when you thought I might've turned on you. I've *been* where you are now, and I know about doubting people, about hating that you can't trust like you used to, and maybe being afraid you won't ever be able to again. I had my Kurt." She glanced his way. "And you had your Steve Carmichael."

As her meaning sank in, Jack looked down. Something dark inside him twisted, tried to push outward, but he held it back.

"Except I never slept with good ol' Steve," he said, his tone deliberately light.

Diana watched him, her expression unreadable.

Uncomfortable, he looked away again. "Right. It's not something to joke about, it's just that I—"

"Hide behind smiles—the 'go to hell, you can't hurt me' attitude." Her voice was quiet, but even and firm. "It didn't work that way for me. All I felt for the first few months after turning him in was this incredible rage. And I had some pretty vivid revenge fantasies, too. I'm sure you know what I mean."

A sudden, uneasy awareness seemed to crawl beneath his skin.

"I'd known for a whole week what Kurt had been doing, before he was arrested," she said, her tone almost conversational.

"You did what you had to," he said, and fisted his hands to stop the thousand pricklings of fear.

"And then some." She leaned forward again, and for an instant, the intensity of her tension seemed to shimmer between them. "I let him make love to me that morning, just hours before I walked him into a trap. How's that for cold and hard and calculated? And he never even saw it coming, I was that good."

"Diana." His jaw clenched with the effort not to touch her, to comfort her. "You don't have to tell me this."

Nor was he sure he wanted to hear it. The son of a bitch was already in prison, but Jack couldn't shake this intense need to smash his fist into the man's face for her sake, for the satisfaction of making him hurt. Hurt hard.

"Yes, I do." Fresh tears glimmered in her eyes. "Because the rage, the need for revenge, to see them suffer for what they did . . . it doesn't last, Jack."

For a fleeting moment he held her gaze, then he had to look away.

"It doesn't last," she repeated, quietly. "And then you either see the truth and accept it, or you choose the big denial and run for it. I did that for a while, but the truth was always there, and it haunts me, Jack. I can't forget that look of disbelief and pain on his face when the police burst through that hotel door, and he realized I'd set him up. I can't forget, because when I'm honest with myself, it hurt to do that. It hurt a lot."

Silence fell between them, except for the whisper of the wind, the ever-present rumble and roar of the surf.

"I denied that I'd ever loved him, told myself that he had no feelings for me at all—it was just an act, he got caught up in his own lies, and the only reason I'd want to believe otherwise was so that I wouldn't feel like a total loser." She let out a small, shaky sigh. "I don't regret what I did, and believe with all my heart he deserved what he got, but there was something real between us. He *did* love me, as much as he was capable of loving anyone, which made what I did that much worse and harder to live with. But instead of admitting that, I let myself just wallow in the hatred and anger, because I told myself I deserved to wallow. I never let myself feel grief, never let myself cry for what I lost. Not until tonight."

"Ah, Jesus, sweetheart, you can't—"

"No! Let me finish. I'm *glad* I finally had a few tears for me and Kurt. That's what I meant when I said crying was a good thing. It's taken me over two years to make peace with myself, to forgive him, to bring it to an end, and I just . . . I want you to do the same with Steve."

Denial, rejection—anger—enveloped him, and he shook his head.

"It's not the same thing."

"Then you're lying to yourself, the same as I did." She touched his arm. "All your anger, Jack . . . where do you think it came from? People can't hurt you like that unless you loved them in some way."

And just like that, as if a wall suddenly exploded into dust, the hurt and denial and frustrated fury rolled through him. His throat tightened, blood roared in his ears, and he leaned over so she couldn't see his face. He struggled to breathe evenly, to control the tangle of emotions. Finally, he looked up, focusing on a distant blinking light in the blackness.

"He treated me like part of the family, had me over to his house more times than I can remember. I even played with his grandkids. We went fishing out in the Gulf four or five times a year, met in the bar to talk shop. He always told me how proud he was of my discoveries, and he—"

He fisted his hands hard, trying to focus on something other than the tightness in his throat, the heat burning at the back of his eyes.

"He was a friend," Diana said quietly.

Not trusting himself to speak, he only nodded.

At length, she added, "You have to end this, Jack. You know that."

Again, he nodded.

"What are you going to do?"

He took a long breath. "I don't know."

"You can take it to the police."

"Like you did?" Jack looked at her, and immediately felt like a bastard when he saw the lines of tension on her face.

"It's an option, but can you do it? And is that what you want?"

"No. We both know he'd never see the inside of a courtroom, and that's why I decided to beat him at his own game. I don't want to lose my job, or any chance to ever dig at Tikukul again. It's *my* city, nobody else's." Jack turned slightly, facing her. "And I don't want to disappoint those who love me or depend on me."

"But you can't go on waging this little war. Eventually it'll drag you down and cost you everything. You either walk away from it, or you go to the cops and take your chances . . . but you have to do something."

"Once I get back from Egypt, I'll talk to Steve. He won't be able to do anything to me at that point. My hunch is that he'll stop if I confront him."

"You really believe that?"

"I'm on to him, Diana. I can get my own workers, warn my crew. Ever since that tomb was looted, I've kept a close watch on the site. This past season I lost nothing, as far as I know."

"Maybe you should've confronted him at the start."

"I thought about it, but at the time I was too damn angry. And hurt. I wanted to watch the son of a bitch squirm. I wanted him to get a taste of what it was like, and I wanted him to know it was someone he knew and trusted like a son."

The word tasted bitter on his tongue.

Diana was right: Something good inside of him *had* died when the man he'd considered a friend had turned out to be a liar who'd set him up and moved him around like a pawn.

And Diana was right about everything else, too.

"I can't go on doing this anymore." He slowly let out his breath. "At first, it was like a rush. The fear and risk of getting in and out of those houses without being caught made my heart pound, and then there was a burst of relief, of satisfaction, when the job was done. I spent a lot of time convincing myself I was doing the right thing, but I'd bet the people I robbed don't feel the same way."

A small frown settled between her brows. It bothered her, thinking about the people he'd robbed. If they were faceless and nameless, it was so much easier to justify his actions. But this had never been a lark, he'd been a real thief. He'd left behind victims of a crime, knowing exactly how they'd feel in the aftermath—because he'd been victimized himself.

Yet he'd done it anyway—and hated it. God, yes, Diana understood him better than he understood himself; sensed what he'd kept bottled inside, reluctant to face.

"How did you find out who'd bought the pieces that were stolen from your tombs?" she asked at length.

He smiled briefly. "Good old Ed Jones, who's so good at making everything legal and tidy and loophole free. He has an office in an old mansion near the Garden District, and the security system is a joke. I broke in one night and helped myself to Ed's tediously meticulous files."

"You stole them?"

"No, I just took good notes—names, addresses, descriptions. The collectors who bought their pieces in good faith had them insured, and they didn't lose any money. Those who didn't—"

"Knew they were looted to begin with." Diana leaned back, resting her elbows on the step behind her. "And got what they deserved. It's justice, but I'm not sure it's worth the price you've paid for it."

"It's something I'll have to live with. I regret invading the homes and lives of those people who hadn't done anything wrong, and my only consolation is knowing they can always go out and buy another pot for their collection. For them, it's a temporary loss."

Unlike his. What had happened on that hot, humid jungle night was so personal that even now, over two years later, the pain still felt sharp and raw.

"Remember what I told you about jaguars being protectors of the dead?"

"I remember."

"That's how I saw myself—as the voice for those who can no longer speak. Some protector I was." A bitter pang of failure twisted inside. "What I lost when that tomb was looted was priceless, and when data like that is ruined, it's gone for good."

She took his hand, then asked quietly, "Whose tomb was it?"

"The man who built Tikukul." Jack looked away, swallowing back the sudden lump in his throat. "Jaguar Claw the Great."

The sound of her soft sigh carried to him. "I'm so very, very sorry."

That pretty much summed up everything. She didn't dodge the finality of it, and for some reason, her simple expression of sympathy helped dull the hurt. Of course people would go on looting, galleries would continue to sell antiquities, collectors would continue to buy them—and to the average guy on the street, it didn't seem such a big deal that a few old bones were pulverized, or that bits of pottery, gold, and jade were stolen. But for his ancient Mayan king, it was like dying all over again, this death more final than the last.

For Jack, the loss was absolute.

"He was a god to his people, a genius, and a visionary. I had so much to learn from him . . . he had so much to tell me," Jack said, his voice low. "And now he'll never talk to me."

Diana knelt in front of him, her gaze solemn. She reached up and wrapped her arms around his neck and held him close, fingers stroking his hair in a soothing gesture.

As he embraced her, his hands sliding upward under her shirt—wanting the anchoring reality of her warmth, the rightness of feeling her bare skin—Jack realized she wasn't wearing anything underneath.

And he wanted to make love to her again, right there outside under the stars and moonlight, with the wind on their skin. Not out of lust—but to make complete the connection growing between them.

Holding back that driving need, he said quietly, "I've known a lot of women, Diana, but you're the only one who's understood me at all."

EIGHTEEN

...

Trying not to yawn, Diana wrapped her arms around Jack's waist as he started the motorcycle, then turned it toward the road.

Since they'd arrived at Grand Isle, they'd spent a lot of time in bed—no surprise there—and when not fooling around, they'd strolled along the beach, or splashed around in the water. He took her out for lunch and dinner, and the seafood was among the best she'd ever tasted—and she'd dined in some of the world's finest restaurants.

She liked the casualness of the island community, and how everybody seemed to know Jack. Not because he was a semifamous archaeologist, had been in *People* magazine, or on cable TV, but because he was David and Lorna Austin's kid. It was a side to Jack she'd not seen before, and she found it strongly appealing.

Now, with the wind blowing through her hair, she scooted against him as he headed toward Grand Isle Park. Lazily, she rubbed his belly, and he glanced back at her over his shoulder, grinning.

She snuggled close again, cheek against his back, and let her dreamy fantasies wander wherever they wanted.

Relaxed best described her mood, and languid—and very thoroughly loved. Nearly every other thought touched on Jack, and whenever she caught him looking at her, she saw the heat in his eyes.

Oh, yeah, he was crazy about her, and she was crazy about him—if a little too wary to call it love.

The sun beat down hotly on her skin, but the wind felt cool, smelling of sea air. She closed her eyes, resting her chin on his shoulder, face tipped toward the sky, and soaked in the warmth and scents, letting her body feel every bump on the road, the vibration of the bike's engine against her, and the delicious feel of Jack in her arms.

Lust was so uncomplicated: the hunger for his touch, his mouth on every part of her body, the feel of him moving inside her, and the care he took in making sure she had her satisfaction again and again.

Love was scarier, and not only because she didn't know how all this would end. She *wanted* it to end with her and Jack together, but life had taught her you don't always get what you want.

Jack kicked up the speed a little and she opened her eyes, watching the passing blur of cars, buildings, and trees.

After that night on the porch, they'd avoided discussing troubling subjects—like what would happen if things went bad, and he got caught. Hopefully by now he understood that she'd stand by him, no matter what, but she should make it clear.

A chill nibbled at her contented mood, but she firmly shook it off. No brooding, and no ruining the moment by going all glum or depressed.

Of course they couldn't go on hiding from reality forever, and their idyll here would end soon. Which meant she had to get Jack to tell her his plans, because she had no intention of letting him out of her sight until he was safe on that plane to Cairo.

Maybe Jack believed Steve Carmichael wouldn't risk going after him, but Diana didn't share his optimism. People like Carmichael believed their wealth and status allowed them to do whatever they pleased, and, for the most part, they assumed correctly.

The motorcycle slowed, signaling their arrival at the park. After stopping the bike, Jack grabbed the bag packed with snacks, water bottles, sunblock, towels, and swimsuits, and slung it over his shoulder. Then he slipped his arm around her waist, gave her a quick kiss on the top of her head, and said, "Let's go."

At the casual intimacy of that kiss, Diana smiled up at him, slipped her arm around his waist as well, and gave him a quick squeeze.

Oh, God, who was she kidding? She *was* falling in love with him. Absolutely, positively, no turning back now.

"What?" Jack asked, catching her look.

"Nothing. Just thinking how sexy you look."

He winked. "Hold that thought for later, sweet thing."

At the visitor center, they read up on Jean Lafitte and his pirates. As Jack leaned over to examine a picture, she took in his hard-edged looks, the day's worth of dark beard stubble, and grinned.

"You know, you'd make a pretty good pirate," she said, keeping her voice low so no one around them would hear.

He glanced at her, one brow raised. "You have a few plundering and pillaging fantasies?"

Her gaze touched on his lips, then blatantly checked out the rest of him. "Hmmm . . . maybe."

"Great. Now she tells me." He looked around at the busy room with a resigned expression. "Hold that thought for later, too. We're going to have a busy night."

After leaving the visitor center, they climbed to the top of the observation tower to view the coastline and inlets of Barataria Bay, Lafitte's favorite lurking spot, then strolled hand in hand along the huge fishing pier, crowded with people busily casting and reeling. Then Jack led her along the boardwalk trails over lagoons and ponds, accompanied by mothers pushing babies in strollers, herds of children, and other romantically inclined couples, young and not so young.

After a couple of hours they returned to the beach, changed in the public bathhouse, and staked out their territory on the sand.

Jack eyed her with undisguised appreciation. "Have I told you how much I like that swimsuit?"

"Only about a hundred times so far."

"It makes me hot."

After a brief survey of his baggy swim shorts, she arched a brow. "Behave. This is a public beach."

He laughed, then took off at a run for the water.

Diana raced after him and almost managed to over-take him. The water soothed her sun-heated skin as she and Jack played, splashing around, sometimes groping each other under the cover of water, and getting competitive while swimming. Jack won most of the races, but she'd never been much of a swimmer. He'd also brought along a big inner tube, and they took turns inflating it with a small hand pump. They waded back out into the water, hopped up on it, and settled back, legs and arms dangling over the sides, heads pillowed on the rim, bottoms in the water.

A long hour passed as they bobbed and rocked on the waves, dozing on and off in the hot sun, making small talk, and listening to the laughter of children and the whine of motorboats. As the sun started to sink against the horizon they paddled back to the beach, then flopped down on their towels amid other sunbathers and colorful tents belonging to overnight campers.

Diana rubbed more sunscreen over her skin, which was turning a little pink despite her efforts—a drawback of being a natural blond. Jack sprawled on his towel beside her, and she enjoyed having a chance just to sit and admire him. Before long, something about his pose struck her as familiar. With a slow smile, she remembered where she'd seen him lying spread-eagled like that, damp and sweaty and looking deliciously rough-edged.

She didn't realize Jack had been watching her from beneath lowered lashes until he said, "Whatever you're smiling about, I hope it's something dirty."

"You wish." Diana gave him a playful poke. "Actually, I was thinking about that shot of you in *People*."

"Oh, please," he said with a groan. "That stupid picture is something I'd like to forget."

Intrigued, she scooted closer. "Embarrassed?"

"Wouldn't you be?" Jack sat up. "The pose was my idea. I meant it as a visual joke . . . me sacrificing my academic integrity for this gossip rag. I had no idea the picture would end up looking so—"

"Erotic?" Diana said. "Sexually suggestive?"

"Right." Jack rummaged around the backpack until he found the last bottle of water, still scowling. "For Christ's sake, it looked like the photographer was focusing on my dick!"

"Hmmm, yes. I did notice that."

He snorted derisively, then took a long drink of water. After wiping his arm over his mouth, he grumbled, "I'm a professor. I'm supposed to inspire a passion for *knowledge*."

"I bet your class attendance improved, though."

The look he gave her was answer enough. She took the bottle and drank deeply before handing it back. Several minutes passed as they sat close to each other, not quite touching, staring out across the water. Then Diana leaned against him, resting her head on his chest, and sighed.

"We have to leave tomorrow, don't we?" When he didn't respond, she looked up at him. He was still staring out at the ocean. "Jack?"

"How'd you know?"

"One of the disadvantages of boinking a PI. We're intuitive, people-savvy types." Mostly, anyway. "Seriously? You've been very . . . attentive. You were so gentle making love to me this morning, and now this whole afternoon of quiet time together, relaxing. It's kind of a no-brainer, Jack."

"Seems like I can't keep any secrets from you."

At his answer, all her insides knotted up with disappointment—and worry.

"Oh, you've managed to keep plenty," she said, with a touch of sarcasm. "Like where you stashed all those artifacts you stole. Or where you've been keeping the crates from the ship."

"The grave goods are in my lab."

Amazed—and more than a little annoyed—Diana turned to face him. "I didn't see anything suspicious when I was there. What'd you do?"

"Doctored the files." Jack at least had the grace to look guilty. "Which isn't too hard when you're dealing with a collection of evidence from the same location. And nobody argues with the site director who's been working the place for ten years."

"What about the crates?"

"Never left the ship."

Diana absently rubbed her thumb across her bottom lip. "Really? I can't wait to hear this one."

Jack looked up from her mouth, and gave her one of his slow, damn-I'm-good smiles. "Audrey loves her job. For the most part, that's a good thing. Except she talks about it a lot, and sometimes to people she shouldn't. Like me."

"Yes, I'd say the poor woman's schmooze-o-meter is in serious need of a tune up."

His eyebrows shot up at her comment. "I'd called

Steve about a grant report, and while I was waiting
for him to get on the line, Audrey filled me in on
how work at the gallery was progressing, and then
she went on about a shipment coming into port a
month before the big opening party. I recognized
from her descriptions a number of pieces that had
gone missing from Tikukul. My guess is that Steve
kept them out of sight until the heat died down and
officials were focusing on more recent thefts."

Perplexed, and intrigued, Diana leaned forward.
"So how'd you pull it off? I mean, we're talking an
international port here. You can't just walk in and
out, free as you please."

"I made up a story about how I needed to go
home for a week, then hustled my ass back to New
Orleans and waited for the ship to dock. When it
did, I pretended to be a deliveryman. If you wear a
uniform, you can get into almost any place without
people noticing you or asking many questions. But I
guess that's a trick you've pretty much mastered."

It sounded like he was still a little sore about how
she'd wriggled her way into his house. Diana held
back a sigh. "And then what?"

"Then I bribed the first mate to move the crates to
another part of the cargo hold and return them to the
ship's home port in Peru. I added that if he didn't,
I'd make sure Customs received an anonymous tip
about illegal smuggling."

She sent him an incredulous look. "Wow. You
play rough, don't you?"

"I didn't have time for anything subtle." Jack
rubbed at his jaw, his beard rasping. "I had some
help. One of the Guatemalan archaeologists I work

with knows what's going on. Tomas picked up the crates in Peru and returned them to the museum he works for in Guatemala City."

"Even in Peru, there had to be legal paperwork for customs officers to clear."

"Audrey always let me use her office phone to make private calls. I pulled forms and company letterhead out of her files, copied the original paperwork, and changed it to look like the crates were being returned to Guatemala City. A delivery mixup. Happens all the time," he said, his tone dry. "As long as the paperwork looks good, there's no reason to question a crate of Mayan artifacts going to a major museum, in care of one of that museum's staff archaeologists. I was betting the investigation would focus locally, and no one would be in any rush to notify officials in Peru."

Diana shook her head in amazement. "Very sneaky and simple, which is probably why it worked. Did you also have the ship's officer leave behind the jack of spades?"

"He was more than happy to cooperate in any way that would point blame away from himself. The cops knew about my earlier thefts, so that was another way to make sure they'd focus the investigation in the area rather than check the rest of the ship. What I didn't count on was that they'd leave the jack of spades detail out of the news reports. I wanted Steve to read about it in the papers and figure out what was going on. I don't think Steve made the connection for sure until I grabbed that little box full of big surprises from his office."

For a long moment, Diana stared at him in astonishment. "I'm not sure what to say, except that you'd have made a hell of a professional thief."

He grunted, and took another drink. "If everything goes to hell, and I end up in prison, I'll remember that when I get out. I'll start wearing spandex and a mask. Captain Relic, savior of plundered antiquities, dedicated to vigilante justice."

Diana sent him a reproachful look, amazed that he could joke about something this serious. But with Jack, the humor could hide any number of concerns. "I want to tell you something."

Alerted by her serious tone, his smile faded.

"If things do go bad, I want you to know I'll be there for you."

A look of surprise crossed his face, then something very much like gratitude, before he wiped away all expression. "Stand by your man and all that. Nice, if outdated."

"Jack, please. Just understand that if it happens, it happens. We'll deal with it. And I'll be there for you."

"Thanks." His jaw tensed, then he took a quick breath. "Look, I'm not going to get caught, and the only people who'll ever know I was more than a mild-mannered Mayan archaeologist will be you and Steve. And maybe that cop who was in your office, wearing the smiley-face tie. What's with that guy, anyway?"

"That guy's a very smart cop, despite his atrocious taste in ties. Don't underestimate him." She narrowed her eyes at him. "You're certain Carmichael doesn't know you're really going to Cairo?"

He returned her stare without so much as blinking. "As sure as I can be."

A bit evasive, which she didn't like. "When does your plane leave?"

Jack looked away, mouth thinning.

"I see," she said icily. "You don't want to tell me."

"It would be best if you didn't know."

Anger shot through her. "Dammit, Jack, I'm already about as involved as I can get. Telling me when your plane is leaving won't matter at this point."

He continued to avoid looking at her. "I got you into this mess, so I'm going to make sure you don't get into trouble for having the heart to help me out."

"I can take care of myself."

"I know you're smart and strong, Diana, and from the way you were beating up your punching bag, you can probably kick my ass. But none of that means you'd stand a chance against Steve's money and influence. Don't even try to argue with me on this."

Her inner alarms blared a warning. "You expect him to try to stop you, and you want to keep me out of the way."

Again, the muscle in his jaw flexed.

"Jack, answer me!"

"Yes, I want you out of his line of fire. I told you that already, and I keep telling you why." Finally, he turned, his eyes heated. "Why the hell won't you trust me?"

A twinge of doubt rose at the back of her mind. Small, and brief—but she'd felt it, all the same.

Angry at Jack, at herself for not believing in him 200 percent like she should, Diana snapped, "I'm trying, dammit, but it would help a lot if you'd trust me back."

He couldn't hide the struggle on his face, and an abrupt sadness tugged at her—because she knew exactly what was going through his mind, exactly what made him hesitate.

After all, how many times had it gone through hers? Rebuilding trust wouldn't be easy or quick for either of them.

Finally, he said, "My plane leaves tomorrow, early in the afternoon. Delta, flying from Atlanta to New York, and then to Cairo."

Relief rushed over her, and a sting of tears. She blinked several times, then reached over to take his hand, squeezing it. "Thank you."

"I don't want you there," he said quietly, his face intent, even a little angry. "You stay out of the way, got that? I mean it, Diana. It's my battle, not yours."

Not anymore.

"Diana," he said sharply, his gaze hardening.

"All right."

She made her tone just grudging enough so that her acquiescence sounded genuine—after all, she was a lot better at lying than he was. For once, she could feel good about that.

Though Jack wouldn't like it, she intended to be at that airport, guarding his back. He'd yell at her afterward, but she knew without a doubt that if their positions were reversed, he'd do the same for her.

"I'm getting hungry," he said, changing the subject with his usual lack of finesse. "Let's go back, shower up and change, and head off to that Cajun joint we ate at last night."

"Sounds good to me."

Jack nodded, but didn't move. He continued to watch her with that dark, piercing intensity that always made her faintly uneasy. Then he leaned forward and kissed her hard and long and deeply.

Afterward, Diana helped him pack, trying to ignore her gathering disquiet, and they walked to the bathhouse to change. On the ride back to the beach house, she pressed close against him, hands under his tank, fingers lightly caressing him . . . right now, she couldn't get enough of touching him.

Back at the cottage, getting ready took longer than expected because Jack joined her in the shower. He ended up making love to her in the tub, slipping and sliding and laughing, splashing water and shampoo suds all over the floor.

By the time they finally made it to the restaurant, it was after the dinner rush. He ordered a seafood sampler platter while she ordered blackened catfish, and her tongue was still burning when they returned to the cottage.

"Maybe a glass of chilled wine will cool it off," Jack suggested.

She climbed the steps, fanning her tongue with her hand. "Do you thee blitherth?"

"No blisters. Now stick it back in your mouth, because you're turning me on."

Diana smiled. "I've noticed it doesn't take much to get you all hot and bothered."

"I told you I was easy."

He also looked particularly attackable just now. He'd dressed up for dinner, which meant he'd buttoned his shirt over his tank *and* tucked it into a pair of jeans, while she'd worn the sundress he'd bought—which had added a new challenge to riding the bike and not flashing the neighborhood. All through dinner he'd eyed the laced front, undressing her with his gaze.

Now, standing in the air-conditioned coolness of the living room, the lights dim, Jack's wicked grin roused a deep, inner warmth. Diana smiled. "That wine you mentioned? I'd love some."

"I'll grab a bottle."

"Are you trying to get me tipsy so you can have your way with me?"

He laughed. "It saves time, sweet thing. We can cut right to the good stuff."

"Works for me."

Nothing about Jack Austin was subtle, and that earthy honesty appealed to her. It made her feel sure of herself, every bit a woman. Jack made her feel softer, made her laugh, and when she was with him it was so easy to forget about work and worries, to put all her obligations and pressures into a better perspective.

It had been a long time—too long—since she'd let herself have fun.

Jack showed her what it meant to work hard and play hard, too. Rebuilding her career and her reputation was fine and dandy, as was the healthy bank account and stock portfolio, and the closetful of great clothes, but she wanted more out of her life than just being good at a job. Like most people, she really wanted companionship, friendship, and love—a person to be with, to call her own, to grow old with.

And she had a chance right now to have all that with Jack—providing nothing went wrong at the eleventh hour.

After Jack returned with the glasses and wine, he poured her glass first, then lifted his in a toast, one side of his mouth curving in a half smile. "To beginnings and journeys and discovery."

An odd toast, but captivating, and Diana touched her glass to his with a gentle *tink* sound before taking a small sip.

"My turn." She raised her glass, and frowned, thinking. "I'm not as creative as you. All I can think of is: to us."

His smile widened—without a doubt, that smile was the most beautiful part of him—and clinked glasses with her again. "You're a direct kind of girl. Me, I'm a tease and a major pain in the ass, or so my sisters always say."

He finished off his wine quickly, and taking that as a cue, she tossed back the rest of hers as well.

"More?"

Diana shook her head. "I'm fine, thanks."

Jack plucked the glass from her fingers and set both on the table beside him. Then he turned back to her.

The wall clock counted off the seconds of silence. He didn't make any move, and Diana wasn't sure what to do. After a while she glanced around the room, wondering if she should laugh, tell him to stop looking at her that way, or if she should walk away or kiss him. She should do something, *anything* than just stand here like this.

Finally, holding back a smile, she said, "So."

"So." He still didn't move. "You want to watch some TV?"

The question surprised her—and disappointed her, as she'd been expecting something involving bodily contact and lots of bare skin.

Jack walked up to her in that lazy cat-stalking way of his, then leaned over slightly, and asked in a low voice, "When was the last time you made out on a couch?"

"A long time. I can't really remember."

"Me, either." He nudged her toward the over-stuffed couch, with its cotton slipcovers. "Let's do it."

On a fluttery thrill of anticipation, Diana followed him to the couch—where he promptly sat as far from her as possible, grabbed the remote, and turned on the television.

Diana eyed him as he surfed channels, confusion crowding out her anticipation. Feeling acutely awkward—something she'd not experienced in a good long while—she debated whether she should scoot closer, or—

"*Shields up!*"

The yell came from the television, and she jumped.

"*Fire!*"

Over a pulsating whine, she turned to Jack. "*Star Trek?*"

"Hey, it's classic."

"Ah, yes, Captain James T. Kirk, intergalactic stud, big on blowing up things and boinking green girls." Diana blew out a breath, cheeks puffing. "Where's that wine? I think I need something more to drink."

Jack reached behind him to retrieve her glass and the wine. He filled it as Scotty yelled something dire about dilithium crystals and warp drives, then he settled back on his side of the couch. She raised a brow, sipping her wine, and finally shifted her attention to the TV, where actors were flinging themselves from one side of the bridge to the other as the camera rocked.

Then, very casually, Diana untied the laces at the top of her dress. "Special effects sure have come a long way, huh?"

"Yeah." Jack looked over at her, watching as she tugged at the laces. "Good idea. I think I'll get comfortable, too."

Much to her surprise—and a bit of pique as well—he just unbuttoned his shirt and pulled the tails from his pants. Then he returned to watching TV.

What on earth was he up to?

She finished off her wine and put the glass down on the floor by the couch. Fine; two could play this game. With exaggerated casualness, she loosened the laces even more, revealing a healthy amount of cleavage. Several seconds passed before he transferred his attention from the TV to the front of her dress.

With a blatantly fake yawn, Jack leaned back, then stretched—an expansive and equally calculated stretch that ended with him resting his arm along the back of the couch, behind her shoulders.

Diana almost giggled, and eased closer.

The Federation boys and girls were getting their butts kicked, but between the heady effects of the wine and nearness of Jack's body, she didn't care. He now sat a mere inch or two from her, shoulder by shoulder, hip by hip, thigh by thigh—not touching, but so close. The visceral pull of him was like a hand reaching out and tugging on her heart.

She tingled as if she'd passed through an electrical current, a warm, muzzy buzz that left her all achy and hot, wanting Jack to kiss her, knowing she could make the first move herself, but wanting him to do it.

"Now, Mr. Sulu! Fire!"

Jack leaned closer, and brushed his fingertips along her bare shoulder.

A delicious warmth curled through her. All her senses focused on that soft touch, as she stared unseeingly at the TV.

"Gotcha," Jack said, his words a tickle of breath against her temple.

Sweet anticipation stole over her as she waited for the kiss. After several seconds, she glanced his way. "Yeah. Dumb, skanky aliens in bad makeup."

His fingers touched her shoulder again, moving lower, lightly tracing the swell of her breasts above the loose neckline. Without even realizing what she was doing, Diana pressed closer in encouragement.

Her mouth suddenly dry, she swallowed, and said, "That'll teach them to mess with Kirk."

What was he waiting for? Goose bumps rippled along her skin where he stroked her, where his warm breath caressed her forehead.

Jack shifted, and for a split second she went still

when his leg pressed against hers—frozen to the spot like a nervous virgin.

Why hadn't she noticed before how large and broad he was, how much physically stronger? She glanced at his full bottom lip, the strong line of his nose and jaw, the dark beard stubble, then back down at her hands, clenched in her lap.

"This is crazy," she whispered, overwhelmed by his heat and nearness, by his scent, and terribly aware of his leg touching hers, and that slow, stroking motion of his fingers on her breast.

"Crazy," he agreed, his voice a low rumble, his lips barely touching the skin of her cheek.

"Worse than my first time . . . I was just sixteen and didn't even know what was coming. Wait, wrong word! Oh my God, I'm *babbling*, and I—"

Jack kissed her, his mouth gentle, intent. No probing tongue, only the pressure of lips, lazy and sure and so, so good. Her eyes fluttered closed as his callused palm cupped her chin, and the dry warmth of his lips brushed hers, tasting of Chardonnay, sweet and smooth.

Jack deepened the kiss, one arm closing around her shoulders, pulling her against his chest, his other hand resting on her hip. Diana wrapped her arms around his neck, pressing closer, wanting him to touch her where she ached.

They'd made love so many times already, but by acting like they were on a first date, making her remember years back to when she'd been untouched and naive, he'd made it feel like their first time.

Like she was his one and only, ever and always.

Jack touched his tongue to her lip, and she opened

to him, arching against his hand with a muffled sigh as he cupped her breast through her dress. He made a low growl in response, slipped his hand down the neckline, and lightly touched her.

"You're not wearing a bra."

"Give the boy a prize. He finally noticed. Why don't you just untie it?" Breaking away, she met his eyes. "I know you want to. I saw you staring at the laces all through dinner."

"I'm tempted," he said with a slow grin. "But staying dressed is part of making out on the couch. In case Mom and Dad come home."

"We're alone here, Jack. Nobody's going to interrupt us."

His amused smile told her he wasn't interested in logic. "Remember what it was like, making out like crazy, half-afraid your mom might walk in on you? Or a cop would come along and shine a flashlight into the car?"

Diana laughed, and kissed him again as his thumb brushed across her taut nipple.

"My sisters used to wage guerrilla warfare on my love life, and I learned to achieve maximum enjoyment while shedding a minimum of clothing. Just in case they burst through the door at a crucial moment."

She could see where he was headed with this, and it did bring back fuzzy memories of fumbling around in the dark, of awkwardness and frustration, excitement and a bit of anxiety to spice it up.

"And you're wearing a dress, which is a plus," Jack murmured, moving until he was lying on the couch and she was on top of him.

"Skirts hide a multitude of sins." She lowered her mouth toward his. "I get it."

She kissed him hungrily, feeling the tension of his muscles under her hands, the hardness of his erection through his jeans, pressing against her where she perched on his lap. She wiggled her hips to tease him—payback for making her squirm earlier.

When she sat back, a smile played at the corners of Jack's mouth, his brow arched in speculation, his expression intently expectant. She couldn't help grinning back at him.

"I hope that smile means you're planning on putting me out of my misery."

"Mmmm, I suppose so."

Aware of her gaping neckline, she leaned over until his nose was just inches from her cleavage. Jack's focus shifted, and his smiled turned wolfish.

"I'm gonna make you pay for this," he said with a growl.

"Oooh, I'm shivering, I'm so scared. See?" She wriggled her shoulders dramatically and the neckline slipped off one shoulder, baring most of a breast. He visibly swallowed, his gaze locked on her chest.

He slid his hand through the loosened laces, circling her nipple, teasing it and rolling it between his fingers.

Diana almost whimpered when he pulled his hand away, but then he drew her down against him, kissing her again, his tongue circling her mouth, stroking her tongue. She rubbed against his erection for a long, delicious moment, then moved until she could touch him, fingers lingering over the snap, stroking the zipper until he sucked in his breath sharply through his clenched teeth. She let herself have fun, walking her fingers along his zipper—up and down, up and down—until he laughed.

"Are you gonna do something useful with that or not?" he demanded.

After flashing him a wicked grin, Diana scooted back and *slowly* opened the zipper, revealing the swell of his erection.

She sent him a look from beneath half-lowered lashes. "Oooh, Jack, you're so bad. No underwear?"

"Give the girl a prize. She finally noticed."

"I suppose I'd better make up for my lack of attentiveness," she murmured, and with his help managed to remove her panties without getting off the couch.

"Right front pocket." Perspiration dotted his upper lip. "Make it quick."

Diana slipped her hand in his pocket, searching until she found a condom. She pulled it out, ripped it open, then slipped it over his erection as he watched, a flush of anticipation heating her body. Then she moved back over Jack, legs braced on either side of him, hands on his shoulders, hips poised over his, enjoying the feel of his hot, bare skin beneath hers, the hard press of his erection against her inner thigh.

She slowly lowered her hips, taking him deeply inside her, closing her eyes and sighing with pleasure as he slid his hands beneath her skirt and gripped her bottom.

"That's nice," she murmured, smiling. "I like how you touch me."

"I want to touch you all over," Jack said, his voice tight. "God, you're incredible."

She didn't answer, concentrated on the feelings tightening deep inside her. He let her experiment, moving fast or slow, leaning forward, then back. She ran her hands along his chest, beneath his tank, teasing him as she rocked above him. When she leaned forward he kissed her skin between her breasts, then tongued her nipples through the fabric, which made her shiver with need.

Jack was breathing hard, and she knew he wouldn't last much longer. Wanting them to come together, she leaned forward, and whispered, "Help me along."

He moved his hand lower, his fingers finding where they joined, and as he pumped his hips upward, breathing harshly, his fingers coaxed her faster and harder, and the feel of him inside her, coupled with the touch of his fingers, quickly triggered her climax. She came with a gasp as the jolt of release rocked over her, sharp and sweet and strong. She felt his release, heard him say her name in a low groan as the pleasure continued to pulse through her body, then slowly ebbed after what seemed like forever, and yet not long enough.

Gasping for breath, Diana collapsed on his chest, and Jack's arms closed tightly around her. The thudding of his heartbeat and heat of his body lulled her into closing her eyes. He ran one hand along the back of her thighs, skimming her bare bottom, and the friction of his callused palm was almost more than her sensitized skin could bear.

"Damn," he said. "I don't remember any make-out session on the couch being anywhere near that good."

"There's something to be said for experience." Diana smiled, still listening to the steady beating of his heart. The scent of his musky warmth curled deep inside her, sharply arousing, and when she pulled up his shirt to kiss his belly, he tasted salty and dark.

"That was wonderful," she said with a sigh.

For a long while, they lay in silence as his pulse slowed, and his breathing steadied.

Finally, after another leisurely kiss, Jack scooped her up into his arms and carried her, giggling like a girl, into the bedroom, and fell on top of her with a growl as the bed springs creaked in protest.

"You know what?" he asked.

Something in his voice, or perhaps the stillness of his body, made her breath catch.

"I think I'm crazy in love with you, Sheena."

Her chest squeezed tight, and her belly made a funny little flip.

"Well, guess what?" She kept her voice light, but couldn't disguise the slight tremble. "I think I'm falling in love with you, too."

"Good. It always helps to have the same game plan."

His gaze darkened, but a split second later he flashed her a boyish, open grin that sent a powerful rush of need and love shooting through her. Diana grabbed his head and pulled him down for a deep kiss.

Jack made love to her again before she fell asleep,

her back pressed to his front, his arms around her, legs entwined, thoroughly content and satiated. Her last conscious thought, through a drowsy haze, was almost giddy: *He loves me . . . and everything is going to be fine.*

NINETEEN

...

The rumbling roar of an engine broke through Diana's warm veil of sleep. She stirred, reaching behind her for Jack's body—and found nothing but cool, empty sheets.

In an instant she came fully awake, muscles tensing as she sat up. She quickly rolled out of bed, taking in the red digital numbers on the clock—4:30. She ran for the front of the beach house, but she was too late. The roar of the motorcycle was already fading when she reached the window, and all she saw was the red glow of taillights disappearing around a corner.

She stared out at the darkness, not wanting to believe the obvious. For several seconds she struggled with what he'd done, scattered fragments of excuses rushing to mind . . . and then anger rolled over her, dark and hot.

"Lying son of a *bitch*!" The words started low, and ended in a furious yell as she banged her fist against the wall, hardly feeling the sting of pain.

Shaking from the force of her anger, she turned from the window and stalked back to the bedroom.

She should've seen it coming; should've known he'd pull a dumb-ass stunt like this.

"Dammit," she spat, snapping on the light in the bedroom. She quickly pulled on a shirt, icy fear edging out her fury, then she sat down on the bed.

"Think," she whispered fiercely as she struggled to regain her calm and control.

Okay. Jack was gone—he was getting better at lying, after all—leaving her without any means of transportation on an island that was a two-hour drive to New Orleans. He'd lied about his plane departing early in the afternoon, but she had a hunch the rest of it was true.

Carmichael must know Jack's travel plans, and if she were Carmichael and planning on setting up Jack for a fall, she'd simply pay somebody from security to stop him the minute he walked through the terminal gate. A quick search, the discovery of a suspicious item, a call to the police—and it would all be over. Carmichael would get his box back and, as a bonus, eliminate Jack as a threat.

Or better yet, it would give Carmichael the perfect excuse to "save" Jack, thinking Jack would then be so grateful that he'd do whatever Carmichael wanted. And if not, at least it would be a good threat to keep hanging over his head as an assurance against future good behavior and cooperation.

"Oh, Jack, how could you have been so stupid," she said, on another spurt of furious panic.

Except Jack *wasn't* stupid. He'd known all along

this could happen—and that's why he'd left her behind. Not to prevent her from following, but to delay her long enough to keep her off the playing field and out of Carmichael's way.

All right; she had to get to New Orleans, fast, and while he might have a jump on her, she had an advantage—a phone.

Diana reached across to the nightstand, grabbed the phone, dialed a number she knew by heart, and waited. On the fifth ring, somebody picked up with a sleepy, slurred, "What the . . . 'Lo?"

A male voice. Frowning, she said, "Who's this?"

A pause, as if he wasn't entirely sure he knew the answer. "Mike?"

Ah, Van Dyke Mike. Diana hadn't realized he'd taken to sleeping at Luna's. "Mike, this is Diana. Is Luna there? I need to talk to her. It's important."

"Yeah, um, sure. Hold on."

There was the sound of squeaking mattress springs, a muffled, querulous protest, and Mike said, "Hey, baby, it's for you. It's your boss."

More fumbling, then Luna's sleep-roughened voice asked, "Diana? What's wrong?"

"Everything. I need your help."

A moment's silence followed, and when Luna spoke again, she sounded completely alert. "What do you want me to do?"

"I need you at the airport to stop Jack Austin from getting on a plane."

"Professor *Austin*? But what—"

"Luna, I don't have time for explanations. Please, just hear me out." With an effort, Diana kept her voice calm. "I'm pretty sure he's taking a Delta flight this morning to Atlanta, probably sometime between seven and eight. Delta flies out of Concourse D, if I remember right, so get over there and wait for him to arrive. Stop him. I don't care what you have to do, but no matter what, do not let him go through security."

"Oh."

Diana could hear Luna's breathing, imagined her stunned expression and wide, dark eyes.

"Do you understand?" Diana pressed.

"Um, yes. Go the airport. Find Professor Austin. Don't let him go through security. What's going on?"

"Something you're better off not knowing about."

"Ooookay . . . can I take Mike with me?"

"That'd be good. With two of you, it'll be easier to locate Jack and keep him busy. I'll be there as soon as I can find a ride, but I'm in Grand Isle. It'll take a couple hours."

Which meant she'd have to make a call to one more person, no matter how much she wanted to avoid that.

"Okay. Me and Mike will be there."

"Thanks, Luna. I owe you both big-time."

Diana hurriedly dressed, a single thought running over and over through her mind: how the hell was she going to get to New Orleans?

Commandeer a ride or a car, of course. How else?

The first option to come to mind was the restaurant up the road—one of those little dives that catered to the fact that fishermen and oil drillers didn't have nine-to-five hours. Jack had mentioned in passing that when the oil rig workers had a few days off, they often left to visit relatives. Maybe she'd find somebody getting ready to head to New Orleans—or someone who'd be willing to take a detour.

She flew out of the beach house, taking only her purse, and ran flat out toward the little diner. Breathing heavily, she charged up the steps and pushed open the door.

The instant she walked inside, the low buzz of male conversation halted.

With her wild hair, and wearing jeans, running shoes, and Jack's wine red Hawaiian print shirt, she probably looked a fright—not to mention not quite sane—but to hell with it.

"A friend of mine is in trouble, and I have to help him. I need a ride to New Orleans, fast. I have $250 in my purse, and I'm willing to double that."

A heavy silence met this rushed, breathless announcement.

The heavyset older man working the counter spoke first. "Aren't you that gal staying with the Austin boy?"

The Austin *boy*? Diana blinked in surprise, still gulping air, then nodded. "Yes."

"Jack in trouble?"

Again she nodded, hands on her hips, suddenly light-headed, and telling herself it wasn't because she was out of shape—it was the heat, the desperate all-out run, too much wine, too much sex, and not enough sleep.

And sheer terror.

"Hell, I've known Dave and Lorna for years, and

their kids, too. You've come to the right place, and you can forget about the money. Around here, we look after our own." The man turned toward the open door leading to the kitchen area, and bellowed, "Darryl, get out here!"

Darryl turned out to be a younger, slimmer, and neater version of the counterman—except for the cast on his left arm, and a healing cut on his cheek.

"My boy works the shrimp boats, but he had himself an accident and he's laid up for a bit." To his son, the man said tersely, "This here lady needs a ride to N'Awlins, and she's in a hurry."

If Darryl was surprised by a request to haul a strange woman halfway across the state at the crack of dawn, it didn't show on his face. He turned to Diana as he fished out a cigarette from his shirt pocket, then said, "C'mon."

Just like that. No questions. Nothing.

Almost shaking with relief, Diana followed and climbed up the running board of a mud-spattered, older-model Ford pickup with huge wheels, a roll bar, and floodlights mounted on the front, and sat next to the laconic Darryl in the truck's pristine interior.

Darryl opened the window, lit the cigarette, then started the truck and took off as if he had a boot full of lead.

Diana hurriedly buckled her seat belt, wedging her purse between her feet so its contents wouldn't spill out the next time he took a hairpin curve, and tried not to dwell on how he'd ended up with a broken arm and cut face to begin with.

"I appreciate your help, Darryl—my name's Diana, by the way—but I'd prefer if we didn't end up getting pulled over by any state troopers."

Darryl sucked in a lung full of nicotine, then jerked his chin upward. "Got a fuzzbuster."

"Oh. Okay." The dark, nearly empty highway stretched out ahead of them, surrounded by murky black bayou. Hopefully all the cops were busy elsewhere.

And speaking of cops, she couldn't put off that other call any longer. She glanced at Darryl, who was resting his cast on the open window, driving one-handed, cigarette dangling from his mouth, and looking far too relaxed for someone going 90 mph, then pulled her cell phone from her purse.

"I have to call a friend."

She dug out her address book and dialed Bobby's phone. It rang a few times, then he picked up—and he didn't sound any more awake than Luna had. "Yeah?"

"Bobby, it's Diana."

He muttered something crude. "You know what the hell time it is?"

Since it was an idiotic question, all she said was, "I need your help."

"Where are you?"

"At the moment I'm in a pickup with a guy named Darryl, doing about ninety on Highway 1."

A short silence, and when he spoke again, his voice was clear and cool. "Okay. Where *were* you? I called your office Friday, and your secretary said she didn't know where you were, but that you'd headed out of town. I was getting a little concerned, darlin'."

"I was in Grand Isle with Jack Austin. Bobby, I need you to meet me at the airport. I think Jack's in trouble, and I have a feeling I'm going to need someone with a badge behind me."

"What'd he do?"

Again, Diana glanced at Darryl, puffing on his cigarette and seemingly indifferent to her conversation. "He hasn't done anything yet, but I need to stop him before he goes through security with something that'll be really hard to explain . . . if you catch my meaning."

He swore again. "Do you want me to try and grab him at his place first? Have a squad pick him up?"

Diana hesitated, thinking quickly. Jack had left all his clothing behind, but she doubted he'd ride all the way to his cottage, then turn around and head back to Kenner and the airport. As for a patrol car pulling Jack over . . . if she brought in outside help, there were no guarantees she could control the outcome. She didn't dare risk it.

"No to both," she said. "I don't want to bring in the police on this, except for you, and I don't think he's going home. He planned this trip a while ago, so I'm guessing he has everything he needs with him. Can you just meet me at the Delta terminal?"

"When?"

Diana checked her watch, then the speedometer. "We should be there by seven at the latest." Unless they got busted for speeding. "Is that okay?"

"I'll be there." He paused. "Are we expecting company?"

"Seems a good possibility."

"Okay. I'll make sure to come fully accessorized."

His comment made her smile despite the gnawing tension, and she said good-bye, disconnected, and returned the phone to her purse.

"Boyfriend troubles?" Darryl asked, not taking his eyes from the road.

"You could say that."

"He ain't trying to skip outta town on you or something?"

"No."

Darryl glanced her way, and for the first time he smiled. He had a nice smile, despite the scabbed-over gash on his face. "What's he driving? How much of a jump does he got on me?"

"He's on a white Honda, one of the big sport touring bikes, about thirty minutes ahead of us. I'm betting he can go a lot faster than your truck."

"Don't bet too much. I'll catch him."

Although she didn't believe it, Diana nodded, and leaned forward in the seat—as if by doing so she could make the truck get to Jack faster.

Then she'd kick his very fine butt clear into the next parish for scaring her to death like this.

To Jack, the ride to the airport seemed to take a lot longer than it should've, considering that he'd practically rocketed along the entire distance.

An invisible chain of guilt had dragged behind him all the way, tying him to a pink cottage where he'd left a beautiful woman sleeping alone. A woman he'd just admitted to loving, a woman who'd asked him not to ever let her down—and he'd tricked her anyway.

Halfway to the airport he knew he'd made a mistake, but it was too late to turn back, and no amount of telling himself that he had to make that plane, that everything would work out in the end, helped him feel any better. Diana might not forgive him for what he'd done, and a chilly unease hung over him the rest of the way to the airport.

Diana *could* take care of herself, and keeping her out of Steve's way by force or dirty tricks wasn't the answer, even if it had seemed to be a short while ago.

She would be mad as hell when she figured out what he'd done, and Jack knew she wouldn't sit meekly behind. And if he'd really wanted to sneak away, he should've walked the bike down the road before starting the engine, but he hadn't.

Maybe it had been his way of alerting her, not as direct as leaving a note behind, but pretty much the same thing. She'd know where he was going, and it would be her choice to follow him or not.

He'd kept glancing over his shoulder the entire way, half-fearing to see the flashing lights of a squad car ordering him to pull over, half-hoping that somehow she'd followed him. But even if she'd managed to find a car or talk someone into driving her to the airport, he had too big a lead.

And that was a good thing, he reminded himself yet again.

The sky had lightened to gray by the time Jack pulled into the airport and parked the bike in the long-term parking lot. After pulling off his helmet, he rolled his head to ease the ache in his shoulder and neck muscles, then swung off the bike and headed into the terminal.

A familiar prickling of adrenaline propelled

through him as the automatic doors whooshed open to admit him.

Steve would try to stop him, and he was ready. This time, for once, he had all the cards, and no way in hell was he going to fold.

Jack made his way into the terminal, glancing at his watch. Just past 6:45. His flight was leaving at 7:30.

Everything was proceeding according to his plan.

The terminal wasn't empty, but not as busy as it could've been on a Monday morning. He walked quickly past the check-in counters along the ticket lobby, heading straight for the concourse and security gate.

Jack took a long, deep breath, preparing himself for the inevitable. Steve would either have him intercepted as he went through security, or just before he boarded the plane. He hoped it'd be the former, as all he had on him now was his wallet—and the locker key.

Ahead, a businessman laid his luggage on the conveyor and walked through the metal detector, smiling a polite greeting at the security guards— two women and an older man, all watching Jack's approach.

Which one of them had Steve promised a fat reward for reeling in his renegade archaeologist?

This is it . . .

Just as he put his hand in his pocket to pull out his keys, an unfamiliar female voice called from behind him: "Professor Austin! Hey!"

He stopped and turned on reflex. "Jesus," he muttered, staring at the small group hurrying toward him.

Young, and all in shades of black, purple, and red. Spiked hair, dark makeup. Leather.

What was this? Refugees from the set of *Buffy the Vampire Slayer*?

Then he recognized the slender woman in the short black leather skirt, black fishnet stockings, and red lace top as Diana's secretary, although he couldn't remember her name.

A damn vampire cavalry had arrived to rescue him, which meant Diana must've called out the troops shortly after he'd left the cottage.

Which also meant she was on her way to the airport. If not already there.

The others in the airport made way for the group of Goth kids, and behind them, he spied two burly security guards following, their faces grim and intent.

Great.

For a split second he considered making a run for it anyway, but sanity prevailed—not to mention a healthy spurt of anger. He hadn't wanted to draw attention to himself, but with the Vampire Brat Pack closing on him, going unnoticed was pretty much impossible now.

The secretary reached him first. Behind her stood three young men and a wild-haired woman wearing a black leather vest—sans shirt—and a sparkly, purple flounced skirt. One man was stocky and black, his head shaved, nose and eyebrow pierced, and his tight black T-shirt revealed heavily tattooed arms. The other two men were white, the first sullen and dark-haired, decked out in black denim and knit, while the other was tall and thin, peroxide blond hair cut short, and with a black mustache and goatee beard. He also wore all black: canvas trench coat, clunky boots with lots of showy buckles, tight leather pants, and a mesh tank that revealed pale skin beneath. He sported earrings and a nose stud.

Jack took a quick breath when they surrounded him. "Okay. Don't take this wrong, but who the hell are you people?"

"I'm Luna, remember me? I'm—"

"Diana's assistant, yeah, I remember. So who're they?"

"That's Iris." Luna pointed to the wild-haired woman. "The black dude's Dawayne, this is Tyler, and the guy in the coat is Mike."

"If you have a message from Diana, make it quick," Jack said. "I'm in a hurry."

"Um, no message, Professor Austin. We just can't let you go into the gate area. Sorry."

Annoyed, Jack glanced past the group toward the approaching security guards. "How do you plan on doing that? Sit on me? Tie me up?"

"If that's what it takes, man," said Dawayne, his voice a deep, lazy rumble, "then that's what we do."

"Not unless you want to get arrested. Two security guards are right behind you." Jack reined in his impatience. "Look. I know what Diana is trying to do here, but she's wrong. You guys back off and let me take care of things."

"Can't do that," said Mike the Trench Coat, his tone void of emotion. "We get busted, you get busted with us. We're all cool with that."

It took an effort, but Jack didn't move, not even

when the two security guards stepped between him and Diana's crew.

"Are these people bothering you, Dr. Austin?" asked the older of the two guards.

Dr. Austin?

Jack stared hard at Steve's flunkies. They hadn't been trying to intercept the vampires; they'd been trying to get to him first.

"No," he said curtly. "I just need a minute alone with this woman."

Without waiting for a response, Jack grabbed Luna's arm and yanked her after him as he moved a short distance from the group. Mike frowned, making motions to follow, but a look from the thick-necked security guard made him reconsider.

These kids dressed like toughs, and were probably mouthy and full of shit half the time, but they weren't dangerous or violent. In a confrontation, they'd give way—and follow his orders, if he handled them right.

"I have to get to my plane," Jack said tightly, looking Luna in the eye. "If I don't, things will get ugly, I promise you that."

"She says you're in trouble, Professor Austin."

"This is the kind of trouble I have to face head-on, not avoid. It works better that way."

"I was told to stop you, no matter what."

"She's wrong."

The girl looked both uncertain and stubborn, and her gaze darted toward her friends. Then she took a deep breath, and squared her shoulders. "Maybe, but I'm following the boss's orders."

"Luna," Jack said after a moment, his tone almost gentle. "I'm going through that gate. The only way to stop me is to knock me down, and I guarantee I won't make it easy."

She chewed her lip, frowning.

Damn. He really didn't want a fight, but if he didn't—

"Jack! There you are."

At the sound of that faint Texas twang, Jack slowly turned.

"It's about time, buddy. You're late for our meeting."

On the other side of the security gate stood Steve Carmichael, dressed in a crisp dark suit, looking every inch the powerful multimillionaire that nobody, but nobody, dared mess with.

As Jack's gaze locked with Steve's, he was unable to hold back a small, wry smile. It seemed he'd been a touch premature in assuming everything was going according to his plan.

Well, he'd just do what he did best: improvise.

"Sorry, Steve. I had a few delays." Jack turned back to the group behind him, caught Luna's attention, and mouthed the words: *Follow me.*

These kids could help him simply by being five pairs of very observant eyes.

Then he faced Steve again and walked forward. The guards at the gate went alert, gazes sharp. Steve smiled pleasantly, and Jack was suddenly aware of the tension behind him, in front of him, thick enough to cut.

If he made one wrong move, the security guards

wouldn't hesitate to take him down—assuming the kids behind him didn't grab him first.

With a deceptive casualness, he tossed his keys and pocket change into the plastic tray, and caught the flash of annoyance on Steve's face when he saw the locker key.

Jack passed through the metal detector, and although no alarm sounded, the two women watched him with a piercing intensity. A smug smile had replaced Steve's annoyance by the time Jack stopped in front of him.

For a long moment he held the gaze of the man he'd once thought his friend. Nobody moved. Even the pervasive din around them seemed to have faded, all the world having narrowed to him and Steve, staring each other down. High Noon at Concourse D.

"Looks like we may have a change of plans," Steve said at length, his voice pitched for Jack's ears alone. "I appear to have underestimated you."

"Again," Jack said, with fierce satisfaction, as Steve's smile faltered. "And I have a plane to catch, so we'll have to keep this short and sweet."

Diana arrived in time to see Jack saunter through the security gate. She swore under her breath, then looked over at Bobby as she quickened her pace—not quite running, but close to it. "That guy in the expensive suit by Jack? That's Steve Carmichael."

"Sounds like you didn't expect to see him here."

"No." Hired grunts, yes . . . the top banana, hardly. "And now I don't know what to think."

She couldn't see Jack any longer, but Luna and her friends had followed Jack as well.

Why the hell hadn't Luna stopped him like she'd ordered?

With a stab of unease, she noticed two thick-set security guards closing in behind Luna's group—after a short nod from Carmichael.

A major confrontation looked inevitable, and she grimaced, glancing down at her jeans and Jack's Hawaiian shirt, which practically hung down to her knees.

Noticing the direction of her gaze, Bobby asked, "What's wrong?"

"Just an attack of nerves. I'd feel a lot tougher and badder if I had on a really expensive suit and a pair of killer heels."

He gave a short bark of laughter. "I thought you were going for the *Magnum P.I.* look." When she glared at him, he shrugged. "Don't worry. You're prettier than Tom Selleck. And not as hairy, either."

She actually smiled despite the pounding tension, and by then they'd reached the security gate. Bobby displayed his shield along with his gun for the security guards, and since he was a cop, he was allowed to pass through the gate armed.

"Something wrong, Detective?" asked one of the women at the security area.

"Nope." Bobby flashed his good ol' Alabama boy grin. "My friend is running late. I'm just here to see her off before I head to work."

Despite his casual explanation, Diana could tell the guards remained suspicious. Not that she could blame them; the confrontation between Jack and

Luna's pals had to strike them as out of the ordinary.

Diana passed through security without any trouble, and with Bobby at her side walked swiftly through the crowded concourse.

It didn't take long to find Jack; all she had to do was look for Luna's crowd, who couldn't blend in even if they tried. She spotted the black-clad knot huddled outside a snack shop, looking uncertain for all their menacing posturing and clothing.

When Luna caught sight of Diana and Bobby, her eyes widened. She grabbed Mike's arm, pointing, and her friends turned as well. Diana recognized Iris, the card reader from Jackson Square.

"Isn't that your secretary? What's she doing here?" Bobby asked.

"I called and told her to find Jack and corral him."

"Doesn't look like she quite got the corral part."

"She's a little in awe of Jack, and I wouldn't put it past him to use that to his advantage."

"Okay." Bobby glanced over at her. "So am I the good cop, the bad cop, or no cop at all? What's the plan, *kemo sabe*?"

"I don't have one," she admitted. "Except to keep from having another lover end up in prison. I'm going to take a cue from Jack Austin on this, and fly by the seat of my pants."

"That's my favorite kind of plan." A beatific smile lit Bobby's face. "I love this John Wayne shit."

TWENTY

...

Jack sat across from Steve. To casual passersby they probably looked like two old friends getting together for a quick chat before one of them left on a trip.

Most people wouldn't notice that the two security guards behind Steve, and the group of tough-looking kids behind him, were all part of a quiet war being waged over steaming Styrofoam cups and untouched pastries in an airport coffee shop.

"What's with the gang in black?" Carmichael asked, his tone genuinely curious as he glanced over Jack's shoulder.

"They're just some people who want to see me make my flight." He leaned back, picking up his coffee. "I have to say I was surprised to see you here. Since when do you personally take care of the dirty work?"

"Since you made things personal between us." Carmichael folded his arms over his chest, raising a brow. "You've put me in a very uncomfortable position. I hope you understand that."

"Me?" Jack sipped at the hot, bitter coffee, hardly tasting it. It took almost all his concentration to keep from unleashing his temper. "Seems you managed that all by yourself. You started this. I'm just finishing it."

"You were never a stupid man, Jack. Don't start now."

"I could say the same for you."

Jack maintained eye contact—and for the first time that he could ever remember, Steve looked away first, although he covered it with a soft laugh. "You have nothing on me."

"And again, that goes both ways."

"Not entirely. You stole my box, my very precious and rare box, and I can prove it."

"I'd like to see you try to explain that in front of a judge." Jack smiled as he slowly leaned forward. "Fact is, you can't afford to, and the only reason you're here right now is a last-ditch effort to muscle me into going along with your bullshit plans. But it's not going to happen. I'm getting on my plane in a few minutes, and you won't give me any trouble about it."

"You're so sure of that?" Anger flashed in the older man's eyes, along with a shadow of disbelief—or maybe it was simple astonishment.

"I've never been more sure of anything in my life."

And that was one whopper of a lie.

"So what's the point of it all? The thefts, the jack of spades . . . which, by the way, was quite clever of you. I always admired your joie de vivre, your relentless good humor."

Jack ignored the last mocking comment. "I'm taking back control of my work, that's what. Maybe I can't stop you from smuggling, but I can make damn sure you won't use me or Tikukul anymore. This game's mine, and I'm calling your bluff."

"You can't. Not without revealing your own illegal proclivities. The first law of survival, my friend, is to never back yourself into a corner."

"Don't call me friend," Jack said coldly, gratified to see amazement cross Steve's face. "And if revealing that I'm a thief is what it takes to bring you down, then that's what I'll do."

A shadow of doubt flickered in Steve's eyes before he shook his head. "You don't have the guts for that."

"Wrong again, Steve."

Even if it meant facing a conviction, he'd do it to stop the looting and to expose Steve Carmichael's lies.

Very quietly, he added, "I've come this far; I may as well see it to the end. And while I might not be able to escape the consequences, I'm betting the tide of sympathy will swing my way and I'll never see the inside of a prison cell. I will stop you—and I will protect what's mine."

Steve's gaze shifted over Jack's shoulder, and whatever he saw made him smile. "You're forgetting one thing. I have a long reach, a lot of friends in high places. I made you, Jack, and I can unmake you. And those close to you."

Jack put down his cup to answer, when a smooth, feminine voice from behind him said, "The Jack you made is now public. To tear him down, you'll have to do it publicly. Somehow, I have a feeling you won't want to risk that, Mr. Carmichael."

"Well, well," Steve said, his tone amused. "Looks like some late-arriving baggage. I believe it's yours, Jack."

As a sinking sensation settled in the pit of his belly, Jack twisted around in his chair to face Diana. He'd wanted to spare her this petty ugliness, yet he was absurdly happy to see her—even if she looked totally pissed off. And beautiful, in a narrow-eyed, stern-jawed kind of way, the high color in her cheeks nearly matching the color of her shirt.

Her cop friend stood beside her, hands on his hips to push his navy suit coat back and casually reveal not only his detective shield, but his service piece. He wore a tie with little Betty Boops on it, which seemed all the more surreal considering the pack of pseudovampires gathered at his back.

Not even in his wildest imaginings could he have come up with a more bizarre scenario than this for his final showdown with Steve.

Finally, Jack found his voice, and demanded, "What the hell are you doing here?"

"It's called teamwork, Jack. A concept we're both a little rusty with." To Steve she said coolly, "I hope you don't mind if Detective Halloran and I join you?"

"Please do." Steve made an expansive gesture, then glanced at the two security guards who stood close at hand, obviously waiting for orders.

Intercepting him at the security gate had fizzled, but they could still stop him as he headed to the jetway, with some excuse to detain him and search him and his baggage. He wasn't in the clear yet—and wouldn't be until he was actually sitting in that plane and on his way to Atlanta.

The PA system crackled, and a woman's voice said: *"Attention, please. At this time we would like to begin preboarding passengers for Delta Airlines flight 788 with service to Atlanta through gate 3-D."*

That was his flight. Time was running short.

Diana sat down on his right, the detective on his left. The vampire cavalry moved closer, acting more sure of themselves. Tyler draped his arms around Iris, while Luna stood between Trench Coat Mike and Dawayne—and everybody in the coffee shop stared at them with various shades of unease.

"How long were you standing behind me?" Jack demanded.

"We heard enough of the good stuff to know what's going on," answered the blond cop in his easy drawl. He had pale, cold eyes, and despite the weird tie and casual sprawl, he radiated an air of violence.

Jack tamped down a renewed rush of anger. Christ; Steve was so damn sure he was above the law that he'd threatened him while a cop stood easily within hearing distance.

"Too many people." Jack looked back toward Steve. "A cop, a private investigator, and all those kids. Anything you do will be witnessed by every one of them."

As if on cue, Luna stepped closer, and her friends followed. They gathered behind him, Diana, and Halloran. Luna even went so far as to rest one hand on Jack's shoulder, and her other on Diana's. From the corner of his eye, Jack could see the black polish on her short nails. Iris moved languidly toward Steve, trailing a longer nail—hers painted bloodred—across the tabletop.

As she approached Steve, the older security guard hurried forward to block her, and asked in a gruff voice, "Sir?"

Steve's gaze tracked the faces behind Jack. While he wasn't smiling, he didn't look concerned, either—a man too used to doing whatever he wanted, getting whatever he wanted. A man who didn't consider himself in the wrong.

"It's all right."

Without a word, the security guard retreated—and Jack caught the uneasy look that passed between him and the other guard.

Iris leaned forward, smiling. She broke off a piece of Steve's untouched pastry, and popped it into her mouth. "Stale," she said in a mournful tone. "So terribly stale."

After a brief, bemused look, Steve ignored her.

Halloran eased his chair back, presumably to allow himself room to respond if things got ugly. While part of Jack registered these details, his focus remained on Diana, on the tension on her face, the concern for him in her eyes that she couldn't hide.

"I'm rather disappointed in you, Ms. Belmaine," Steve said mildly. "I believed I'd hired a pragmatic, and instead I bought a lovesick fool. But I suppose I can't blame you. Jack has a knack for getting into the beds of even the smartest women. Though this was record time, even for him."

On a burst of raw fury, Jack lunged toward Carmichael, but Diana, Halloran, and Luna forced him back down.

"Jack, sit," Diana ordered sharply, glaring as she placed a restraining hand on his chest. Keeping it there, she leaned over the table toward Steve, and said in a quieter voice, "The pragmatic part of this lovesick fool knows that bringing any suit against you is pointless, as you'd probably just get off with a fine and some community service. But it's over, Carmichael. Your supply line just dried up, and now you're going to let Jack get on his plane."

"I'm not the one acting violently." Carmichael looked pointedly at Jack. "This man is a menace. A terrible thing, air rage. He needs to be detained, so I'm afraid letting him go isn't an option."

"Oh, I think it is." Diana tipped her head toward Halloran. "This guy next to me is Detective Halloran. He's an honest cop, but," she paused for emphasis, "he's also a genius when it comes to bending rules."

Several seconds passed before Steve asked, "Are you threatening me?"

"Uh-uh," Halloran said. "Not me. I'm sworn to protect and serve. But when it comes to this lovely lady here, I don't believe I have much control over what she might do. And she's a feisty little thing."

Jack let himself relax a fraction, amazed that all these people were here to help him. Strangers, all of them, helping him simply because Diana had asked. Because it was the right thing to do.

It went a long way in restoring his faith in people, in believing that trust and integrity were alive and well—even with these kids who dressed like punks.

"I'm not threatening you, either, only laying out all the facts." Diana smiled pleasantly. "Right now, I'm tending toward the good old anonymous tip. I bet a reporter or two at the *Picayune* would love to take on a story like this. Think of all that attention, Mr. Carmichael, unrelenting and focused on your every move, every single day, week after week, month after month."

Taken aback by the fierceness in her voice, Jack turned toward Diana, hit by a bolt of pure admiration for this woman at his side.

God, he loved her.

Above the airport din came a faint voice on the PA: *"Ladies and gentleman, we are now boarding Delta Airlines flight 788 . . ."*

"That's my plane." Jack stood, and Diana also came to her feet. He stared down at Steve. "If you're going to do anything, you better do it now. I'm in a hurry."

Steve glanced at the two waiting security guards, and Halloran slowly stood. He fixed the two uneasy guards with a piercing stare. "You're not needed here any longer, boys. Move on along."

Steve's thugs didn't like that "boys" crack at all.

"I don't follow your orders," said the younger of the two guards, moving forward, his demeanor suddenly menacing, his thick shoulders hunched.

Dawayne said, "Awright, a fight! I could use me some action."

Diana grabbed the kid by his powerful arm. "Throw the first punch, and I'll kick your ass myself."

Offended, Dawayne turned, taking in Diana from head to toe. The look on his face told her he wasn't too impressed by her threat. "And if he throws the first punch?"

"Then you can beat him senseless; I don't care. Just don't hit first."

Jack didn't move, unused to other people getting him out of his tight spots.

"Mr. Carmichael?" the older security guard asked, his skin a grayish color, perspiration gleaming on his forehead. "What would you like us to do, sir? Take Dr. Austin into custody?"

"Touch me, and you'll regret it," Jack said evenly. "So what's it going to be, Steve? This is getting old."

Almost as an echo, a voice close by said, ". . . Steve Carmichael, isn't it? I wonder what the trouble is . . ."

Steve's gaze flicked briefly to a nearby table, his face tight with barely controlled fury, and then he turned his attention to the guards. "There's nothing wrong. You can go."

"But—"

"I said go." Steve smiled as he said it, but he spoke through clenched teeth.

Reluctantly, the guards left, and as a final act of bravado the younger one sauntered between Dawayne and Trench Coat Mike, shouldering aside the two young men.

Mike whirled and made to go after him, eyes glittering with temper and testosterone, but Luna hauled him back by the tail of his coat.

A charged silence fell as Steve stared first at Diana, then at Bobby. Finally, he turned his attention back to Jack, and demanded flatly, "What do you want from me?"

What Steve meant was: *What can I give you so that you'll keep your mouth shut?*

Relief rushed over Jack. He'd *won*. Even if there'd be no legal consequences or public scandal for what Steve had done, Jack had hit him where it hurt the most—his pride and ego—and that was good enough for him.

"You keep funding me," Jack answered. "Until I find a new sponsor, which shouldn't be too hard, considering all the media exposure you've conveniently provided."

Steve nodded once; a short, tight gesture.

"I want complete control over my digs, and that includes hiring the workers. Nothing, and I mean *nothing*, goes missing. If even one potsherd disappears, I send a letter to the newspaper."

Again, a brief nod. "Anything else?"

"Yes, there is one more thing." Jack leaned over, fists on the table. "I want my mask back, you son of a bitch."

Beside him Diana stiffened, her eyes widening in understanding. "The mask in the Jade Jaguar. My God," she whispered. "Your lost king?"

He nodded, holding his anger in check with an effort. "It was the one thing I couldn't steal back. The gallery was beyond my B&E skills."

"A mask." Halloran sauntered over to Steve, standing close. "And one that doesn't belong to you. Tsk-tsk. I do believe, sir, that you're about to make a generous donation to the government of Guatemala."

Iris leaned against the table at Steve's other side and bent to stare into his face. He jerked back, glaring.

"You have a dark aura," she said, her accent heavy. "But this policeman is right. You must atone, or face ruination. So it is written; so it shall be."

Holding back a smile, Jack glanced at Diana, who wore a carefully blank expression.

Halloran tapped Steve's shoulder. "Get up. You and me are gonna take a ride back to your gallery and have a look at this mask—along with anything else that strikes my fancy."

"I have no intention of—"

"You don't want to go there." Halloran held up his hand and, amazingly, Steve shut up. "And you don't want to start pretending that I won't be keeping a very close eye on business at your gallery. If you're a smart man, you'll behave yourself."

"Now that's something I've heard before," Diana murmured, and smiled.

Steve's mouth thinned as he stood, and when he looked at Jack, dark fury glittering in his eyes.

"Let's go, Mr. Carmichael."

Steve stalked off with Halloran at his side, and they were soon lost in the crowd.

"Well, that was fun," Diana said after a moment, slanting a glance up toward Jack. "What do you think? Can I kiss my fee good-bye?"

"I wouldn't count on him paying you, no." Jack stepped close and took her by the shoulders. "Did you just rescue me?"

"Uh-huh." A smile, tentative at first, then smug. "Looks that way, doesn't it?"

The airport PA system crackled again: *"Delta Airlines flight 788 with service to Atlanta is now in the final boarding process through gate 3-D. Any remaining passengers should immediately report to the gate area."*

Damn; he needed a few more minutes to make things right with her—he couldn't leave without doing that.

Diana was still smiling, but he didn't miss the mix of emotion in her eyes, all the excitement, worry, and something of a lingering anger. She opened her mouth to speak again, but before she could do so, Jack pulled her close and kissed her—deeply and thoroughly, until they had to come up for air. Behind him, somebody let out a loud whistle, and Luna crowed, "Yeah, baby!"

Pulling back, Diana said in a shaky voice, "I think you have a plane to catch."

A sudden thought came to Jack—crazy, but then most of his best ideas were crazy—and he grinned.

"I'm serious—if you want to be on that plane, you better haul ass over to gate 3-D. You still have a passport in that purse?"

She blinked in surprise at his abrupt question. "Yes."

"Good. Come to Cairo with me."

Her mouth dropped, then she sucked in her breath and shook her head. "Jack, I can't do that."

"Why? You have some big plans you didn't tell me about? We'll be back in a few days. On Thursday night."

"Oh God, you're *serious?* But I . . . I have reports and cases I should've finished by now, and—"

"I can take care of them, Boss." Luna flashed a

sudden smile, an oddly wholesome one in contrast to her clothes and dark makeup. "I'll cover for you if you promise to fill me in on all the details. And I do mean *all* the details."

Diana still looked overwhelmed. "But I don't have any clothes. And what about a visa? I'm sure I need one, and if—"

"We'll have a long layover in Atlanta; we can catch a cab and go buy you a few things. And you can get a visa when we land in Cairo. I've done it before, and I'm sure you have, too." Completely charmed by her blush, her flustered expression, he added in a cajoling tone, "Come on, Diana. We have some unfinished business to take care of, too."

Annoyance edged out her shock. "Not to mention you owe me a big, fat apology!"

"Considering how long it'll take to fly to Egypt, we'll have plenty of time to talk. And kiss and make up." Jack ran his gaze slowly over her, smiling. Something about her all but drowning in one of his old shirts turned him on, big-time. "Did I tell you just how sexy you look wearing my shirt?"

"Not here, Jack." Her cheeks turned a fascinating shade of pink. "All right. It appears I don't have anything to do that can't wait a few days. And come to think of it, it's been a while since I gave myself a vacation." She turned to Luna. "Thanks. I owe you one."

"Down-and-dirty details will do," Luna said cheerfully as Jack seized Diana's hand and pulled her toward him. "But if you can't swing that, a raise is okay, too. Bye now, and have fun!"

They ran to a nearby row of lockers. Stopping in front of one, Jack pulled the corresponding key out of his pocket, opened the door, and hauled out a small carry-on bag.

Diana sighed. "You had it here all along."

"Since last week." He hurriedly shrugged into a suit coat, and made a halfhearted attempt to smooth away the wrinkles.

"And our troublesome little box?"

"Right in here." He patted the luggage. "Inside a box wrapped in happy birthday paper with a big yellow bow and a card taped to the side addressed to Aunt Lucy."

"Who's Aunt Lucy?"

"Beats the hell out of me." Jack grabbed the suitcase in one hand, Diana's hand in the other, and they took off at a run.

"God, Jack," Diana gasped out, "I can't believe I'm doing this!"

The ticket agent couldn't believe it, either, and barely concealed her annoyance at having to print out a ticket at the last minute.

While they waited, Jack glanced down at his hand, still holding Diana's, and when he looked up again, he caught her watching him with a soft smile.

"You're a closet romantic, Jack," she murmured. "You know that, right?"

His lips twitched in a reluctant smile. "Shhh. Don't tell."

"I doubt it's much of a secret to anybody who's known you for more than five minutes." She playfully poked him with her elbow. "Not that it lets you off the hook for stranding me in a cottage with a bunch of flamingos. You should've trusted me to cover your butt."

"I know, and I'm sorry. I wanted to keep you safe, and halfway to the airport I realized I'd been an idiot, but it was too late to go back. Besides, I'm not used to depending on anybody but myself. This teamwork thing . . . you're right, it doesn't come easy for me." Seeing her uncertainty, he added quickly, "But we'll work on it."

A sudden brightness glimmered in her eyes, and Jack grimaced. "Hooboy, please tell me those are the good kind."

She laughed, then sniffed. "Most definitely the good kind."

"*Excuse* me." The ticket agent cleared her throat. "Here's your ticket, ma'am. You both can board now. And quickly, please. I'm closing the door in one minute."

As Diana took her ticket, Jack placed his hand at the small of her back, then steered her toward the jetway.

Right before they boarded the plane, Diana stopped and surprised him with a quick, hard kiss.

"What was that for?" he asked, over the whine of jet engines.

"For the guy who stole my heart. And the best part of it is that you don't ever have to give it back."

"Good. Because I wasn't planning on it."

He returned her kiss, already imagining the many ways they could pass those dry, hot hours in Cairo. "I meant what I said that night, you know. From now on, you're the only one for me. And I'm the only one for you."

"Oooh," Diana purred, leaning against him so that her breast brushed his arm. "I love it when you get all alpha on me. This is going to be such fun."

"Always. That I can promise you." Under the amused gazes of the pilots and cabin crew, Jack took her hand. Squeezing it lightly, he stepped into the plane with her at his side, and grinned. "Let the fun begin."

EPILOGUE

...

Yawning widely, Diana shuffled into her sunny kitchen, sniffing at the scents of warm toast and brewing coffee. Jack wasn't much of a cook, but he could whip up a mean plate of buttered toast.

He was already sitting at the breakfast bar, his coffee and cereal bowl in front of him, and he glanced up from the newspaper as she walked in. Hair tousled, badly in need of a shave, he looked sexy and lovable wearing men's cotton pajama bottoms with a football motif. She was wearing the top—and nothing else.

"Morning, beautiful."

"Morning," she said, her voice still raspy with sleep, as she sat on the stool beside him. "Aren't we disgustingly cute. We match."

Amusement gleamed in his dark eyes. "Yeah, that we certainly do."

He slid a cereal bowl her way, along with a spoon, jug of milk, and a box of Cocoa Krispies. Then he poured her a cup of coffee, and set it in front of her.

"You take such good care of me, Jack," Diana murmured, and took a grateful gulp of coffee.

Hot and strong. Just perfect.

It had been four months since they'd returned from their uneventful adventure in Cairo—uneventful in the sense of trouble; the stay at the hotel had been plenty eventful. Lately they'd fallen into a comfortable routine, whether staying at her condo or at his cottage. With some compromise and ingenuity, meshing two busy lives and schedules had turned out to be easier than she'd expected.

It never failed to amaze and humble her, how easily they fit into each other's lives.

"Your buddy Halloran's been busy," Jack said.

Diana put down her cup. "What do you mean?"

He thumbed past a couple pages in the newspaper, then folded it and handed it to her.

"Steve Carmichael sold the Jade Jaguar." She scanned the short article in the business section. "Huh. I really didn't think he'd do it."

"Considering two-thirds of his stock was looted, I'm not surprised. I'd say he got out while the going was good."

"He's still funding you for this year's excavation, right?"

"Oh, yeah. And I got a call from my friend Tomas. The archaeologist from Guatemala City, remember?" When she nodded, he added, "The mask is going on display at the end of next month, courtesy of an 'anonymous donor.'"

"That's a nice bit of justice on this fine, sunny morning." She handed the newspaper back, smiling with satisfaction. "And it looks like Audrey Spencer is staying on to manage the gallery under its new owners. I'm glad to hear that."

"Me too."

"I'll have to give Bobby a call and find out what he did."

"Have some breakfast first."

"I am, I am . . . jeez, you're pushy this morning."

Yawning again, waiting for the caffeine to kick in, Diana grabbed the box of Cocoa Krispies and started pouring out puffy brown rice bits—until something very non-Krispie-like fell into her bowl with a heavy clunk, scattering cereal and rattling the bowl on the counter.

For several seconds, Diana stared blankly at it. A box wrapped in plain brown paper?

"Uh-oh. Somebody at the cereal factory fell asleep at the quality control wheel."

When Jack didn't answer, she turned to him. He was eating his cereal, but his cheeks bunched suspiciously.

"Did you hear me? Maybe you shouldn't be eating that."

He made a strange sound, and finally her "something-is-smelly-in-Denmark" intuition kicked in.

"Laughing and eating at the same time isn't a good idea—and *what* are you up to now? Did you put that in there?"

Even as she asked the question, she realized that the thing in her bowl had a jewelry-box look to it—and a light-headed sensation suddenly swept over her.

"Oh, Jack," she whispered. "You didn't."

Diana picked up the box, surprised by its weight. She took a quick breath, then peeled back a corner of the brown paper—and saw why it was so heavy.

The tiny box, no more than a couple inches high and wide, was made of alabaster, its lid carved with an Egyptian papyrus motif painted in red and black.

Stunned, she looked up again. "Jack—"

"I didn't steal it," he said quickly. "In case you were wondering."

"I wasn't, and it's lovely . . . should I open it?"

"It sure as hell would put me out of my misery if you did."

She smiled at his rueful tone, and carefully lifted the lid. Inside, a gold ring set with a large, sparkling diamond nestled on a cushion of black velvet.

"Ohmigod," she squeaked. "Ohmigod!"

"Okay," he said slowly, drawing out the word. "Is this good? You're not going to pass out on me, are you?"

She nodded, then quickly shook her head. "Yes . . . no, I mean I'm fine. This is . . . Jack, it's the most . . . I don't know what to say!"

"Maybe it would help if I actually asked the question." He took her hands, then leaned closer until they were eye to eye. "Diana, would you marry me?"

This was really happening; she wasn't dreaming. It took her a second or two to find her voice. "Yes . . . most definitely, yes."

"Thank God." Relief crossed his face, and he let out his breath. "I've been sweating this for weeks, but that look on your face was worth the wait."

As he took the ring from the box and slipped it on her finger, his hands shook slightly. "Love you."

"Love you, too." Even knowing he could see her happiness, she added softly, "It's beautiful, Jack. Thank you. I am the luckiest woman in the world."

Sudden tears welled, and Diana looked at her hand, feeling a little odd with this new, unfamiliar weight, watching the diamond facets sparkle in the sunlight at her every movement. After a moment, her composure back in place, she asked, "Where did you get the little box?"

"Buying a chunk of alabaster was easy. Finding an artist was harder. Luckily, I work in a university with an art department."

"You had it specially made? Oh, Jack, you didn't have to do that."

"I know, but I thought it would be fitting, seeing as how a little box full of big surprises brought us together."

Her tears fell then; touched by his efforts that showed, more than words, how much he loved her. After wiping them away, she laughed and launched herself at him, landing on his lap. The stool rocked precariously, but Diana didn't care if they ended up on the kitchen floor; all she wanted was to wrap her arms around his neck, her legs around his waist, and kiss him breathless.

Finally, she had to break away and come up for air. Still smiling widely, she said, "Okay, I have to ask: Why a cereal box?"

"Because," he said, his hands lazily rubbing her back, "you understand me and put up with me, and

I love you for that. But when I found out you share my secret passion for Cocoa Krispies, I knew I had to marry you. Because if that doesn't mean we're destined for eternal love, I don't know what does."

AUTHOR NOTE

...

I want to thank two people who were kind enough to help me with research for this book: New Orleans native and fellow Avon author Nancy Wagner (Hailey North), who took pictures of the Tulane campus for me and sent bunches of New Orleans-related info, and Marelou Azares, who helped me out with kickboxing information.

A number of the places mentioned in this book do exist, including the Jaguar Jungle in the Audubon Park Zoo. Tikukul is a figment of my imagination, but it's based rather loosely on the existing ruins of the Mayan city of Tikal. Any errors or dramatic license I may have taken with facts are mine alone.

To this day, the parentage of Tutankhamen remains a mystery. The "family heirlooms" in the book are based on actual artifacts discovered by Howard Carter in the pharaoh's tomb in 1922. A two-inch solid gold figure of a squatting king, often identified as Amenhotep III, was found inside a miniature gilded sarcophagus, along with a lock of auburn hair attributed to his queen, Tiye, since the sarcophagus was inscribed with her name. It didn't seem like too much of a stretch to use similar small mementoes, and attribute them to the most mysterious and fascinating figures in Egyptian history: the heretic pharaoh Akhenaton and his beautiful queen, Nefertiti.

Four stars of romance soar this November!

WHEN IT'S PERFECT by Adele Ashworth
An Avon Romantic Treasure

Miss Mary Marsh's quiet world is sent spinning the moment dashing Marcus Longfellow comes striding into her life. The Earl of Renn believes the young miss is hiding something, and a sensuous seduction will surely reveal her secrets. But is his growing passion for her interfering with his perfect plan?

I'VE GOT YOU, BABE by Karen Kendall
An Avon Contemporary Romance

Vanessa Tower has never met anyone like Christopher "Crash" Dunmoor, the sexy adventurer who can ignite sparks in her with just a smile. Will the gorgeous bookworm convince the confirmed loner that love is the most tantalizing adventure of all?

HIGHLAND ROGUES: THE WARRIOR BRIDE
by Lois Greiman
An Avon Romance

Lachlan MacGowan is suspicious of the mysterious "Hunter"—and shocked to discover this warrior is really a woman! Beneath the soldier's garb, Rhona is a proud beauty . . . and she is determined to resist the striking rogue who has laid siege to her heart.

HIS BRIDE by Gayle Callen
An Avon Romance

Gwyneth Hall has heard the dark rumors about Sir Edmund Blackwell, the man she is betrothed to but has never seen. Yet burning kisses from the gorgeous "devil" may be more than she bargained for . . .

REL 1002